JULIA QUINN

Lost Duke The of Wyndham

AVON

An Imprint of HarperCollins*Publishers*

AVON BOOKS
An Imprint of HarperCollins*Publishers*
10 East 53rd Street
New York, New York 10022-5299

Copyright © 2008 by Julie Cotler Pottinger
ISBN 978-0-06-087610-4
www.avonromance.com

First Avon Books paperback printing: June 2008

Avon Trademark Reg. U.S. Pat. Off. and in Other Countries, Marca Registrada, Hecho en U.S.A.
HarperCollins® is a registered trademark of HarperCollins Publishers.

Printed in the U.S.A.

10 9 8 7 6 5 4 3 2 1

For my mom,
who makes all things possible.

And also for Paul,
even though she once introduced us
as her son and daughter-in-law. Sheesh.

Chapter One

*G*race Eversleigh had been the companion to the dowager Duchess of Wyndham for five years, and in that time she had learned several things about her employer, the most pertinent of which was this:

Under her grace's stern, exacting, and haughty exterior did *not* beat a heart of gold.

Which was not to say that the offending organ was black. Her grace the dowager Duchess of Wyndham could never be called completely evil. Nor was she cruel, spiteful, or even entirely mean-spirited. But Augusta Elizabeth Candida Debenham Cavendish had been born the daughter of a duke, she had married a duke, and then given birth to another. Her sister was now a member of a minor royal family in some central European country whose name Grace could never quite pronounce, and her brother owned most of East Anglia. As far as the dowager was concerned, the world was a stratified place, with a hierarchy as clear as it was rigid.

Wyndhams, and especially Wyndhams who used to be Debenhams, sat firmly at the top.

And as such, the dowager expected certain behavior and deference to be paid. She was rarely kind, she did not tolerate stupidity, and her compliments were never falsely given. (Some might say they were never given at all, but Grace had, precisely twice, borne witness to a curt but honest "well done"—not that anyone believed her when she mentioned it later.)

But the dowager had saved Grace from an impossible situation, and for that she would always possess Grace's gratitude, respect, and most of all, her loyalty. Still, there was no getting around the fact that the dowager was something less than cheerful, and so, as they rode home from the Lincolnshire Dance and Assembly, their elegant and well-sprung coach gliding effortlessly across the midnight-dark roads, Grace could not help but be relieved that her employer was fast asleep.

It had been a lovely night, truly, and Grace knew she should not be so uncharitable. Upon arrival, the dowager had immediately retired to her seat of honor with her cronies, and Grace had not been required to attend to her. Instead, she had danced and laughed with all of her old friends, she had drunk three glasses of punch, she had poked fun at Thomas—always an entertaining endeavor; he was the current duke and certainly needed a bit less obsequiousness in his life. But most of all she had smiled. She had smiled so well and so often that her cheeks hurt.

The pure and unexpected joy of the evening had left her body humming with energy, and she was now perfectly happy to grin into the darkness, listening to the soft snore of the dowager as they made their way home.

Grace closed her eyes, even though she did not think herself sleepy. There was something hypnotic about the motion of the carriage. She was riding backwards —she always did— and the rhythmic clip-clop of the horses' hooves was making her drowsy. It was strange. Her eyes were tired, even though the rest of her was not. But perhaps a nap would not be such a misplaced endeavor—as soon as they returned to Belgrave, she would be required to aid the dowager with—

Crack!

Grace sat up straight, glancing over at her employer, who, miraculously, had not awakened. What was that sound? Had someone—

Crack!

This time the carriage lurched, coming to a halt so swiftly that the dowager, who was facing front as usual, was jerked off her seat.

Grace immediately dropped to her knees next to her employer, her arms instinctively coming around her.

"What the devil?" the dowager snapped, but fell silent when she caught Grace's expression.

"Gunshots," Grace whispered.

The dowager's lips pursed tightly, and then she yanked off her emerald necklace and thrust it at Grace. "Hide this," she ordered.

"Me?" Grace practically squeaked, but she shoved the jewels under a cushion all the same. And all she could think was that she would dearly like to smack a little sense into the esteemed Augusta Wyndham, because if she were killed because the dowager was too cheap to hand over her jewels—

The door was wrenched open.

"Stand and deliver!"

Grace froze, still crouched on the floor next to the dowager. Slowly, she lifted her head to the doorway, but all she could see was the silvery end of a gun, round and menacing, and pointed at her forehead.

"Ladies," came the voice again, and this time it was a bit different, almost polite. The speaker then stepped forward out of the shadows, and with a graceful motion swept his arm in an arc to usher them out. "The pleasure of your company, if you will," he murmured.

Grace felt her eyes dart back and forth—an exercise in futility, to be sure, as there was clearly no avenue of escape. She turned to the dowager, expecting to find her spitting with fury, but instead she had gone white. It was then that Grace realized she was shaking.

The dowager was shaking.

Both of them were.

The highwayman leaned in, one shoulder resting against the door frame. He smiled then—slow and lazy, and with the charm of a rogue. How Grace could see all of that when half of his face was covered with his mask, she did not know, but three things about him were abundantly clear:

He was young.

He was strong.

And he was dangerously lethal.

"Ma'am," Grace said, giving the dowager a nudge. "I think we should do as he says."

"I do love a sensible woman," he said, and smiled again. Just a quirk this time—one devastating little lift at the corner of his mouth. But his gun remained high, and his charm did little to assuage Grace's fear.

And then he extended his other arm. *He extended his arm.* As if they were embarking at a house party. As if he were a country gentleman, about to inquire about the weather.

"May I be of assistance?" he murmured.

Grace shook her head frantically. She could not touch him. She did not know *why*, precisely, but she knew in her bones that it would be utter disaster to put her hand in his.

"Very well," he said with a small sigh. "Ladies today are so very capable. It breaks my heart, really." He leaned in, almost as if sharing a secret. "No one likes to feel superfluous."

Grace just stared at him.

"Rendered mute by my grace and charm," he said, stepping back to allow them to exit. "It happens all the time. Really, I shouldn't be allowed near the ladies. I have such a vexing effect on you."

He was mad. That was the only explanation. Grace didn't care how pretty his manners were, he had to be mad. And he had a gun.

"Although," he mused, his weapon rock steady even as his words seemed to meander through the air, "some would surely say that a mute woman is the least vexing of all."

Thomas would, Grace thought. The Duke of Wyndham—who had years ago insisted that she use his given name at Belgrave after a farcical chorus of *your grace, Miss Grace, your grace*—had no patience for chitchat of any sort.

"Ma'am," she whispered urgently, tugging on the dowager's arm.

The dowager did not say a word, nor did she nod, but she took Grace's hand and allowed herself to be helped down from the carriage.

"Ah, now that is much better," the highwayman said, grinning widely now. "What good fortune is mine to have stumbled upon two ladies so divine. Here I thought I'd be greeted by a crusty old gentleman."

Grace stepped to the side, keeping her eyes trained on his face. He did not look like a criminal, or rather, her idea of a criminal. His accent screamed education and breeding, and if he was not recently washed, well, she could not smell it.

"Or perhaps one of those dreadful young toads, stuffed into a waistcoat two sizes too small," he mused, rubbing his free hand thoughtfully against his chin. "You know the sort, don't you?" he asked Grace. "Red face, drinks too much, thinks too little."

And to her great surprise, Grace found herself nodding.

"I thought you would," he replied. "They're rather thick on the ground, sadly."

Grace blinked and just stood there, watching his mouth. It was the only bit of him she *could* watch, with his mask covering the upper portion of his face. But his lips were so full of movement, so perfectly formed and expressive, that she almost felt she *could* see him. It was odd. And mesmerizing. And more than a little unsettling.

"Ah, well," he said, with the same deceptive sigh of ennui Grace had seen Thomas utilize when he wished to change the subject. "I'm sure you ladies realize that this isn't a social call." His eyes flicked toward Grace, and he let loose a devilish smile. "Not entirely."

Grace's lips parted.

His eyes—what she could see of them through the mask—grew heavy-lidded and seductive.

"I do enjoy mixing business and pleasure," he murmured. "It's not often an option, what with all those portly young gentlemen traveling the roads."

She knew she should gasp, or even spit forth a protest, but the highwayman's voice was so smooth, like the fine brandy she was occasionally offered at Belgrave. There was a very slight lilt to it, too, attesting to a childhood spent far from Lincolnshire, and Grace felt herself sway, as if she could fall forward, lightly, softly, and land somewhere else. Far, far from here.

Quick as a flash his hand was at her elbow, steadying her. "You're not going to swoon, are you?" he asked, his fingers offering just the right amount of pressure to keep her on her feet.

Without letting her go.

Grace shook her head. "No," she said softly.

"You have my heartfelt thanks for that," he replied. "It would be lovely to catch you, but I'd have to drop my gun, and we couldn't have that, could we?" He turned to the dowager with a chuckle. "And don't you go thinking about it. I would be more than happy to catch you as well, but I don't believe either of you would wish to leave my associates in charge of the firearms."

It was only then that Grace realized there were three other men. Of course there had to be—he could not have orchestrated this by himself. But the rest of them had been so silent, choosing to remain in the shadows.

And she had not been able to take her eyes off their leader.

"Has our driver been harmed?" Grace asked, mortified that she was only now thinking of his welfare. Neither he nor the footman who had served as an outrider were anywhere in sight.

"Nothing that a spot of love and tenderness won't cure," the highwayman assured her. "Is he married?"

What was he talking about? "I—I don't think so," Grace replied.

"Send him to the public house, then. There is a rather buxom maid there who— Ah, but what am I thinking? I am among ladies." He chuckled. "Warm broth, then, and perhaps a cold compress. And then after that, a day off to find that spot of love and tenderness. The other fellow, by the way"—he flicked his head toward a nearby cluster of trees—"is over there. Perfectly unharmed, I assure you, although he might find his bindings tighter than he prefers."

Grace flushed, and she turned to the dowager, amazed that she wasn't giving the highwayman a dressing down for such lewd talk. But the dowager was still as pale as sheets, and she was staring at the thief as if she'd seen a ghost.

"Ma'am?" Grace said, instantly taking her hand. It was cold and clammy. And limp. Utterly limp. "Ma'am?"

"What is your name?" the dowager whispered.

"My name?" Grace repeated in horror. Had she suffered an apoplexy? Lost her memory?

"*Your* name," the dowager said with greater force, and it was clear this time that she was addressing the highwayman.

But he only laughed. "I am delighted by the attentions of so lovely a lady, but surely you do not think I would reveal my name during what is almost certainly a hanging offense."

"I need your name," the dowager said.

"And I'm afraid that I need your valuables," he replied. He motioned to the dowager's hand with a respectful tilt of his head. "That ring, if you will."

"Please," the dowager whispered, and Grace's head snapped around to face her. The dowager rarely said thank you, and she *never* said please.

"She needs to sit down," Grace said to the highwayman, because surely the dowager was ill. Her health was excellent, but she was well past seventy and she'd had a shock.

"I don't need to sit down," the dowager said sharply, shaking Grace off. She turned back to the highwayman, yanked off her ring, and held it out. He plucked it from her hand, rolling it about in his fingers before depositing it in his pocket.

Grace held silent, watching the exchange, waiting for him to ask for more. But to her surprise, the dowager spoke first.

"I have another reticule in the carriage," she said—slowly, and with a strange and wholly uncharacteristic deference. "Please allow me to retrieve it."

"As much as I would like to indulge you," he said smoothly, "I must decline. For all I know, you've two pistols hidden under the seat."

Grace swallowed, thinking of the jewels.

"And," he added, his manner growing almost flirtatious, "I can tell you are that most maddening sort of female." He sighed with dramatic flair. "Capable. Oh, admit it." He gave the dowager a subversive little smile. "You are an expert rider, a crack shot, and you can recite the complete works of Shakespeare backwards."

If anything, the dowager grew even more pale at his words.

"Ah, to be twenty years older," he said with a sigh. "I should not have let you slip away."

"Please," the dowager begged. "There is something I must give to you."

"Now *that's* a welcome change of pace," he remarked. "People so seldom wish to hand things over. It does make one feel unloved."

Grace reached for the dowager. "Please let me help you," she insisted. The dowager was not well. She could not be well. She was never humble, and did not beg, and—

"Take her!" the dowager suddenly cried out, grabbing Grace's arm and thrusting her at the highwayman. "You may hold her hostage, with a gun to the head if you desire. I promise you, I shall return, and I shall do it unarmed."

Grace swayed and stumbled, the shock of the moment rendering her almost insensible. She fell against the highwayman, and one of his arms came instantly around her. The embrace was strange, almost protective, and she knew that he was as stunned as she.

They both watched as the dowager, without waiting for his acquiescence, climbed quickly into the carriage.

Grace fought to breathe. Her back was pressed up against him, and his large hand rested against her abdomen, the tips of his fingers curling gently around her right hip. He was warm, and she felt hot, and dear heaven above, she had never—*never*—stood so close to a man.

She could smell him, feel his breath, warm and soft against her neck. And then he did the most amazing thing. His lips came to her ear, and he whispered, "She should not have done that."

He sounded . . . *gentle*. Almost sympathetic. And stern, as if he did not approve of the dowager's treatment of her.

"I am not used to holding a woman such," he murmured in her ear. "I generally prefer a different sort of intimacy, don't you?"

She said nothing, afraid to speak, afraid that she would try to speak and discover she had no voice.

"I won't harm you," he murmured, his lips touching her ear.

Her eyes fell on his gun, still in his right hand. It looked angry and dangerous, and it was resting against her thigh.

"We all have our armor," he whispered, and he

moved, shifted, really, and suddenly his free hand was at her chin. One finger lightly traced her lips, and then he leaned down and kissed her.

Grace stared in shock as he pulled back, smiling gently down at her.

"That was far too short," he said. "Pity." He stepped back, took her hand, and brushed another kiss on her knuckles. "Another time, perhaps," he murmured.

But he did not let go of her hand. Even as the dowager emerged from the carriage, he kept her fingers in his, his thumb rubbing lightly across her skin.

She was being seduced. She could barely think—she could barely *breathe*—but this, she knew. In a few minutes they would part ways, and he would have done nothing more than kiss her, and she would be forever changed.

The dowager stepped in front of them, and if she cared that the highwayman was caressing her companion, she did not speak of it. Instead, she held forth a small object. "Please," she implored him. "Take this."

He released Grace's hand, his fingers trailing reluctantly across her skin. As he reached out, Grace realized that the dowager was holding a miniature painting. It was of her long-dead second son.

Grace knew that miniature. The dowager carried it with her everywhere.

"Do you know this man?" the dowager whispered.

The highwayman looked at the tiny painting and shook his head.

"Look closer."

But he just shook his head again, trying to return it to the dowager.

"Might be worth something," one of his companions said.

He shook his head and gazed intently at the dowager's face. "It will never be as valuable to me as it is to you."

"No!" the dowager cried out, and she shoved the miniature toward him. "Look! I beg of you, *look*! His eyes. His chin. His mouth. *They are yours.*"

Grace sucked in her breath.

"I am sorry," the highwayman said gently. "You are mistaken."

But she would not be dissuaded. "His voice is your voice," she insisted. "Your tone, your humor. I know it. I know it as I know how to breathe. He was my son. *My son.*"

"Ma'am," Grace interceded, placing a motherly arm around her. The dowager would not normally have allowed such an intimacy, but there was nothing normal about the dowager this evening. "Ma'am, it is dark. He is wearing a mask. It cannot be he."

"Of course it's not he," she snapped, pushing Grace violently away. She rushed forward, and Grace nearly fell with terror as every man steadied his weapon.

"Don't hurt her!" she cried out, but her plea was unnecessary. The dowager had already grabbed the highwayman's free hand and was clutching it as if he was her only means of salvation.

"This is my son," she said, her trembling fingers holding forth the miniature. "His name was John Cavendish, and he died twenty-nine years ago. He had brown hair, and blue eyes, and a birthmark on his shoulder." She swallowed convulsively, and her voice fell to a whisper. "He adored music, and he could not eat strawberries. And he could . . . he could . . ."

The dowager's voice broke, but no one spoke. The air was thick and tense with silence, every eye on the old woman until she finally got out, her voice barely a whisper, "He could make anyone laugh."

And then, in an acknowledgment Grace could never have imagined, the dowager turned to her and added, "Even me."

The moment stood suspended in time, pure, silent, and heavy. No one spoke. Grace wasn't even sure if anyone breathed.

She looked at the highwayman, at his mouth, at that expressive, devilish mouth, and she *knew* that something was not right. His lips were parted, and more than that, they were still. For the first time, his mouth was without movement, and even in the silvery light of the moon she could tell that he'd gone white.

"If this means anything to you," the dowager continued with quiet determination, "you may find me at Belgrave Castle awaiting your call."

And then, as stooped and shaking as Grace had ever seen her, she turned, still clutching the miniature, and climbed back into the carriage.

Grace held still, unsure of what to do. She no longer felt in danger—strange as that seemed, with three guns still trained on her and one —the highwayman's, *her* highwayman's—resting limply at his side. But they had turned over only one ring—surely not a productive haul for an experienced band of thieves, and she did not feel she could get back into the carriage without permission.

She cleared her throat. "Sir?" she said, unsure of how to address him.

"My name is not Cavendish," he said softly, his voice reaching her ears alone. "But it once was."

Grace gasped.

And then, with movements sharp and swift, he leaped atop his horse and barked, "We are done here."

And Grace was left to stare at his back as he rode away.

Chapter Two

everal hours later Grace was sitting in a chair in the corridor outside the dowager's bedchamber. She was beyond weary and wanted nothing more than to crawl into her own bed, where she was quite certain she would toss and turn and fail to find slumber, despite her exhaustion. But the dowager was so overset, and indeed had rung so many times that Grace had finally given up and dragged the chair to its present location. In the last hour she had brought the dowager (who would not leave her bed) a collection of letters, tucked at the bottom of a locked drawer; a glass of warm milk; a glass of brandy; another miniature of her long-dead son John; a handkerchief that clearly possessed some sort of sentimental value; and another glass of brandy, to replace the one the dowager had knocked over while anxiously directing Grace to fetch the handkerchief.

It had been about ten minutes since the last summons. Ten minutes to do nothing but sit and wait in the chair, thinking, thinking . . .

Of the highwayman.

Of his kiss.

Of Thomas, the current Duke of Wyndham. Whom she considered a friend.

Of the dowager's long-dead middle son, and the man who apparently bore his likeness. *And* his name.

His name. Grace took a long, uneasy breath. His *name*.

Good God.

She had not told the dowager this. She had stood motionless in the middle of the road, watching the highwayman ride off in the light of the partial moon. And then, finally, when she thought her legs might actually function, she set about getting them home. There was the footman to untie, and the coachman to tend to, and as for the dowager—she was so clearly upset that she did not even whisper a complaint when Grace put the injured coachman inside the carriage with her.

And then she joined the footman atop the driver's seat and drove them home. She wasn't a particularly experienced hand with the reins, but she could manage.

And she'd had to manage. There was no one else to do it. But that was something she was good at.

Managing. Making do.

She'd got them home, found someone to tend to the coachman, and then tended to the dowager, and all the while she'd thought—

Who *was* he?

The highwayman. He'd said his name had once been Cavendish. Could he be the dowager's grandson? She had been told that John Cavendish died without issue, but he wouldn't have been the first young nobleman to litter the countryside with illegitimate children.

Except he'd said his name was Cavendish. Or rather, *had* been Cavendish. Which meant—

Grace shook her head blearily. She was so tired she could barely think, and yet it seemed all she could *do* was think. What did it mean that the highwayman's name was Cavendish? Could an illegitimate son bear his father's name?

She had no idea. She'd never met a bastard before, at least not one of noble origins. But she'd known others who had changed their names. The vicar's son had gone to live with relatives when he was small, and the last time he'd been back to visit, he'd introduced himself with a different surname. So surely an illegitimate son could call himself whatever he wanted. And even if it was not legal to do so, a highwayman would not trouble himself with such technicalities, would he?

Grace touched her mouth, trying to pretend she did not love the shivers of excitement that rushed through her at the memory. He had kissed her. It had been her first kiss, and she did not know who he was.

She knew his scent, she knew the warmth of his skin, and the velvet softness of his lips, but she did not know his name.

Not all of it, at least.

"Grace! Grace!"

Grace stumbled to her feet. She'd left the door ajar

so she could better hear the dowager, and sure enough, her name was once again being called. The dowager must still be overset—she rarely used Grace's Christian name. It was harder to snap out in a demanding manner than *Miss Eversleigh*.

Grace rushed back into the room, trying not to sound weary and resentful as she asked, "May I be of assistance?"

The dowager was sitting up in bed—well, not quite sitting up. She was mostly lying down, with just her head propped up on the pillows. Grace thought she looked terribly uncomfortable, but the last time she had tried to adjust her position she'd nearly got her head bit off.

"Where have you been?"

Grace did not think the question required an answer, but she said, nonetheless, "Just outside your door, ma'am."

"I need you to get me something," the dowager said, and she didn't sound as imperious as she did agitated.

"What is it you would like, your grace?"

"I want the portrait of John."

Grace stared at her, uncomprehending.

"Don't just stand there!" the dowager practically screamed.

"But ma'am," Grace protested, jumping back, "I've brought you all three of the miniatures, and—"

"No, no, no," the dowager cried, her head swinging back and forth on the pillows. "I want the portrait. From the gallery."

"The portrait," Grace echoed, because it was half three in the morning, and perhaps she was addled by exhaustion, but she *thought* she'd just been asked to remove a life-sized portrait from a wall and carry it up two flights of stairs to the dowager's bedchamber.

"You know the one," the dowager said. "He's standing next to the tree, and he has a sparkle in his eye."

Grace blinked, trying to absorb this. "There is only the one, I think."

"Yes," the dowager said, her voice almost unbalanced in its urgency. "There is a sparkle in his eye."

"You want me to bring it here."

"I have no other bedchamber," the dowager snapped.

"Very well." Grace swallowed. Good Lord, how was she going to accomplish this? "It will take a bit of time."

"Just drag a chair over and yank the bloody thing down. You don't need—"

Grace rushed forward as the dowager's body convulsed in a spasm of coughing. "Ma'am! Ma'am!" she said, bringing her arm around her to set her upright. "Please, ma'am. You must try to be more settled. You are going to hurt yourself."

The dowager coughed a few last times, took a long swallow of her warm milk, then cursed and took her brandy instead. That, she finished entirely. "I'm going to hurt *you*," she gasped, thunking the glass back down on her bedside table, "if you don't get me that portrait."

Grace swallowed and nodded. "As you wish, ma'am." She hurried out, sagging against the corridor wall once she was out of the dowager's sight.

It had begun as such a lovely evening. And now

look at her. She'd had a gun pointed at her heart, been kissed by a man whose next appointment was surely with the gallows, and now the dowager wanted her to wrestle a life-sized portrait off the gallery wall.

At half three in the morning.

"She can't possibly be paying me enough," Grace mumbled under her breath as she made her way down the stairs. "There couldn't possibly exist enough money—"

"Grace?"

She stopped short, stumbling off the bottom step. Large hands immediately found her upper arms to steady her. She looked up, even though she knew who it had to be. Thomas Cavendish was the grandson of the dowager. He was also the Duke of Wyndham and thus without question the most powerful man in the district. He was in London nearly as often as he was here, but Grace had got to know him quite well during the five years she'd acted as companion to the dowager.

They were friends. It was an odd and completely unexpected situation, given the difference in their rank, but they were friends.

"Your grace," she said, even though he had long since instructed her to use his given name when they were at Belgrave. She gave him a tired nod as he stepped back and returned his hands to his sides. It was far too late for her to ponder matters of titles and address.

"What the devil are you doing awake?" he asked. "It's got to be after two."

"After three, actually," she corrected absently, and then—good heavens, *Thomas*.

She snapped fully awake. What should she tell him? Should she say anything at all? There would be no hiding the fact that she and the dowager had been accosted by highwaymen, but she wasn't quite certain if she should reveal that he *might* have a first cousin racing about the countryside, relieving the local gentry of their valuables.

Because, all things considered, he might not. And surely it did not make sense to concern him needlessly.

"Grace?"

She gave her head a shake. "I'm sorry, what did you say?"

"Why are you wandering the halls?"

"Your grandmother is not feeling well," she said. And then, because she desperately wanted to change the subject: "You're home late."

"I had business in Stamford," he said brusquely.

His mistress. If it had been anything else, he would not have been so oblique. It was odd, though, that he was here now. He usually spent the night. Grace, despite her respectable birth, was a servant at Belgrave, and as such privy to almost all of the gossip. If the duke stayed out all night, she generally knew about it.

"We had an . . . exciting evening," Grace said.

He looked at her expectantly.

She felt herself hesitate, and then—well, there was really nothing to do but say it. "We were accosted by highwaymen."

His reaction was swift. "Good God," he exclaimed. "Are you all right? Is my grandmother well?"

"We are both unharmed," Grace assured him, "although our driver has a nasty bump on his head. I took the liberty of giving him three days to convalesce."

"Of course." He closed his eyes for a moment, looking pained. "I must offer my apologies," he said. "I should have insisted that you take more than one outrider."

"Don't be silly. It's not your fault. Who would have thought—" She cut herself off, because really, there was no sense in assigning blame. "We are unhurt," she repeated. "That is all that matters."

He sighed. "What did they take?"

Grace swallowed. She couldn't very well tell him they'd stolen nothing but a ring. Thomas was no idiot; he'd wonder why. She smiled tightly, deciding that vagueness was the order of the day. "Not very much," she said. "Nothing at all from me. I imagine it was obvious I am not a woman of means."

"Grandmother must be spitting mad."

"She is a bit overset," Grace hedged.

"She was wearing her emeralds, wasn't she?" He shook his head. "The old bat is ridiculously fond of those stones."

Grace declined to scold him for his characterization of his grandmother. "She kept the emeralds, actually. She hid them under the seat cushion."

He looked impressed. "She did?"

"*I* did," Grace corrected, unwilling to share the glory. "She thrust them at me before they breached the vehicle."

He smiled slightly, and then, after a moment of somewhat awkward silence, said, "You did not mention why you're up and about so late. Surely you deserve a rest as well."

"I . . . er . . ." There seemed to be no way to avoid telling him. If nothing else, he'd notice the massive empty spot on the gallery wall the next day. "Your grandmother has a strange request."

"All of her requests are strange," he replied immediately.

"No, this one . . . well . . ." Grace's eyes flicked up in exasperation. How was it her life had come to this? "I don't suppose you'd like to help me remove a painting from the gallery."

"A painting."

She nodded.

"From the gallery."

She nodded again.

"I don't suppose she's asking for one of those modestly sized square ones."

"With the bowls of fruit?"

He nodded.

"No." When he did not comment, she added, "She wants the portrait of your uncle."

"Which one?"

"John."

He nodded, smiling slightly, but without any humor. "He was always her favorite."

"But you never knew him," Grace said, because the way he'd said it—it almost sounded as if he'd witnessed her favoritism.

"No, of course not. He died before I was born. But my father spoke of him."

It was clear from his expression that he did not wish to discuss the matter further. Grace could not think of anything more to say, however, so she just stood there, waiting for him to collect his thoughts.

Which apparently he did, because he turned to her and asked, "Isn't that portrait life-sized?"

Grace pictured herself wrestling it from the wall. "I'm afraid so."

For a moment it looked as if he might turn toward the gallery, but then his jaw squared and he was once again every inch the forbidding duke. "No," he said firmly. "You will not get that for her this evening. If she wants the bloody painting in her room, she can ask a footman for it in the morning."

Grace wanted to smile at his protectiveness, but by this point she was far too weary. And besides that, when it came to the dowager, she had long since learned to follow the road of least resistance. "I assure you, I want nothing more than to retire this very minute, but it is easier just to accommodate her."

"Absolutely not," he said imperiously, and without waiting, he turned and marched up the stairs. Grace watched him for a moment, and then, with a shrug, headed off to the gallery. It couldn't be that difficult to take a painting off a wall, could it?

But she made it only ten paces before she heard Thomas bark her name.

She sighed, stopping in her tracks. She should have known better. The man was as stubborn as his grand-mother, not that he would appreciate the comparison.

She turned and retraced her steps, hurrying along

when she heard him call out for her again. "I'm right here," she said irritably. "Good gracious, you'll wake the entire house."

He rolled his eyes. "Don't tell me you were going to get the painting by yourself."

"If I don't, she will ring for me all night, and then I will never get any sleep."

He narrowed his eyes. "Watch me."

"Watch you what?" she asked, baffled.

"Dismantle her bell cord," he said, heading upstairs with renewed determination.

"Dismantle her . . . Thomas!" She ran up behind him, but of course could not keep up. "Thomas, you can't!"

He turned. Grinned even, which she found somewhat alarming. "It's my house," he said. "I can do anything I want."

And while Grace digested that on an exhausted brain, he strode down the hall and into his grandmother's room. "What," she heard him bite off, "do you think you're doing?"

Grace let out a breath and hurried after him, entering the room just as he was saying, "Good heavens, are you all right?"

"Where is Miss Eversleigh?" the dowager asked, her eyes darting frantically about the room.

"I'm right here," Grace assured her, rushing forward.

"Did you get it? Where is the painting? I want to see my son."

"Ma'am, it's late," Grace tried to explain. She inched forward, although she wasn't sure why. If the dowager started spouting off about the highwayman and his resemblance to her favorite son, it wasn't as if she would be able to stop her.

But still, the proximity at least gave the illusion that she might be able to prevent disaster.

"Ma'am," Grace said again, gently, softly. She gave the dowager a careful look.

"You may instruct a footman to procure it for you in the morning," Thomas said, sounding slightly less imperious than before, "but I will not have Miss Eversleigh undertaking such manual labor, and certainly not in the middle of the night."

"I need the painting, Thomas," the dowager said, and Grace almost reached out to take her hand. She sounded pained. She sounded old. And she certainly did not sound like herself when she said, "Please."

Grace glanced at Thomas. He looked uneasy. "Tomorrow," he said. "First thing, if you wish it."

"But—"

"No," he interrupted. "I am sorry you were accosted this evening, and I shall certainly do whatever is necessary—*within reason*—to facilitate your comfort and health, but this does not include whimsical and ill-timed demands. Do you understand me?"

They stared at each other for so long that Grace wanted to flinch. Then Thomas said sharply, "Grace, go to bed." He didn't turn around.

Grace held still for a moment, waiting for what, she didn't know—disagreement from the dowager? A thunderbolt outside the window? When neither was forthcoming, she decided she could do nothing more that evening and left the room. As she walked slowly down the hall, she could hear them arguing—nothing violent, nothing impassioned. But then, she'd not have expected that. Cavendish tempers ran cold, and they were far more likely to attack with a frozen barb than a heated cry.

Grace let out a long, uneven breath. She would never get used to this. Five years she had been at Belgrave, and still the resentment that ran back and forth between Thomas and his grandmother shocked her.

And the worst part was—there wasn't even a reason! Once, she had dared to ask Thomas *why* they held each other in such contempt. He just shrugged, saying that it had always been that way. She'd disliked his father, Thomas said, his father had hated him, and he himself could have done quite well without either of them.

Grace had been stunned. She'd thought families were meant to love each other. Hers had. Her mother, her father . . . She closed her eyes, fighting back tears. She was being maudlin. Or maybe it was because she was tired. She didn't cry about them any longer. She missed them—she would *always* miss them. But the great big gaping hole their deaths had rent in her had healed.

And now . . . well, she'd found a new place in this world. It wasn't the one she'd anticipated, and it wasn't the one her parents had planned for her, but it came with food and clothing, and the opportunity to see her friends from time to time.

But sometimes, late at night as she lay in her bed, it was just so hard. She knew she should not be ungrateful—she was living in a *castle*, for heaven's sake. But she had not been brought up for this. Not the servitude, and not the sour dispositions. Her father had been a country gentleman, her mother a well-liked member of the local community. They had raised her with love and laughter, and sometimes, as they sat before the fire in the evening, her father would sigh and say that she was going to have to remain a spinster, because surely there was no man in the county good enough for his daughter.

And Grace would laugh and say, "What about the rest of England?"

"Not there, either!"

"France?"

"Good heavens, not."

"The Americas?"

"Are you trying to kill your mother, gel? You know she gets seasick if she so much as *sees* the beach."

And they all somehow knew that Grace would marry someone right there in Lincolnshire, and she'd live down the road, or at least just a short ride away, and she would be happy. She would find what her parents had found, because no one expected her to marry for any reason other than love. She'd have babies, and her house would be full of laughter, and she would be happy.

She'd thought herself the luckiest girl in the world.

But the fever that had struck the Eversleigh house was cruel, and when it broke, Grace was an orphan. At seventeen, she could hardly remain on her own, and indeed, no one had been sure what to do with her until her father's affairs were settled and the will was read.

Grace let out a bitter laugh as she pulled off her wrinkled clothing and readied herself for bed. Her father's directives had only made matters worse. They were in debt; not deeply so, but enough to render her a burden. Her parents, it seemed, had always lived slightly above their means, presumably hoping that love and happiness would carry them through.

And indeed they had. Love and happiness had stood up nicely to every obstacle the Eversleighs had faced.

Except death.

Sillsby—the only home Grace had ever known—was entailed. She'd known that, but not how eager her cousin Miles would be to assume residence. Or that he was still unmarried. Or that when he pushed her against a wall and jammed his lips against hers, she was supposed to let him, indeed *thank* the toad for his gracious and benevolent interest in her.

Instead she had shoved her elbow into his ribs and her knee up against his—

Well, he hadn't been too fond of her after that. It was the only part of the whole debacle that still made her smile.

Furious at the rebuff, Miles had tossed her out on her ear. Grace had been left with nothing. No home, no money, and no relations (she refused to count him among the last).

Enter the dowager.

News of Grace's predicament must have traveled fast through the district. The dowager had swooped in like an icy goddess and whisked her away. Not that there had been any illusion that she was to be a pampered guest. The dowager had arrived with full retinue, stared down Miles until he squirmed (literally; it had been a most enjoyable moment for Grace), and then declared to her, "You shall be my companion."

Before Grace had a chance to accept or decline, the dowager had turned and left the room. Which just confirmed what they all knew—that Grace had never had a choice in the matter to begin with.

That had been five years ago. Grace now lived in a castle, ate fine food, and her clothing was, if not the latest stare of fashion, well-made and really quite pretty. (The dowager was, if nothing else, at least not cheap.)

She lived mere miles from where she had grown up, and as most of her friends still resided in the district, she saw them with some regularity—in the village, at church, on afternoon calls. And if she didn't have a family of her own, at least she had not been forced to have one with Miles.

But much as she appreciated all the dowager had done for her, she wanted something more.

Or maybe not even more. Maybe just something else.

Unlikely, she thought, falling into bed. The only options for a woman of her birth were employment and marriage. Which, for her, meant employment. The men of Lincolnshire were far too cowed by the dowager to ever make an overture in Grace's direction. It was well-known that Augusta Cavendish had no desire to train a new companion.

It was even more well-known that Grace hadn't a farthing.

She closed her eyes, trying to remind herself that

the sheets she'd slid between were of the highest quality, and the candle she'd just snuffed was pure beeswax. She had every physical comfort, truly.

But what she wanted was. . .

It didn't really matter what she wanted. That was her last thought before she finally fell asleep.

And dreamed of a highwayman.

Chapter Three

Five miles away, in a small posting inn, a man sat in his room, alone, with a bottle of expensive French brandy, an empty glass, a very small case of clothing, and a woman's ring.

His name was Jack Audley; formerly Captain John Audley of His Majesty's army; formerly Jack Audley of Butlersbridge, County Cavan, Ireland; formerly Jack Cavendish-Audley of the same place; and formerly—as formerly as one could get, as it was at the time of his christening—John Augustus Cavendish.

The miniature had meant nothing to him. He could barely see it in the night, and he'd yet to find a portraitist who could capture a man's essence on a miniature painting, anyway.

But the ring. . .

With an unsteady hand, he poured himself another drink.

He hadn't looked closely at the ring when he took it from the old lady's hands. But now, in the privacy of his rented room, he'd looked. And what he'd seen had shaken him to his bones.

He'd seen that ring before. On his own finger.

His was a masculine version, but the design was identical. A twisted flower, a tiny swirled D. He'd never known what it meant, as he'd been told that his father's name was John Augustus Cavendish, no capital D's to be found anywhere.

He still didn't know what the D stood for, but he knew that the old lady did. And no matter how many times he tried to convince himself that this was just a coincidence, he knew that this evening, on a deserted Lincolnshire road, he'd met his grandmother.

Good Lord.

He looked down at the ring again. He'd propped it up on the table, its face winking up at him in the candlelight. Abruptly, he twisted his own ring and yanked it off. He couldn't remember the last time his finger had been bare. His aunt had always insisted that he keep it close; it was the only keepsake they had of his father.

His mother, they told him, had been clutching it in her shivering fingers when she was pulled from the frigid waters of the Irish Sea.

Slowly, Jack held the ring out, carefully setting it down next to its sister. His lips flattened slightly as he regarded the pair. What had he been thinking? That when he got the two side by side he'd see that they were actually quite different?

He'd known little of his father. His name, of course,

and that he was the younger son of a well-to-do English family. His aunt had met him but twice; her impression had been that he was somewhat estranged from his relations. He spoke of them only laughingly, in that manner people used when they did not wish to say anything of substance.

He hadn't much money, or so his aunt assumed. His clothes were fine, but well-worn, and as far as anyone could tell, he'd been wandering the Irish countryside for months. He'd said he had come to witness the wedding of a school friend and liked it so much that he stayed. His aunt saw no reason to doubt this.

In the end, all Jack knew was this: John Augustus Cavendish was a well-born English gentleman who'd traveled to Ireland, fallen in love with Louise Galbraith, married her, and then died when the ship carrying them to England had sunk off the coast of Ireland. Louise had washed ashore, her body bruised and shivering, but alive. It was over a month before anyone realized she was pregnant.

But she was weak, and she was devastated by grief, and her sister—the woman who had raised Jack as her own—said it was more of a surprise that Louise survived the pregnancy than it was that she finally succumbed at his birth.

And that fairly well summed up Jack's knowledge of his paternal heritage. He thought about his parents from time to time, wondering who they'd been and which had gifted him with his ready smile, but in truth, he'd never yearned for anything more. At the age of two days he'd been given to William and Mary Audley, and if they had ever loved their own children more, they never allowed him to know it. Jack had grown up the de facto son of a country squire, with two brothers, a sister, and twenty acres of rolling pasture, perfect for riding, running, jumping—anything a young boy could fancy.

It had been a marvelous childhood. Damn near perfect. If he was not leading the life he'd anticipated, if he sometimes lay in bed and wondered what the hell he was doing robbing coaches in the dead of night—at least he knew that the road to this point had been paved with his own choices, his own flaws.

And most of the time, he was happy. He was reasonably cheerful by nature, and really, one could do worse than playing Robin Hood along rural British roads. At least he felt as if he had some sort of purpose. After he and the army had parted ways, he'd not known what to do with himself. He was not willing to return to his life as a soldier, and yet, what else was he qualified to do? He had two skills in life, it seemed: He could sit a horse as if he'd been born in the position, and he could turn a conversation with enough wit and flair to charm even the crustiest of individuals. Put together, robbing coaches had seemed the most logical choice.

Jack had made his first theft in Liverpool, when he'd seen a young toff kick a one-handed former soldier who'd had the temerity to beg for a penny. Somewhat buoyed by a rather potent pint of ale, Jack had followed the fellow into a dark corner, pointed a gun a his heart, and walked off with his wallet.

The contents of which he had then dispersed among the beggars on Queens Way, most of whom had fought for—and then been forgotten by—the good people of England.

Well, ninety per cent of the contents had been dispersed. Jack had to eat, too.

After that, it had been an easy step to move to highway robbery. It was so much more elegant than the life of footpad. And it could not be denied that it was much easier to get away on horseback.

And so that was his life. It was what he did. If he'd gone back to Ireland, he would probably be married by now, sleeping with one woman, in one bed, in one house. His life would be County Cavan, and his world a far, far smaller place than it was today.

His was a roaming soul. That was why he did not go back to Ireland.

He splashed a bit more brandy into his glass. There were a hundred reasons why he did not go back to Ireland. Fifty, at least.

He took a sip, then another, then drank deeply until he was too sotted to continue his dishonesty.

There was one reason he did not go back to Ireland. One reason, and four people he did not think he could face.

Rising from his seat, he walked to the window and looked out. There wasn't much to see—a small barn for horses, a thickly leaved tree across the road. The moonlight had turned the air translucent—shimmery and thick, as if a man could step outside and lose himself.

He smiled grimly. It was tempting. It was always tempting.

He knew where Belgrave Castle was. He'd been in

the county for a week; one could not remain in Lincolnshire that long without learning the locations of the grand houses, even if one wasn't a thief out to rob their inhabitants. He could take a look, he supposed. He probably *should* take a look. He owed it to someone. Hell, maybe he owed it to himself.

He hadn't been interested in his father *much* . . . but he'd always been interested a little. And he was here.

Who knew when he'd be in Lincolnshire again? He was far too fond of his head to ever stay in one place for long.

He didn't want to talk to the old lady. He didn't want to introduce himself and make explanations or pretend that he was anything other than what he was—

A veteran of the war.

A highwayman.

A rogue.

An idiot.

An occasionally sentimental fool who knew that the softhearted ladies who'd tended the wounded had it all wrong—sometimes you *couldn't* go home again.

But dear Lord, what he wouldn't give just to take a peek.

He closed his eyes. His family would welcome him back. That was the worst of it. His aunt would put her arms around him. She would tell him it wasn't his fault. She would be so understanding.

But she would not understand. That was his final thought before he fell asleep.

And dreamed of Ireland.

* * *

The following day dawned bright and mockingly clear. Had it rained, Jack wouldn't have bothered to go. He was on horseback, and he'd spent enough of his life pretending he didn't mind that he was soaked to the skin. He did not ride in the rain if he did not have to. He'd earned that much, at least.

But he was not meant to meet up with his cohorts until nightfall, so he did not have an excuse for *not* going. Besides, he was just going to *look*. Maybe see if there was some way he could leave the ring for the old lady. He suspected it meant a great deal to her, and even though he could have probably got a hefty sum for it, he knew he would not be able to bring himself to sell it.

And so he ate a hearty breakfast—accompanied by a noxious beverage the innkeeper swore would clear his head, not that Jack had said anything other than, "Eggs," before the fellow said, "I'll get what you need." Amazingly, the concoction worked (hence the ability to digest the hearty breakfast), and Jack mounted his horse and took off toward Belgrave Castle at an unhurried pace.

He'd ridden about the area frequently over the last few days, but this was the first time he found himself curious at his surroundings. The trees seemed more interesting to him for some reason—the shape of the leaves, the way they showed their backs when the wind blew. The blossoms, too. Some were familiar to him, identical to the ones that bloomed in Ireland. But others were new, perhaps native to the dales and fens of the region.

It was odd. He wasn't sure what he was meant to be thinking about. Perhaps that this vista was what his father had seen every time he'd ridden along the same road. Or maybe that, but for a freak storm in the Irish Sea, these might be the flowers and trees of his own childhood. Jack did not know whether his parents would have made their home in England or Ireland. They were apparently going over to introduce his mother to the Cavendish family when their ship had gone down. Aunt Mary had said that they were planning to decide where to live after Louise had a chance to see a bit of England.

Jack paused and plucked a leaf off a tree, for no reason other than whimsy. It wasn't as green as the ones at home, he decided. Not that it mattered, of course, except that in a strange way, it did.

He tossed the leaf to the ground and with a snort of impatience, took off at a greater speed. It was ludicrous that he felt even a niggle of guilt at going over to see the castle. Good God, it wasn't as if he was going to introduce himself. He did not want to find a new family. He owed the Audleys far more than that.

He just wanted to see it. From afar. To see what might have been, what he was glad *hadn't* been.

But maybe should have been.

Jack took off at a gallop, letting the wind blow the memories away. The speed was cleansing, almost forgiving, and before he knew it he was at the end of the drive. And all he could think was—

Good *Lord*.

* * *

Grace was exhausted.

She'd slept the night before, but not much, and not well. And even though the dowager had chosen to spend the morning in bed, Grace had not been afforded that luxury.

The dowager was powerfully demanding, whether vertical, horizontal, or, should she ever figure out how to hold the position, at a slant.

And so even though she tossed and turned, and refused to lift her head from the pillow, she still managed to summon Grace six times.

The first hour.

Finally, she had become engrossed in a batch of letters Grace had dug up for her at the bottom of her late husband's old desk, tucked in a box labeled: JOHN, ETON.

Saved by school papers. Who would have thought?

Grace's moment of rest was interrupted not twenty minutes later, however, by the arrival of the Ladies Elizabeth and Amelia Willoughby, the pretty, blond daughters of the Earl of Crowland, longtime neighbors and, Grace was always delighted to note, friends.

Elizabeth especially. They were of an age, and before Grace's position in the world had plummeted with the death of her parents, had been considered proper companions. Oh, everyone knew that Grace would not make a match like the Willoughby girls— she would never have a London season, after all. But when they were all in Lincolnshire, they were, if not equals, then at least on something of the same level. People weren't so fussy at the Dance and Assembly.

And when the girls were alone, rank was never something they noticed.

Amelia was Elizabeth's younger sister. Just by a year, but when they were all younger, it had seemed a massive gulf, so Grace did not know her nearly so well. That would change soon, though, she supposed. Amelia was betrothed to Thomas, and had been from the cradle. It would have been Elizabeth, except she was promised to another young lord (also in infancy; Lord Crowland was not one to leave matters to chance). Elizabeth's fellow, however, had died quite young. Lady Crowland (who was not one for tact) had declared it all very inconvenient, but the papers binding Amelia to Thomas had already been signed, and it was deemed best to leave matters as they were.

Grace had never discussed the engagement with Thomas—they were friends, but he would never talk about something so personal with her. Still, she had long suspected that he found the entire situation rather convenient. A fiancée did keep marriage-minded misses (and their mamas) at bay. Somewhat. It was quite obvious that the ladies of England believed in hedging their bets, and poor Thomas could not go anywhere without the women attempting to put themselves in the best possible light, just in case Amelia should, oh, disappear.

Die.

Decide she didn't wish to be a duchess.

Really, Grace thought wryly, as if Amelia had any choice in the matter.

But even though a wife would be a far more effective deterrent than a fiancée, Thomas continued to drag his feet, which Grace thought dreadfully insensitive of him. Amelia was one-and-twenty, for heaven's sake. And according to Lady Crowland, at least four men would have offered for her in London if she had not been marked as the future Duchess of Wyndham.

(Elizabeth, sister that she was, said it was closer to three, but still, the poor girl had been dangling like a string for years.)

"Books!" Elizabeth announced as they entered the hall. "As promised."

At her behest, Elizabeth's mother had borrowed several books from the dowager. Not that Lady Crowland actually read the books. Lady Crowland read very little outside the gossip pages, but returning them was a fine pretext to visit Belgrave, and she was always in favor of anything that placed Amelia in the vicinity of Thomas.

No one had the heart to tell her that Amelia rarely even *saw* Thomas when she was at Belgrave. Most of the time, she was forced to endure the dowager's company—*company*, however, being perhaps too generous a word to describe Augusta Cavendish whilst standing before the young lady who was meant to carry on the Wyndham line.

The dowager was very good at finding fault. One might even call it her greatest talent.

And Amelia was her favorite subject.

But today she had been spared. The dowager was still upstairs, reading her dead son's Latin conjugations, and so Amelia had ended up sipping tea while Grace and Elizabeth chatted.

Or rather, Elizabeth chatted. It was all Grace could

do to nod and murmur in the appropriate moments. One would think her tired mind would go utterly blank, but the opposite was true. She could not stop thinking about the highwayman. And his kiss. And his identity. And his kiss. And if she would meet him again. And that he'd kissed her. And—

And she *had* to stop thinking about him. It was madness. She looked over at the tea tray, wondering if it would be rude to eat the last biscuit.

"—certain you are well, Grace?" Elizabeth said, reaching forward to clasp her hand. "You look very tired."

Grace blinked, trying to focus on her dear friend's face. "I'm sorry," she said reflexively. "I am quite tired, although that is not an excuse for my inattention."

Elizabeth grimaced. She knew the dowager. They all did. "Did *she* keep you up late last night?"

Grace nodded. "Yes, although, truthfully, it was not her fault."

Elizabeth glanced to the doorway to make sure no one was listening before she replied, "It is always her fault."

Grace smiled wryly. "No, this time it really wasn't. We were . . ." Well, really, was there any reason not to tell Elizabeth? Thomas already knew, and surely it would be all over the district by nightfall. "We were accosted by highwaymen, actually."

"Oh, my heavens! Grace!" Elizabeth hastily set down her teacup. "No wonder you appear so distracted!"

"Hmmm?" Amelia had been staring off into space, as she frequently did while Grace and Elizabeth were nattering on, but this had clearly got her attention.

"I am quite recovered," Grace assured her. "Just a bit tired, I'm afraid. I did not sleep well."

"What happened?" Amelia asked.

Elizabeth actually shoved her. "Grace and the dowager were accosted by highwaymen!"

"Really?"

Grace nodded. "Last night. On the way home from the assembly." And then she thought—*Good Lord, if the highwayman is really the dowager's grandson, and he is legitimate, what happens to Amelia?*

But he wasn't legitimate. He couldn't be. He might very well be a Cavendish by blood, but surely not by birth. Sons of dukes did not leave legitimate offspring littering the countryside. It simply did not happen.

"Did they take anything?" Amelia asked.

"How can you be so dispassionate?" Elizabeth demanded. "They pointed a gun at her!" She turned to Grace. "Did they?"

Grace saw it again in her mind—the cold round end of the pistol, the slow, seductive gaze of the highwayman. He wouldn't have shot her. She knew that now. But still, she murmured, "They did, actually."

"Were you terrified?" Elizabeth asked breathlessly. "I would have been. I would have swooned."

"I wouldn't have swooned," Amelia remarked.

"Well, of course you wouldn't," Elizabeth said irritably. "You didn't even gasp when Grace told you about it."

"It sounds rather exciting, actually." Amelia looked at Grace with great interest. "Was it?"

And Grace—Good heavens, she felt herself blush.

Amelia leaned forward, her eyes lighting up. "Was he handsome, then?"

Elizabeth looked at her sister as if she were mad. "Who?"

"The highwayman, of course."

Grace stammered something and pretended to drink her tea.

"He *was*," Amelia said triumphantly.

"He was wearing a *mask*," Grace felt compelled to point out.

"But you could still tell that he was handsome."

"No!"

"Then his accent was terribly romantic. French? Italian?" Amelia's eyes grew even wider. *"Spanish."*

"You've gone mad," Elizabeth said.

"He didn't *have* an accent," Grace retorted. Then she thought of that lilt, that devilish little lift in his voice that she couldn't quite place. "Well, not much of one. Scottish, perhaps? Irish? I couldn't tell, precisely."

Amelia sat back with a happy sigh. "A highwayman. How romantic."

"Amelia Willoughby!" Elizabeth scolded. "Grace was just attacked at gunpoint, and you are calling it romantic?"

Amelia opened her mouth to reply, but just then they heard footsteps in the hall.

"The dowager?" Elizabeth whispered to Grace, looking very much as if she'd like to be wrong.

"I don't think so," Grace replied. "She was still abed when I came down. She was rather . . . ehrm . . . distraught."

"I should think so," Elizabeth remarked. Then she gasped. "Did they make away with her emeralds?"

Grace shook her head. "We hid them. Under the seat cushions."

"Oh, how clever!" Elizabeth said approvingly. "Amelia, wouldn't you agree?" Without waiting for an answer, she turned back to Grace. "It was your idea, wasn't it?"

Grace opened her mouth to retort that she would have happily handed them over, but just then Thomas walked past the open doorway to the sitting room.

Conversation stopped. Elizabeth looked at Grace, and Grace looked at Amelia, and Amelia just kept looking at the now empty doorway. After a moment of held breath, Elizabeth turned to Amelia and said, "I think he does not realize we are here."

"I don't care," Amelia declared, and Grace believed her.

"I wonder where he went," Grace murmured, although she did not think anyone heard her. They were all still watching the doorway, waiting to see if he'd return.

There was a grunt, and then a crash. Grace stood, wondering if she ought to go investigate.

"Bloody hell," she heard Thomas snap.

Grace winced, glancing over at the others. They had risen to their feet as well.

"Careful with that," she heard Thomas say.

And then, as the three ladies watched in silence, the painting of John Cavendish moved past the open doorway, two footmen struggling to keep it upright and balanced.

"Who was that?" Amelia asked once the portrait had gone by.

"The dowager's middle son," Grace murmured. "He died twenty-nine years ago."

"Why are they moving the portrait?"

"The dowager wants it upstairs," Grace replied, thinking that ought to be answer enough. Who knew why the dowager did anything?

Amelia was apparently satisfied with this explanation, because she did not question her further. Or it could have been that Thomas chose that moment to reappear in the doorway.

"Ladies," he said.

They all three bobbed curtsies.

He nodded in that way of his, when he was clearly being nothing but polite. "Pardon." And then he left.

"Well," Elizabeth said, and Grace wasn't certain whether she was trying to express outrage at his rudeness or simply fill the silence. If it was the latter, it didn't work, because no one said anything more until Elizabeth finally added, "Perhaps we should leave."

"No, you can't," Grace replied, feeling dreadful for having to be the bearer of such bad news. "Not yet. The dowager wants to see Amelia."

Amelia groaned.

"I'm sorry," Grace said. And meant it.

Amelia sat down, looked at the tea tray and announced, "I'm eating the last biscuit."

Grace nodded. Amelia would need sustenance for the ordeal ahead. "Perhaps I should order more?"

But then Thomas returned *again*. "We nearly lost

it on the stairs," he said to Grace, shaking his head. "The whole thing swung to the right and nearly impaled itself on the railing."

"Oh, my."

"It would have been a stake through the heart," he said with grim humor. "It would have been worth it just to see her face."

Grace prepared to rise and make her way upstairs. If the dowager was awake, that meant her visit with the Willoughby sisters was over. "Your grandmother rose from bed, then?"

"Only to oversee the transfer. You're safe for now." He shook his head, rolling his eyes as he did so. "I cannot believe she had the temerity to demand that you fetch it for her last night. Or," he added quite pointedly, "that you actually thought you could do it."

Grace thought she ought to explain. "The dowager requested that I bring her the painting last night," she told Elizabeth and Amelia.

"But it was huge!" Elizabeth exclaimed.

"My grandmother always favored her middle son," Thomas said, with a twist of his lips that Grace would not have called a smile. He glanced across the room, and then, as if suddenly realizing his future bride was present, said, "Lady Amelia."

"Your grace," she responded.

But he couldn't possibly have heard her. He was already back to Grace, saying, "You will of course support me if I lock her up?"

"Thom—" Grace began, cutting herself off at the last moment. She supposed that Elizabeth and Amelia knew that he had given her leave to use his given name while at Belgrave, but still, it seemed disrespectful to do so when others were present.

"Your grace," she said, enunciating each word with careful resolve. "You must grant her extra patience this day. She is distraught."

Grace sent up a prayer for forgiveness as she let everyone think the dowager had been upset by nothing more than an ordinary robbery. She wasn't *precisely* lying to Thomas, but she suspected that in this case the sin of omission could prove equally dangerous.

She made herself smile. It felt forced.

"Amelia? Are you unwell?"

Grace turned. Elizabeth was watching her sister with concern.

"I'm perfectly fine," Amelia snapped, which was enough, of course, to show that she was not.

The pair bickered for a moment, their voices low enough so Grace could not make out their exact words, and then Amelia rose, saying something about needing some air.

Thomas stood, of course, and Grace rose to her feet as well. Amelia passed by and even reached the doorway before Grace realized that Thomas did not intend to follow.

Good heavens, for a duke, his manners were abominable. Grace elbowed him in the ribs. Someone had to, she told herself. No one ever stood up to the man.

Thomas shot her a dirty look, but he obviously realized that she was in the right, because he turned to Amelia, nodded his head the barest of inches, and said, "Allow me to escort you."

They departed, and Grace and Elizabeth sat silently for at least a minute before Elizabeth said resignedly, "They are not a good match, are they?"

Grace glanced at the door, even though they had long since departed. She shook her head.

It was huge. It was a castle, of course, and meant to be imposing, but *really.*

Jack stood, open-mouthed.

This was huge.

Funny how no one had mentioned that his father was from a ducal family. Had anyone even known? He had always assumed his father had been the son of some jolly old country squire, maybe a baronet or possibly a baron. He had always been told that he was sired by John Cavendish, not Lord John Cavendish, as he must have been styled.

And as for the old lady . . , Jack had realized that morning that she had never given her name, but surely she was the duchess. She was far too imperious to be a maiden aunt or widowed relation.

Good Lord. He was the grandson of a duke. How was that possible?

Jack stared at the structure before him. He was not a complete provincial. He'd traveled widely whilst in the army and had gone to school with the sons of Ireland's most notable families. The aristocracy was not unknown to him. He did not consider himself uncomfortable in their midst.

But this. . .

This was huge.

How many rooms in the place? There had to be

over a hundred. And what was the provenance? It didn't look quite medieval, despite the crenellations at the top, but it was certainly pre-Tudor. Something important must have happened there. Houses did not get this big without stumbling into the occasional historic event. A treaty, maybe? Perhaps a royal visit? It sounded like the sort of thing that would have been mentioned in school, which was probably why he didn't know it.

A scholar he was not.

The view of the castle as he'd approached had been deceptive. The area was heavy with trees, and the turrets and towers seemed to twinkle in and out of sight as he moved through the foliage. It was only when he reached the end of the drive that it had come completely into view—massive and amazing. The stone was gray in color, with a hint of a yellow undertone, and although its angles were mostly squared off, there was nothing boring about the facade. It dipped and rose, jutted out and swept back in. No long Georgian wall of windows was this.

Jack couldn't even imagine how long it would take a newcomer to find his way around inside. Or how long it would take to find the poor fellow once he got himself lost.

And so he stood and stared, trying to take it in. What would it have been like to grow up there? His father had done so, and by all accounts he'd been a nice enough fellow. Well, by *one* account, he supposed—his Aunt Mary was the only person he knew who'd known his father well enough to pass along a story or two.

Still, it was difficult to imagine a family living

there. His own home in Ireland had not been small by any standards, but still, with four children it often felt as if they were constantly crashing into one another. You couldn't go ten minutes or even ten steps without being swept into a conversation with a cousin or a brother or an aunt or even a dog. (He'd been a good dog, God rest his furry little soul. Better than most people.)

They had *known* each other, the Audleys. It was, Jack had long since decided, a very good—and very uncommon—thing.

After a few minutes there was a small flurry of movement at the front door, then three women emerged. Two were blond. It was too far away to see their faces, but he could tell by the way they moved that they were young, and probably quite pretty.

Pretty girls, he'd long since learned, moved differently than the plain ones. It did not matter if they were aware of their beauty or not. What they *weren't* was aware of their plainness. Which the plain ones always were.

Jack quirked a half smile. He supposed he was a bit of a scholar of women. Which, he'd often tried to convince himself, was as noble a subject as any.

But it was the third girl—the last to emerge from the castle—who captured his breath and held him motionless, unable to look away.

It was the girl from the carriage the night before. He was sure of it. The hair was the right color—shiny and dark, but it wasn't such a unique shade that it couldn't be found elsewhere. He knew it was her because . . . because . . .

Because he did.

He *remembered* her. He remembered the way she moved, the way she felt pressed up against him. He remembered the soft breath of the air between their bodies when she'd moved away.

He'd liked her. He didn't often get the chance to like or dislike the people he waylaid, but he'd been thinking to himself that there was something rather appealing about the flash of intelligence in her eyes when the old lady had shoved her at him, giving him permission to hold a gun to her head.

He'd not approved of that. But he'd appreciated it all the same, because touching her, holding her—it had been an unexpected pleasure. And when the old lady returned with the miniature, his only thought had been that it was a pity he didn't have time to kiss her properly.

Jack held himself quietly as he watched her move in the drive, glancing over her shoulder, then leaning forward to say something to the other girls. One of the blondes linked arms with her and led her off to the side. They were friends, he realized with surprise, and he wondered if the girl—his girl, as he was now thinking of her—was something more than a companion. A poor relation, maybe? She was certainly not a daughter of the house, but it seemed she was not quite a servant.

She adjusted the straps of her bonnet, and then she (What was her name? He wanted to know her name) pointed to something in the distance. Jack found himself glancing the same way, but there were too many trees framing the drive for him to see whatever had captured her interest.

And then she turned.

Faced him.

Saw him.

She did not cry out, nor did she flinch, but he knew that she saw him in the way she. . .

In the way she simply *was*, he supposed, because he could not see her face from such a distance. But he knew.

His skin began to prickle with awareness, and it occurred to him that she'd recognized him, too. It was preposterous, because he was all the way down the drive, and not wearing his highwayman's garb, but he knew that she knew she was staring at the man who had kissed her.

The moment—it could only have lasted seconds—stretched into eternity. And then somewhere behind him a bird cawed, snapping him from his trance, and one thought pounded through his head.

Time to go.

He never stayed in one spot for long, but here—this place—it was surely the most dangerous of all.

He gave it one last look. Not of longing; he did not long for this. And as for the girl from the carriage—he fought down something strange and acrid, burning in his throat—he would not long for her, either.

Some things were simply untenable.

"Who was that man?"

Grace heard Elizabeth speak, but she pretended not

to. They were sitting in the Willoughbys' comfortable carriage, but their happy threesome now numbered four.

The dowager had, upon rising from her bed, taken one look at Amelia's sun-kissed cheeks (Grace did think that she and Thomas had taken quite a long walk together, all things considered), and gone into a barely intelligible tirade about the proper decorum of a future duchess. It was not every day one heard a speech containing dynasty, procreation, and sunspots—all in one sentence.

But the dowager had managed it, and now they were *all* miserable, Amelia most of all. The dowager had got it into her head that she needed to speak with Lady Crowland—most probably about the supposed blemishes on Amelia's skin—and so she invited herself along for the ride, giving instructions to the Wyndham stables to ready a carriage and send it after them for the return journey.

Grace had come along, too. Because, quite frankly, she didn't have any choice.

"Grace?" It was Elizabeth again.

Grace sucked in her lips and positively glued her eyes to a spot on the seat cushion just to the left of the dowager's head.

"Who was it?" Elizabeth persisted.

"No one," Grace said quickly. "Are we ready to depart?" She looked out the window, pretending to wonder why they were delayed on the drive. Any moment now they would leave for Burges Park, where the Willoughbys lived. She had been dreading the journey, short though it was.

And then she'd seen *him*.

The highwayman. Whose name wasn't Cavendish. But once was.

He had left before the dowager emerged from the castle, turning his mount in a display of horsemanship so expert that even she, who was no equestrienne, recognized his skill.

But he had seen her. And he had recognized her. She was certain of it.

She'd *felt* it.

Grace tapped her fingers impatiently against the side of her thigh. She thought of Thomas, and of the enormous portrait that had passed by the doorway of the sitting room. She thought of Amelia, who had been raised since birth to be the bride of a duke. And she thought of herself. Her world might not be quite what she wanted, but it was hers, and it was safe.

One man had the power to send it all crashing down.

Which was why, even though she would have traded a corner of her soul for just one more kiss from a man whose name she did not know, when Elizabeth remarked that it looked as if she knew him, she said, sharply, "I do not."

The dowager looked up, her face pinched with irritation. "What are you talking about?"

"There was a man at the end of the drive," Elizabeth said, before Grace could deny anything.

The dowager's head snapped back in Grace's direction. "Who was it?" she demanded.

"I don't know. I could not see his face." Which wasn't a lie. Not the second part, at least.

"Who was it?" the dowager thundered, her voice rising over the sound of the wheels beginning their rumble down the drive.

"I don't know," Grace repeated, but even she could hear the cracks in her voice.

"Did you see him?" the dowager asked Amelia.

Grace's eyes caught Amelia's. Something passed between them.

"I saw no one, ma'am," said Amelia.

The dowager dismissed her with a snort, turning the full weight of her fury on Grace. "Was it he?"

Grace shook her head. "I don't know," she stammered. "I couldn't say."

"Stop the carriage," the dowager yelled, lurching forward and shoving Grace aside so she could bang on the wall separating the cabin and the driver. "Stop, I tell you!"

The carriage came to a sudden stop, and Amelia, who had been sitting face front beside the dowager, tumbled forward, landing at Grace's feet. She tried to get up but was blocked by the dowager, who had reached across the carriage to grab Grace's chin, her long, ancient fingers digging cruelly into her skin.

"I will give you one more chance, Miss Eversleigh," she hissed. "Was it he?"

Forgive me, Grace thought.

She nodded.

Chapter Four

Ten minutes later Grace was in the Wyndham carriage, alone with the dowager, trying to remember just why she'd told Thomas he shouldn't commit his grandmother to an asylum. In the last five minutes the dowager had:

Turned the carriage around.

Shoved Grace out and to the ground, where she'd landed awkwardly on her right ankle.

Sent the Willoughby sisters on their way without the slightest explanation.

Had the Wyndham carriage brought around.

Outfitted aforementioned carriage with six large footmen.

Had Grace tossed inside. (The footman doing the tossing had apologized as he'd done so, but still.)

"Ma'am?" Grace asked hesitantly. They were speeding along at a rate that could not be considered safe, but the dowager kept banging her walking stick against the wall, bellowing at the driver to move faster.

"Ma'am? Where are we going?"

"You know very well."

Grace waited one careful moment, then said, "I'm sorry, ma'am, I don't."

The dowager speared her with an angry stare.

"We don't know where he is," Grace pointed out.

"We will find him."

"But, ma'am—"

"Enough!" the dowager ground out. Her voice was not loud, but it contained sufficient passion to silence Grace immediately. After a moment passed, she stole a glance at the older woman. She was sitting ramrod straight—too straight, really, for a ride in the carriage, and her right hand was bent and angled like a claw, pulling back the curtain so she might see outside.

Trees.

That's all there was to see. Grace couldn't imagine why the dowager was staring out so intently.

"If you saw him," the dowager said, her low voice cutting into Grace's thoughts, "then he is still in the district."

Grace said nothing. The dowager wasn't looking at her, in any case.

"Which means," the icy voice continued, "that there are only a very few places he might be. Three posting inns in the vicinity. That is all."

Grace rested her forehead in her hand. It was a sign of weakness, something she usually tried not to display in front of the dowager, but there was no maintaining a stiff facade now. They were going to kidnap him. She, Grace Catriona Eversleigh, who had never so much as nicked a ha'penny ribbon from a fair, was going to be party to what had to be a high crime. "Dear Lord," she whispered.

"Shut up," the dowager snapped, "and make yourself useful."

Grace grit her teeth. How the devil did the dowager think she *could* be useful? Surely any manhandling that needed doing would be performed by the footmen, each of whom stood, as per Belgrave regulations, five feet eleven inches tall. And no, she did not mistake their purpose on the journey. When she had looked askance at the dowager, the reply had been a terse, "My grandson might need convincing."

Now, the dowager growled, "Look out the window," speaking to her as if she'd turned idiot overnight. "You got the best look at him."

Dear God, she would gratefully forfeit five years off her life just to be anywhere but inside this carriage. "Ma'am, I said—he was at the end of the drive. I didn't really see him."

"You did last night."

Grace had been trying not to look at her, but at that, she could not help but stare.

"I saw you kissing him," the dowager hissed. "And I will warn you now. Don't try to rise above your station."

"Ma'am, he kissed *me*."

"He is my grandson," the dowager spat, "and he may very well be the true Duke of Wyndham, so do not be getting any ideas. You are valued as my companion, but *that is all*."

Grace could not find the outrage to react to the insult. Instead, she could only stare at the dowager in horror, unable to believe that she had actually spoken the words.

The true Duke of Wyndham.

Even the very suggestion of it was scandalous. Would she throw over Thomas so easily, strip him of his birthright, of his very name? Wyndham was not just a title Thomas held, it was who he was.

But if the dowager publicly championed the highwayman as the true heir . . . dear God, Grace could not even imagine the depth of the scandal it would create. The impostor would be proven illegitimate, of course—there could be no other outcome, surely—but the damage would be done. There would always be those who whispered that *maybe* Thomas wasn't really the duke, that maybe he ought not be so secure in his conceits, because he wasn't truly entitled to them, was he?

Grace could not imagine what this would do to him. To all of them.

"Ma'am," she said, her voice quavering slightly. "You cannot think that this man could be legitimate."

"Of course I can," the dowager snapped. "His manners were impeccable—"

"He was a highwayman!"

"One with a fine bearing and perfectly correct accent," the dowager retorted. "Whatever his current station, he was brought up properly and given a gentleman's education."

"But that does not mean—"

"My son died on a boat," the dowager interrupted,

her voice hard, "after he'd spent eight months in Ireland. Eight bloody months that were supposed to be four weeks. He went to attend a wedding. A wedding." Her body seemed to harden as she paused, her teeth grinding together at the memory. "And not even of anyone worth mentioning. Just some school friend whose parents bought themselves a title and bludgeoned their way into Eton, as if that could make them better than they were."

Grace's eyes widened. The dowager's voice had descended into a low, venomous hiss, and without even meaning to, Grace moved closer to the window. It felt toxic to be so close to her right now.

"And then . . ." the dowager continued. "And then! All I received was a three-sentence note, written in someone else's hand, reporting that he was having such a fine time that he believed he was going to remain."

Grace blinked. "He didn't write it himself?" she asked, unsure why she found this detail so curious.

"He signed it," the dowager said brusquely. "And sealed it with his ring. He knew I couldn't decipher his scrawl." She sat back, her face contorting with decades old anger and resentment. "Eight months," she muttered. "Eight stupid, useless months. Who is to say he did not marry some harlot over there? He had ample time."

Grace watched her for several moments. Her nose was in the air, and she gave every indication of haughty anger, but something was not quite right. Her lips were pinching and twisting, and her eyes were suspiciously bright.

"Ma'am—" Grace said gently.

"Don't," the dowager said, her voice sounding as if it might crack.

Grace considered the wisdom of speaking, then decided there was too much at stake to remain silent. "Your grace, it simply cannot be," she began, somehow maintaining her courage despite the withering expression on the dowager's face. "This is not a humble country entail. This is not Sillsby," she added, swallowing the lump that formed in her throat at the mention of her childhood home. "We are speaking of Belgrave. Of a dukedom. Heirs apparent do not simply vanish into the mist. If your son had had a son, we would have known."

The dowager stared at her for an uncomfortably sharp moment, then said, "We will try the Happy Hare first. It is the least uncouth of all the local posting inns." She settled back against the cushion, staring straight ahead as she said, "If he is anything like his father, he will be too fond of his comforts for anything less."

Jack was already feeling like an idiot when a sack was thrown over his head.

So this was it, then. He knew he'd stayed too long. The whole ride back he'd berated himself for the fool he was. He should have left after breakfast. He should have left at dawn. But no, he had to get drunk the night before, and then he had to ride out to that bloody castle. And then he'd seen *her*.

If he hadn't seen *her*, he would never have remained

at the end of the drive for so long. And then he wouldn't have ridden off with such speed. And had to rest and water his mount.

And he certainly wouldn't have been standing by the trough like a bloody bull's-eye when someone attacked him from behind.

"Bind him," a gruff voice said.

It was enough to set every pore in his body into fighting mode. A man did not spend his life so close to the noose without preparing for those two words.

It didn't matter that he couldn't see. It didn't matter that he had no idea who they were or why they'd come for him. He fought. And he knew how to fight, clean *and* dirty. But there were three of them at least, possibly more, and he managed only two good punches before he was facedown in the dirt, his hands yanked behind his back and bound with . . .

Well, it wasn't rope. Almost felt like silk, truth be told.

"Sorry," one of his captors mumbled, which was odd. Men in the business of tying up other men rarely thought to offer apologies.

"Think nothing of it," Jack returned, then cursed himself for his insolence. All his little quip earned him was a mouth full of burlap dust.

"This way," someone said, helping him to his feet.

And Jack could do nothing but obey.

"Er, if you please," the first voice said—the one who'd ordered him bound.

"Care to tell me where I'm going?" Jack inquired.

There was quite a bit of hemming and hawing. Minions. These were minions. He sighed. Minions never knew the important things.

"Er, can you step up?"

And then, before Jack could oblige, or even say, "Beg pardon," he was roughly hoisted into the air and tumbled into what had to be a carriage.

"Put him on a seat," a voice barked. He knew that voice. It was the old lady. His grandmother.

Well, at least he wasn't off to be hanged.

"Don't suppose someone will see to my horse," Jack said.

"See to his horse," the old lady snapped.

Jack allowed himself to be moved onto a seat, not a particularly easy maneuver, bound and blindfolded as he was.

"Don't suppose you'll untie my hands," he said.

"I'm not stupid," was the old lady's reply.

"No," he said with a false sigh. "I didn't think you were. Beauty and stupidity never go as hand in hand as one might wish."

"I am sorry I had to take you this way," the old lady said. "But you left me no choice."

"No choice," Jack mused. "Yes, of course. Because I've done so much to escape your clutches up to now."

"If you had intended to call upon me," the old lady said sharply, "you would not have ridden off earlier this afternoon."

Jack felt himself smile mockingly. "She told you, then," he said, wondering why he'd thought she might not.

"Miss Eversleigh?"

So that was her name.

"She had no choice," the old lady said dismissively, as if the wishes of Miss Eversleigh were something she rarely considered.

And then Jack felt it. A slight brush of air beside him. A faint rustle of movement.

She was there. The elusive Miss Eversleigh. The silent Miss Eversleigh.

The delicious Miss Eversleigh.

"Remove his hood," he heard his grandmother order. "You're going to suffocate him."

Jack waited patiently, affixing a lazy smile onto his face—it was not, after all, the expression they would expect, and thus the one he most wished to display. He heard her make a noise—Miss Eversleigh, that was. It wasn't a sigh exactly, and not a groan, either. It was something he couldn't quite place. Weary resignation, perhaps. Or maybe—

The hood came off, and he took a moment to savor the cool air on his face.

Then he looked at her.

It was mortification. That's what it had been. Poor Miss Eversleigh looked miserable. A more gracious gentleman would have turned away, but he wasn't feeling overly charitable at the moment, and so he treated himself to a lengthy perusal of her face. She was lovely, although not in any predictable manner. No English rose was she, not with that glorious dark hair and shining blue eyes that tilted up ever-so-slightly at the edges. Her lashes were dark and sooty, in stark contrast to the pale perfection of her skin.

Of course, that paleness might have been a result of her extreme discomfort. The poor girl looked as if she might cast up her accounts at any moment.

"Was it that bad, kissing me?" he murmured.

She turned scarlet.

"Apparently so." He turned to his grandmother and said in his most conversational tone, "I hope you realize this is a hanging offense."

"I am the Duchess of Wyndham," she replied with a haughty lift of her brow. "Nothing is a hanging offense."

"Ah, the unfairness of life," he said with a sigh. "Wouldn't you agree, Miss Eversleigh?"

She looked as if she wanted to speak. Indeed, the poor girl was most definitely biting her tongue.

"Now if *you* were the perpetrator in this little crime," he continued, allowing his eyes to slide insolently from her face to her bosom and back, "this would all be so very different."

Her jaw tightened.

"It would be," he murmured, allowing his gaze to fall to her lips, "rather lovely, I think. Just think—you, me, alone in this exceedingly luxurious carriage." He sighed contentedly and sat back. "The imagination runs wild."

He waited for the old lady to defend her. She did not.

"Care to share your plans for me?" he asked, propping one ankle over the opposite knee as he slouched in his seat. It wasn't an easy position to achieve, with his hands still stuck behind him, but he was damned if he'd sit up straight and polite.

The old lady turned to him, her lips pinched. "Most men would not complain."

He shrugged. "I am not most men." Then he offered a half smile and turned to Miss Eversleigh. "A rather banal rejoinder on my part, wouldn't you say? So obvious. A novice could have come up with it." He shook his head as if disappointed. "I do hope I'm not losing my touch."

Her eyes widened.

He grinned. "You think I'm mad."

"Oh, yes," she said, and he rather enjoyed her voice again, washing warmly over him.

"It's something to consider." He turned to the old lady. "Does madness run in the family?"

"Of course not," she snapped.

"Well, that's a relief. Not," he added, "that I am acknowledging a connection. I don't believe I wish to be associated with cutthroats such as yourself. Tsk tsk. Even I have never resorted to kidnapping." He leaned forward, as if imparting a very grave confidence to Miss Eversleigh. "It's very bad form, you know."

And he thought—oh, how *lovely*—that he saw her lips twitch. Miss Eversleigh had a sense of humor. She was growing more delectable by the second.

He smiled at her. He knew how to do it, too. He knew exactly how to smile at a woman to make her feel it deep inside.

He smiled at her. And she blushed.

Which made him smile even more.

"Enough," the old lady snapped.

He feigned innocence. "Of what?"

He looked at her, at this woman who was most

probably his grandmother. Her face was pinched and lined, the corners of her mouth pulled down by the weight of an eternal frown. She'd look unhappy even if she smiled, he thought. Even if somehow she managed to get that mouth to form a crescent in the correct direction—

No, he decided. It wouldn't work. She'd never manage it. She'd probably expire from the exertion.

"Leave my companion alone," she said tersely.

He leaned toward Miss Eversleigh, giving her a lopsided smile even though she was quite determinedly looking away. "Was I bothering you?"

"No," she said quickly. "Of course not."

Which couldn't have been further from the truth, but who was he to quibble?

He turned back to the old lady. "You didn't answer my question."

She lifted an imperious brow. *Ah*, he thought, completely without humor, *that was where he got the expression*.

"What do you plan to do with me?" he asked.

"Do with you." She repeated the words curiously, as if she found them most strange.

He lifted a brow right back at her, wondering if she'd recognize the gesture. "There are a great many options."

"My dear boy," she began. Her tone was grand. Condescending. As if he'd only needed this to realize that he ought to be licking her boots. "I'm going to give you the world."

* * *

Grace had just about managed to regain her equilibrium when the highwayman, after a lengthy and thoughtful frown, turned to the dowager and said, "I don't believe I'm interested in your world."

A bubble of horrified laughter burst forth from her throat. Oh dear heavens, the dowager looked ready to spit.

Grace clamped a hand over her mouth and turned away, trying not to notice that the highwayman was positively grinning at her.

"Apologies," he said to the dowager, not sounding the least bit contrite. "But can I have *her* world instead?"

Grace's head snapped back around in time to see him nodding in her direction. He shrugged. "I like you better."

"Are you never serious?" the dowager bit off.

And then he changed. His body did not move from its slouch, but Grace could feel the air around him coiling with tension. He was a dangerous man. He hid this well with his lazy charm and insolent smile. But he was not a man to be crossed. She was sure of it.

"I'm always serious," he said, his eyes never leaving those of the dowager. "You'd do well to take note of that."

"I'm so sorry," Grace whispered, the words slipping out before she had a chance to consider them. The gravity of the situation was bearing down on her with uncomfortable intensity. She had been so worried about Thomas and what this would all mean for him. But in that moment it was brought home to her that there were two men caught in this web.

And whatever this man was, whoever he was, he did not deserve this. Perhaps he would want life as a Cavendish, with its riches and prestige. Most men would. But he deserved the choice. Everyone deserved a choice.

She looked over at him then, forcing herself to bring her eyes to his face. She had been avoiding his gaze as much as she could, but her cowardice suddenly felt distasteful.

He must have felt her watching him, because he turned. His dark hair fell forward over his brow, and his eyes—a spectacular shade of mossy green—grew warm. "I do like you better," he murmured, and she thought—hoped?—that she saw a flicker of respect in his gaze.

And then, quick as a blink, the moment was gone. His mouth slid into that cocky half smile and he let out a pent-up breath before saying, "It's a compliment."

It was on the tip of her tongue to say, *Thank you*, as ridiculous as that seemed, but then he shrugged—one shoulder only, as if that was all he could be bothered with—and added, "Of course, I would imagine that the only person I would like *less* than our esteemed countess—"

"Duchess," the dowager snapped.

He paused, gave her a blandly haughty stare, then turned back to Grace. "As I was saying, the only person I would like less than *her*"—he jerked his head toward the dowager, not even honoring her with a direct glance—"would be the French menace himself, so I suppose it's not *that* much of a compliment, but I did want you to know that it was sincerely given."

Grace tried not to smile, but he always seemed to be looking at her as if they were sharing a joke, just the two of them, and she knew that it was making the dowager more furious by the second. A glance across the carriage confirmed this; the dowager looked even more starched and upset than usual.

Grace turned back to the highwayman, as much out of self-preservation as anything else. The dowager showed every sign of an imminent tirade, but after her performance the night before, Grace knew that she was far too besotted with the idea of her long-lost grandson to make him her target.

"What is your name?" Grace asked him, since it seemed the most obvious question.

"My name?"

Grace nodded.

He turned to the dowager with an expression of great scolding. "Funny that *you* haven't asked me yet." He shook his head. "Shameful manners. All the best kidnappers know their victims' names."

"I am not kidnapping you!" the dowager burst out.

There was an uncomfortable moment of silence, and then his voice emerged like silk. "I misunderstand the bindings, then."

Grace looked warily at the dowager. She'd never appreciated sarcasm unless it emerged from her own lips, and she would never allow him the last word. And indeed, when she spoke, her words were clipped and stiff, and colored blue with the blood of one secure in her own superiority. "I am restoring you to your proper place in this world."

"I see," he said slowly.

"Good," the dowager said briskly. "We are in accord, then. All that remains is for us to—"

"My proper place," he said, cutting her off.

"Indeed."

"In the world."

Grace realized that she was holding her breath. She could not look away, could not take her eyes off his when he murmured, "The conceit. It's remarkable."

His voice was soft, almost thoughtful, and it cut to the bone. The dowager turned sharply toward the window, and Grace searched her face for something— anything—that might have shown her humanity, but she remained stiff and hard, and her voice betrayed no emotion when she said, "We are almost home."

They were turning down the drive, passing the very spot where Grace had seen him earlier that afternoon.

"So you are," the highwayman said, glancing out the window.

"You will come to regard it as home," the dowager stated, her voice imperious and exacting and, more than anything else, final.

He did not respond. But he didn't need to. They all knew what he was thinking.

Never.

Chapter Five

"Lovely house," Jack said, as he was led—hands still bound—through the grand entrance of Belgrave. He turned to the old lady. "Did you decorate? It has that woman's touch."

Miss Eversleigh was trailing behind, but he could hear her choke back a bubble of laughter.

"Oh, let it out, Miss Eversleigh," he called over his shoulder. "Much better for your constitution."

"This way," the dowager ordered, motioning for him to follow her down the hall.

"Should I obey, Miss Eversleigh?"

She did not reply, smart girl that she was. But he was far too furious for circumspect sympathy, so he took his insolence one step further. "Yoo-hoo! Miss Eversleigh! Did you hear me?"

"Of course she heard you," the dowager snapped angrily.

Jack paused, cocking his head as he regarded the dowager. "I thought you were overjoyed to make my acquaintance."

"I am," she bit off.

"Hmmm." He turned to Miss Eversleigh, who had caught up to them during the exchange. "I don't think she sounds overjoyed, Miss Eversleigh. Do you?"

Miss Eversleigh's eyes darted from him to her employer and back before she said, "The dowager duchess is most eager to accept you into her family."

"Well said, Miss Eversleigh," he applauded. "Insightful and yet circumspect." He turned back to the dowager. "I hope you pay her well."

Two red spots appeared on the dowager's cheeks, in such stark relief to the white of her skin that he would have sworn she'd used rouge if he hadn't seen the angry marks appear with his own eyes. "You are dismissed," she ordered, not even looking at Miss Eversleigh.

"I am?" he feigned. "Lovely." He held out his bound wrists. "Would you mind?"

"Not you, *her.*" His grandmother's jaw clenched. "As you well know."

But Jack was not in the mood to be accommodating, and in that moment he did not even care to maintain his usual jocular facade. And so he looked her in the eye, his green meeting her icy, icy blue, and as he spoke, he felt a shiver of déjà vu. It was almost as if he were back on the Continent, back in battle, his shoulders straight and his eyes narrowed as he faced down the enemy.

"She stays."

They froze, all three of them, and Jack's eyes did not waver from the dowager's as he continued. "You brought her into this. She will remain through to the end."

He half expected Miss Eversleigh to protest. Hell, any sane person would have run as far as possible from the upcoming confrontation. But she stood utterly still, her arms stick-straight at her sides, her only movement her throat as she swallowed.

"If you want me," he said quietly, "you will take her as well."

The dowager sucked a long, angry breath through her nose and jerked her head to the side. "Grace," she barked, "the crimson drawing room. *Now.*"

Her name was Grace. He turned and looked at her. Her skin was pale and her eyes were wide and assessing.

Grace. He liked it. It fit her.

"Don't you want to know my name?" he called out to the dowager, who was already stalking down the hall.

She stopped and turned, as he knew she would.

"It's John," he announced, enjoying the way the blood drained from her face. "Jack to friends"—he looked at Grace with heavy-lidded seduction in his eyes—"and *friends*."

He could have sworn he felt her shiver, which delighted him.

"Are we?" he murmured.

Her lips parted a full second before she managed to make a sound. "Are we what?"

"Friends, of course."

"I—I—"

"Will you leave my companion alone!" the dowager barked.

He sighed and shook his head toward Miss Eversleigh. "She's so domineering, don't you think?"

Miss Eversleigh blushed. Truly, it was the prettiest pink he'd ever seen.

"Pity about these bindings," he continued. "We do seem to be caught in a romantic moment, your employer's acidic presence aside, and it would be far easier to drop one exquisite kiss on the back of your hand were I able to lift it with one of mine."

This time he was certain she shivered.

"Or your mouth," he whispered. "I might kiss your mouth."

There was a lovely silence, broken rather rudely by: *"What the devil?"*

Miss Eversleigh jumped back a foot or three, and Jack turned to see an extremely angry man striding his way.

"Is this man bothering you, Grace?" he demanded.

She shook her head quickly. "No, no, he's not. But—"

The newcomer turned to Jack with furious blue eyes. Furious blue eyes that rather closely resembled those of the dowager, save for the bags and wrinkles. "Who are you?"

"Who are *you?*" Jack countered, instantly disliking him.

"I am Wyndham," he shot back. "And you are in my home."

Jack blinked. A cousin. His new family was growing more charming by the second. "Ah. Well, in that case, I am Jack Audley. Formerly of His Majesty's esteemed army, more recently of the dusty road."

"Who are these Audleys?" the dowager demanded, crossing back over. "You are no Audley. It is there in your face. In your nose and chin and in every bloody feature save your eyes, which are quite the wrong color."

"The wrong color?" Jack responded, acting hurt. "Really?" He turned to Miss Eversleigh. "I was always told the ladies *like* green eyes. Was I misinformed?"

"You are a Cavendish!" the dowager roared. "You are a Cavendish, and I demand to know why I was not informed of your existence."

"What the *devil* is going on?" Wyndham demanded.

Jack thought it wasn't his duty to answer, so he happily kept quiet.

"Grace?" Wyndham asked, turning to Miss Eversleigh.

Jack watched the exchange with interest. They were friends, but were they *friendly*? He could not be sure.

Miss Eversleigh swallowed with noticeable discomfort. "Your grace," she said, "perhaps a word in private?"

"And spoil it for the rest of us?" Jack chimed in, because after what he'd been subjected to, he didn't much feel that anyone deserved a moment of privacy. And then, to achieve maximum irritation, he added, "After all I've been through . . ."

"He is your cousin," the dowager announced sharply.

"He is the highwayman," Miss Eversleigh said.

"Not," Jack added, turning to display his bound hands, "here of my own volition, I assure you."

"Your grandmother thought she recognized him last night," Miss Eversleigh told the duke.

"I *knew* I recognized him," the dowager snapped. Jack resisted the urge to duck as she flicked her hand at him. "Just look at him."

Jack turned to the duke. "I was wearing a mask." Because really, he shouldn't have to take the blame for this.

He smiled cheerfully, watching the duke with interest as he brought his hand to his forehead and pressed his temples with enough force to crush his skull. And then, just like that, his hand fell away and he yelled, "Cecil!"

Jack was about to make a quip about another lost cousin, but at that moment a footman—presumably named Cecil—came skidding down the hall.

"The portrait," Wyndham bit off. "Of my uncle."

"The one we just brought up to—"

"Yes. In the drawing room. *Now!*"

Even Jack's eyes widened at the furious energy in his voice.

And then—it was like acid in his belly—he saw Miss Eversleigh lay a hand on the duke's arm. "Thomas," she said softly, surprising him with her use of his given name, "please allow me to explain."

"Did you know about this?" Wyndham demanded.

"Yes, but—"

"Last night," he said icily. "Did you know last night?"

Last night?

"I did, but Thomas—"

What happened last night?

"Enough," he spat. "Into the drawing room. All of you."

Jack followed the duke, and then, once the door was shut behind them, held up his hands. "D'you think you might . . . ?" he asked. Rather conversationally, if he did say so himself.

"For the love of Christ," Wyndham muttered. He grabbed something from a writing table near the wall and then returned. With one angry swipe, he cut through the bindings with a gold letter opener.

Jack looked down to make sure he wasn't bleeding. "Well done," he murmured. Not even a scratch.

"Thomas," Miss Eversleigh was saying, "I really think you ought to let me speak with you for a moment before—"

"Before what?" Wyndham snapped, turning on her with what Jack deemed rather unbecoming fury. "Before I am informed of another long-lost cousin whose head may or may not be wanted by the Crown?"

"Not by the Crown, I think," Jack said mildly. He had his reputation to think of, after all. "But surely a few magistrates. And a vicar or two." He turned to the dowager. "Highway robbery is not generally considered the most secure of all possible occupations."

His levity was appreciated by no one, not even poor Miss Eversleigh, who had managed to incur the fury of both Wyndhams. Rather undeservedly, too, in his opinion. He hated bullies.

"Thomas," Miss Eversleigh implored, her tone once

again causing Jack to wonder just what, precisely, existed between those two. "Your grace," she corrected, with a nervous glance over at the dowager, "there is something you need to know."

"Indeed," Wyndham bit off. "The identities of my true friends and confidantes, for one thing."

Miss Eversleigh flinched as if struck, and at that moment Jack decided that he'd had quite enough. "I suggest," he said, his voice light but steady, "that you speak to Miss Eversleigh with greater respect."

The duke turned to him, his eyes as stunned as the silence that descended over the room. "I *beg* your pardon."

Jack hated him in that moment, every prideful little aristocratic speck of him. "Not used to being spoken to like a man, are we?" he taunted.

The air went electric, and Jack knew he probably should have foreseen what would come next, but the duke's face had positively twisted into fury, and Jack somehow could not seem to move as Wyndham launched himself forward, his hands wrapping themselves around his throat as the both of them went crashing down to the carpet.

Cursing himself for a fool, Jack tried to get traction as the duke's fist slammed into his jaw. Pure animalistic survival set in, and he tensed his belly into a hard knot. With one lightning-quick movement he threw his torso forward, using his head as a weapon. There was a satisfying crack as he struck Wyndham's jaw, and Jack took advantage of his stunned state to roll them over and reverse their positions.

"Don't . . . you. . . . *ever* strike me again," Jack

growled. He'd fought in gutters, on battlefields, for his country and for his life, and he'd *never* had patience for men who threw the first punch.

He took an elbow in the belly and was about to return the favor with a knee to the groin when Miss Eversleigh leapt into the fray, wedging herself between the two men with nary a thought to propriety or her own safety.

"Stop it! Both of you!"

Jack managed to nudge Wyndham's upper arm just in time to stop his fist from reaching her cheek. It would have been an accident, of course, but then he'd have had to kill him, and that *would* have been a hanging offense.

"You should be ashamed of yourself," Miss Eversleigh scolded, looking straight at the duke.

He merely raised a brow and said, "You might want to remove yourself from my, er . . ." He looked down at his midsection, upon which she was now seated.

"Oh!" She jumped up, and Jack would have defended her honor except that he had to admit he'd have said the same thing were he seated under her. Not to mention that she was still holding his arm.

"Tend to my wounds?" he asked, making his eyes big and green and brimming with the world's most effective expression of seduction. Which was, of course, *I need you. I need you and if you would only care for me I will forswear all other women and melt at your feet and quite possibly become filthy rich and if you'd like even royal all in one dreamy swoop.*

It never failed.

Except, apparently, now. "You have no wounds,"

she snapped, thrusting him away. She looked over at Wyndham, who had risen to his feet beside her. "And neither do you."

Jack was about to make a comment about the milk of human kindness, but just then the dowager stepped forward and smacked her grandson—that would be the grandson of whose lineage they were quite certain—in the shoulder.

"Apologize at once!" she snapped. "He is a guest in our house."

A guest. Jack was touched.

"*My* house," the duke snapped back.

Jack watched the old lady with interest. She wouldn't take well to that.

"He is your first cousin," she said tightly. "One would think, given the lack of close relations in our family, that you would be eager to welcome him into the fold."

Oh, right. The duke was just *brimming* with joy.

"Would someone," Wyndham bit off, "do me the service of explaining just how this man has come to be in my drawing room?"

Jack waited for someone to offer an explanation, and then, when none was forthcoming, offered his own version. "She kidnapped me," he said with shrug, motioning toward the dowager.

Wyndham turned slowly to his grandmother. "You kidnapped him," he said, his voice flat and strangely devoid of disbelief.

"Indeed," she replied, her chin butting up in the air. "And I would do it again."

"It's true," Miss Eversleigh said. And then she delighted him by turning in his direction and saying, "I'm sorry."

"Accepted, of course," Jack said graciously.

The duke, however, was not amused. To the extent that poor Miss Eversleigh felt the need to defend her actions with, "She *kidnapped* him!"

Wyndham ignored her. Jack was *really* starting to dislike him.

"And forced me to take part," Miss Eversleigh muttered. She, on the other hand, was quickly becoming one of his favorite people.

"I recognized him last night," the dowager announced.

Wyndham looked at her disbelievingly. "In the dark?"

"Under his mask," she answered with pride. "He is the very image of his father. His voice, his laugh, every bit of it."

Jack hadn't thought this a particularly convincing argument himself, so he was curious to see how the duke responded.

"Grandmother," he said, with what Jack had to allow was remarkable patience, "I understand that you still mourn your son—"

"Your uncle," she cut in.

"My uncle." He cleared his throat. "But it has been thirty years since his death."

"Twenty-nine," she corrected sharply.

"It has been a long time," Wyndham said. "Memories fade."

"Not mine," she replied haughtily, "and certainly not the ones I have of John. *Your* father I have been more than pleased to forget entirely—"

"In that we are agreed," Wyndham interrupted, leaving Jack to wonder at *that* story. And then, looking as if he very much still wished to strangle someone (Jack would have put his money on the dowager, since he'd already had the pleasure), Wyndham turned and bellowed, "Cecil!"

"Your grace!" came a voice from the hall. Jack watched as two footmen struggled to bring a massive painting around the corner and into the room.

"Set it down anywhere," the duke ordered.

With a bit of grunting and one precarious moment during which it seemed the painting would topple what was, to Jack's eye, an extremely expensive Chinese vase, the footmen managed to find a clear spot and set the painting down on the floor, leaning it gently against the wall.

Jack stepped forward. They all stepped forward. And Miss Eversleigh was the first to say it.

"Oh my God."

It was him. Of course it wasn't *him*, because it was John Cavendish, who had perished nearly three decades earlier, but by *God*, it looked exactly like the man standing next to her.

Grace's eyes grew so wide they hurt, and she looked back and forth and back and forth and—

"I see no one is disagreeing with me now," the dowager said smugly.

Thomas turned to Mr. Audley as if he'd seen a ghost. "Who *are* you?" he whispered.

But even Mr. Audley was without words. He was just staring at the portrait, staring and staring and staring, his face white, his lips parted, his entire body slack.

Grace held her breath. Eventually he'd find his voice, and when he did, surely he'd tell them all what he'd told her the night before.

My name isn't Cavendish.

But it once was.

"My name," Mr. Audley stammered, "my given name . . ." He paused, swallowed convulsively, and his voice shook as he said, "My full name is John Rollo Cavendish-Audley."

"Who were your parents?" Thomas whispered.

Mr. Audley—Mr. *Cavendish*-Audley—didn't answer.

"Who was your father?" Thomas's voice was louder this time, more insistent.

"Who the bloody hell do you think he was?" Mr. Audley snapped.

Grace's heart pounded. She looked at Thomas. He was pale and his hands were shaking, and she felt like such a traitor. She could have told him. She could have warned him.

She had been a coward.

"Your parents," Thomas said, his voice low. "Were they married?"

"What is your implication?" Mr. Audley demanded, and for a moment Grace feared that they would come to blows again. Mr. Audley brought to mind a caged beast, poked and prodded until he could stand it no more.

"Please," she pleaded, jumping between them yet again. "He doesn't know," she said. Mr. Audley couldn't know what it meant if he was indeed legitimate. But Thomas did, and he'd gone so still that Grace thought he might shatter. She looked at him, and at his grandmother. "Someone needs to explain to Mr. Audley—"

"Cavendish," the dowager snapped.

"Mr. Cavendish-Audley," Grace said quickly, because she did not know how to style him without offending *someone* in the room. "Someone needs to tell him that . . . that . . ."

She looked to the others for help, for guidance, for something, because surely this was not her duty. She was the only one of them there not of Cavendish blood. Why did *she* have to make all of the explanations?

She looked at Mr. Audley, trying not to see the portrait in his face, and said, "Your father—the man in the painting, that is—assuming he *is* your father—he was his grace's father's . . . *elder* brother."

No one said anything.

Grace cleared her throat. "So, if . . . if your parents were indeed lawfully married—"

"They were," Mr. Audley all but snapped.

"Yes, of course. I mean, not of course, but—"

"What she means," Thomas cut in sharply, "is that if you are indeed the legitimate offspring of John Cavendish, then you are the Duke of Wyndham."

And there it was. The truth. Or if not the truth, then

the possibility of the truth, and no one, not even the dowager, knew what to say. The two men—the two dukes, Grace thought with a hysterical bubble of laughter—simply stared at each other, taking each other's measure, and then finally Mr. Audley's hand seemed to reach out. It shook, quivered like the dowager's when she was attempting to find purchase, and then finally, when it settled on the back of a chair, his fingers grasped tightly. With legs that were clearly unsteady, Mr. Audley sat down.

"No," he said. "No."

"You will remain here," the dowager directed, "until this matter can be settled to my satisfaction."

"No," Mr. Audley said with considerably more conviction. "I will not."

"Oh, yes, you will," she responded. "If you do not, I will turn you in to the authorities as the thief you are."

"You wouldn't do that," Grace blurted out. She turned to Mr. Audley. "She would never do that. Not if she believes that you are her grandson."

"Shut up!" the dowager growled. "I don't know what you think you are doing, Miss Eversleigh, but you are not family, and you have no place in this room."

Mr. Audley stood. His bearing was sharp, and proud, and for the first time Grace saw within him the military man he'd said he once was. When he spoke, his words were measured and clipped, completely unlike the lazy drawl she had come to expect from him.

"Do not speak to her in that manner ever again."

Something inside of her melted. Thomas had defended her against his grandmother before; indeed, he'd long been her champion. But not like this. He valued her friendship, she knew that he did. But this . . . this was different. She didn't hear the words.

She felt them.

And as she watched Mr. Audley's face, her eyes slid to his mouth. It came back to her . . . the touch of his lips, his kiss, his breath, and the bittersweet shock when he was through, because she hadn't wanted it . . . and then she hadn't wanted it to end.

There was perfect silence, stillness even, save for the widening of the dowager's eyes. And then, just when Grace realized that her hands had begun to tremble, the dowager bit off, "I am your grandmother."

"That," Mr. Audley replied, "remains to be determined."

Grace's lips parted with surprise, because no one could doubt his parentage, not with the proof propped up against the drawing room wall.

"What?" Thomas burst out. "Are you now trying to tell me that you *don't* think you are the son of John Cavendish?"

Mr. Audley shrugged, and in an instant the steely determination in his eyes was gone. He was a highwayman rogue again, devil-may-care and completely without responsibility. "Frankly," he said, "I'm not so certain I wish to gain entry into this charming little club of yours."

"You don't have a choice," the dowager said.

"So loving," Mr. Audley said with sigh. "So thoughtful. Truly, a grandmother for the ages."

Grace clamped a hand over her mouth, but her

choked laughter came through nonetheless. It was so inappropriate . . . in so many ways . . . but it was impossible to keep it in. The dowager's face had gone purple, her lips pinched until the lines of anger drew up to her nose. Not even Thomas had ever provoked such a reaction, and heaven knew, he had tried.

She looked over at him. Of everyone in the room, surely he was the one with the most at stake. He looked exhausted. And bewildered. And furious, and amazingly, about to laugh. "Your grace," she said hesitantly. She didn't know what she wanted to say to him. There probably wasn't anything *to* say, but the silence was just awful.

He ignored her, but she knew he'd heard, because his body stiffened even more, then shuddered when he let out a breath. And then the dowager—oh why would she never learn to leave well enough alone?—bit off his name as if she were summoning a dog.

"Shut *up*," he snapped back.

Grace wanted to reach out to him. Thomas was her friend, but he was—and he always had been—so far above her. And now she was standing here, hating herself because she could not stop thinking about the other man in the room, the one who might very well steal Thomas's very identity.

And so she did nothing. And hated herself even more for it.

"You should remain," Thomas said to Mr. Audley. "We will need—"

Grace held her breath as Thomas cleared his throat.

"We will need to get this sorted out."

They all waited for Mr. Audley's response. He seemed to be assessing Thomas, taking his measure. Grace prayed he would realize just how difficult it must have been for Thomas to speak to him with such civility. Surely he would respond in kind. She wanted him so badly to be a good person. He'd kissed her. He'd defended her. Was it too much to hope that he was, underneath it all, a white knight?

Chapter Six

Jack had always prided himself on being able to spot the irony in any situation, but as he stood in the Belgrave drawing room—correction, *one* of the Belgrave drawing rooms, surely there were dozens—he could find nothing but stark, cold reality.

He'd spent six years as an officer in His Majesty's army, and if he'd learned one thing from his years on the battlefield, it was that life could, and frequently did, turn on a single moment. One wrong turn, one missed clue, and he could lose an entire company of men. But once he returned to Britain, he'd somehow lost sight of that. His life was a series of small decisions and insignificant encounters. It was true that he was living a life of crime, which meant he was always dancing a few steps ahead of the hangman's noose, but it wasn't the same. No one's life depended upon his actions. No one's livelihood, even.

There was nothing serious about robbing coaches. It was a game, really, played by men with too much education and too little direction. Who would have thought that one of his insignificant decisions—to take the Lincoln road north instead of south—would lead to this? Because one thing was for certain, his carefree life on the road was over. He suspected that Wyndham would be more than happy to watch him ride away without a word, but the dowager would not be so accommodating. Miss Eversleigh's assurances aside, he was quite certain the old bat would go to extensive lengths to keep him on a leash. Maybe she would not turn him over to the authorities, but she could certainly tell the world that her long-lost grandson was gadding about the countryside robbing coaches. Which would make it *damned* difficult to continue in his chosen profession.

And if he was truly the Duke of Wyndham . . .

God help them all.

He was beginning to hope that his aunt had lied. Because no one wanted him in a position of such authority, least of all himself.

"Could someone please explain . . ." He took a breath and stopped, pressing his fingers against his temples. It felt as if an entire battalion had marched across his forehead. "Could someone explain the family tree?" Because shouldn't someone have *known* if his father had been the heir to a dukedom? His aunt? His mother? Himself?

"I had three sons," the dowager said crisply. "Charles was the eldest; John, the middle; and Reginald the last. Your father left for Ireland just after Reginald married"—her face took on a visible expression of distaste, and she jerked her head toward Wyndham— "*his* mother."

"She was a Cit," Wyndham said, with no expression whatsoever. "Her father owned factories. Piles and piles of them." One of his brows lifted. Very slightly. "We own them now."

The dowager's lips tightened, but she did not acknowledge his interruption. "We were notified of your father's death in July of 1790."

Jack nodded tightly. He had been told the same.

"One year after that, my husband and my eldest son died of a fever. I did not contract the ailment. My youngest son was no longer living at Belgrave, so he, too, was spared. Charles had not yet married, and we believed John to have died without issue. Thus Reginald became duke." She paused, but other than that expressed no emotion. "It was not expected."

Everyone looked at Wyndham. He said nothing,

"I will remain," Jack said quietly, because he didn't see as he had any other choice. And maybe it wouldn't hurt to learn a thing or two of his father. A man ought to know where he comes from. That was what his uncle had always said. Jack was beginning to wonder if he'd been offering forgiveness—in advance. Just in case he decided one day that he wished to be a Cavendish.

Of course, Uncle William hadn't met *these* Cavendishes. If he had, he might've revised that statement entirely.

"Most judicious of you," the dowager said, clapping her hands together. "Now then, we—"

"But first," Jack cut in, "I must return to the inn to collect my belongings." He glanced around the drawing room, almost laughing at the opulence. "Meager though they are."

"Nonsense," the dowager said briskly. "Your things will be replaced." She looked down her nose at his traveling costume. "With items of far greater quality, I might add."

"I wasn't asking your permission," Jack said lightly. He did not like to allow his anger to reveal itself in his voice. It did put a man at a disadvantage.

"Nonethe—"

"Furthermore," Jack added, because really, he didn't wish to hear her voice any more than he had to, "I must make explanations to my associates." At that he looked over at Wyndham. "Nothing approaching the truth," he added dryly, lest the duke assume that he intended to spread rumors throughout the county.

"Don't disappear," the dowager directed. "I assure you, you will regret it."

"There's no worry of that," Wyndham said blandly. "Who would disappear with the promise of a dukedom?"

Jack's jaw tightened, but he forced himself to let it pass. The afternoon did not need another fistfight.

And then—bloody hell—the duke abruptly added, "I will accompany you."

Oh, good God. That was the last thing he needed. Jack swung around to face him, lifting one dubious brow. "Need I worry for my safety?"

Wyndham stiffened visibly, and Jack, who had been

trained to notice even the smallest of details, saw that both of his fists clenched at his sides. So he'd insulted the duke. At this point, and considering the bruises he was likely to find staining his throat, he didn't care.

He turned to Miss Eversleigh, offering her his most self-effacing smile. "I am a threat to his very identity. Surely any reasonable man would question his safety."

"No, you're wrong!" she cried out. "You misjudge him. The duke—"

She shot a horrified look at Wyndham, and they all were forced to share her discomfort when she realized what she'd said. But she plowed on, determined girl that she was.

"He is as honorable a man as I have ever met," she continued, her voice low and fervent. "You would never come to harm in his company."

Her cheeks had flushed with passion, and Jack was struck by the most acidic thought. *Was* there something between Miss Eversleigh and the duke? They resided in the same house, or castle, as it were, with only an embittered old lady for company. And while the dowager was anything but senile, Jack could not imagine that there was any lack of opportunity to engage in a dalliance under her nose.

He watched Miss Eversleigh closely, his eyes falling to her lips. He'd surprised himself when he kissed her the night before. He hadn't meant to, and he certainly had never done such a thing before whilst attempting to rob a coach. It had seemed the most natural thing in the world—to touch her chin, tilt her face up toward his, and brush his lips against hers.

It had been soft, and fleeting, and it had taken him until this moment to realize just how deeply he wanted more.

He looked at Wyndham, and his jealousy must have shown on his face because his newly discovered cousin looked coolly amused as he said, "I assure you, whatever violent urges I possess, I shall not act upon them."

"That is a terrible thing to say," Miss Eversleigh responded.

"But honest," Jack acknowledged with a nod. He did not like this man, this duke who had been brought up to view the world as his private domain. But he appreciated honesty, no matter the source.

And as Jack looked him in the eye, there seemed to develop an unspoken agreement. They did not have to be friends. They did not even have to be friendly. But they would be honest.

Which suited Jack just fine.

By Grace's calculations, the men ought to have returned within ninety minutes, two hours at most. She had not spent much time in a saddle, so she was not the best judge of speed, but she was fairly certain that two men on horseback could reach the posting inn in something less than an hour. Then Mr. Audley would need to retrieve his belongings, which could not take very long, could it? And then—

"Get away from the window," the dowager snapped.

Grace's lips tightened with irritation, but she managed to return her expression to one of placidity before she turned around.

"Make yourself useful," the dowager said.

Grace glanced this way and that, trying to decode the dowager's order. She always had something specific in mind, and Grace hated it when she was forced to guess.

"Would you like me to read to you?" she asked. It was the most pleasant of her duties; they were currently reading *Pride and Prejudice*, which Grace was enjoying immensely, and the dowager was pretending not to like at all.

The dowager grunted. It was a *no* grunt. Grace was fluent in this method of communication. She took no particular pride in this skill.

"I could pen a letter," she suggested. "Weren't you planning to respond to the recent missive from your sister?"

"I can write my own letters," the dowager said sharply, even though they both knew her spelling was atrocious. Grace always ended up rewriting all of her correspondence before it was posted.

Grace took a deep breath and then let it out slowly, the exhale shuddering through her. She did not have the energy to untangle the inner workings of the dowager's mind. Not today.

"I'm hot," the dowager announced.

Grace did not respond. She was hoping none was necessary. And then the dowager picked something up off a nearby table. A fan, Grace realized with dismay, just as the dowager snapped it open.

Oh, please, no. Not now.

The dowager regarded the fan, a rather festive blue one, with Chinese paintings in black and gold. Then she snapped it back shut, clearly just to make it easier for her to hold it before her like a baton.

"You may make me more comfortable," she said.

Grace paused. It was only for a moment, probably not even a full second, but it was her only means of rebellion. She could not say no, and she could not even allow her distaste to show in her expression. But she could pause. She could hold her body still for just enough time to make the dowager wonder.

And then, of course, she stepped forward.

"I find the air quite pleasant," she said once she had assumed her position at the dowager's side.

"That is because you are pushing it about with the fan."

Grace looked down at her employer's pinched face. Some of the lines were due to age, but not the ones near her mouth, pulling her lips into a perpetual frown. What had happened to this woman to make her so bitter? Had it been the deaths of her children? The loss of her youth? Or had she simply been born with a sour disposition?

"What do you think of my new grandson?" the dowager asked abruptly.

Grace froze, then quickly regained her composure and resumed fanning. "I do not know him well enough to form an opinion," she answered carefully.

The dowager continued to look straight ahead as she answered, "Nonsense. All of the best opinions are formed in an instant. You know that very well. 'Else you'd be married to that repulsive little cousin of yours, wouldn't you?"

Grace thought of Miles, ensconced in her old home. She had to admit, every now and then the dowager got things exactly right.

"Surely you have something to say, Miss Eversleigh."

The fan rose and fell three times before Grace decided upon, "He seems to have a buoyant sense of humor."

"Buoyant." The dowager repeated the word, her voice curious, as if she were testing it out on her tongue. "An apt adjective. I should not have thought of it, but it is fitting."

It was about as close to a compliment as the dowager ever got.

"He is rather like his father," the dowager continued.

Grace moved the fan from one hand to the other, murmuring, "Is he?"

"Indeed. Although if his father had been a bit more . . . *buoyant*, we'd not be in this mess, would we?"

Grace choked on air. "I'm so sorry, ma'am. I should have chosen my words more carefully."

The dowager did not bother to acknowledge the apology. "His levity is much like his father. My John was never one to allow a serious moment to pass him by. He had the most cutting wit."

"I would not say that Mr. Audley is cutting," Grace said. His humor was far too sly.

"His name is not Mr. Audley, and of course he is," the dowager said sharply. "You're too besotted to see it."

"I am not besotted," Grace protested.

"Of course you are. Any girl would be. He is most handsome. Pity about the eyes, though."

"What I am," Grace said, resisting the urge to point out that there was nothing wrong with green eyes, "is overset. It has been a most exhausting day. And night," she added after a thought.

The dowager shrugged. "My son's wit was legendary," she said, setting the conversation back to where she wished it. "You wouldn't have thought it cutting, either, but that was simply because he was far too clever. It is a brilliant man who can make insult without the recipient even realizing."

Grace thought that rather sad. "What is the point, then?"

"The point?" The dowager blinked several times in rapid succession. "Of what?"

"Of insulting someone." Grace shifted the fan again, then shook out her free hand; her fingers were cramped from clutching the handle. "Or I should say," she amended, since she was quite sure the dowager could find many good reasons to cut someone down, "of insulting someone with intention of their not noticing it?"

The dowager still did not look at her, but Grace could see that she rolled her eyes. "It is a source of pride, Miss Eversleigh. I wouldn't expect you to understand."

"No," Grace said softly. "I wouldn't."

"You don't know what it means to excel at something." The dowager pursed her lips and stretched her neck slightly from side to side. "You couldn't know."

Which had to be as cutting an insult as any, except

that the dowager seemed completely unaware she'd done it.

There was irony in there somewhere. There had to be.

"We live in interesting times, Miss Eversleigh," the dowager commented.

Grace nodded silently, turning her head to the side so that the dowager, should she ever choose to turn her head in her direction, would not see the tears in her eyes. Her parents had lacked the funds to travel, but theirs had been wandering hearts, and the Eversleigh home had been filled with maps and books about far-away places. Like it was yesterday, Grace remembered the time they had all been sitting in front of the fire, engrossed in their own reading, and her father looked up from his book and exclaimed, "Isn't this marvelous? In China, if you wish to insult someone, you say, 'May you live in interesting times.'"

Grace suddenly did not know if the tears in her eyes were of sorrow or mirth.

"That is enough, Miss Eversleigh," the dowager said suddenly. "I am quite cooled."

Grace shut the fan, then decided to set it down on the table by the window so she would have a reason to cross the room. Dusk hung only lightly in the air, so it was not difficult to see down the drive. She was not certain why she was so eager to have the two men back—possibly just as proof that they had not killed each other on the trip. Despite defending Thomas's sense of honor, she had not liked the look in his eyes. And she had certainly never known him to attack someone. He'd looked positively feral when he lunged for Mr. Audley. If Mr. Audley had been less of a fighting man himself, she was quite certain Thomas would have done him permanent harm.

"Do you think it will rain, Miss Eversleigh?"

Grace turned. "No."

"The wind is picking up."

"Yes." Grace waited until the dowager turned her attention to a trinket on the table next to her, and then she turned back to the window. Of course the moment she did, she heard—

"I hope it rains."

She held still. And then she turned. "I beg your pardon?"

"I hope it rains." The dowager said it again, so very matter-of-fact, as if anyone would wish for precipitation while two gentlemen were out on horseback.

"They will be drenched," Grace pointed out.

"They will be forced to take each other's measure. Which they will have to do sooner or later. Besides, my John never minded riding in the rain. In fact, he rather enjoyed it."

"That does not mean that Mr.—"

"Cavendish," the dowager inserted.

Grace swallowed. It helped her catch her patience. "Whatever he wishes to be called, I don't think we may assume that he enjoys riding in the rain just because his father did. Most people do not."

The dowager did not seem to wish to consider this. But she acknowledged the statement with, "I know nothing of the mother, that is true. She could be responsible for any number of adulterations."

"Would you care for tea, ma'am?" Grace asked. "I could ring for it."

"What do we know of her, after all? Almost certainly Irish, which could mean any number of things, all of them dreadful."

"The wind is picking up," Grace said. "I shouldn't want you to get chilled."

"Did he even tell us her name?"

"I don't believe so." Grace sighed, because direct questions made it difficult to pretend she wasn't a part of this conversation.

"Dear Lord." The dowager shuddered, and her eyes took on an expression of utter horror. "She could be *Catholic.*"

"I have met several Catholics," Grace said, now that it was clear that her attempts to divert the subject had failed. "It was strange," she murmured. "None had horns."

"*What* did you say?"

"Just that I know very little about the Catholic faith," Grace said lightly. There was a reason she often directed her comments to a window or wall.

The dowager made a noise that Grace could not quite identify. It sounded like a sigh, but it was probably more of a snort, because the next words from her mouth were: "We shall have to get that taken care of." She leaned forward, pinching the bridge of her nose with her fingers and looking extremely put out. "I suppose I shall have to contact the archbishop."

"Is that a problem?" Grace asked.

The dowager's head shook with distaste. "He is a

beady little man who will be lording this over me for years."

Grace leaned forward. Was that movement she saw in the distance?

"Heaven knows what sorts of favors he shall demand," the dowager muttered. "I suppose I shall have to let him sleep in the State Bedroom, just so he can say he slept on Queen Elizabeth's sheets."

Grace watched as the two men on horseback came into view. "They are back," she said, and not for the first time that evening, wondered just what role she was meant to play in this drama. She was not family; the dowager was certainly correct in that. And despite Grace's relatively lofty position within the household, she was not included in matters pertaining to family or title. She did not expect it, and indeed she did not want it. The dowager was at her worst when matters of dynasty arose, and Thomas was at his worst when he had to deal with the dowager.

She should excuse herself. It did not matter that Mr. Audley had insisted upon her presence. Grace knew her position, and she knew her place, and it was not in the middle of a family affair.

But every time she told herself it was time to go, that she ought to turn from the window and inform the dowager that she would leave her to talk with her grandsons in private, she could not make herself move. She kept hearing—no, *feeling*—Mr. Audley's voice.

She stays.

Did he need her? He might. He knew nothing of the

Wyndhams, nothing of their history and the tensions that ran through the house like a vicious, intractable spiderweb. He could not be expected to navigate his new life on his own, at least not right away.

Grace shivered, hugging her arms to her chest as she watched the men dismount in the drive. How strange it was to feel needed. Thomas liked to say he needed her, but they both knew that was untrue. He could hire anyone to put up with his grandmother. Thomas needed no one. Nothing. He was marvelously self-contained. Confident and proud, all he really needed was the occasional pinprick to burst the bubble that surrounded him. He knew this, too, which was what saved him from being entirely insufferable. He'd never said as much, but Grace knew it was why they had become friends. She was possibly the only person in Lincolnshire who did not bow and scrape and say only what she thought he wished to hear.

But he didn't *need* her.

Grace heard footsteps in the hall and turned, stiffening nervously. She waited for the dowager to order her gone. She even looked at her, raising her brows ever so slightly as if in a dare, but the dowager was staring at the door, determinedly ignoring her.

When the men arrived, Thomas walked in first.

"Wyndham," the dowager said briskly. She never called him anything but his title.

He nodded in response. "I had Mr. Audley's belongings sent up to the blue silk bedroom."

Grace shot a careful look over at the dowager to gauge her reaction. The blue silk bedroom was one of the nicer guest bedchambers, but it was not the largest or most prestigious. It was, however, just down the hall from the dowager.

"Excellent choice," the dowager replied. "But I must repeat. Do not refer to him as Mr. Audley in my presence. I don't know these Audleys, and I don't care to know them."

"I don't know that they would care to know you, either," commented Mr. Audley, who had entered the room behind Thomas.

The dowager lifted a brow, as if to point out her own magnificence.

"Mary Audley is my late mother's sister," Mr. Audley stated. "She and her husband, William Audley, took me in at my birth. They raised me as their own and, *at my request*, gave me their name. I don't care to relinquish it." He looked coolly at the dowager, as if daring her to comment.

She did not, much to Grace's surprise.

And then he turned to her, offering her an elegant bow. "You may refer to me as Mr. Audley if you wish, Miss Eversleigh."

Grace bobbed a curtsy. She was not certain if this was a requirement, since no one had any clue as to his rank, but it seemed only polite. He had bowed, after all.

She glanced at the dowager, who was glaring at her, and then at Thomas, who somehow managed to look amused and annoyed at the same time.

"She can't sack you for using his legal name," Thomas said with his usual hint of impatience. "And if she does, I shall retire you with a lifelong bequest and have her sent off to some far-flung property."

Mr. Audley looked at Thomas with surprise and approval before turning to Grace and smiling. "It's tempting," he murmured. "How far can she be flung?"

"I am considering adding to our holdings," Thomas replied. "The Outer Hebrides are lovely this time of year."

"You're despicable," the dowager hissed.

"Why do I keep her on?" Thomas wondered aloud. He walked over to a cabinet and poured himself a drink.

"She is your grandmother," Grace said, since someone had to be the voice of reason.

"Ah yes, blood." Thomas sighed. "I'm told it's thicker than water. Pity." He looked over at Mr. Audley. "You'll soon learn."

Grace half expected Mr. Audley to bristle at Thomas's tone of condescension, but his face remained blandly unconcerned. Curious. It seemed the two men had forged some sort of truce.

"And now," Thomas announced, looking squarely at his grandmother, "my work here is done. I have returned the prodigal son to your loving bosom, and all is right with the world. Not *my* world," he added, "but someone's world, I'm sure."

"Not mine," Mr. Audley said, when no one else seemed inclined to comment. And then he unleashed a smile—slow, lazy, and meant to paint himself as the careless rogue he was. "In case you were interested."

Thomas looked at him, his nose crinkling in an expression of vague indifference. "I wasn't."

Grace's head bobbed back to Mr. Audley. He was

still smiling. She looked to Thomas, waiting for him to say something more.

He dipped his head toward her in wry salute, then tossed back his liquor in one shockingly large swallow. "I am going out."

"Where?" demanded the dowager.

Thomas paused in the doorway. "I have not yet decided."

Which meant, Grace was sure, *anywhere but here*.

Chapter Seven

And that, Jack decided, was his cue to leave as well.

Not that he had any great love for the duke. Indeed, he'd had quite enough of his marvelous lordliness for one day and was perfectly happy to see his back as he left the room. But the thought of remaining here with the dowager. . .

Even Miss Eversleigh's delightful company was not enough of a temptation to endure more of *that*.

"I believe I shall retire as well," he announced.

"Wyndham did not retire," the dowager said peevishly. "He went out."

"Then *I* shall retire," Jack said. He smiled blandly. "End of sentence."

"It's barely dark," the dowager pointed out.

"I'm tired." It was true. He was.

"My John used to stay up until the wee hours," she said softly.

Jack sighed. He did not want to feel sorry for this woman. She was hard, ruthless, and thoroughly un-likable. But she had, apparently, loved her son. His father. And she'd lost him.

A mother shouldn't outlive her children. He knew this as well as he knew how to breathe. It was un-natural.

And so instead of pointing out that her John had most likely never been kidnapped, strangled, black-mailed, and stripped of his (albeit paltry) livelihood, all in one day, he walked forward and set her ring—the very one he had all but snatched from her finger—on the table next to her. His own was in his pocket. He was not quite prepared to share its existence with her. "Your ring, madam," he said.

She nodded, then took it into her hands.

"What is the D for?" he asked. His whole life, he'd wondered. He might as well gain something from this debacle.

"Debenham. My birth surname."

Ah. It made sense. She'd have given her own heir-looms to her favorite son.

"My father was the Duke of Runthorpe."

"I am not surprised," he murmured. She could decide for herself if that was a compliment. He bowed. "Good evening, your grace."

The dowager's mouth tightened with disappoint-ment. But she seemed to recognize that if there had been a battle that day, she was the only one who had emerged victorious, and she was surprisingly gracious as she said, "I shall have supper sent up."

Jack nodded and murmured his thanks, then turned to exit.

"Miss Eversleigh will show you to your room."

At that Jack snapped to attention, and when he looked Miss Eversleigh's way, he saw that she had, too.

He had been expecting a footman. Possibly the butler. This was a delightful surprise.

"Is that a problem, Miss Eversleigh?" the dowager asked. Her voice sounded sly, a little bit taunting.

"Of course not," Miss Eversleigh replied. Her eyes were clouded but not entirely unreadable. She was surprised. He could see it by the way her lashes seemed to reach a little higher toward her brows. She was not used to being ordered to tend to anyone except the dowager. Her employer, he decided, did not like to share her. And as his eyes fell again to her lips, he decided that he was in complete accord. If she were his, if he had any right to her . . . he would not wish to share her, either.

He wanted to kiss her again. He wanted to touch her, just a soft brush of hand against skin, so fleeting that it could only be deemed accidental.

But more than any of that, he wanted use of her name.

Grace.

He liked it. He found it soothing.

"See to his comfort, Miss Eversleigh."

Jack turned to the dowager with widening eyes. She sat like a statue, her hands folded primly in her lap, but the corners of her mouth were tilted ever so slightly up, and her eyes looked cunning and amused.

She was giving Grace to him. As clear as day, she was telling him to make use of her companion, if that was his desire.

Good Lord. What sort of family had he fallen into?

"As you wish, ma'am," Miss Eversleigh replied, and in that moment Jack felt soiled, almost dirty, because he was quite certain she had no idea that her employer was attempting to whore her off on him.

It was the most appalling sort of bribe. *Stay the night, and you can have the girl.*

It sickened him. Doubly so, because he wanted the girl. He just didn't want her given to him.

"It is most kind of you, Miss Eversleigh," he said, feeling as if he had to be extra polite to make up for the dowager. They reached the door, and then, before he forgot, he turned back. He and the duke had spoken only tersely on their outing, but on one matter they had been in accord. "Oh, by the by, should anyone ask, I am a friend of Wyndham's. From years gone by."

"From university?" Miss Eversleigh suggested.

Jack fought back a grim chuckle. "No. I did not attend."

"You did not attend!" the dowager gasped. "I was led to believe you'd had a gentleman's education."

"By whom?" Jack inquired, ever so politely.

She sputtered at that for a moment, and then finally she scowled and said, "It is in your speech."

"Felled by my accent." He looked at Miss Eversleigh and shrugged. "Pommy R's and proper H's. What's a man to do?"

But the dowager was not prepared to let the subject drop. "You *are* educated, are you not?"

It was tempting to claim he'd been schooled with the local lads, if only to witness her reaction. But he owed his aunt and uncle better than that, and so he turned to the dowager and said, "Portora Royal, followed by two months at Trinity College—Dublin, that is, not Cambridge—and then six years serving in His Majesty's army and protecting *you* from invasion." He cocked his head to the side. "I'll take those thanks now, if you will."

The dowager's lips parted with outrage.

"No?" He lifted his brows. "Funny how no one seems to care that they still speak English and curtsy to good King George."

"I do," Miss Eversleigh said. And when he looked at her, she blinked and added, "Er, thank you."

"You're welcome," he said, and it occurred to him that this was the first time he'd had cause to say it. Sadly, the dowager was not unique in her sense of entitlement. Soldiers were occasionally feted, and it was true that the uniforms were quite effective when attracting the ladies, but no one ever thought to say thank you. Not to him, and especially not to the men who'd suffered permanent injury or disfigurement.

"Tell everyone we shared fencing lessons," Jack said to Miss Eversleigh, ignoring the dowager as best he could. "It's as good a ruse as any. Wyndham says he's passable with a sword?"

"I do not know," she said.

Of course she wouldn't. But no matter. If Wyndham had said he was passable, then he was almost certainly a master. They would be well-matched if ever they had to offer proof of their lie. Fencing had been his best subject in school. It was probably the only reason they had kept him to age eighteen.

"Shall we?" he murmured, tilting his head toward the door.

"The blue silk bedroom," the dowager called out sourly.

"She does not like to be left out of a conversation, does she?" Jack murmured, so that only Miss Eversleigh could hear.

He'd known she could not answer, not with her employer so close, but he saw her eyes dart away, as if trying to hide her amusement.

"You may retire for the night as well, Miss Eversleigh," the dowager directed.

Grace turned in surprise. "You don't wish for me to attend to you? It's early yet."

"Nancy can do it," she replied with a pinch of her lips. "She's an acceptable hand with buttons, and what's more, she doesn't say a word. I find that to be an exceptionally good trait in a servant."

As Grace held her tongue more often than not, she decided to take that as a compliment, rather than the rear-door insult it was meant to be. "Of course, ma'am," she said, bobbing a demure curtsy. "I shall see you in the morning, then, with your chocolate and the newspaper."

Mr. Audley was already at the door and was holding out his hand to motion for her to precede him, so she walked out into the hall. She had no idea what the dowager was up to, giving her the rest of the evening off, but she was not going to argue further.

"Nancy is her maid," she explained to Mr. Audley once he reached her side.

"I'd guessed."

"It's most odd." She shook her head. "She—"

Mr. Audley waited rather patiently for her to finish her sentence, but Grace decided the better of it. She had been going to say that the dowager hated Nancy. In fact, the dowager complained most bitterly and at painful length each time she had a day out and Nancy served as a substitute.

"You were saying, Miss Eversleigh?" he murmured.

She almost told him. It was strange, because she barely knew him, and furthermore, he could not possibly be interested in the trivialities of the Belgrave household. Even if he did become the duke—and the thought of it still made her somewhat sick to her stomach—well, it wasn't as if *Thomas* could have identified any of the housemaids. And if asked which ones his grandmother disliked, he'd surely have said, *All of them*.

Which, Grace thought with a wry smile, was probably true.

"You're smiling, Miss Eversleigh," Mr. Audley remarked, looking very much as if he were the one with a secret. "Do tell why."

"Oh, it's nothing," she said. "Certainly nothing that would be of interest to you." She motioned toward the staircase at the rear of the hall. "Here, the bedchambers are this way."

"You *were* smiling," he said again, falling in step beside her.

For some reason that made her smile anew. "I did not say that I wasn't."

"A lady who doesn't dissemble," he said approvingly. "I find myself liking you more with every passing minute."

Grace pursed her lips, eyeing him over her shoulder. "That does not indicate a very high opinion of women."

"My apologies. I should have said a *person* who does not dissemble." He flashed her a smile that shook her to her toes. "I would never claim that men and women are interchangeable, and thank heavens for that, but in matters of truthiness, neither sex earns high marks."

She looked at him in surprise. "I don't think truthiness is a word. In fact, I'm quite certain it is not."

"No?" His eyes darted to the side. Just for a second—not even a second, but it was long enough for her to wonder if she'd embarrassed him. Which couldn't be possible. He was so amazingly glib and comfortable in his own skin. One did not need more than a day's acquaintance to realize that. And indeed, his smile grew jaunty and lopsided, and his eyes positively twinkled as he said, "Well, it should be."

"Do you often make up words?"

He shrugged modestly. "I try to restrain myself."

She looked at him with considerable disbelief.

"I do," he protested. He clasped one hand over his heart, as if wounded, but his eyes were laughing. "Why is it no one ever believes me when I tell them I am a moral and upstanding gentleman, on this earth with the *every* intention of following *every* rule."

"Perhaps it is because most people make your acquaintance when you order them out of a carriage with a gun?"

"True," he acknowledged. "It does color the relationship, doesn't it?"

She looked at him, at the humor lurking in his emerald eyes, and she felt her lips tickle. She wanted to laugh. She wanted to laugh the way she'd laughed when her parents were alive, when she'd had the freedom to seek out life's absurdities and the time to make merry over them.

It almost felt as if something were waking up within her. It felt lovely. It felt *good.* She wanted to thank him, but she'd sound the veriest fool. And so she did the next best thing.

She apologized.

"I'm sorry," she said, pausing at the base of the stairs.

That seemed to surprise him. "You're sorry?"

"I am. For . . . today."

"For kidnapping me." He sounded amused, vaguely so. Perhaps even condescending.

"I didn't mean to," she protested.

"You *were* in the carriage," he pointed out. "I do believe that any court of law would brand you an accomplice."

Oh, *that* was more than she could take. "This would, I assume, be the same court of law that sent you to the gallows earlier that same morning for pointing a loaded gun at a duchess."

"Tsk tsk. I told you it wasn't a hanging offense."

"No?" she murmured, echoing his earlier tone precisely. "It ought to be."

"Oh, you think?"

"If truthiness gets to be a word, then accosting a duchess with a gun ought to be enough to get one hanged."

"You're quick," he said admiringly.

"Thank you," she said, then admitted, "I'm out of practice."

"Yes." He glanced down the hall toward the drawing room, where the dowager was presumably still enthroned upon her sofa. "She does keep you rather silent, doesn't she?"

"Loquaciousness is not considered becoming in a servant."

"Is that how you see yourself?" His eyes met hers, searching her so deeply she almost stepped away. "A servant?"

And then she did step away. Because whatever it was he was going to find in her, she wasn't so sure *she* wanted to see it. "We should not loiter," she said, motioning for him to follow her up the stairs. "The blue silk bedroom is lovely. Very comfortable, and with excellent morning light. The artwork in particular is superb. I think you will like it."

She was babbling, but he was kind enough not to remark upon it, instead saying, "I'm sure it will be an improvement over my current lodgings."

She glanced over at him with surprise. "Oh. I had assumed—" She broke off, too embarrassed to remark that she'd thought him a homeless nomad.

"A life of posting inns and grassy fields," he said with

an affected sigh. "Such is the fate of a highwayman."

"Do you enjoy it?" She surprised herself, both by asking it and also by how very curious she was in the answer.

He grinned. "Robbing coaches?"

She nodded.

"It depends on who is in the coach," he said softly. "I very much enjoyed not robbing you."

"*Not* robbing me?" She turned then, and the ice, which had been cracked, was officially broken.

"I didn't take a thing, did I?" he returned, all innocence.

"You stole a kiss."

"That," he said, leaning forward with great cheek, "was freely given."

"Mr. Audley . . ."

"I do wish you'd call me Jack," he sighed.

"Mr. Audley," she said again. "I did not—" She looked quickly about, then lowered her voice to an urgent whisper. "I did not . . . *do* . . . what you said I did."

He smiled lazily. "When did 'kiss' become such a dangerous word?"

She clamped her lips together because truly there was no way she would gain the upper hand in this conversation.

"Very well," he said. "I shan't torment you."

It would have been a kind and generous statement if he hadn't followed it with: "Today."

But even then, she smiled. It was difficult not to, in his presence.

They were in the upper hall now, and Grace turned

toward the family apartments where he would be staying. They moved along in silence, giving her ample time to consider the gentleman beside her. She did not care what he'd said about not completing university. He was extremely intelligent, unique vocabulary notwithstanding. And there was no arguing against his charm. There was no reason he should not be gainfully employed. She could not ask him why he was robbing coaches, however. It was far too forward on so short an acquaintance.

It was ironic, that. Who would have thought she'd be worried about manners and propriety with a thief?

"This way," she said, motioning for him to follow her to the left.

"Who sleeps down there?" Mr. Audley asked, peering in the opposite direction.

"His grace."

"Ah," he said darkly. "His grace."

"He is a good man," Grace said, feeling she must speak up for him. If Thomas had not behaved as he ought, it was certainly understandable. From the day of his birth, he'd been raised to be the Duke of Wyndham. And now, with the flimsiest of fate twists, he'd been informed that he might be nothing more than plain Mr. Cavendish.

If Mr. Audley had had a rough day, well then, surely Thomas's was worse.

"You admire the duke," Mr. Audley stated. Grace couldn't quite tell if this was a question; she didn't think so. But either way, his tone was dry, as if he thought she was somewhat naive for doing so.

"He is a good man," she repeated firmly. "You will

agree with me, once you further your acquaintance."

Mr. Audley let out an amused little puff of breath. "You sound like a servant now, starched and prim and properly loyal."

She scowled at him, but he clearly did not care, because he was already grinning and saying, "Are you going to defend the dowager next? I should like to hear you do it, because I'm most curious as to how, exactly, one would attempt such a feat."

Grace could not imagine that he might actually expect her to reply. She turned, though, so he could not see her smile.

"I could not manage it myself," he continued, "and I'm told I have a most silver tongue." He leaned forward, as if imparting a grave secret. "It's the Irish in me."

"You're a Cavendish," she pointed out.

"Only half." And then he added, "Thank God."

"They're not so bad."

He let out a chuckle. "They're not so bad? That's your rousing defense?"

And then heaven help her, she could not think of a single good thing to say except, "The dowager would give her life for the family."

"Pity she has not done so already."

Grace shot him a startled look. "You sound just like the duke."

"Yes, I'd noticed they had a warm and loving relationship."

"Here we are," Grace said, pushing open the door to his chamber. She stepped back then. It could not be proper for her to accompany him into his room.

Five years she'd been at Belgrave, and she'd never once stepped foot inside Thomas's chambers. She might not have much in this world, but she had her self-respect, and her reputation, and she planned to keep a firm hold on both.

Mr. Audley peeked in. "How very blue," he remarked.

She could not help but smile. "And silken."

"Indeed." He stepped inside. "You're not going to join me?"

"Oh, no."

"Didn't think you would. Pity. I'm going to have to loll about all on my own, rolling in all this silken blue splendor."

"The dowager was right," Grace said with a shake of her head. "You're never serious."

"Not true. I'm quite frequently serious. It's up to you to figure out when." He shrugged as he wandered over to the writing desk, his fingers trailing idly along the blotter until they slid off the edge and back to his side. "I find it convenient to keep people guessing."

Grace said nothing, just watched him inspect his room. She ought to go. She rather thought she *wanted* to go, actually; all day she'd been longing to crawl into bed and go to sleep. But she stayed. Just watching him, trying to imagine what it was like to see all of this for the first time.

She had entered Belgrave Castle as a servant. He was quite possibly its master.

It had to be strange. It had to be overwhelming. She didn't have the heart to tell him that this wasn't the fanciest or most ostentatious guest bedchamber. Not even close.

"Excellent art," he commented, tilting his head as he regarded a painting on the wall.

She nodded, her lips parting, then closing again.

"You were about to tell me it's a Rembrandt."

Her lips parted again, but this time in surprise. He hadn't even been looking at her. "Yes," she admitted.

"And this?" he asked, turning his attention to the one underneath. "Caravaggio?"

She blinked. "I don't know."

"I do," he said, in a tone that was somehow both impressed and grim. "It's a Caravaggio."

"You are a connoisseur?" she asked, and she noticed that her toes had somehow crossed the threshold of the room. Her heels were still safe and proper, resting on the corridor floor, but her toes. . .

They itched in her slippers.

They longed for adventure.

She longed for adventure.

Mr. Audley moved to another painting—the east wall was full of them—and murmured, "I would not say that I am a connoisseur, but yes, I do like art. It's easy to read."

"To read?" Grace stepped forward. What an odd statement.

He nodded. "Yes. Look here." He pointed to a woman in what looked like a post-Renaissance work. She was seated upon a lavish chair, cushioned in dark velvet, edged with thick, twisting gold. Perhaps a throne? "Look at the way the eyes look down," he said. "She is watching this other woman. But she is not looking at her face. She's jealous."

"No, she's not." Grace moved to his side. "She's angry."

"Yes, of course. But she's angry because she's jealous."

"Of her?" Grace responded, pointing to the "other" woman in the corner. Her hair was the color of wheat, and she was clad in a filmy Grecian robe. It ought to have been scandalous; one of her breasts seemed poised to pop out at any moment. "I don't think so. Look at her." She motioned to the first woman, the one on the throne. "She has everything."

"Everything material, yes. But this woman"—he motioned to the one in the Grecian robe—"has her husband."

"How can you even know she is married?" Grace squinted and leaned in, inspecting her fingers for a ring, but the brushwork was not fine enough to make out such a small detail.

"Of *course* she is married. Look at her expression."

"I see nothing to indicate wifeliness."

He lifted a brow. "Wifeliness?"

"I'm quite certain it's a word. More so than truthiness, in any case." She frowned. "And if she is married, then where is the husband?"

"Right there," he said, touching the intricate gilt frame, just beyond the woman in the Grecian robe.

"How can you possibly know that? It's beyond the edge of the canvas."

"You need only to look at her face. Her eyes. She is gazing at the man who loves her."

Grace found that intriguing. "Not at the man she loves?"

"I can't tell," he said, his head tilting slightly.

They stood in silence for a moment, then he said, "There is an entire novel in this painting. One need only take the time to read it."

He was right, Grace realized, and it was unsettling, because he wasn't supposed to be so perceptive. Not him. Not the glib, jaunty highwayman who couldn't be bothered to find a proper profession.

"You're in my room," he said.

She stepped back. Abruptly.

"Steady now." His arm shot out and his hand found her elbow.

She couldn't scold him, not really, because she would have fallen. "Thank you," she said softly.

He didn't let go.

She'd regained her balance. She was standing straight.

But he didn't let go.

And she did not pull away.

Chapter Eight

𝒜nd so he kissed her. He couldn't help it.

No, he couldn't stop it. His hand was on her arm, and he could feel her skin, feel the soft warmth of it, and then when he looked down, her face was tilted toward his, and her eyes, deep and blue but so completely unmysterious, were gazing up at him, and in truth there was no way—simply no way—he could do anything in that moment *but* kiss her.

Anything else would have been a tragedy.

There was an art to kissing—he'd long known that, and he'd been told he was an expert. But this kiss, with this woman—the one time it should have been art, it was all breathless nerves, because never in his life had he wanted someone in quite the manner he wanted Miss Grace Eversleigh.

And never had he wanted quite so much to get it all right.

He couldn't scare her. He had to please her. He wanted her to want him, and he wanted her to want to *know* him. He wanted her to cling to him, to need him, to whisper in his ear that he was her hero and she'd never want to so much as breathe the air near another man.

He wanted to taste her. He wanted to devour her. He wanted to drink in whatever it was that made her *her,* and see if it would transform him into the man he sometimes thought he ought to be. In that moment she was his salvation.

And his temptation.

And everything in between.

"Grace," he whispered, his voice brushing across her lips. "Grace," he said again, because he loved saying it.

She moaned in response, a soft whimpering sound that told him everything he wanted to know.

He kissed her softly. Thoroughly. His lips and tongue found every corner of her soul, and then he wanted more.

"Grace," he said again, his voice hoarser now. His hands slid around to her back, pressing her against him so he could feel her body as a part of the kiss. She was not corseted under her gown, and every lush curve became known to him, every warm contour. He wanted more than the shape of her, though. He wanted the taste, the smell, the touch.

The kiss was seduction.

And he was the one being seduced.

"Grace," he said again, and this time she whispered—
"*Jack.*"

It was his undoing. The sound of his name on her lips, the single, soft syllable—it shot through him like no *Mr. Audley* ever could. His mouth grew urgent and he pressed her more tightly to his body, too far gone to care that he'd gone hard against her.

He kissed her cheek, her ear, her neck, moving down to the hollow of her collarbone. One of his hands moved along the side of her rib cage, the pressure plumping her breast up until the upper curve was so close to his lips, so tantalizingly—

"No . . ."

It was more of a whisper than anything else, but still, she pushed him away.

He stared at her, his breath rushed and heavy. Her eyes were dazed, and her lips looked wet and well-kissed. His body was thrumming with need, and his eyes slid down to her belly, as if he could somehow see through the folds of her dress, down, down to the V where her legs met.

Whatever he'd been feeling just then—it tripled. Dear God, he hurt with it.

With a shuddering groan, he tore his gaze back up to her face. "Miss Eversleigh," he said, since the moment called for *some*thing, and there was no way he was going to apologize. Not for something that good.

"Mr. Audley," she replied, touching her lips.

And he realized, in a single blinding moment of pure terror, that everything he saw on her face, every stunned blink of her eyes—he felt it, too.

But no, that was impossible. He'd just met her, and beyond that, he did not *do* love. Amendment: he did not do the heart-pounding, mind-fogging, overabundance of lust that was so often confused with love.

He loved women, of course. He liked them, too, which he was aware made him rather unique among men. He loved the way they moved, and he loved the sounds they made, whether they were melting in his arms or clucking their disapproval. He loved how each one smelled different, and how each moved differently, and how even so, there was something about them all as a group that seemed to brand them together. *I am woman*, the air around them seemed to say. *I am most definitely not you.*

And thank heavens for that.

But he had never loved a woman. And he did not have any inclination to do so. Attachments were messy things, given to all sorts of unpleasantries. He preferred to move from affaire to affaire. It fit his life—and his soul—much better.

He smiled. Just a little one. Exactly the sort one would expect from a man like him at a time like this. Perhaps with a little extra tilt in one corner. Just enough to lend some wry wit to his tone when he said, "You stepped into my room."

She nodded, but the motion was so slow he couldn't be sure she even realized she was doing it. When she spoke, there was a certain dazedness to it, as if perhaps she was talking to herself. "I won't do it again."

Now, *that* would be a tragedy. "I wish you would," he said, offering her his most disarming smile. He reached out, and before she could guess his intentions, took her hand and raised it to his lips. "It was certainly," he murmured, "the most pleasant welcome of my day here at Belgrave."

He did not let go of her fingers as he added, "I very much enjoyed discussing that painting with you."

It was true. He had always liked the smart women best.

"As did I," she answered, and then she gave her hand a gentle tug, forcing him to relinquish his hold. She took a few steps toward the door, then paused, turning partway around as she said, "The collection here rivals any of the great museums."

"I look forward to viewing it with you."

"We shall begin in the gallery."

He smiled. She was clever. But just before she reached the door, he called out, "Are there nudes?"

She froze.

"I was wondering," he said innocently.

"There are," she replied, but she did not turn around. He longed to see the color of her cheeks. Vermillion, or merely pink?

"In the gallery?" he asked, because surely it would be impolite to ignore his query. He wanted to see her face. One last time.

"Not in the gallery, no," she said, and she did turn then. Just enough so he could see the sparkle in her eyes. "It is a portrait gallery."

"I see." He made his expression appropriately grave. "No nudes, then, please. I confess to a lack of desire to see Great-Grandfather Cavendish *au naturel.*"

Her lips pressed together, and he *knew* it was with humor, not disapproval. He wondered just what it would take to nudge her further, to dislodge the laughter that was surely bubbling at the base of her throat.

"Or, good heavens," he murmured, "the dowager."

She sputtered at that.

He brought a hand to his forehead. "My eyes," he moaned. "My eyes."

And then, bloody hell, he missed it. She laughed. He was sure that she did, even though it was more of a choking sound than anything else. But he had his hand over his eyes.

"Good night, Mr. Audley."

He returned his hand to its proper place at his side. "Good night, Miss Eversleigh." And then—and he would have sworn he'd been prepared to allow her to depart— he heard himself call out, "Will I see you at breakfast?"

She paused, her hand on the outer doorknob. "I expect so, if you are an early riser."

He absolutely was not.

"Absolutely I am."

"It is the dowager's favorite meal," she explained.

"Not the chocolate and the newspaper?" He wondered if he remembered everything she'd said that day. Quite possibly.

She shook her head. "That is at six. Breakfast is laid at seven."

"In the breakfast room?"

"You know where it is, then?"

"Haven't a clue," he admitted. "But it seemed a likely choice. Will you meet me here, to escort me down?"

"No," she said, her voice dipping slightly with amusement (Or exasperation? He couldn't be sure), "but I will arrange to have someone else lead you there."

"Pity." He sighed. "It won't be the same."

"I should hope not," she said, slowly shutting the door between them. And then, through the wood, he heard, "I plan to send a footman."

He laughed at that. He loved a woman with a sense of humor.

At precisely six the following morning, Grace entered the dowager's bedroom, holding the heavy door open for the maid who had followed her with the tray from the kitchen.

The dowager was awake, which was no great surprise. She always woke early, whether the summer sun was slipping in around the curtain edges, or the winter gloom hung heavy on the morning. Grace, on the other hand, would have gladly slept until noon if permitted. She'd taken to sleeping with her drapes open since her arrival at Belgrave—the better to let the sunlight batter her eyelids open every morning.

It didn't work very well, nor did the chiming clock she'd installed upon her bedside table years earlier. She thought she would have adapted to the dowager's schedule by this point, but apparently her inner timepiece was her one rebellion—the last little bit of her that refused to believe that she was, and forever would be, companion to the dowager Duchess of Wyndham.

All in all, it was a good thing she'd befriended the

housemaids. The dowager might have Grace to start her day, but Grace had the maids, who took turns each morning, slipping into her room and shaking her shoulder until she moaned, "Enough . . ."

How strange about Mr. Audley. She would never have pegged him for a morning person.

"Good morning, your grace," Grace said, moving to the windows. She pulled open the heavy velvet curtains. It was overcast, with a light mist, but the sun seemed to be making a good effort. Perhaps the clouds would burn off by afternoon.

The dowager sat up straight against her pillows, queenly in her elaborately styled, domed canopy bed. She was nearly done with her series of morning exercises, which consisted of a flexing of the fingers, followed by a pointing of the toes, finishing with a twisting of her neck to the left and right. She never stretched it side to side, Grace had noticed. "My chocolate," she said tersely.

"Right here, ma'am." Grace moved to the desk, where the maid had left the tray before hurrying off. "Be careful, ma'am. It's hot."

The dowager waited while Grace arranged the tray on her lap, then smoothed out the newspaper. It was only two days old (three was standard in this region) and had been neatly ironed by the butler.

"My reading glasses."

They were already in Grace's hand.

The dowager perched them on the tip of her nose, taking a gingerly sip of her chocolate as she perused the paper. Grace sat in the straight-back chair by the desk. It was not the most convenient location—the dowager was as demanding in the morning as she was the rest of the day, and would surely have her hopping up and down and across the room to her bed. But Grace was not permitted to actually sit *next* to the bed. The dowager complained that it felt as if Grace were trying to read over her shoulder.

Which was true, of course. Grace now had the newspaper transferred to her room once the dowager was through with it. It was still only two and a half days old when she read it, which was twelve hours better than anyone else in the district.

It was strange, really, the things that made one feel superior.

"Hmmm."

Grace tilted her head but did not inquire. If she inquired, the dowager would never tell.

"There was a fire at Howath Hall," the dowager said.

Grace was not certain where that was. "I do hope no one was injured."

The dowager read a few more lines, then answered, "Just a footman. And two maids." And then a moment later: "The dog perished. Oh my, that *is* a shame."

Grace did not comment. She did not trust herself to engage in early morning conversations until she'd had her own cup of chocolate, which she was generally not able to do until breakfast at seven.

Her stomach rumbled at the thought. For someone who detested mornings as she did, she'd come to adore breakfast fare. If they could only serve kippers and eggs for supper each evening, she'd have been in heaven.

She glanced at the clock. Only fifty-five more minutes. She wondered if Mr. Audley was awake.

Probably. Morning people never awoke with only ten minutes to spare before breakfast.

She wondered what he looked like, all sleepy and rumpled.

"Is something wrong, Miss Eversleigh?" the dowager sharply inquired.

Grace blinked. "Wrong, ma'am?"

"You . . . *chirped.*" She said this with considerable distaste, as if handling something with a particularly foul smell.

"I'm so sorry, ma'am," Grace said quickly, looking down at her hands folded in her lap. She could feel her cheeks growing warm, and she had a feeling that even in the morning light *and* with the dowager's diminished vision, her blush would be clearly visible.

Really, she should not be imagining Mr. Audley, and especially not in any state of dishabille. Heaven only knew what sorts of inappropriate sounds she would make the next time.

But he *was* handsome. Even when all she'd seen of him was the lower half of his face and his mask, that much had been clear. His lips were the sort that always held a touch of humor. She wondered if he even knew how to frown. And his eyes . . . Well, she hadn't been able to see those that first night, and that was almost certainly a good thing. She'd never seen anything quite so emerald. They far outshone the dowager's emeralds, which, Grace was still chagrined to remember, she'd risked her life (in theory, at least) to keep safe.

"Miss Eversleigh!"

Grace jerked upright. "Ma'am?"

The dowager pierced with a stare. "You snorted."

"I did?"

"Are you questioning my hearing?"

"Of course not, ma'am." The dowager abhorred the notion that any part of her might be susceptible to the usual impairments of age. Grace cleared her throat. "I apologize, ma'am. I was not aware. I must have, ehrm, breathed heavily."

"Breathed heavily." The dowager appeared to find that as appealing as she had Grace's earlier chirp.

Grace touched a hand lightly to her chest. "A bit of congestion, I'm afraid."

The dowager's nostrils flared as she peered down at the cup in her hands. "I do hope you did not breathe on my chocolate."

"Of course not, ma'am. The kitchen maids always carry the tray up."

The dowager evidently did not find any reason to ponder that further, and she turned back to her newspaper, leaving Grace alone once more with her thoughts of Mr. Audley.

Mr. *Audley*.

"Miss Eversleigh!"

At that Grace stood. This was getting ridiculous. "Yes, ma'am?"

"You sighed."

"I sighed?"

"Do you deny it?"

"No," Grace replied. "That is to say, I did not notice that I sighed, but I certainly allow that I *could* have done so."

The dowager waved an irritated hand in her direction. "You are most distracting this morning."

Grace felt her eyes light up. Did this mean she'd escape early?

"Sit down, Miss Eversleigh."

She sat. Apparently not.

The dowager set down her newspaper and pressed her lips together. "Tell me about my grandson."

And the blush returned. "I beg your pardon?"

The dowager's right eyebrow did a rather good imitation of a parasol top. "You did show him to his room last night, didn't you?"

"Of course, ma'am. At your directive."

"Well? What did he say? I am eager to learn what sort of man he is. The future of the family may very well rest in his hands."

Grace thought guiltily of Thomas, whom she'd somehow forgotten in the past twelve hours. He was everything a duke ought to be, and no one knew the castle as he did. Not even the dowager. "Er, don't you think that might be a bit premature, your grace?"

"Defending my other grandson, are we?"

Grace's eyes widened. Something about the dowager's tone sounded positively malevolent. "I consider his grace a friend," she said carefully. "I would never wish him ill."

"Pfft. If Mr. Cavendish—and don't you dare call

him Mr. Audley—really is the legitimate issue of my John, then you are hardly wishing Wyndham ill. The man ought to be grateful."

"For having his title pulled from beneath his feet?"

"For having had the good fortune to have had it for as long as he did," the dowager retorted. "If Mr.—oh, bloody hell, I'm going to call him John—"

Jack, Grace thought.

"If John really is *my* John's legitimate son, then Wyndham never really had the title to begin with. So one could hardly call it stripping."

"Except that he has been told since birth that it is his."

"That's not my fault, is it?" scoffed the dowager. "And it has hardly been since birth."

"No," Grace allowed. Thomas had ascended to the title at the age of twenty, when his father perished of a lung ailment. "But he has known since birth that it would one day be his, which is much the same thing."

The dowager grumbled a bit about that, using the same peevish undertone she always used when presented with an argument to which she had no ready contradiction. She gave Grace one final glare and then picked up her newspaper again, snapping it upright in front of her face.

Grace took advantage of the moment to let her posture slip. She did not dare close her eyes.

And sure enough, only ten seconds passed before the dowager brought the paper back down and asked sharply, "Do you think he will make a good duke?"

"Mr. Au—" Grace caught herself just in time. "Er, our new guest?"

The dowager rolled her eyes at her verbal acrobatics. "Call him Mr. Cavendish. It is his name."

"But it is not what he wishes to be called."

"I don't give a damn what he wishes to be called. He is who he is." The dowager took a long gulp of her chocolate. "We all are. And it's a good thing, too."

Grace said nothing. She'd been forced to endure the dowager's lectures on the natural order of man far too many times to risk provoking a repeat performance.

"You did not answer my question, Miss Eversleigh."

Grace took a moment to decide upon her reply. "I really could not say, ma'am. Not on such a short acquaintance."

It was mostly true. It was difficult to think of anyone besides Thomas holding the title, but Mr. Audley—for all his lovely friendliness and humor—seemed to lack a certain gravitas. He was intelligent, certainly, but did he possess the acumen and judgment necessary to run an estate the size of Wyndham? Belgrave might have been the family's primary domicile, but there were countless other holdings, both in England and abroad. Thomas employed at least a dozen secretaries and managers to aid him in his stewardship, but he was no absentee landlord. If he had not walked every inch of the Belgrave lands, she would wager that he'd come close. And Grace had substituted for the dowager on enough of her duties around the estate to know that Thomas knew nearly all of his tenants by name.

Grace had always thought that a remarkable achievement for one brought up as he had been, with a constant emphasis on the Wyndham place in the hierarchy of man. (Just below the king, and well above *you*, thank you very much.)

Thomas liked to present to the world the image of a slightly bored, sophisticated man of the *ton*, but there was quite a bit more to him. It was why he was so very good at what he did, she supposed.

And why it was so callous of the dowager to treat him with such a lack of regard. Grace supposed that one had to possess feelings in order to have a care for those of others, but really, the dowager had quite gone beyond her usual selfishness.

Grace had no idea whether Thomas had returned the night before, but if he hadn't . . . well, she wouldn't blame him.

"More chocolate, Miss Eversleigh."

Grace stood and refilled the dowager's cup from the pot she'd left on the bedside table.

"What did you talk about last night?"

Grace decided to feign obtuseness. "I retired early." She tilted the pot back, careful not to drip. "With your very kind permission."

The dowager scowled. Grace avoided the expression by returning the chocolate pot to its spot on the table. It took her an impressively long time to get it just so.

"Did he speak of me?" the dowager asked.

"Er, not so very much," Grace hedged.

"Not very much or not at all?"

Grace turned. There was only so much interrogation she could avoid before the dowager lost her temper. "I'm certain he *mentioned* you."

"What did he say?"

Good heavens. How was she meant to say that he'd

called her an old bat? And if he hadn't called her that, then he'd probably called her something worse. "I don't recall precisely, ma'am," Grace said. "I'm terribly sorry. I was not aware you wished for me to take note of his words."

"Well, next time, do so," the dowager muttered. She turned to her newspaper, then looked up toward the window, her mouth in a straight, recalcitrant line. Grace stood still, her hands clasped in front of her, and waited patiently while the dowager fussed and turned and sipped and ground her teeth, and then—it was hard to believe, but Grace thought she might actually feel *sorry* for the older woman.

"He reminds me of you," she said, before she could think the better of it.

The dowager turned to her with delighted eyes. "He does? How?"

Grace felt her stomach drop, although she was not certain if this was due to the uncharacteristic happiness on the dowager's face or the fact that she had no idea what to say. "Well, not completely, of course," she stalled, "but there is something in the expression."

But after about ten seconds of smiling blandly, it became apparent to Grace that the dowager was waiting for more. "His eyebrow," she said, in what she thought was a stroke of genius. "He lifts it like you do."

"Like this?" The dowager's left brow shot up so fast Grace was surprised it did not fly off her face.

"Er, yes. Somewhat like that. His are . . ." Grace made awkward motions near her own brows.

"Bushier?"

"Yes."

"Well, he is a man."

"Yes." *Oh, yes.*

"Can he do both?"

Grace stared at her blankly. "Both, ma'am?"

The dowager began lifting and dropping her brows in alternation. Left, right, left, right. It was a singularly bizarre spectacle.

"I do not know," Grace said. Quickly. To cut her off.

"Very strange," the dowager said, returning both of her brows back to where Grace hoped she'd keep them. "My John could not do it."

"Heredity is very mysterious," Grace agreed. "My father could not do this"—she took her thumb and bent it back until it touched her forearm—"but he said his father could."

"Aah!" The dowager turned aside in disgust. "Put it back! Put it back!"

Grace smiled and said with perfect mildness, "You will not wish to see what I can do with my elbow, then."

"Good Lord, no." The dowager snorted and waved toward the door. "I am through with you. Go see to breakfast."

"Shall I have Nancy help you dress?"

The dowager let out the most amazingly long-suffering sigh, as if a lifetime of aristocratic privilege was just too much. "Yes," she agreed gracelessly, "if only because I can't bear to look at your thumb."

Grace chuckled. And she must have been feeling especially bold, because she did not even attempt to stifle it.

"Are you laughing at me, Miss Eversleigh?"

"Of course not!"

"Don't," the dowager said sharply, "even *think* about saying you're laughing *with* me."

"I was just laughing, ma'am," Grace said, her face twitching with the smile she could not keep contained. "I do that sometimes."

"I have never witnessed it." Said as if this meant it couldn't possibly be true.

Grace could not say any of the three rejoinders that immediately sprang to mind—

That is because you are not listening, your grace.

That is because I rarely have cause to laugh in your presence.

or

What of it?

So instead she smiled—warmly, even. Now this *was* strange. She'd spent so much of her time swallowing her retorts, and it always left a bitter taste in her mouth.

But not this time. This time she felt light. Unfettered. If she could not speak her mind to the dowager, she didn't much care. She had too much to look forward to this morning.

Breakfast. Bacon and eggs. Kippers. Toast with butter and marmalade, too, and. . .

And him.

Mr. Audley.

Jack.

Chapter Nine

Jack staggered out of bed at precisely fourteen minutes before seven. Waking had been an elaborate undertaking. He had, after Miss Eversleigh had departed the night before, rung for a maid and given her strict orders to rap on his door at fifteen minutes past six. Then, as she was leaving, he thought the better of it and revised his directive to six sharp raps at the appointed time, followed by another twelve fifteen minutes later.

It wasn't as if he was going to make it out of bed on the first attempt, anyway.

The maid had also been informed that if she did not see him at the door within ten seconds of the second set of raps, she was to enter the room and not depart until she was certain he was awake.

And finally, she was promised a shilling if she did not breathe a word of this to anyone.

"And I'll know if you do," he warned her, with his most disarming smile. "Gossip always makes its way back to me."

It was true. No matter the house, no matter the establishment, the maids *always* told him everything. It was amazing how far one could travel on nothing but a smile and a puppy-dog expression.

Unfortunately for Jack, however, what his plan boasted in strategy, it lacked in eventual execution.

Not that the maid could be blamed. She carried out her part to the letter. Six sharp raps at fifteen minutes past six. Precisely. Jack managed to pry one eye about two-thirds of the way open, which proved to be just enough to focus upon the clock on his bedside table.

At half six he was snoring anew, and if he only counted seven of the twelve raps, he was fairly certain the fault was his, not hers. And really, one had to admire the poor girl's adherence to plan when faced with his somewhat surly *No*, followed by:

Go away;

Ten more minutes;

I said, ten more minutes; and

Don't you have a bloody pot to scrub?

At fifteen minutes before seven, as he teetered on his belly at the edge of his bed, one arm hanging limply over the side, he finally managed to get both eyes open, and he saw her, sitting primly in a chair across the room.

"Er, is Miss Eversleigh awake?" he mumbled, rubbing the sleep from his left eye. His right eye seemed to have shut again, trying to pull the rest of him along with it, back into sleep.

"Since twenty minutes before six, sir."

"Chipper as a bloody mockingbird, too, I'm sure."

The maid held her tongue.

He cocked his head, suddenly a bit more awake. "Not so chipper, eh?" So Miss Eversleigh was *not* a morning person. The day was growing brighter by the second.

"She's not so bad as you," the maid finally admitted.

Jack pushed his legs over the side and yawned. "She'd have to be dead to achieve *that*."

The maid giggled. It was a good, welcome sound. As long as he had the maids giggling, the house was his. He who had the servants had the world. He'd learned that at the age of six. Drove his family crazy, it did, but that just made it all the sweeter.

"How late do you imagine she would sleep if you didn't wake her?" he asked.

"Oh, I couldn't tell you *that*," the maid said, blushing madly.

Jack did not see how Miss Eversleigh's sleep habits might constitute a confidence, but nonetheless he had to applaud the maid for her loyalty. This did not mean, however, that he would not make every attempt to win her over.

"What about when the dowager gives her the day off?" he asked, rather offhandedly.

The maid shook her head sadly. "The dowager never gives her the day off."

"Never?" Jack was surprised. His newfound grandmother was exacting and self-important and a host of other annoying faults, but she'd struck him as, at the heart, somewhat fair-minded.

"Just afternoons," the maid said. And she leaned forward, looking first to her left and then her right, as if there might actually be someone else in the room who could hear her. "I think she does it just because she knows that Miss Eversleigh is not partial to mornings."

Ah, now that *did* sound like the dowager.

"She gets twice as many afternoons," the maid went on to explain, "so it does even out in the end."

Jack nodded sympathetically. "It's a shame."

"Unfair."

"So unfair."

"And poor Miss Eversleigh," the maid went on, her voice growing in animation. "She's ever so kind. Lovely to all the maids. Never forgets our birthdays and gives us gifts that she says are from the dowager, but we all know it's her."

She looked up at him then, so Jack rewarded her with an earnest nod.

"And all she wants, poor dear, is one morning every other week to sleep until noon."

"Is that what she said?" Jack murmured.

"Only once," the maid admitted. "I don't think she would recall. She was very tired. I think the dowager had her up quite late the night before. Took me twice as long as usual to rouse her."

Jack nodded sympathetically.

"The dowager never sleeps," the maid went on.

"Never?"

"Well, I'm sure she must. But she doesn't seem to need very much of it."

"I knew a vampire bat once," Jack murmured.

"Poor Miss Eversleigh must adhere to the dowager's schedule," the maid explained.

Jack continued on with the nodding. It seemed to be working.

"But she does not complain," the maid said, clearly eager to defend her. "She would never complain about her grace."

"Never?" If he had lived at Belgrave as long as Grace, he'd have been complaining forty-eight hours a day.

The maid shook her head with a piety that would have been quite at home on a vicar's wife. "Miss Eversleigh is not one for gossip."

Jack was about to point out that everyone gossiped, and despite what they might say, everyone enjoyed it. But he did not want the maid to interpret this as a critique of her current behavior, so he nodded yet again, prodding her on with: "Very admirable."

"Not with the help, at least," the maid clarified. "Maybe with her friends."

"Her friends?" Jack echoed, padding across the room in his nightshirt. Clothing had been laid out for him, freshly washed and pressed, and it did not take more than a glance to see that they were of the finest quality.

Wyndham's, most probably. They were of a similar size. He wondered if the duke knew that his closet had been raided. Probably not.

"The Ladies Elizabeth and Amelia," the maid said. "They live on the other side of the village. In the other big house. Not as big as this, mind you."

"No, of course not," Jack murmured. He decided

that this maid, whose name he really ought to learn, would be his favorite. A wealth of knowledge, she was, and all one had to do was let her get off her feet for a moment and into a comfortable chair.

"Their father's the Earl of Crowland," the maid went on, nattering away even as Jack stepped into his dressing room to don his clothing. He supposed some men would refuse to wear the duke's attire after their altercation the day before, but it seemed to him an impractical battle to pick. Assuming he was not going to succeed in luring Miss Eversleigh into a wild orgy of abandon (at least not today), he would have to dress. And his own clothes were rather worn and dusty.

Besides, maybe it would irk his dukeliness. And Jack had judged that to be a noble pursuit, indeed.

"Does Miss Eversleigh get to spend time with the Ladies Elizabeth and Amelia very often?" he called out, pulling on his breeches. Perfect fit. How fortunate.

"No. Although they were here yesterday."

The two girls he'd seen her with in the front drive. The blond ones. Of course. He should have realized they were sisters. He *would* have realized it, he supposed, if he'd been able to tear his eyes away from Miss Eversleigh long enough to see beyond the color of their hair.

"Lady Amelia is to be our next duchess," the maid continued.

Jack's hands, which were doing up the buttons on Wyndham's extraordinarily well-cut linen shirt, stilled. "Really," he said. "I did not realize the duke was betrothed."

"Since Lady Amelia was a baby," the maid supplied. "We'll be having a wedding soon, I think. We've got to, really. She's getting long in the tooth. I don't think her parents'll stand for much more delay."

Jack had thought both girls had looked youthful, but he *had* been some distance away.

"Twenty-one, I think she is."

"That old?" he murmured dryly.

"I'm seventeen," the maid said with a sigh.

Jack decided not to comment, as he could not be sure whether she wished to be seen as older or younger than her actual years. He stepped out of the dressing room, putting the finishing touches on his cravat.

The maid jumped to her feet. "Oh, but I should not gossip."

Jack gave her a reassuring nod. "I won't say a word. I give you my vow."

She dashed toward the door, then turned around and said, "My name is Bess." She bobbed a curtsy. "If you need anything."

Jack smiled then, because he was quite certain her offer was completely innocent. There was something rather refreshing in that.

A minute after Bess left, a footman arrived, as promised by Miss Eversleigh, to escort him down to the breakfast room. He proved not nearly as informative as Bess (the footmen never were, at least not to him), and the five-minute walk was made in silence.

The fact that the trip required five minutes was not lost on Jack. If Belgrave had seemed unconscionably huge from afar, then the inside was a positive labyrinth. He was fairly certain he'd seen less than a tenth of it, and already he'd located three staircases. There were turrets, too; he'd seen them from the outside, and almost certainly dungeons as well.

There had to be dungeons, he decided, taking what had to be the sixth turn since descending the staircase. No self-respecting castle would be without them. He decided he'd ask Grace to take him down for a peek, if only because the subterranean rooms were probably the only ones that could be counted upon not to have priceless old masters hanging on the walls.

A lover of art he might be, but *this*—he nearly flinched when he brushed past an El Greco—was simply too much. Even his dressing room had been hung wainscot to ceiling with priceless oils. Whoever had decorated *there* had an appalling fondness for cupids. Blue silk bedroom, his foot. The place ought to be renamed *Corpulent Babies, Armed with Quivers and Bows Room*. Subtitled: *Visitors Beware*.

Because, really, there ought to be a limit on how many cupids one could put in one small dressing room.

They turned a final corner, and Jack nearly sighed in delight as the familiar smells of an English breakfast wafted past his nose. The footman motioned to an open doorway, and Jack walked through it, his body tingling with an unfamiliar anticipation, only to find that Miss Eversleigh had not yet arrived.

He looked at the clock. One minute before seven. Surely that was a new, postmilitary record.

The sideboard had already been laid, so he took a plate, filled it to heaping, and chose a seat at the table. It had been some time since he'd breakfasted in a proper house. His meals of late had been taken at inns and in rented rooms, and before that on the battlefield. It felt luxurious to sit with his meal, almost decadent.

"Coffee, tea, or chocolate, sir?"

Jack had not had chocolate for more time than he could remember, and his body nearly shuddered with delight. The footman took note of his preference and moved to another table, where three elegant pots sat in a row, their arched spouts sticking up like a line of swans. In a moment Jack was rewarded with a steaming cup, into which he promptly dumped three spoonfuls of sugar and a splash of milk.

There were, he decided, taking one heavenly sip, some advantages to a life of luxury.

He was nearly through with his food when he heard footsteps approaching. Within moments Miss Eversleigh appeared. She was dressed in a demure white frock—no, not white, he decided, more of a cream color, rather like the top of a milk bucket before it was skimmed. Whatever the hue was, it matched the swirling plaster that adorned the door frame perfectly. She needed only a yellow ribbon (for the walls, which were surprisingly cheerful for such an imposing home) and he would have sworn the room had been decorated just for that moment.

He stood, offering her a polite bow. "Miss Eversleigh," he murmured. He liked that she was blushing. Just a little, which was ideal. Too much, and that would mean she was embarrassed. A bare hint of pale pink, however, meant that she was looking forward to the encounter.

And perhaps thought she ought not to be.

Which was even better.

"Chocolate, Miss Eversleigh?" the footman asked.

"Oh, yes, please, Graham." She sounded most relieved to get her beverage in hand. And indeed, when she finally sat across from him, her plate nearly as full as his, she sighed with delight.

"You don't take sugar?" he asked, surprised. He'd never met a woman—and very few men, for that matter—with a taste for unsweetened chocolate. He couldn't abide it himself.

She shook her head. "Not in the morning. I need it undiluted."

He watched with interest—and, to be honest, a fair bit of amusement—as she alternately sipped the brew and breathed in the scent of it. Her hands did not leave her cup until she'd drained the last drop, and then Graham, who obviously knew her preferences well, was at her side in an instant, refilling without even a hint of a request.

Miss Eversleigh, Jack decided, was definitely not a morning person.

"Have you been down long?" she asked, now that she had imbibed a full cup.

"Not long." He gave a rueful glance to his plate, which was almost clean. "I learned to eat quickly in the army."

"By necessity, I imagine," she said, taking a bite of her coddled eggs.

He let his chin dip very slightly to acknowledge her statement.

"The dowager will be down shortly," she said.

"Ah. So you mean that we must learn to converse

quickly as well, if we wish to have any enjoyable discourse before the descent of the duchess."

Her lips twitched. "That wasn't exactly what I meant, but—" She took a sip of her chocolate, not that that hid her smile. "—it's close."

"The things we must learn to do quickly," he said with a sigh.

She looked up, fork frozen halfway to her mouth. A small blob of egg fell to her plate with a slap. Her cheeks were positively flaming with color.

"I didn't mean *that*," he said, most pleased with the direction of her thoughts. "Good heavens, I would never do *that* quickly."

Her lips parted. Not quite an O, but a rather attractive little oval nonetheless.

"Unless, of course I had to," he added, letting his eyes grow heavy-lidded and warm. "When faced with the choice of speed versus abstinence—"

"Mr. Audley!"

He sat back with a satisfied smile. "I was wondering when you'd scold me."

"Not soon enough," she muttered.

He picked up his knife and fork and cut off a piece of bacon. It was thick and pink and perfectly cooked. "And once again, there it is," he said, popping the meat into his mouth. He chewed, swallowed, then added, "My inability to be serious."

"But you claimed that wasn't true." She leaned in— just an inch or so, but the motion seemed to say—*I'm watching you.*

He almost shivered. He liked being watched by her.

"You said," she continued, "that you were frequently serious, and that it is up to me to figure out when."

"Is that what I said?" he murmured.

"Something rather close to it."

"Well, then." He leaned in closer, too, and his eyes captured hers, green on blue, across the breakfast table. "What do you think? Am I being serious right now?"

For a moment he thought she might answer him, but no, she just sat back with an innocent little smile and said, "I really couldn't say."

"You disappoint me, Miss Eversleigh."

Her smile turned positively serene as she returned her attention to the food on her plate. "I couldn't possibly render judgment on a subject so unfit for my ears," she murmured.

He laughed aloud at that. "You have a very devious sense of humor, Miss Eversleigh."

She appeared to be pleased by the compliment, almost as if she'd been waiting for years for someone to acknowledge it. But before she could say anything (if indeed she'd *intended* to say something), the moment was positively assaulted by the dowager, who marched into the breakfast room trailed by two rather harried and unhappy looking maids.

"What are you laughing about?" she demanded.

"Nothing in particular," Jack replied, deciding to spare Miss Eversleigh the task of making conversation. After five years in the dowager's service, the poor girl deserved a respite. "Just enjoying Miss Eversleigh's enchanting company."

The dowager shot them both a sharp look. "My

plate," she snapped. One of the maids rushed to the sideboard, but she was halted when the dowager said, "Miss Eversleigh will see to it."

Grace stood without a word, and the dowager turned to Jack and said, "She is the only one who does it properly." She shook her head and let out a short-tempered little puff of air, clearly lamenting the levels of intelligence commonly found in the servants.

Jack said nothing, deciding this would be as good a time as any to invoke his aunt's favorite axiom: *If you can't say something nice, say nothing at all.*

Although it *was* tempting to say something extraordinarily nice about the servants.

Grace returned, plate in hand, set it down in front of the dowager, and then gave it a little twist, turning the disk until the eggs were at nine o'clock, closest to the forks.

Jack watched the entire affair, first curious, then impressed. The plate had been divided into six equal, wedge-shaped sections, each with its own food selection. Nothing touched, not even the hollandaise sauce, which had been dribbled over the eggs with careful precision. "It's a masterpiece," he declared, arching forward. He was trying to see if she'd signed her name with the hollandaise.

Grace gave him a look. One that was not difficult to interpret.

"Is it a sundial?" he asked, all innocence.

"What are you talking about?" the dowager grumbled, picking up a fork.

"No! Don't ruin it!" he cried out—as best he could without exploding with laughter.

But she jabbed a slice of stewed apple all the same.

"How could you?" Jack accused.

Grace actually turned in her chair, unable to watch.

"What the devil are you talking about?" the dowager demanded. "Miss Eversleigh, why are you facing the window? What is he about?"

Grace twisted back around, hand over her mouth. "I'm sure I do not know."

The dowager's eyes narrowed. "I think you do know."

"I assure you," Grace said, "I never know what he is about."

"Never?" Jack queried. "What a sweeping comment. We've only just met."

"It feels like so much longer," Grace said.

"Why," he mused, "do I wonder if I have just been insulted?"

"If you've been insulted, you shouldn't have to wonder at it," the dowager said sharply.

Grace turned to her with some surprise. "That's not what you said yesterday."

"What did she say yesterday?" Mr. Audley asked.

"He is a Cavendish," the dowager said simply. Which, to her, explained everything. But she apparently held little faith in Grace's deductive abilities, and so she said, as one might speak to a child, "We are different."

"The rules don't apply," Mr. Audley said with a shrug. And then, as soon as the dowager was looking away, he winked at Grace. "What did she say yesterday?" he asked again.

Grace was not sure she could adequately paraphrase, given that she was so at odds with the overall sentiment, but she couldn't very well ignore his direct question twice, so she said, "That there is an art to insult, and if one can do it without the subject realizing, it's even more impressive."

She looked over to the dowager, waiting to see if she would be corrected. "It does not apply," the dowager said archly, "when one is the *subject* of the insult."

"Wouldn't it still be art for the other person?" Grace asked.

"Of course not. And why should I care if it were?" The dowager sniffed disdainfully and turned back to her breakfast. "I don't like this bacon," she announced.

"Are your conversations always this oblique?" Mr. Audley asked.

"No," Grace answered, quite honestly. "It has been a most exceptional two days."

No one had anything to add to that, probably because they were all in such agreement. But Mr. Audley did fill the silence by turning to the dowager and saying, "I found the bacon to be superb."

To that, the dowager replied, "Is Wyndham returned?"

"I don't believe so," Grace answered. She looked up to the footman. "Graham?"

"No, miss, he is not at home."

The dowager pursed her lips into an expression of irritated discontent. "Very inconsiderate of him."

"It is early yet," Grace said.

"He did not indicate that he would be gone all night."

"Is the duke normally required to register his schedule with his grandmother?" Mr. Audley murmured, clearly out to make trouble.

Grace gave him a peeved look. Surely this did not require a reply. He smiled in return. He enjoyed vexing her. This much was becoming abundantly clear. She did not read too much into it, however. The man enjoyed vexing everyone.

Grace turned back to the dowager. "I am certain he will return soon."

The dowager's expression did not budge in its irritation. "I had hoped that he would be here so that we might talk frankly, but I suppose we may proceed without him."

"Do you think that's wise?" Grace asked before she could stop herself. And indeed, the dowager responded to her impertinence with a withering stare. But Grace refused to regret speaking out. It was not right to make determinations about the future in Thomas's absence.

"Footman!" the dowager barked. "Leave us and close the doors behind you."

Once the room was secure, the dowager turned to Mr. Audley and announced, "I have given the matter great thought."

"I really think we should wait for the duke," Grace cut in. Her voice sounded a little panicked, and she wasn't sure why she was quite so distressed. Perhaps it was because Thomas was the one person who had made her life bearable in the past five years. If it hadn't been for him, she'd have forgotten the sound of her own laughter.

She liked Mr. Audley. She liked him rather too much, in all honesty, but she would not allow the dowager to hand him Thomas's birthright over breakfast.

"Miss Eversleigh—" the dowager bit off, clearly beginning a blistering set-down.

"I agree with Miss Eversleigh," Mr. Audley put in smoothly. "We should wait for the duke."

But the dowager waited for no one. And her expression was one part formidable and two parts defiant when she said, "We must travel to Ireland. Tomorrow if we can manage it."

Chapter Ten

Jack's usual response when delivered unpleasant tidings was to smile. This was his response to pleasant news as well, of course, but anyone could grin when offered a compliment. It took talent to curve one's lips in an upward direction when ordered, say, to clean out a chamber pot or risk one's life by sneaking behind enemy lines to determine troop numbers.

But he generally managed it. Excrement . . . moving defenseless among the French . . . he always reacted with a dry quip and a lazy smile.

This was not something he'd had to cultivate. Indeed, the midwife who'd brought him into the world swore to her dying day that he was the only baby she'd ever seen who emerged from his mother's womb smiling.

He disliked conflict. He always had, which had made his chosen professions—the military, followed by gen-

teel crime—somewhat interesting. But firing a weapon
at a nameless frog or lifting a necklace from the neck
of an overfed aristocrat—this was not conflict.

Conflict—to Jack—was personal. It was a lover's be-
trayal, a friend's insult. It was two brothers vying for
their father's approval, a poor relation forced to swallow her pride. It involved a sneer, or a shrill voice, and
it left a body wondering if he'd offended someone.

Or disappointed another.

He had found, with a near one hundred percent success rate, that a grin and a jaunty remark could defuse
almost any situation. Or change any topic. Which
meant that he very rarely had to discuss matters that
were not of his choosing.

Nonetheless, this time, when faced with the dowager and her unexpected (although, really, he should
have expected it) announcement, all he could do was
stare at her and say, "I beg your pardon?"

"We must go to Ireland," she said again, in that
obey-me tone he expected *she* had been born with.
"There is no way we shall get to the bottom of the
matter without visiting the site of the marriage. I
assume Irish churches keep records?"

Good God, did she think *all* of them were illiterate?
Jack forced down a bit of bile and said quite tightly,
"Indeed."

"Good." The dowager turned back to her breakfast,
the matter good and settled in her mind. "We shall
find whoever performed the ceremony and obtain the
register. It is the only way."

Jack felt his fingers bending and flexing beneath the

table. It felt as if his blood were going to burst through his skin. "Wouldn't you prefer to send someone in your stead?" he inquired.

The dowager regarded him as she might an idiot. "Who could I possibly trust with a matter of such importance? No, it must be me. And you, of course, and Wyndham, since I expect he will want to see whatever proof we locate as well."

The usual Jack would never have let such a comment pass without his own, exceedingly ironic, *One would think,* but this current Jack—the one who was desperately trying to figure out how he might travel to Ireland without being seen by his aunt, uncle, or any of his cousins—actually bit his lip.

"Mr. Audley?" Grace said quietly.

He didn't look at her. He refused to look at her. She'd see far more in his face than the dowager ever would.

"Of course," he said briskly. "Of course we must go." Because really, what else could he say? *Terribly sorry, but I can't go to Ireland, as I killed my cousin*?

Jack had been out of society for a number of years, but he was fairly certain this would not be considered good breakfast table conversation.

And yes, he knew that he had not pulled a trigger, and yes, he knew that he had not forced Arthur to buy a commission and enter the army along with him, and yes—and this was the worst of it—he knew that his aunt would never even dream of blaming him for Arthur's death.

But he had known Arthur. And more importantly, Arthur had known him. Better than anyone. He'd

known his every strength—and his every weakness—
and when Jack had finally closed the door on his disastrous university career and headed off to the military,
Arthur had refused to allow him to go alone.

And they both knew why.

"It might be somewhat ambitious to try to depart
tomorrow," Grace said. "You will have to secure passage, and—"

"Bah!" was the dowager's response. "Wyndham's
secretary can manage it. It's about time he earned his
wages. And if not tomorrow, then the next day."

"Will you wish for me to accompany you?" Grace
asked quietly.

Jack was just about to interject that, *damn* yes, she'd
be going, or else he would not, but the dowager gave
her a haughty look and replied, "Of course. You do not
think I would make such a journey without a companion? I cannot bring maids—the gossip, you know—
and so I will need someone to help me dress."

"You know that I am not very good with hair," Grace
pointed out, and to Jack's horror, he laughed. It was
just a short little burst of it, tinged with a loathsome
nervous edge, but it was enough for both ladies to stop
their conversation, and their meal, and turn to him.

Oh. Brilliant. How was he to explain this? *Don't
mind me, I was simply laughing at the ludicrousness
of it all. You with your hair, me with my dead cousin.*

"Do you find my hair amusing?" the dowager asked
sharply.

And Jack, because he had absolutely nothing to
lose, just shrugged and said, "A bit."

The dowager let out an indignant huff, and Grace positively glared at him.

"Women's hair always amuses me," he clarified. "So much work, when all anyone really wants is to see it down."

They both seemed to relax a bit. His comment may have been risqué, but it took the personal edge off the insult. The dowager tossed one last irritated look in his direction, then turned to Grace to continue their previous conversation. "You may spend the morning with Maria," she directed. "She will show you what to do. It can't be that difficult. Pull one of the scullery maids up from the kitchen and practice upon her. She'll be grateful for the opportunity, I'm sure."

Grace looked not at all enthused, but she nodded and murmured, "Of course."

"See to it that the kitchen work does not suffer," the dowager said, finishing the last of her stewed apples. "An elegant coiffure is compensation enough."

"For what?" Jack asked.

The dowager turned to him, her nose somehow looking pointier than usual.

"Compensation for what?" he restated, since he felt like being contrary.

The dowager stared at him a moment longer, then must have decided he was best ignored, because she turned back to Grace. "You may commence packing my things once you are done with Maria. And after that, see to it that a suitable story is set about for our absence." She waved her hand in the air as if it were a trifle. "A hunting cottage in Scotland will do nicely.

The Borders, I should think. No one will believe it if you say I went to the Highlands."

Grace nodded silently.

"Somewhere off the well-trod path, however," the dowager continued, looking as if she were enjoying herself. "The last thing I need is for one of my friends to attempt to see me."

"Do you have many friends?" Jack asked, his tone so perfectly polite that she'd be wondering all day if she'd been insulted.

"The dowager is much admired," Grace said quickly, perfect little companion that she was.

Jack decided not to comment.

"Have you ever been to Ireland?" Grace asked the dowager. But Jack caught the angry look she shot him before turning to her employer.

"Of course not." The dowager's face pinched. "Why on earth would I have done so?"

"It is said to have a soothing effect on one's temperament," Jack said.

"Thus far," the dowager retorted, "I am not much impressed with its influences upon one's manners."

He smiled. "You find me impolite?"

"I find you impertinent."

Jack turned to Grace with a sad sigh. "And here I thought I was meant to be the prodigal grandson, able to do no wrong."

"Everyone does wrong," the dowager said sharply. "The question is how little wrong one does."

"I would think," Jack said quietly, "that it is more important what one does to rectify the wrong."

"Or perhaps," the dowager snapped angrily, "one could manage not to make the mistake in the first place."

Jack leaned forward, interested now. "What did my father do that was so very very wrong?"

"He died," she said, and her voice was so bitter and full of chill that Jack heard Grace suck in her breath from across the table.

"Surely you cannot blame him for that," Jack murmured. "A freak storm, a leaky boat . . ."

"He should never have stayed so long in Ireland," the dowager hissed. "He should never have gone in the first place. He was needed here."

"By you," Jack said softly.

The dowager's face lost some of its usual stiffness, and for a moment he thought he saw her eyes grow moist. But whatever emotion came over her, it was swiftly tamped down, and she stabbed at her bacon and bit off, "He was needed here. By all of us."

Grace suddenly stood. "I will go find Maria now, your grace, if that is amenable."

Jack rose along with her. There was no way she was leaving him alone with the dowager. "I believe you promised me a tour of the castle," he murmured.

Grace looked from the dowager to him and back again. Finally the dowager flicked her hand in the air and said, "Oh, take him about. He should see his birthright before we leave. You may have your session with Maria later. I will remain and await Wyndham."

But as they reached the doorway, they heard her add softly, "If that is indeed still his name."

*　*　*

Grace was too angry to wait politely outside the doorway, and indeed, she was already halfway down the hall before Mr. Audley caught up with her.

"Is this a tour or a race?" he asked, his lips forming that now familiar smile. But this time it did nothing but raise her ire.

"Why did you bait her?" she burst out. "Why would you do such a thing?"

"The comment about her hair, do you mean?" he asked, and he gave her one of those annoying innocent whatever-could-I-have-done-wrong looks. When of course he had to have known, perfectly well.

"Everything," she replied hotly. "We were having a perfectly lovely breakfast, and then you—"

"You might have been having a perfectly lovely breakfast," he cut in, and his voice held a newly sharp edge. "I was conversing with Medusa."

"Yes, but you didn't have to make things worse by provoking her."

"Isn't that what his holiness does?"

Grace stared at him in angry confusion. "What are you talking about?"

"Sorry." He shrugged. "The duke. I've not noticed that he holds his tongue in her presence. I thought to emulate."

"Mr. Aud—"

"Ah, but I misspoke. He's not holy, is he? Merely perfect."

She could do nothing but stare. What had Thomas done to earn such contempt? By all rights Thomas should be the one in a blackened mood. He probably *was*, to be fair, but at least he'd taken himself off to be furious elsewhere.

"His grace, it is, isn't it?" Mr. Audley continued, his voice losing none of its derision. "I'm not so uneducated that I don't know the correct forms of address."

"I never said you were. Neither, I might add, did the dowager." Grace let out an irritated exhale. "She shall be difficult all day now."

"She isn't normally difficult?"

Good heavens, she wanted to hit him. Of course the dowager was normally difficult. He knew that. What could he possibly have to gain by remarking upon it other than the enhancement of his oh so dry and wry persona?

"She shall be worse," she ground out. "And I shall be the one to pay for it."

"My apologies, then," he said, and he offered a contrite bow.

Grace felt suddenly uncomfortable. Not because she thought he was mocking her, but rather because she was quite sure he was not. "It was nothing," she mumbled. "It is not your place to worry over my situation."

"Does Wyndham?"

Grace looked up at him, somehow captured by the directness of his gaze. "No," she said softly. "Yes, he does, but no . . ."

No, he didn't. Thomas did look out for her, and had, on more than one occasion, interceded when he felt she was being treated unfairly, but he never held his tongue with his grandmother just to keep the peace. And Grace would never dream of asking him to. Or scold him for not doing so.

He was the duke. She could not speak to him that way, no matter their friendship.

But Mr. Audley was. . .

She closed her eyes for a moment, turning away so he could not see the turmoil on her face. He was just Mr. Audley for now, not so very far above her. But the dowager's voice, soft and menacing, still rang in her ears—

If that is indeed still his name.

She was speaking of Thomas, of course. But the counterpart was true as well. If Thomas was not Wyndham, then Mr. Audley *was.*

And this man . . . this man who had kissed her twice and made her dream of something beyond the walls of this castle—he would *be* this castle. The dukedom wasn't just a few words appended to the end of one's name. It was lands, it was money, it was the very history of England placed upon one man's shoulders. And if there was one thing she had learned during her five years at Belgrave, it was that the aristocracy were different from the rest of humanity. They were mortals, true, and they bled and cried just like everyone else, but they carried within them something that set them apart.

It didn't make them *better.* No matter the dowager's lectures on the subject, Grace would never believe that. But they were different. And they were shaped by the knowledge of their history and their roles.

If Mr. Audley's birth had been legitimate, then he was the Duke of Wyndham, and she was an overreaching spinster for even dreaming of his face.

Grace took a deep, restorative breath, and then,

once her nerves were sufficiently calmed, turned back to him. "Which part of the castle would you like to see, Mr. Audley?"

He must have recognized that this was not the time to press her, and so he answered cheerfully, "Why, all of it, of course, but I imagine that is not feasible for a single morning. Where do you suggest we begin?"

"The gallery?" He had been so interested in the paintings in his room the night before. It seemed a logical place to start.

"And gaze upon the friendly faces of my supposed ancestors?" His nostrils flared, and for a moment he almost looked as if he'd swallowed something distasteful. "I think not. I've had enough of my ancestors for one morning, thank you very much."

"These are dead ancestors," Grace murmured, hardly able to believe her cheek.

"Which is how I prefer them, but not this morning."

She glanced across the hall to where she could see sunlight dappling in through a window. "I could show you the gardens."

"I'm not dressed for it."

"The conservatory?"

He tapped his ear. "Made of tin, I'm afraid."

She pressed her lips together, waited a moment, then said, "Do *you* have any location in mind?"

"Many," he answered promptly, "but they'd leave your reputation in tatters."

"Mr. Au—"

"Jack," he reminded her, and somehow there was less space between them. "You called me Jack last night."

Grace did not move, despite the fact that her heels were itching to scoot backwards. He was not close enough to kiss her, not even close enough to accidentally brush his hand against her arm. But her lungs felt suddenly devoid of air, and her heart had begun to race, beating erratically in her chest.

She could feel it forming on her tongue—*Jack*. But she could not say it. Not in this moment, with the image of him as the duke still fresh in her mind. "Mr. Audley," she said, and although she tried for sternness, she did not quite manage it.

"I am heartbroken," he said, and he did it with the exact right note of levity to restore her equilibrium. "But I shall carry on, painful though it may be."

"Yes, you look to be in despair," she murmured.

One of his brows rose. "Do I detect a hint of sarcasm?"

"Just a hint."

"Good, because I assure you"—he thumped one hand against his heart—"I am dying on the inside."

She laughed, but she tried to hold it in, so it came out more like a snort. It should have been embarrassing; with anyone else it *would* have been. But he had set her back at ease, and instead she felt herself smile. She wondered if he realized what a talent it was—to return any conversation to a smile. "Come with me, Mr. Audley," she said, motioning for him to accompany her down the hall. "I shall show you my very favorite room."

"Are there cupids?"

She blinked. "I beg your pardon?"

"I was attacked by cupids this morning," he said with a shrug, as if such a thing were a common day occurrence. "In my dressing room."

And again she smiled, this time even more broadly. "Ah. I'd forgotten. It's a bit much, isn't it?"

"Unless one is partial to naked babies."

Again her laughter snorted out.

"Something in your throat?" he asked innocently.

She answered him with a dry look, then said, "I believe the dressing room was decorated by the present duke's great-grandmother."

"Yes, I'd assumed it wasn't the dowager," he said cheerfully. "She doesn't seem the sort for cherubs of any stripe."

The image *that* brought forth was enough to make her laugh aloud.

"Finally," he said, and at her curious look, added, "I thought you were going to choke on it earlier."

"You seem to have regained your good mood as well," she pointed out.

"It requires only the removal of my presence from *her* presence."

"But you only just met the dowager yesterday. Surely you've had a disagreeable moment before that."

He flashed her a broad grin. "Happy since the day I was born."

"Oh, come now, Mr. Audley."

"I never admit to my black moods."

She raised her brows. "You merely experience them?"

He chuckled at that. "Indeed."

They walked companionably toward the rear of the house, Mr. Audley occasionally pressing her for information of their destination.

"I shan't tell you," Grace said, trying to ignore the giddy sense of anticipation that had begun to slide through her. "It sounds like nothing special in words."

"Just another drawing room, eh?"

To anyone else, perhaps, but for her it was magical.

"How many are there, by the way?" he asked.

She paused, trying to count. "I am not certain. The dowager is partial to only three, so we rarely use the others."

"Dusty and molding?"

She smiled. "Cleaned every day."

"Of course." He looked about him, and it occurred to her that he did not seem cowed by the grandeur of his surroundings, just . . . amused.

No, not amused. It was more of a wry disbelief, as if he were still wondering if he could trade this all in and get himself kidnapped by a different dowager duchess. Perhaps one with a smaller castle.

"Penny for your thoughts, Miss Eversleigh," he said. "Although I'm sure they are worth a pound."

"More than that," she said over her shoulder. His mood was infectious, and she felt like a coquette. It was unfamiliar. Unfamiliar and lovely.

He held up his hands in surrender. "Too steep a price, I'm afraid. I am but an impoverished highwayman."

She cocked her head. "Wouldn't that make you an unsuccessful highwayman?"

"Touché," he acknowledged, "but alas, untrue. I have had a most lucrative career. The life of a thief suits my talents perfectly."

"Your talents are for pointing guns and removing necklaces off ladies' necks?"

"I *charm* the necklaces off their necks." He shook his head in a perfect imitation of offense. "Kindly make the distinction."

"Oh, please."

"I charmed *you*."

She was all indignation. "You did not."

He reached out, and before she could step away, he'd grasped her hand and raised it to his lips. "Recall the night in question, Miss Eversleigh. The moonlight, the soft wind."

"There was no wind."

"You're spoiling my memory," he growled.

"There was no wind," she stated. "You are romanticizing the encounter."

"Can you blame me?" he returned, smiling at her wickedly. "I never know who is going to step through the carriage door. Most of the time I get a wheezy old badger."

Grace's initial inclination was to ask him if *badger* referred to a man or a woman, but she decided this would only encourage him. Plus, he was still holding her hand, his thumb idly stroking her palm, and she was finding that such intimacies severely restricted her talents for witty repartee.

"Where are you taking me, Miss Eversleigh?" His voice was a murmur, brushing softly against her skin.

He was kissing her again, and her entire arm shivered with the excitement of it.

"It is just around the corner," she whispered. Because her voice seemed to have abandoned her. It was all she could do to breathe.

He straightened then, but did not release her hand. "Lead on, Miss Eversleigh."

She did, tugging him gently as she moved toward her destination. To everyone else, it was just a drawing room, decorated in shades of cream and gold, with the occasional accent of the palest, mintiest of greens. But Grace's dowager-inflicted schedule had given her cause to enter in the morning, when the eastern sun still hung low on the horizon.

The air shimmered in the early morning, somehow golden with the light, and when it streamed through the windows in this far-flung, unnamed drawing room, the world somehow sparkled. By midmorning it would be just an expensively decorated room, but now, while the larks were still chirping softly outside, it was magic.

If he didn't see that. . .

Well, she did not know what it would mean if he did not see that. But it would be disappointing. It was a small thing, meaningless to anyone but her, and yet. . .

She wanted him to see it. The simple magic of the morning light. The beauty and grace in the one room at Belgrave that she could almost imagine was hers.

"Here we are," she said, a little breathless with the anticipation. The door was open, and as they approached, she could see the light slanting out, landing gently on the smooth surface of the floor. There was such a golden hue to it, she could see every speck of dust that hung floating in the air.

"Is there a private choir?" he teased. "A fantastical menagerie?"

"Nothing so ordinary," she replied. "But close your eyes. You should see it all at once."

He took her hands and, still facing her, placed them over his eyes. It brought her achingly close to him, her arms stretched up, the bodice of her dress just a whisper away from his finely tailored coat. It would be so easy to lean forward, to sigh into him. She could let her hands drop and close her own eyes, tilting her face toward his. He would kiss her, and she would lose her breath, her will, her very desire to, in that moment, be only herself.

She wanted to melt into him. She wanted to be a part of him. And the strangest part was—right there, right then, with the golden light rippling down upon them—it seemed the most natural thing in the world.

But his eyes were closed, and for him, one little piece of the magic was missing. It had to have been, because if he had felt everything that was floating around her—through her—he never would have said, his voice utterly charming—

"Are we there yet?"

"Almost," she said. She should have been grateful that the moment was broken. She should have been relieved that she did not do something she was sure to regret.

But she wasn't. She wanted her regrets. She wanted

them desperately. She wanted to do something she knew she should not, and she wanted to lie in bed at night letting the memory keep her warm.

But she was not brave enough to initiate her own downfall. Instead, she led him to the open doorway and said softly, "Here we are."

Chapter Eleven

What Jack saw took his breath away.

"No one comes here but me," Grace said softly. "I don't know why."

The light, the ripple through the air as the sun slid through the uneven glass of the ancient windows . . .

"In the winter especially," she continued, her voice just a little hesitant, "it's magic. I can't explain it. I think the sun dips lower. And with the snow . . ."

It was the light. It had to be. It was the way the light trembled, and fell on *her*.

His heart clenched. Like a fist it hit him—this need, this overwhelming urge . . . He could not speak. He could not even begin to articulate it, but—

"Jack?" she whispered, and it was just enough to break his trance.

"Grace." It was just one word, but it was a benediction. This went beyond desire, it was need. It was an indefinable, inexplicable, living, pulsing thing within him that could only be tamed by her. If he didn't hold her, didn't touch her in that very moment, something within him would die.

To a man who tried to treat life as an endless series of ironies and witticisms, nothing could have been more terrifying.

He reached out and roughly pulled her to him. He was not delicate, nor was he gentle. He couldn't be. He couldn't manage it, not now, not when he needed her so desperately.

"Grace," he said again, because that's what she was to him. It was impossible that he'd known her but a day. She was his grace, his Grace, and it was like she had always been there within him, waiting for him to finally open his eyes and find her.

His hands cupped her face. She was a priceless treasure, and yet he could not force himself to touch her with the reverence she deserved. Instead, his fingers were clumsy, his body rough and pounding. Her eyes—so clear, so blue—he thought he might drown in them. He *wanted* to drown in them, to lose himself within her and never leave.

His lips touched hers, and then—of this he was certain—he was lost. There was nothing more for him but this woman, in this moment, maybe even for all his moments thereafter.

"Jack," she sighed. It was the first time all morning she'd used his name, and it sent waves of desire pulsing through his already taut body.

"Grace," he said in return, because he was afraid to say anything else, afraid that for the first time in his life his glib tongue would fail him, and his words would come out wrong. He'd say something and it would mean too little, or perhaps he'd say something and it would mean too much. And then she would know, if by some miracle she did not already, that she had bewitched him.

He kissed her hungrily, passionately, with all the fire within him. His hands slid down her back, memorizing the gentle slope of her spine, and when he reached the more lush curves of her bottom, he could not help it—he pressed her more firmly against him. He was aroused, and wound more tightly than he'd ever imagined possible, and all he could think—if he was thinking at all—was that he needed her close, closer. Whatever he could get, whatever he could have—right now he would take it.

"Grace," he said again, one of his hands moving to the spot where her dress touched her skin, just at her collarbone.

She flinched at his touch, and he stilled, barely able to imagine how he would tear himself away. But her hand covered his, and she whispered, "I was surprised."

It was only then that he once again breathed.

Fingers shaking, he traced the delicately scalloped edge of her bodice. Her pulse seemed to leap beneath his touch, and never in his life had he been so aware of a single sound—the quiet rasp of air, brushing across her lips.

"You are so beautiful," he whispered, and the amazing thing was that he was not even looking at her face. It was merely her skin, the pale, milky hue of it, the soft blush of pink that followed his fingers.

Softly, gently, he bowed his head and brushed his lips along the hollow at the base of her throat. She gasped then, or maybe it was a moan, and her head slowly fell back in silent agreement. Her arms were around him and her hands in his hair, and then, without even considering what it meant, he swept her into his arms and carried her across the room, to the low, wide settee that sat near the window, bathed in the magical sunlight that had seduced them both.

For a moment, kneeling at her side, he could do nothing but look at her, then one of his trembling hands reached forth to stroke her cheek. She was staring up at him, and in her eyes there was wonder, and anticipation, and yes, a little nervousness.

But there was also trust. She wanted him. Him. No one else. She had never been kissed before, of that he was certain. She could have done. Of that he was even more certain. A woman of Grace's beauty did not reach her age without having refused (or rebuffed) multiple advances.

She had waited. She had waited for him.

Still kneeling beside her, he bent to kiss her, his hand moving down the side of her face to her shoulder, then to her hip. His passion grew deeper, and hers, too; she was returning his kiss with an unschooled eagerness that left him breathless with desire.

"Grace, Grace," he moaned, his voice lost in the warmth of her mouth. His hand found the hem of her dress and then slid under, grasping the slender circle of her ankle. And then up . . . up . . . to her knee. And higher. Until he could bear it no longer, and he moved to the settee himself, partially covering her with his own body.

His lips had moved to her neck, and he felt her sharply indrawn breath on his cheek. But she did not say no. She did not cover his hand with hers and bring him to a stop. She did nothing but whisper his name and arch her hips beneath him.

She couldn't have known what the movement had meant, could never have known what it would do to him, but that ever-so-slight pressure beneath him, rising up against his own desire, brought him to the very peak of need.

He kissed his way down her neck, to the gentle swell of her breast, his lips finding the very spot at the edge of her bodice that his fingers had so recently traveled. He lifted himself away from her, just a bit, just enough so he could slide his finger under the hem and slide it down, or maybe push her up—whichever was needed to free her to his devotion.

But just when his hand had moved toward his destination, just when he'd had one glorious second to cup the fullness of her, skin to skin, the stiff edge peaking in his palm, she cried out. Softly, with surprise.

And dismay.

"No, I can't." With jerky movements she scrambled to her feet, righting her dress. Her hands were shaking. More than shaking. They seemed filled with a foreign, nervous energy, and when he looked in her eyes, it was as if a knife had pierced him.

It was not revulsion, it was not fear. What he saw was anguish.

"Grace," he said, moving toward her. "What is wrong?"

"I'm sorry," she said, stepping back. "I—I shouldn't have. Not now. Not until—" One of her hands flew up to cover her mouth.

"Not until . . . ? Grace? Not until what?"

"I'm sorry," she said again, confirming his belief that those were the worst two words in the English language. She bobbed a quick, perfunctory curtsy. "I must go."

And then she ran from the room, leaving him quite alone. He stared at the empty doorway for a full minute, trying to figure out just what had happened. And it was only when he finally stepped into the hall that he realized he hadn't a clue how to get back to his bedchamber.

Grace dashed through Belgrave, half walking, half skipping . . . running . . . whatever it was she needed to do to reach her room with the most equal balance of dignity and speed. If the servants saw her—and she couldn't imagine they didn't; they seemed positively everywhere this morning—they must have wondered at her distress.

The dowager would not expect her. Surely she would think she was still showing Mr. Audley the house. Grace had at least an hour before she might need to show her face.

Dear God, what had she done? If she had not finally remembered herself, remembered who he was, and who he might be, she would have let him continue. She'd wanted it. She'd wanted it with a fervor that had shocked her. When he'd taken her hand, when he'd pulled her to him, he awakened something within her.

No. It had been awakened two nights earlier. On that moonlit night, standing outside the carriage, something had been born within her. And now . . .

She sat upon her bed, wanting to bury herself in the covers but instead just sitting there, staring at the wall. There was no going back. One couldn't ever *not* have been kissed once the deed was done.

With a nervous breath, maybe even a frantic laugh, she covered her face with her hands. Could she possibly have chosen anyone less suitable with whom to fall in love? Not that this was the measure of her feelings, she hastened to reassure herself, but she was not so much of a fool that she could not recognize her leanings. If she let herself . . . If she let him . . .

She would fall in love.

Good heavens.

Either he was a highwayman, and now she was destined to be the consort of an outlaw, or he was the true Duke of Wyndham, which meant—

She laughed because really, this was funny. It had to be funny. If it wasn't funny, then it could only be tragic, and she didn't think she could manage that just now.

Wonderful. Perhaps she was falling in love with the Duke of Wyndham. Now that was appropriate. Let's see, how many ways was this a disaster? He was her employer, for one, he owned the house in which she lived, and his rank was so far above hers as to be nearly immeasurable.

And then there was Amelia. She and Thomas certainly did not suit, but she had every right to expect that she would be the Duchess of Wyndham upon her marriage. Grace could not imagine how crass and overreaching she would appear to the Willoughbys—her good friends—if she were seen to be throwing herself at the new duke.

Grace closed her eyes and touched the tips of her fingers to her lips. If she breathed deeply enough she almost relaxed. And she could almost still feel his presence, his touch, the warmth of his skin.

It was awful.

It was wonderful.

She was a fool.

She lay down, let out a long, weary breath. Funny how she'd hoped for change, for something to break the monotony of her days attending to the dowager. Life was a mocking sort of thing, wasn't it? And love . . .

Love was the cruelest joke of all.

"Lady Amelia is here to see you, Miss Eversleigh."

Grace jolted upright, blinking furiously. She must have fallen asleep. She could not recall the last time she had done so at midday. "Lady Amelia?" she echoed, surprised. "With Lady Elizabeth?"

"No, miss," the maid informed her. "She is alone."

"How curious." Grace sat up, flexing her feet and hands to awaken her body. "Please tell her I shall be right there." She waited for the maid to depart, then went to her small mirror to straighten her hair. It was worse than she'd feared, although she could not be certain whether it had been mussed in sleep or by Mr. Audley.

She felt her skin flush at the memory, and she groaned at that. Gathering her determination, she re-pinned her hair and left the room, walking as briskly as she could, as if speed and a set of squared shoulders could keep all of her worries at bay.

Or at the very least, make her look as if she did not care.

It did seem odd that Amelia would come to Belgrave without Elizabeth. Grace did not know that she had ever done so before. Certainly not to see *her*. Grace wondered if her original intention had been to call upon Thomas, who was, as far as she knew, still out.

She hurried down the stairs, then turned to make for the front drawing room. But she'd not taken more than a dozen steps before someone grabbed her arm and yanked her into a side room.

"Thomas!" she exclaimed. It was indeed he, somewhat haggard and sporting a nasty bruise under his left eye. His appearance was a shock; she had never seen him looking so rumpled before. His shirt was wrinkled, his cravat missing, and his hair had most definitely not been styled à la Brutus.

Or even à la human.

And then there were his eyes, which were most uncharacteristically red-rimmed.

"What happened to you?"

He put a finger to his lips and shut the door. "Were you expecting someone else?" he asked, and her cheeks grew warm. Indeed, when she'd felt a strong male hand close around her arm and pull, she had assumed it was Mr. Audley, trying to steal a kiss.

Her flush grew deeper as she realized she had been disappointed to realize that it was not.

"No, of course not," she said quickly, even though

she suspected he knew she was lying. She quickly glanced around the room to see if they were alone. "What is wrong?"

"I needed to speak with you before you see Lady Amelia."

"Oh, then you know she is here?"

"I brought her," he confirmed.

Her eyes widened. That was news. He had been out all night and was considerably worse for the wear. She glanced at a nearby clock. It was not yet even noon. When could he have collected Amelia? And where?

And why?

"It is a long story," he said, clearly to cut her off before she could ask any questions. "But suffice it to say, she will inform you that you were in Stamford this morning, and you invited her back to Belgrave."

Her brows rose. If he was asking her to lie, it was very serious, indeed. "Thomas, any number of people know quite well that I was not in Stamford this morning."

"Yes, but her mother is not among that number."

Grace wasn't sure if she should be shocked or delighted. Had he compromised Amelia? Why else would they need to lie to her mother? "Er, Thomas . . ." she began, unsure of how to proceed. "I feel I must tell you, given the number of delays thus far, I would imagine that Lady Crowland would be delighted to know—"

"Oh for God's sake, it is nothing like that," he muttered. "Amelia assisted me home when I was"—he blushed then. Blushed! *Thomas*!—"impaired."

Grace bit her lip to keep from smiling. It was quite remarkable what a pleasant image that was—Thomas allowing himself to be anything less than perfectly composed. "That was most charitable of her," she said, perhaps a little too primly. But really, it couldn't be helped.

He glared at her, which only made it more difficult to maintain an even face.

She cleared her throat. "Have you, er, considered tidying up?"

"No," he snapped, "I rather enjoy looking like a slovenly fool."

Grace winced at that.

"Now listen," he continued, looking terribly determined. "Amelia will repeat what I have told you, but it is imperative that you not tell her about Mr. Audley."

"I would never do that," Grace said quickly. "It is not my place."

"Good."

"But she will want to know why you were, er . . ." Oh, dear, how to put it politely?

"You don't know why," he said firmly. "Just tell her that. Why would she suspect that you would know more?"

"She knows that I consider you a friend," Grace said. "And furthermore, I live here. Servants always know everything. She knows that."

"You're not a servant," he muttered.

"I am and you know it," she replied, almost amused. "The only difference is that I am allowed to wear finer clothing and occasionally converse with the guests. But I assure you, I am privy to all of the household gossip."

For several seconds he did nothing but stare, as if

waiting for her to laugh and say, *Only joking!* Finally
he muttered something under his breath that she was
quite certain she was not meant to understand (and
indeed she did not; servants' gossip was occasionally
risqué, but it was never profane).

"For me, Grace," he said, his eyes boring into hers,
"will you please just tell her you don't know?"

It was the closest she had ever heard him come to
begging, and it left her disoriented and acutely uncomfortable. "Of course," she said quickly. "You have
my word."

He nodded briskly. "Amelia will be expecting you."

"Yes. Yes, of course." Grace hurried to the door, but
when her hand touched the knob, she found she was
not quite ready to go. She turned around, taking one
last look at his face.

He was not himself. No one could blame him; it
had been a most extraordinary two days. But still, it
worried her.

"Will you be all right?" she asked.

And immediately regretted that she had done so.
His face seemed to move, and twist, and she could not
be sure if he was going to laugh or cry. But she did
know that she did not want to be witness to either.

"No, don't answer that," she mumbled, and she ran
from the room.

Chapter Twelve

Jack did (eventually) find his bedchamber, but even though he knew he'd likely still have been happily asleep if he hadn't been determined to join Grace at breakfast, when he lay down atop his covers, intending to take a restorative nap, he found himself unable to do so.

This was profoundly irritating. He had long prided himself on his ability to fall asleep at will. It had come in handy during his years as a soldier. No one ever managed to acquire the correct sleep, either in quality or amount. He would steal his slumber where he could, and his friends had been eternally jealous that he could prop up against a tree, close his eyes, and be asleep within three minutes.

But not, apparently, today, even though he'd traded a knobby tree for the finest mattress money could buy.

He closed his eyes, took his customary long, slow breaths, and . . . nothing.

Nothing but Grace.

He'd like to have said she was haunting him, but that would have been a lie. It wasn't her fault that he was a fool. And in truth, it wasn't just that he was completely desperate for her (although he was, and most uncomfortably, too). He couldn't get her out of his mind because he didn't *want* to get her out of his mind. Because if he stopped thinking about Grace, he would have to start thinking about other things. The possibility of his being the Duke of Wyndham, for one.

Possibility . . . Bah. He knew it was true. His parents had been married. All that was needed was to locate the parish register.

He closed his eyes, trying to push back the overwhelming feeling of dread that was bearing down on him. He should have just lied and said that his parents had never wed. But blast it, he had not known the consequences when he said that they had. No one had told him he'd be crowned the bloody duke. All he'd known was that he was so damned furious with the dowager for kidnapping him and with Wyndham for staring at him like he was something to be swept under the rug.

And then Wyndham had said, in that smarmy, superior voice of his: *If indeed your parents were married. . . .*

Jack had snapped out his reply before he had a chance to consider the consequences of his actions. These people were not better than he was. They had no right to cast aspersions on his parents.

It was too late now, though. Even if he tried to lie

and recant his words, the dowager would not rest until she'd burned a trail through Ireland in search of the marriage documents.

She wanted him to inherit, that much was clear. It was difficult to imagine her caring for anyone, but she had apparently adored her middle son.

His father.

And even though the dowager had not shown any particular fondness for him—not that he had made much of an effort to impress—she clearly preferred him over her other grandson. Jack had no idea what had transpired between the dowager and the current duke, if anything. But there was little affection between the pair.

Jack stood and walked to the window, finally admitting defeat and giving up on the notion of sleep. The morning sun was already bright and high in the sky, and he was suddenly seized by a need to be out of doors, or rather, out of Belgrave. Strange, that one could feel so closed-in in such a massive dwelling. But he did, and he wanted out.

Jack strode across the room and snatched up his coat. It was satisfyingly shabby atop the fine apparel of Wyndham's he'd donned that morning. He almost hoped he bumped into the dowager, just so she could see him all dusty and road-worn.

Almost. But not quite.

With quick, long strides he made his way down to the main hall, just about the only location he knew how to get to. His footsteps were annoyingly loud on the marble as he walked forth. Everything seemed to echo here. It was too big, too impersonal, too—

"Thomas?"

He stopped. It was a female voice. Not Grace. Young, though. Unsure of her surroundings.

"Is that—I'm so sorry." It was indeed a young woman, of medium height, blond, with rather fetching hazel eyes. She was standing near the doorway of the drawing room he had been dragged into the day before. Her cheeks were delightfully pink, with a smattering of freckles he was sure she detested. (All women did, he'd learned.) There was something exceptionally pleasant about her, he decided. If he weren't so obsessed with Grace, he would flirt with her.

"Sorry to disappoint," he murmured, offering her a roguish smile. This wasn't flirting. This was how he conversed with all ladies. The difference was in the intention.

"No," she said quickly, "of course not. It was my mistake. I was just sitting back there." She motioned behind her to a seating area. "You looked rather like the duke as you walked by."

This must be the fiancée, Jack realized. How interesting. It was difficult to imagine why Wyndham was dragging his heels on the marriage. He swept into a gracious bow. "Captain Jack Audley, at your service, ma'am." It had been some time since he'd introduced himself with his military rank, but somehow it seemed the thing to do.

She bobbed a polite curtsy. "Lady Amelia Willoughby."

"Wyndham's fiancée."

"You know him, then? Oh, well, of course you do.

You are a guest here. Oh, you must be his fencing partner."

"He told you about me?" The day grew more interesting by the second.

"Not much," she admitted. She blinked, staring at a spot that was not his eyes. He realized that she was looking at his cheek, which was still discolored from his altercation with her fiancé the day before.

"Ah, this," he murmured, affecting mild embarrassment. "It looks much worse than it actually is."

She wanted to ask about it. He could see it in her eyes. He wondered if she'd seen Wyndham's blackened eye. That would certainly set her curiosity on fire.

"Tell me, Lady Amelia," he said conversationally, "what color is it today?"

"Your cheek?" she asked with some surprise.

"Indeed. Bruises tend to look worse as they age, have you noticed? Yesterday it was quite purple, almost regally so, with a hint of blue in it. I haven't checked in the mirror lately." He turned his head to offer her a better view. "Is it still as attractive?"

Her eyes widened, and for a moment she seemed not to know what to say. Jack wondered if she was unused to men flirting with her. Shame on Wyndham. He had done her a great disservice.

"Er, no," she replied. "I would not call it attractive."

He laughed. "No mincing words for you, eh?"

"I'm afraid those blue undertones of which you were so proud have gone a bit green."

He leaned in with a warm smile. "To match my eyes?"

"No," she said, seemingly immune to his charms, "not with the purple overlaying it. It looks quite horrible."

"Purple mixed with green makes . . . ?"

"Quite a mess."

Jack laughed again. "You are charming, Lady Amelia. But I am sure your fiancé tells you that on every possible occasion."

She did not reply. Not that she could; her only possible answers were yes, which would reveal her conceit, or no, which would reveal Wyndham's negligence. Neither was what a lady wished to show to the world.

"Do you await him here?" he asked, thinking to himself that it was time to end the conversation. Lady Amelia was charming, and he could not deny a certain level of entertainment that came from making her acquaintance without Wyndham's knowledge, but he was still a bit wound up inside, and he was looking forward to time out of doors.

"No, I just—" She cleared her throat. "I am here to see Miss Eversleigh."

Grace?

And who was to say that a man could not acquire a bit of fresh air in a drawing room? One had only to crack open a window.

"Have you met Miss Eversleigh?" Lady Amelia asked.

"Indeed I have. She is most lovely."

"Yes." There was a pause, just long enough for Jack to wonder at it. "She is universally admired," Lady Amelia finished.

Jack thought about making trouble for Wyndham. A simple, murmured, *It must be difficult for you, with so beautiful a lady in residence here at Belgrave,* would go a long way. But it would make equal trouble for Grace, which he was not prepared to do. And so instead he chose the bland and boring: "Are you and Miss Eversleigh acquaintances?"

"Yes. I mean, no. More than that, I should say. I have known Grace since childhood. She is most friendly with my elder sister."

"And surely with you, as well."

"Of course." Lady Amelia acceded. "But more so with my sister. They are of an age, you see."

"Ah, the plight of the younger sibling," he murmured.

"You share the experience?"

"Not at all," he said with a grin. "I was the one ignoring the hangers-on." He thought back to his days with the Audleys. Edward had been but six months younger, and Arthur a mere eighteen months after that. Poor Arthur had been left out of any number of escapades, and yet wasn't it interesting—it was Arthur with whom he had ultimately formed the strongest bond.

Arthur had been uncommonly perceptive. They shared that. Jack had always been good at reading people. He'd had to. Sometimes it was his only means of gathering information. But as a boy he'd viewed Arthur as an annoying little whelp; it wasn't until they were both students at Portora Royal that he realized that Arthur saw everything, too.

And although he had never come out and said it, Jack knew that he'd seen everything in *him* as well.

But he refused to grow maudlin. Not right now, not with a charming lady for company and the promise of another at any moment. And so he pushed more happy thoughts of Arthur to the forefront of his mind and said, "I was the eldest of the brood. A fortuitous position, I think. I should have been most unhappy not to have been in charge."

Lady Amelia smiled at that. "I am the second of five, so I can appreciate your sentiments as well."

"Five! All girls?" he guessed.

"How did you know?"

"I have no idea," he said quite honestly, "except that it is such a charming image. It would have been a shame to have sullied it with a male."

"Is your tongue always this silver, Captain Audley?"

He gave her one of his best half smiles. "Except when it's gold."

"Amelia!"

They both turned. Grace had entered the room.

"And Mr. Audley," she said, looking surprised to see him there.

"Oh, I'm sorry," Lady Amelia said, turning to him. "I thought it was *Captain* Audley."

"It is," he said with a very slight shrug. "Depending upon my mood." He turned to Grace and bowed. "It is indeed a privilege to see you again so soon, Miss Eversleigh."

She blushed. He wondered if Lady Amelia noticed.

"I did not realize you were here," Grace said after bobbing a curtsy.

"There is no reason why you should have done. I

was heading outside for a restorative walk when Lady Amelia intercepted me."

"I thought he was Wyndham," Lady Amelia said. "Isn't that the oddest thing?"

"Indeed," Grace replied, looking acutely uncomfortable.

"Of course I was not paying much attention," Lady Amelia continued, "which I am sure explains it. I only caught sight of him out of the corner of my eye as he strode past the open doorway."

Jack turned to Grace. "It makes so much sense when put that way, does it not?"

"So much sense," Grace echoed. She glanced over her shoulder.

"Are you waiting for someone, Miss Eversleigh?" Jack inquired.

"No, I was just thinking that his grace might like to join us. Er, since his fiancée is here, of course."

"Is he returned, then?" Jack murmured. "I was not aware."

"That is what I have been told," Grace said, and he was certain that she was lying, although he could not imagine why. "I have not seen him myself."

"Alas," Jack said, "he has been absent for some time."

Grace swallowed. "I think I should get him."

"But you only just got here."

"Nonetheless—"

"We shall ring for him," Jack said, since he wasn't going to allow her such an easy escape. Not to mention that he was rather looking forward to the duke discovering him here with both Grace and Lady

Amelia. He crossed the room and gave the bellpull a yank. "There," he said. "It is done."

Grace smiled uncomfortably and moved to the sofa. "I believe I will sit down."

"I will join you," Lady Amelia said with alacrity. She hurried after Grace and took a seat right beside her. Together they sat, stiff and awkward.

"What a fetching tableau the two of you make," he said, because really, how could he not tease them? "And me, without my oils."

"Do you paint, Mr. Audley?" Lady Amelia inquired.

"Alas, no. But I have been thinking I might take some lessons. It is a noble pursuit for a gentleman, wouldn't you say?"

"Oh, indeed."

Silence, then Lady Amelia nudged Grace. "Mr. Audley is a great appreciator of art," Grace blurted out.

"You must be enjoying your stay at Belgrave, then," Lady Amelia said. Her face was the perfect picture of polite interest. He wondered how long it had taken her to hone the expression. As the daughter of an earl, she would have any number of social obligations. He imagined that the expression—placid and unmoving, yet not unfriendly—was quite useful.

"I look forward to touring the collections," Jack replied. "Miss Eversleigh has consented to show them to me."

Lady Amelia turned to Grace as best she could, considering that they were wedged up against one another. "That was very kind of you, Grace."

Grace grunted something that was probably meant to be a response.

"We plan to avoid cupids," Jack said.

"Cupids?" Lady Amelia echoed.

Grace looked the other way.

"I have discovered that I am not fond of them."

Lady Amelia regarded him with a curious mixture of irritation and disbelief.

Jack glanced at Grace to gauge her reaction, then returned his attention to Lady Amelia. "I can see that you disagree, Lady Amelia."

"What is there not to like about cupids?"

He perched himself on the arm of the opposite sofa. "You don't find them rather dangerous?"

"Chubby little babies?"

"Carrying deadly weapons," he reminded her.

"They are not *real* arrows."

He made another attempt to draw Grace into the conversation. "What do you think, Miss Eversleigh?"

"I don't often think about cupids," she said tersely.

"And yet we have already discussed them twice, you and I."

"Because you brought them *up*."

Jack turned to Lady Amelia. "My dressing room is positively awash in them."

Lady Amelia turned to Grace. "You were in his dressing room?"

"Not *with* him," Grace practically snapped. "But I have certainly seen it before."

Jack smiled to himself, wondering what it said about him that he so liked making trouble.

"Pardon," Grace muttered, clearly embarrassed by her outburst.

"Mr. Audley," Lady Amelia said, turning to him with determination.

"Lady Amelia."

"Would it be rude if Miss Eversleigh and I took a turn about the room?"

"Of course not," he said, even though he could see in her face that in fact she did think it was rude. But he did not mind. If the ladies wished to share confidences, he was not going to stand in their way. Besides, he enjoyed watching Grace move.

"Thank you for your understanding," Lady Amelia said, linking her arm through Grace's and pulling them both to their feet. "I do feel the need to stretch my legs, and I fear that your stride would be far too brisk for a lady."

How she uttered that without choking on her tongue, he did not know. But he merely smiled and watched them as they moved as one to the window, leaving him behind and out of earshot.

Chapter Thirteen

$\mathcal{G}$race let Amelia set the pace, and as soon as they were across the room, Amelia began whispering urgently about the events of the morning, and then about Thomas having needed her assistance, and then something about her mother.

Grace just nodded, her eyes constantly darting toward the door. Thomas would be there at any moment, and although she had no idea what she might do to prevent what would surely be a disastrous encounter, she could not possibly think of anything else.

Meanwhile, Amelia kept on whispering. Grace had just enough presence of mind to catch the end, when Amelia said: " . . . I beg of you not to contradict."

"Of course not," Grace said quickly, because surely Amelia had made the same request Thomas had minutes earlier. If not, then she had no idea what she was agreeing to when she added, "You have my word."

At that point, Grace wasn't sure she cared.

They continued walking, lapsing into silence as they promenaded past Mr. Audley, who gave them a rather knowing nod and a smile as they went by.

"Miss Eversleigh," he murmured. "Lady Amelia."

"Mr. Audley," Amelia returned. Grace managed the same, but her voice was unpleasant and croaky.

Amelia began whispering again once they were well past Mr. Audley, but just then Grace heard heavy footsteps in the hall. She twisted about to see, but it was only a footman, passing by with a trunk.

Grace swallowed. Oh, dear heavens, the dowager was already beginning to pack for their trip to Ireland, and Thomas did not even know of her plans. How could she have forgotten to tell him during their interview?

And then she became aware of Amelia, whom she'd somehow managed to forget, even though their arms were linked. "Sorry," she said quickly, since she suspected it was her turn to speak. "Did you say something?"

Amelia shook her head and said, "No." Grace was fairly certain this was a lie, but she was not inclined to argue.

And then . . . more footsteps in the hall.

"Excuse me," Grace said, unable to bear the suspense for one moment longer. She pulled away and hurried to the open doorway. Several more servants were passing by, all clearly in preparations for the upcoming journey to Ireland. Grace returned to Amelia's side and once again took her arm. "It wasn't the duke."

"Is someone going somewhere?" Amelia asked,

watching as two footmen passed the doorway, one with a trunk and another with a hatbox.

"No," Grace said. But she hated lying, and she was terrible at it, so she added, "Well, I suppose someone might be, but I do not know about it."

Which was also a lie. Wonderful. She looked at Amelia and tried to smile cheerfully.

"Grace," Amelia said quietly, looking terribly concerned, "are you all right?"

"Oh, no . . . I mean, yes, I'm quite fine." She tried for the cheerful smile again, and suspected she did a worse job of it than before.

"Grace," Amelia whispered, her voice taking on a new and rather unsettlingly sly tone, "are you in love with Mr. Audley?"

"No!" Oh, good heavens, that was loud. Grace looked over at Mr. Audley. Not that she'd wanted to, but they'd just turned a corner and were facing him again, and she couldn't avoid it. His face was tilted slightly down, but she could see him looking up at her, rather bemused. "Mr. Audley," she said, because with him watching her, it seemed she should acknowledge him, even if he was too far away to hear.

But then, as soon as she had the opportunity, she turned back to Amelia, furiously whispering, "I've only just met him. Yesterday. No, the day before." Oh, she was a ninny. She shook her head and looked firmly in front of her. "I can't recall."

"You've been meeting many intriguing gentlemen lately," Amelia commented.

Grace turned to her sharply. "Whatever can you mean?"

"Mr. Audley . . ." Amelia teased. "The Italian high-wayman."

"Amelia!"

"Oh, that's right, you said he was Scottish. Or Irish. You weren't certain." Amelia's brow scrunched in thought. "Where is Mr. Audley from? He has a bit of lilt as well."

"I do not know," Grace ground out. Where was Thomas? She dreaded his arrival, but the anticipation of it was worse.

And then Amelia—good heavens, *why*?—called out, "Mr. Audley!"

Grace turned and looked at a wall.

"Grace and I were wondering where you are from," Amelia said. "Your accent is unfamiliar to me."

"Ireland, Lady Amelia, a bit north of Dublin."

"Ireland!" Amelia exclaimed. "My goodness, you are far afield."

They'd finished circling the room, but Grace remained standing even after Amelia had disengaged herself and sat down. Then Grace moved toward the door as subtly as she was able.

"How are you enjoying Lincolnshire, Mr. Audley?" she heard Amelia ask.

"I find it most surprising."

"Surprising?"

Grace peered out into the hall, still half listening to the conversation behind her.

"My visit here has not been what I expected," Mr. Audley said, and Grace could well imagine his amused smile as he said *that*.

"Really?" Amelia responded. "What did you expect?

I assure you, we are quite civilized in this corner of England."

"Very much so," he murmured. "More so than is my preference, as a matter of fact."

"Why, Mr. Audley," Amelia responded, "whatever can that mean?"

If he made a reply, Grace did not hear it. Just then she saw Thomas coming down the hall, all tidied up and looking like a duke again.

"Oh," she said, the word slipping from her lips. "Excuse me." She hurried into the hall, waving madly toward Thomas so as not to alert Amelia and Mr. Audley to her distress.

"Grace," he said, moving forward with great purpose, "what is the meaning of this? Penrith told me that Amelia was here to see me?"

He did not slow as he approached, and Grace realized he meant for her to fall in step beside him. "Thomas, wait," she said with hushed urgency, and she grabbed his arm and yanked him to a halt.

He turned to her, one of his brows rising into a haughty arch.

"It's Mr. Audley," she said, pulling him back even farther from the door. "He is in the drawing room."

Thomas glanced toward the drawing room and then back at Grace, clearly not comprehending.

"With Amelia," she practically hissed.

All traces of his unflappable exterior vanished. "What the hell?" he cursed. He looked sharply back toward the drawing room, not that he could possibly have seen inside from his vantage point. "Why?"

"I don't know," Grace said, her voice snapping with

irritation. Why would *she* know why? "He was in there when I arrived. Amelia said she saw him walking by the doorway and thought he was you."

His body shuddered. Visibly. "What did he say?"

"I don't know. I wasn't there. And then I couldn't very well interrogate her in his presence."

"No, of course not."

Grace waited in silence for him to say more. He was pinching the bridge of his nose, and he looked rather as if his head were aching. Trying to offer some sort of *not* unpleasant news, she said, "I'm quite sure that he did not reveal his . . ."

Oh, good heavens. How was she to put it?

" . . . identity to her," she finished with a wince.

Thomas gave her a thoroughly awful look.

"It is not my fault, Thomas," she retorted.

"I did not say that it was." His voice was stiff, and he did not offer any more words before stalking off to the drawing room.

From the moment Grace rushed from the room, neither Jack nor Lady Amelia had uttered a word. It was as if they had reached an unspoken agreement; silence would prevail while they both tried to make out what was being said in the hall.

Jack had always considered himself better than average in the art of eavesdropping, but he was unable to catch even the sound of their whispers. Still, he had a fair idea of what was being said. Grace was warning Wyndham that the evil Mr. Audley had got his claws into the lovely and innocent Lady Amelia. And then Wyndham would curse—under his breath, of course, as he would never be so crass as to do so in front of a lady—and demand to know what had been said.

The whole thing would have been highly entertaining if not for her, and the morning. And the kiss.

Grace.

He wanted her back. He wanted the woman he'd held in his arms, not the one who'd stiffly walked the perimeter of the room with Lady Amelia, eyeing him as if he were going to steal the silver at any moment.

He supposed it was amusing. Somehow. And he supposed he ought to congratulate himself. Whatever she felt for him, it was not disinterest. Which would have been the cruelest response of all.

But for the first time, he was finding that his conquest of a lady was not a game to be played. He did not care about the thrill of the chase, about remaining one enjoyable and entertaining step ahead, about planning the seduction and then carrying it out with flair and flourish.

He simply wanted *her*.

Maybe even forever.

He glanced over at Lady Amelia. She was leaning forward, her head tilted ever so slightly to the side, as if to place her ear at the best possible angle.

"You won't be able to hear them," Jack said.

The look she gave him was priceless. And completely false.

"Oh, don't pretend you weren't trying," he scolded. "I certainly was."

"Very well." Lady Amelia waited for a moment, then asked, "What do you suppose they are talking about?"

Ah, curiosity would always win out with this one. She was more intelligent than she let on at first acquaintance, he decided. He shrugged, feigning ignorance. "Difficult to say. I would never presume to understand the female mind, or that of our esteemed host."

She turned sharply in surprise. "You do not like the duke?"

"I did not say that," Jack replied. But of course they both knew that he had.

"How long do you stay at Belgrave?" she asked.

He smiled. "Eager to be rid of me, Lady Amelia?"

"Of course not. I saw the servants moving trunks about. I thought perhaps they were yours."

He fought to keep his expression even. He did not know why he was surprised that the old biddy had already begun to pack. "I imagine they belong to the dowager," he replied.

"Is she going somewhere?"

He almost laughed at the hopeful expression on her face. "Ireland," he said absently, before it occurred to him that perhaps this woman of all people ought not to be let in on the plans.

Or maybe she was the one person who truly ought to be told. She certainly deserved to know. She deserved a sainthood, in his opinion, if indeed she planned to go through with her marriage to Wyndham. He could not imagine anything less pleasant than spending one's life with such an arrogant prig.

And then, as if summoned by his thoughts, the arrogant prig appeared.

"Amelia."

Wyndham was standing in the doorway in all his ducal splendor. Save for the lovely eye, Jack thought with some satisfaction. It was even gorier than the evening before.

"Your grace," she replied.

"How lovely to see you," Wyndham said once he had joined them. "I see that you have met our guest."

"Yes," Lady Amelia said, "Mr. Audley is quite diverting."

"Quite," Wyndham said. Jack thought he looked as if he had just eaten a radish.

Jack had always hated radishes.

"I came to see Grace," Lady Amelia said.

"Yes, of course," Wyndham replied.

"Alas," Jack put in, enjoying the awkwardness of the exchange, "I found her first."

Wyndham's response was pure icy disdain. Jack smiled in return, convinced that would irritate him far more than anything he could have said.

"I found *him*, actually," Lady Amelia said. "I saw him in the hall. I thought he was you."

"Astounding, isn't it?" Jack murmured. He turned to Lady Amelia. "We are nothing alike."

"No," Wyndham said sharply, "we are not."

"What do you think, Miss Eversleigh?" Jack asked, rising to his feet. It seemed he was the only one who had noticed that she had entered the room. "Do the duke and I share any traits?"

Grace's lips parted for a full second before she spoke. "I'm afraid I do not know you well enough to be an accurate judge."

"Well said, Miss Eversleigh," he replied, offering

her a nod of compliment. "May I infer, then, that you know the duke quite well?"

"I have worked for his grandmother for five years. During that time I have been fortunate enough to learn something of his character."

"Lady Amelia," Wyndham said, clearly eager to cut short the conversation, "may I escort you home?"

"Of course," she said.

"So soon?" Jack murmured, just to make trouble.

"My family will be expecting me," Lady Amelia said, even though she had not made any indication of this before Wyndham had offered to remove her.

"We will leave right now, then," Wyndham said. His fiancée took his arm and stood.

"Er, your grace!"

Jack turned immediately at the sound of Grace's voice. "If I might have a word with you," she said from her position near the door, "before you, er, depart. Please."

Wyndham excused himself and followed her into the hall. They were still visible from the drawing room, although it was difficult—indeed impossible—to glean their conversation.

"Whatever can they be discussing?" Jack said to Lady Amelia.

"I am sure I have no idea," she bit off.

"Nor I," he said, keeping his voice light and breezy. Just for contrast. Life was infinitely more entertaining that way.

And then they heard: "Ireland!"

That was Wyndham, and rather loud, too. Jack leaned forward to get a better view, but the duke took Grace's arm and steered her out of sight. And earshot.

"We have our answer," Jack murmured.

"He can't be upset that his grandmother is leaving the country," Lady Amelia said. "I would think he'd be planning a celebration."

"I rather think Miss Eversleigh has informed him that his grandmother intends that he accompany her."

"To Ireland?" Amelia shook her head. "Oh, you must be mistaken."

He shrugged, feigning indifference. "Perhaps. I am but a newcomer here."

And then she launched into quite the most ambitious speech:

"Aside from the fact that I cannot imagine why the dowager would wish to go to *Ireland*—not that I wouldn't like to see your beautiful country, but it does not seem in character for the dowager, whom I have heard speak disparagingly of Northumberland, the Lake District, and indeed all of Scotland . . ." She paused, presumably to breathe. "Ireland seems a bit of a stretch for her."

He nodded, since it seemed expected.

"But really, it makes no sense that she would wish for his grace to accompany her. They do not care for each other's company."

"How politely said, Lady Amelia," Jack commented. "Does anyone care for their company?"

Her eyes widened in shock, and it occurred to him that perhaps he should have limited his insult to the dowager alone, but just then Wyndham strode back into the room, looking angry and arrogant.

And almost certainly worthy of whatever sort of insult Jack might give to him.

"Amelia," he said with brisk indifference, "I am afraid I will not be able to see you home. I do apologize."

"Of course," she said, as if she could possibly say anything else.

"I shall make every arrangement for your comfort. Perhaps you would like to select a book from the library?"

"Can you read in a coach?" Jack queried.

"Can you not?" she returned.

"I *can*," he replied with great flair. "I can do almost anything in a coach. Or with a coach," he added, with a smile toward Grace, who stood in the doorway.

Wyndham glared at him and grabbed his fiancée's arm, hauling her rather unceremoniously to her feet.

"It was lovely meeting you, Mr. Audley," Lady Amelia said.

"Yes," he said lightly, "it does seem that you are leaving."

"Amelia," the duke said, his voice even more abrupt than before. He led her from the room.

Jack followed them to the doorway, looking for Grace, but she had disappeared. Ah well, perhaps that was for the best.

He glanced toward the window. The skies had darkened, and it appeared that rain would be imminent.

Time for that walk, he decided. The rain would be cold. And wet. And precisely what he needed.

Chapter Fourteen

After five years at Belgrave, Grace had become, if not accustomed, then at least aware of just what could be accomplished with a bit of prestige and a great deal of money. Nonetheless, even she was amazed at how quickly their travel plans fell into place. Within three days a private yacht had been reserved to ferry them from Liverpool to Dublin and then wait at the dock—for as long as necessary, apparently—until they were ready to return to England.

One of Thomas's secretaries had been dispatched to Ireland to arrange for their stay. Grace had felt nothing but pity for the poor man as he was forced to listen to—and then repeat, twice—the dowager's copious and highly detailed instructions. She herself was used to the dowager's ways, but the secretary, accustomed to dealing with a far more reasonable employer, looked nearly ready to cry.

Only the best of inns would do for such a traveling party, and of course they would expect the finest set of rooms in each establishment.

If the rooms were already reserved, the innkeepers would have to make arrangements to place the other travelers elsewhere. The dowager told Grace that she liked to send someone ahead in cases like these. It was only polite to give the innkeepers a bit of notice so they could find alternate accommodations for their other guests.

Grace thought it would have been more polite not to give the boot to people whose only crime was to reserve a room prior to the dowager, but all she could do was offer the poor secretary a sympathetic smile. The dowager wasn't going to change her ways, and besides, she'd already launched into her next set of instructions, which pertained to cleanliness, food, and the preferred dimensions of hand towels.

Grace spent her days dashing about the castle, preparing for the voyage and passing along important messages, since the other three inhabitants seemed determined to avoid one another.

The dowager was as surly and rude as ever, but now there was an underlying layer of giddiness that Grace found disconcerting. The dowager was *excited* about the upcoming journey. It was enough to leave even the most experienced of companions uneasy; the dowager was never excited about anything. Pleased, yes; satisfied, often (although *un*satisfied was a far more frequent emotion). But excited? Grace had never witnessed it.

It was odd, because the dowager did not seem to like

Mr. Audley very well, and it was clear that she respected him not at all. And as for Mr. Audley—he returned the sentiment in spades. He was much like Thomas in that regard. It seemed to Grace that the two men might have been fast friends had they not met under such strained circumstances.

But while Thomas's dealings with the dowager were frank and direct, Mr. Audley was much more sly. He was always provoking the dowager when in her company, always ready with a comment so subtle that Grace could only be sure of his meaning when she caught his secret smile.

There was always a secret smile. And it was always for her.

Even now, just thinking about it, she found herself hugging her arms to her body, as if holding it tightly against her heart. When he smiled at her, she *felt* it—as if it were more than something to be seen. It landed upon her like a kiss, and her body responded in kind—a little flip in her stomach, pink heat on her cheeks. She maintained her composure, because that was what she'd been trained to do, and she even managed her own sort of reply—the tiniest of curves at the corners of her mouth, maybe a change in the way she held her gaze. She knew he saw it, too. He saw everything. He liked to play at being obtuse, but he had the keenest eye for observation she had ever known.

And all through this, the dowager pressed forward, single-minded in her determination to wrest the title from Thomas and give it to Mr. Audley. When the dowager spoke of their upcoming journey, it was never *if* they found proof, it was *when* they found it.

Already she had begun to plan how best to announce the change to the rest of society.

Grace had noticed that she was not particularly discreet about it, either. What was it the dowager had said just the other day—right in front of Thomas? Something about having to redraw endless contracts to reflect the proper ducal name. She had even turned to him and asked if he thought that anything he'd signed while duke was legally binding.

Grace had thought Thomas a master of restraint for not throttling her on the spot. Indeed, all he said was, "It will hardly be my problem should that come to pass." And then, with a mocking bow in the dowager's direction, he left the room.

Grace was not sure why she was so surprised that the dowager did not censor herself in front of Thomas; it wasn't as if she'd shown a care for anyone else's feelings before. But surely this qualified as extraordinary circumstances. Surely even Augusta Cavendish could see where it might be hurtful to stand in front of Thomas and talk about how she planned to go about his public humiliation.

And as for Thomas—he was not himself. He was drinking too much, and when he wasn't closeted in his study, he stalked about the house like a moody lion. Grace tried to avoid him, partly because he was in such poor temper, but mostly because she felt so *guilty* about everything, so unconscionably disloyal for liking Mr. Audley so well.

Which left *him*. Mr. Audley. She'd been spending too much time with him. She knew it but could not seem to help herself. And it really wasn't her fault.

The dowager kept sending her on errands that put her in his sphere.

Liverpool or Holyhead—which port made better sense for their departure? Surely Jack (the dowager still refused to call him Mr. Audley, and he would not respond to anything Cavendish) would know.

What might they expect from the weather? Find Jack and ask his opinion.

Could one obtain a decent pot of tea in Ireland? What about once they'd left the environs of Dublin? And then, after Grace had reported back with *Yes* and *for God's sake* (amended to remove the blasphemy), she was sent on her way again to determine if he even knew how to judge a tea's quality.

It was almost embarrassing to ask him this. It should have been, but by that point they were bursting out laughing just at the sight of each other. It was like that all the time now. He would smile. And then she would smile. And she was reminded just how much better she liked herself when she had reason to smile.

Just now the dowager had ordered her to find him for a full accounting of their proposed route through Ireland, which Grace found odd, since she would have thought the dowager had worked that out by then. But she was not about to complain, not when the task both removed her from the dowager's presence and placed her in Mr. Audley's.

"Jack," she whispered to herself. He was Jack. His name suited him perfectly, dashing and carefree. John was far too staid, and Mr. Audley too formal. She wanted him to be Jack, even though she had not allowed herself to say it aloud to him, not since their kiss.

He had teased her about it—he always teased her about it. He'd prodded and cajoled and told her she must use his given name or he would not respond, but she remained steadfast. Because once she did, she was afraid she could never go back. And she was already so perilously close to losing her heart forever.

It could happen. It *would* happen if she let it. She had only to let go. She could close her eyes and imagine a future . . . with him, and children, and so much laughter.

But not here. Not at Belgrave, with him as the duke.

She wanted Sillsby back. Not the house, since that could never be, but the feeling of it. The comfortable warmth, the kitchen garden that her mother had never been too important to attend. She wanted the evenings in the sitting room—*the* sitting room, she reminded herself, the only one. Nothing that had to be described with a color or a fabric or a location within the building. She wanted to read by the fire with her husband, pointing out bits that amused her, and laughing when he did the same.

That was what she wanted, and when she had the courage to be honest with herself, she knew that she wanted it with him.

But she wasn't often honest with herself. What was the point? He didn't know who he was; how could she know what to dream?

She was protecting herself, holding her heart in armor until she had an answer. Because if he was the Duke of Wyndham, then she was a fool.

* * *

As fine a house as Belgrave was, Jack much preferred to spend time out of doors, and now that his mount had been transferred to the Wyndham stables (where his horse was certainly wallowing in joy over the endless carrots and warm accommodations), he had taken up the habit of a ride each morning.

Not that this was so very far from his prior routine; Jack usually found himself on horseback by late morning. The difference was that before he'd been going somewhere, or, on occasion, fleeing *from* somewhere. Now he was out and about for sport, for constitutional exercise. Strange, the life of a gentleman. Physical exertion was achieved through organized behavior, and not, as the rest of society got it, through an honest day's work.

Or a dishonest one, as the case often was.

He was returning to the house—it was difficult to call it a castle, even though that's what it was; it always made him want to roll his eyes—on his fourth day at Belgrave, feeling invigorated by the soft bite of the wind over the fields.

As he walked up the steps to the main door, he caught himself peering this way and that, hoping for a glimpse of Grace even though it was highly unlikely she'd be out of doors. He was always hoping for a glimpse of Grace, no matter where he was. Just the sight of her made something tickle and fizz within his chest. Half the time she did not even see him, which he did not mind. He rather enjoyed watching her go about her duties. But if he stared long enough—and he always did; there was never any good reason to place his eyes anywhere else—she always sensed him. Eventually, even if he was at an odd angle, or obscured in shadows, she felt his presence, and she'd turn.

He always tried to play the seducer then, to gaze at her with smoldering intensity, to see if she'd melt in a pool of whimpering desire.

But he never did. Because all he could do, whenever she looked back at him, was smile like a lovesick fool. He would have been disgusted with himself, except that she always smiled in return, which never failed to turn the tickle and fizz into something even more bubbly and carefree.

He pushed open the door to Belgrave's front hall, pausing for a moment once he was inside. It took a few seconds to adjust to the abrupt lack of wind, and indeed, his body gave an unprompted little shake, as if to push away the chill. This also gave him time to glance about the hall, and indeed, he was rewarded for his diligence.

"Miss Eversleigh!" he called out, since she was at the far end of the long space, presumably off on another one of the dowager's ridiculous errands.

"Mr. Audley," she said, smiling as she walked toward him.

He shrugged off his coat (presumably purloined from the ducal closet) and handed it to a footman, marveling, as always, at how the servants seemed to materialize from nowhere, always at the exact moment they were needed.

Someone had trained them well. He was close enough to his military days to appreciate this.

Grace reached his side before he had even pulled

off his gloves. "Have you been out for a ride?" she asked.

"Indeed. It's a perfect day for it."

"Even with all the wind?"

"It's best with wind."

"I trust you were reunited with your horse?"

"Indeed. Lucy and I make a fine team."

"You ride a mare?"

"A gelding."

She blinked with curiosity, but not, strangely, surprise. "You named your gelding Lucy?"

He gave his shrug a bit of dramatic flair. "It is one of those stories that loses something in the retelling." In truth, it involved drink, three separate wagers, and a propensity for the contrary that he was not certain he was proud of.

"I am not much of an equestrienne," she said. It was not an apology, just a statement of fact.

"By choice or circumstance?"

"A bit of both," she replied, and she looked a bit curious, as if she'd never thought to ask herself that question.

"You shall have to join me sometime."

She smiled ruefully. "I hardly think that falls within the scope of my duties to the dowager."

Jack rather doubted that. He remained suspicious of the dowager's motives as pertained to Grace; she seemed to thrust Grace in his direction at every possible occasion, like some piece of ripened fruit, dangled before his nose to entice him to stay put. He found it all rather appalling, but wasn't about to deny himself the pleasure of Grace's company just to spite the old bat.

"Bah," he said. "All the best companions go riding with the houseguests."

"Oh." *So* dubious. "Really."

"Well, they do in my imagination, at least."

Grace shook her head, not even trying not to smile. "Mr. Audley . . ."

But he was looking this way and that, his manner almost comically surreptitious. "I think we're alone," he whispered.

Grace leaned in, feeling very sly. "Which means . . . ?"

"You can call me Jack."

She pretended to consider. "No, I don't think so."

"I won't tell."

"Mmmm . . ." Her nose scrunched, and then a matter-of-fact: "No."

"You did it once."

She pressed her lips together, suppressing not a smile, but a full-fledged laugh. "That was a mistake."

"Indeed."

Grace gasped and turned. It was Thomas.

"Where the devil did he come from?" Mr. Audley murmured.

From the small saloon, Grace thought miserably. The entrance was right behind them. Thomas frequently spent time there, reading or tending to his correspondence. He said he liked the afternoon light.

But it wasn't afternoon. And he smelled like brandy.

"A pleasant conversation," Thomas drawled. "One of many, I assume."

"Were you eavesdropping?" Mr. Audley said mildly. "For shame."

"Your grace," Grace began, "I—"

"It's Thomas," he cut in derisively, "or don't you recall? You've used *my* name far more than once."

Grace felt her cheeks grow hot. She'd not been sure how much of the conversation Thomas had heard. Apparently, most of it.

"Is that so?" Mr. Audley said. "In that case, I insist you call me Jack." He turned to Thomas and shrugged. "It's only fair."

Thomas made no verbal reply, although his thunderous expression spoke volumes. Mr. Audley turned back to her and said, "I shall call you Grace."

"You will not," Thomas snapped.

Mr. Audley remained as calm as ever. "Does he always make these decisions for you?"

"This is my house," Thomas returned.

"Possibly not for long," Mr. Audley murmured.

Grace actually lurched forward, so sure was she that Thomas was going to lunge at him. But in the end Thomas only chuckled.

He chuckled, but it was an *awful* sound.

"Just so you know," he said, looking Mr. Audley in the eye, "she doesn't come with the house."

Grace looked at him in shock.

"Just what do you mean by that?" Mr. Audley inquired, and his voice was so smooth, so purposefully polite, that it was impossible not to hear the edge of steel underneath.

"I think you know."

"Thomas," Grace said, trying to intercede.

"Oh, we're back to Thomas, are we?"

"I think he fancies you, Miss Eversleigh," Mr. Audley said, his tone almost cheerful.

"Don't be ridiculous," Grace said immediately. Because he didn't. He couldn't. If Thomas had— Well, he'd had years to make it known, not that anything could have come of it.

Thomas crossed his arms and gave Mr. Audley a stare—the sort that sent most men scurrying for the corners.

Mr. Audley merely smiled. And then he said, "I wouldn't wish to keep you from your responsibilities."

It was a dismissal, elegantly worded and undeniably rude. Grace could not believe it. No one spoke to Thomas that way.

But Thomas smiled back. "Ah, now they are *my* responsibilities?"

"While the house is still yours."

"It's not just a house, Audley."

"Do you think I don't know that?"

No one spoke. Mr. Audley's voice had been a hiss, low and urgent.

And scared.

"Excuse me," Thomas said abruptly, and while Grace watched in silence, he turned and walked back into the small saloon, shutting the door firmly behind him.

After what felt like an eternity, just staring at the white paint on the door, Grace turned back to Mr. Audley. "You should not have provoked him."

"Oh, *I* should not have been provoking?"

She let out a tense breath. "Surely you understand what a difficult position he is in."

"As opposed to mine," he said, in quite the most

awful voice she'd heard him use. "How I *adore* being kidnapped and held against my will."

"No one has a gun to your head."

"Is that what you think?" His tone was mocking, and his eyes said he could not believe her naiveté.

"I don't think you even want it," Grace said. How was it this had not occurred to her before? How had she not seen it?

"Want what?" he practically snapped.

"The title. You don't, do you?"

"The title," he said icily, "doesn't want me."

She could only stare in horror as he turned on his heel and strode off.

Chapter Fifteen

In his wanderings at Belgrave, Jack had, during a rainstorm that had trapped him indoors, managed to locate a collection of books devoted to art. It had not been easy; the castle boasted two separate libraries, and each must have held five hundred volumes at least. But art books, he noticed, tended to be oversized, so he was able to make his task a bit easier by searching out the sections with the tallest spines. He pulled out these books, perused them and, after some trial and error, found what he was looking for.

He didn't particularly wish to remain in the library, however; he'd always found it oppressive to be surrounded by so many books. So he'd gathered up those that looked the most interesting and took them to his new favorite room—the cream and gold drawing room at the back of the castle.

Grace's room. He would never be able to think of it as anything else.

It was to this room that he retreated after his embarrassing encounter with Grace in the great hall. He did not like to lose his temper; to be more precise, he loathed it.

He sat there for hours, tucked into place at a reading table, occasionally rising to stretch his legs. He was on his final volume—a study of the French rococo style—when a footman walked by the open doorway, stopped, then backed up.

Jack looked back at him, arching a brow in question, but the young man said nothing, just scurried off in the direction from which he'd come.

Two minutes later Jack was rewarded for his patience by the sound of feminine footsteps in the hall. Grace's footsteps.

He pretended to be engrossed in his book.

"Oh, you're reading," she said, sounding surprised.

He carefully turned a page. "I do so on occasion."

He could practically hear her roll her eyes as she walked in. "I've been looking everywhere for you."

He looked up and affixed a smile. "And yet here I am."

She stood hesitantly in the doorway, her hands clasped tightly before her. She was nervous, he realized.

He hated himself for that.

He tilted his head in invitation, motioning to the chair beside him.

"What are you reading?" she asked, coming into the room.

He turned his book toward the empty seat at the table. "Have a look."

She did not sit immediately. Rather, she rested her hands at the edge of the table and leaned forward, peering down at the open pages. "Art," she said.

"My second favorite subject."

She gave him a shrewd look. "You wish for me to ask you what your favorite is."

"Am I so obvious?"

"You are only obvious when you wish to be."

He held up his hands in mock dismay. "And alas, it still doesn't work. You have not asked me what my favorite subject is."

"Because," she returned, sitting down, "I am quite certain the answer will contain something highly inappropriate."

He placed one hand on his chest, the dramatic gesture somehow restoring his equilibrium. It was easier to play the jester. No one expected as much from fools. "I am wounded," he proclaimed. "I promise you, I was not going to say that my favorite subject was seduction, or the art of a kiss, or the proper way to remove a lady's glove, or for that matter the proper way to remove—"

"Stop!"

"I was going to say," he said, trying to sound beleaguered and henpecked, "that my favorite subject of late is you."

Their eyes met, but only for a moment. Something unnerved her, and she quickly shifted her gaze to her lap. He watched her, mesmerized by the play of emotions on her face, by the way her hands, which were clasped together atop the table, tensed and moved.

"I don't like this painting," she said quite suddenly.

He had to look back at the book to see which image she referred to. It was a man and a woman out of doors, sitting on the grass. The woman's back was to the canvas, and she seemed to be pushing the man away. Jack was not familiar with it, but he thought he recognized the style. "The Boucher?"

"Ye—*no*," she said, blinking in confusion as she leaned forward. She looked down. "Jean-Antoine Watteau," she read. "*The Faux Pas.*"

He looked down more closely. "Sorry," he said, his voice light. "I'd only just turned the page. I think it does look rather like a Boucher, though. Don't you?"

She gave a tiny shrug. "I'm not familiar enough with either artist to say. I did not study painting—or painters—very much as a child. My parents weren't overly interested in art."

"How is that possible?"

She smiled at that, the sort of smile that was almost a laugh. "It wasn't so much that they weren't interested, just that they were interested in other things *more*. I think that above all they would have loved to travel. Both of them adored maps and atlases of all sorts."

Jack felt his eyes roll up at that. "I hate maps."

"Really?" She sounded stunned, and maybe just a little bit delighted by his admission. "Why?"

He told her the truth. "I haven't the talent for reading them."

"And you, a highwayman."

"What has that to do with it?"

"Don't you need to know where you're going?"

"Not nearly so much as I need to know where I've been." She looked perplexed at that, so he added, "There are certain areas of the country—possibly all of Kent, to be honest—it is best that I avoid."

"This is one of those moments," she said, blinking several times in rapid succession, "when I am not quite certain if you are being serious."

"Oh, very much so," he told her, almost cheerfully. "Except perhaps for the bit about Kent."

She looked at him in incomprehension.

"I might have been understating."

"Understating," she echoed.

"There's a reason I avoid the South."

"Good heavens."

It was such a ladylike utterance. He almost laughed.

"I don't think I have ever known a man who would admit to being a poor reader of maps," she said once she regained her composure.

He let his gaze grow warm, then hot. "I told you I was special."

"Oh, stop." She wasn't looking at him, not directly, at least, and so she did not see his change of expression. Which probably explained why her tone remained so bright and brisk as she said, "I must say, it does complicate matters. The dowager asked me to find you so that you could aid with our routing once we disembark in Dublin."

He waved a hand. "That I can do."

"Without a map?"

"We went frequently during my school days."

She looked up and smiled, almost nostalgically, as

if she could see into his memories. "I'd wager you were *not* the head boy."

He lifted a brow. "Do you know, I think most people would consider that an insult."

Her lips curved and her eyes glowed with mischief. "Oh, but not you."

She was right, of course, not that he was going to let her know it. "And why would you think that?"

"You would never want to be head boy."

"Too much responsibility?" he murmured, wondering if that was what she thought of him.

She opened her mouth, and he realized that she'd been about to say yes. Her cheeks turned a bit pink, and she looked away for a moment before answering. "You are too much of a rebel," she answered. "You would not wish to be aligned with the administration."

"Oh, the *administration*," he could not help but echo with amusement.

"Don't make fun of my choice of words."

"Well," he declared, arching one brow. "I do hope you realize you are saying this to a former officer in His Majesty's army."

This she dismissed immediately. "I should have said that you enjoy *styling* yourself as a rebel. I rather suspect that at heart you're just as conventional as the rest of us."

He paused, and then: "I hope you realize you are saying this to a former highwayman on His Majesty's roads."

How he said this with a straight face, he'd never know, and indeed it was a relief when Grace, after a moment of shock, burst out laughing. Because really, he didn't think he could have held that arch, offended expression for one moment longer.

He rather felt like he was imitating Wyndham, sitting there like such a stick. It unsettled the stomach, really.

"You're dreadful," Grace said, wiping her eyes.

"I try my best," he said modestly.

"And this"—she wagged a finger at him, grinning all the while—"is why you will never be head boy."

"Good God, I hope not," he returned. "I'd be a bit out of place at my age."

Not to mention how *desperately* wrong he was for school. He still had dreams about it. Certainly not nightmares—it could not be worth the energy. But every month or so he woke up from one of those annoying visions where he was back at school (rather absurdly at his current age of eight-and-twenty). It was always of a similar nature. He looked down at his schedule and suddenly realized he'd forgotten to attend Latin class for an entire term. Or arrived for an exam without his trousers.

The only school subjects he remembered with any fondness were sport and art. Sport had always been easy. He need only watch a game for a minute before his body knew instinctively how to move, and as for art—well, he'd never excelled at any of the practical aspects, but had always loved the study of it. For all the reasons he'd talked about with Grace his first night at Belgrave.

His eyes fell on the book, still open on the table between them. "Why do you dislike this?" he asked, motioning to the painting. It was not his favorite, but he did not find anything to offend.

"She does not like him," she said. She was looking down at the book, but he was looking at her, and he was surprised to see that her brow was wrinkled. Concern? Anger? He could not tell.

"She does not want his attentions," Grace continued. "And he will not stop. Look at his expression."

Jack peered at the image a little more closely. He supposed he saw what she meant. The reproduction was not what he would consider superior, and it was difficult to know how true it was to the actual painting. Certainly the color would be off, but the lines seemed clear. He supposed there was something insidious in the man's expression. Still . . .

"But couldn't one say," he asked, "that you are objecting to the content of the painting and not the painting itself?"

"What is the difference?"

He thought for a moment. It had been some time since anyone had engaged him in what might be termed intellectual discourse. "Perhaps the artist wishes to invoke this response. Perhaps his intention is to portray this very scene. It does not mean that he endorses it."

"I suppose." Her lips pressed together, the corners tightening in a manner that he'd not seen before. He did not like it. It aged her. But more than that, it seemed to call to the fore an unhappiness that was almost entrenched. When she moved her mouth like that—angry, upset, resigned—it looked like she would never be happy again.

Worse, it looked like she accepted it.

"You do not have to like it," he said softly.

Her mouth softened but her eyes remained clouded. "No," she said, "I don't." She reached forward and flipped the page, her fingers changing the subject. "I have heard of Monsieur Watteau, of course, and he may be a revered artist, but— Oh!"

Jack was already smiling. Grace had not been looking at the book as she'd turned the page. But he had.

"Oh my . . ."

"Now *that's* a Boucher," Jack said appreciatively.

"It's not . . . I've never . . ." Her eyes were wide— two huge blue moons. Her lips were parted, and her cheeks . . . He only just managed to resist the urge to fan her.

"Marie-Louise O'Murphy," he told her.

She looked up in horror. "You know her?"

He shouldn't have laughed, but truly, he could not help it. "Every schoolboy knows her. *Of* her," he corrected. "I believe she passed on recently. In her dotage, have no fear. Tragically, she was old enough to be my grandmother."

He gazed down fondly at the woman in the painting, lounging provocatively on a divan. She was naked— wonderfully, gloriously, *completely* so—and lying on her belly, her back slightly arched as she leaned on the arm of the sofa, peering over the edge. She was painted from the side, but even so, a portion of the cleft of her buttocks was scandalously visible, and her legs . . .

Jack sighed happily at the memory. Her legs were spread wide, and he was quite certain he had not been the only schoolboy to have imagined settling himself between them.

Many a young lad had lost his virginity (in dreams, but still) to Marie-Louise O'Murphy. He wondered if the lady had ever realized the service she had provided.

He looked up at Grace. She was staring at the painting. He thought—he hoped—she might be growing aroused.

"You've never seen it before?" he murmured.

She shook her head. Barely. She was transfixed.

"She was the mistress of the King of France," Jack told her. "It was said that the king saw one of Boucher's portraits of her—not this one, I think, perhaps a miniature—and he decided he had to have her."

Grace's mouth opened, as if she wanted to comment, but nothing quite came out.

"She came from the streets of Dublin," he said, "or so I'm told. It is difficult to imagine her obtaining the surname O'Murphy anywhere else." He sighed in fond recollection. "We were always so proud to claim her as one of our own."

He moved so that he might stand behind her, leaning over her shoulder. When he spoke, he knew that his words would land on her skin like a kiss. "It's quite provocative, isn't it?"

Still, Grace seemed not to know what to say. Jack did not mind. He had discovered that watching Grace looking at the painting was far more erotic than the painting itself had ever been.

"I always wanted to go see it in person," he commented. "I believe it is in Germany now. Munich, perhaps. But alas, my travels never took me that way."

"I've never seen anything like it," Grace whispered.

"It does make one feel, does it not?"

She nodded.

And he wondered—if he had always dreamed of lying between Mademoiselle O'Murphy's thighs, did Grace now wonder what it was like to *be* her? Did she imagine herself lying on the divan, exposed to a man's erotic gaze?

To *his* gaze.

He would never allow anyone else to see her thus.

Around them, the room was silent. He could hear his own breath, each one more shaky than the last.

And he could hear hers—soft, low, and coming faster with each inhalation.

He wanted her. Desperately. He wanted Grace. He wanted her spread before him like the girl in the painting. He wanted her any way he could have her. He wanted to peel the clothes from her body, and he wanted to worship every inch of her skin.

He could practically feel it, the soft weight of her thighs in his hands as he opened her to him, the musky heat as he moved closer for a kiss.

"Grace," he whispered.

She was not looking at him. Her eyes were still on the painting in the book. Her tongue darted out, moistening the very center of her lips.

She couldn't have known what that did to him.

He reached around her, touching her fingers. She did not pull away.

"Dance with me," he murmured, wrapping his hand around her wrist. He tugged at her gently, urging her to her feet.

"There is no music," she whispered. But she stood. With no resistance, not even a hint of hesitation, she stood.

And so he said the one thing that was in his heart.

"We will make it ourselves."

There were so many moments when Grace could have said no. When his hand touched hers. When he pulled her to her feet.

When he'd asked her to dance, despite the lack of music—that would have been a logical moment.

But she didn't.

She couldn't.

She should have. But she didn't want to.

And then somehow she was in his arms, and they were waltzing, in time with the soft hum of his voice. It was not an embrace that would ever be allowed in a proper ballroom; he was holding her far too close, and with each step he seemed to draw her closer, until finally the distance between them was measured not in inches but in heat.

"Grace," he said, her name a hoarse, needy moan. But she did not hear the last bit of it, that last consonant. He was kissing her by then, all sound lost in his onslaught.

And she was kissing him back. Good heavens, she did not think she had ever wanted anything so much as she did this man, in this moment. She wanted him to surround her, to engulf her. She wanted to lose herself in him, to lay her body down and offer herself up to him.

Anything, she wanted to whisper. *Anything you want.*

Because surely he knew what she needed.

The painting of that woman—the French king's mistress—it had done something to her. She'd been bewitched. There could be no other explanation. She wanted to lie naked on a divan. She wanted to know the sensation of damask rubbing against her belly, while cool, fresh air whispered across her back.

She wanted to know what it felt like to lie that way, with a man's eyes burning hotly over her form.

His eyes. Only his.

"Jack," she whispered, practically throwing herself against him. She needed to feel him, the pressure of him, the strength. She did not want his touch only on her lips; she wanted it everywhere, and everywhere at once.

For a moment he faltered, as if surprised by her sudden enthusiasm, but he quickly recovered, and within seconds he had kicked the door shut and had her pinned up against the wall beside it, never once breaking their kiss.

She was on her toes, pressed so tightly between Jack and the wall that her feet would have dangled in the air if she'd been just an inch higher. His mouth was hungry, and she was breathless, and when he moved down to worship her cheek, and then her throat, it was all she could do to keep her head upright. As it was, her neck was stretching, and she could feel herself arching forward, her breasts aching for closer contact.

This was not their first intimacy, but it was not the same. Before, she'd wanted him to kiss her. She'd wanted to *be* kissed.

But now . . . It was as if every pent-up dream and desire had awoken within her, turning her into some strange fiery creature. She felt aggressive. Strong. And she was so damned *tired* of watching life happen around her.

"Jack . . . Jack . . ." She could not seem to say anything else, not when his teeth were tugging at the bodice of her frock. His fingers were aiding in the endeavor, nimbly unfastening the buttons at her back.

But somehow that wasn't fair. She wanted to be a part of it, too. "Me," she managed to get out, and she moved her hands, which had been reveling in the crisp silkiness of his hair, to his shirtfront. She slid down the wall, pulling him along with her, until they were both on the floor. Without missing a beat, she made frenetic work of his buttons, yanking his shirt aside once she was through.

For a moment she could do nothing but gaze. Her breath was sucked inside of her, burning to get out, but she could not seem to exhale. She touched him, laying her palm against his chest, a whoosh of air finally escaping her lips when she felt his heart leaping beneath his skin. She stroked upward, and then down, marveling at the contact, until one of his hands roughly covered hers.

"Grace," he said. He swallowed, and she could feel that his fingers were trembling.

She looked up, waiting for him to continue. He

could seduce with nothing but a glance, she thought. A touch and she would melt. Did he have any idea the magic he held over her? The power?

"Grace," he said again, his breath labored. "I won't be able to stop soon."

"I don't care."

"You do." His voice was ragged, and it made her want him even more.

"I want you," she pleaded. "I want this."

He looked as if he were in pain. She *knew* she was.

He squeezed her hand, and they both paused. Grace looked up, and their eyes met.

And held.

And in that moment, she loved him. She didn't know what it was he'd done to her, but she was changed. And she loved him for it.

"I won't take this from you," he said in a rough whisper. "Not like this."

Then how? she wanted to ask, but sense was trickling back into her body, and she knew he was right. She had precious little of value in this world—her mother's tiny pearl earrings, a family Bible, love letters between her parents. But she had her body, and she had her pride, and she could not allow herself to give them to a man who was not to be her husband.

And they both knew that if he turned out to be the Duke of Wyndham, then he could never be her husband. Grace did not know all of the circumstances of his upbringing, but she'd heard enough to know that he was familiar with the ways of the aristocracy. He had to know what would be expected of him.

He cupped her face in his hands and stared at her

with a tenderness that took her breath away. "As God is my witness," he whispered, turning her around so he could do up her buttons, "this is the most difficult thing I have ever done in my life."

Somehow she found the strength to smile. Or at the very least, to not cry.

Later that night Grace was in the rose salon, hunting down writing paper for the dowager, who had decided—on the spur of the moment, apparently—that she must send a letter to her sister, the grand duchess of that small European country whose name Grace could never pronounce (or, indeed, remember).

This was a lengthier process than it seemed, as the dowager liked to compose her correspondence aloud (with Grace as audience), debating—at painful length—each turn of phrase. Grace then had to concentrate on memorizing the dowager's words, as she would then be required (not by the dowager; rather, by a general duty to humanity) to recopy the dowager's missive, translating her unintelligible scrawl into something a bit more neat and tidy.

The dowager did not acknowledge that she did this; in fact, the one time Grace offered, she flew into such a huff that Grace had never again whispered a word of it. But considering that her sister's next letter opened with gushes of praise on the dowager's new penmanship, Grace could not imagine that she was completely unaware.

Ah, well. It was one of those things they did not discuss.

Grace did not mind the task this evening. Sometimes it gave her a headache; she did try to do her recopying when the sun was still high and she could enjoy the advantages of natural light. But it was an endeavor that required all of her concentration, and she rather thought that it was exactly what she needed right now. Something to take her mind off . . . well, everything.

Mr. Audley.

Thomas. And how awful she felt.

Mr. Audley.

That painting of that woman.

Mr. Audley.

Jack.

Grace let out a short, loud sigh. For heaven's sake, who was she trying to fool? She knew exactly what she was trying so hard not to think about.

Herself.

She sighed. Maybe she ought to take herself off to the land of the unpronounceable name. She wondered if they spoke English there. She wondered if the Grand Duchess Margareta (née Margaret, and called, she was pertly told by the dowager, Maggs) could possibly be as ill-tempered as her sister.

It did seem unlikely.

Although as a member of the royal family, Maggs presumably had the authority to order someone's head lopped off. The dowager had said they were a bit feudal over there.

Grace touched her head, decided she liked it where it was, and with renewed determination pulled open the top drawer to the escritoire, using perhaps a bit more force than necessary. She winced at the screech of wood against wood, then frowned; this really wasn't such a well-made piece of furniture. Rather out of place at Belgrave, she had to say.

Nothing in the top drawer. Just a quill that looked as if it hadn't seen use since the last King George ruled the land.

She moved to the second, reaching to the back in case anything was hiding in the shadows, and then she heard something.

Someone.

It was Thomas. He was standing in the doorway, looking rather peaked, and even in the dim light she could see that his eyes were bloodshot.

She gulped down a wave of guilt. He was a good man. She hated that she was falling in love with his rival. No, that was not it. She hated that Mr. Audley *was* his rival. No, not that. She hated the whole bloody situation. Every last speck of it.

"Grace," he said. Nothing else, just her name.

She swallowed. It had been some time since they'd conversed on friendly terms. Not that they had been *un*friendly, but truly, was there anything worse than oh-so-careful civility?

"Thomas," she said, "I did not realize you were still awake."

"It's not so late," he said with a shrug.

"No, I suppose not." She glanced up at the clock. "The dowager is abed but not yet asleep."

"Your work is never done, is it?" he asked, entering the room.

"No," she said, wanting to sigh. Then, refusing to

feel sorry for herself, she explained, "I ran out of writing paper upstairs."

"For correspondence?"

"Your grandmother's," she affirmed. "I have no one with whom to correspond." Dear heavens, could that be true? It had never even occurred to her before. Had she written a single letter in the years she'd been here? "I suppose once Elizabeth Willoughby marries and moves away . . ." She paused, thinking how sad that was, that she needed her friend to leave so she might be able to write a letter. " . . . I shall miss her."

"Yes," he said, looking somewhat distracted, not that she could blame him, given the current state of his affairs. "You are good friends, aren't you?"

She nodded, reaching into the recesses of the third drawer. Success! "Ah, here we are." She pulled forth a small stack of paper, then realized that her triumph meant that she had to go tend to her duties. "I must go write your grandmother's letters now."

"She does not write them herself?" he asked with surprise.

Grace almost chuckled at that. "She thinks she does. But the truth is, her penmanship is dreadful. No one could possibly make out what she intends to say. Even I have difficulty with it. I end up improvising at least half in the copying."

She looked down at the pages in her hands, shaking them down against the top of the desk first one way and then on the side, to make an even stack. When she looked back up, Thomas was standing a bit closer, looking rather serious.

"I must apologize, Grace," he said, walking toward her.

Oh, she didn't want this. She didn't want an apology, not when she herself held so much guilt in her heart. "For this afternoon?" she asked, her voice perhaps a little too light. "No, please, don't be silly. It's a terrible situation, and no one could fault you for—"

"For many things," he cut in.

He was looking at her very strangely, and Grace wondered if he'd been drinking. He'd been doing a lot of that lately. She had told herself that she mustn't scold him; truly, it was a wonder he was behaving as well as he was, under the circumstances.

"Please," she said, hoping to put an end to the discussion. "I cannot think of anything for which you need to make amends, but I assure you, if there were, I would accept your apology, with all graciousness."

"Thank you," he said. And then, seemingly out of nowhere: "We depart for Liverpool in two days."

Grace nodded. She knew this already. And surely he should have known that she was aware of the plans. "I imagine you have much to do before we leave," she said.

"Almost nothing," he said, but there was something awful in his voice, almost as if he were daring her to ask his meaning. And there had to be a meaning, because Thomas always had much to do, whether he had a planned departure or not.

"Oh. That must be a pleasant change," she said, because she could not simply ignore his statement.

He leaned forward slightly, and Grace smelled spirits on his breath. *Oh, Thomas.* She ached for him, for what he must be feeling. And she wanted to tell him: *I don't want it, either. I want you to be the duke and Jack to be plain Mr. Audley, and I want all of this just to be over.*

Even if the truth turned out to be not what she prayed for, she wanted to know.

But she couldn't say this aloud. Not to Thomas. Already he was looking at her in that piercing way of his, as if he knew all her secrets—that she was falling in love with his rival, that she had already kissed him—several times—and she had wanted so much more.

She *would* have done more, if Jack had not stopped her.

"I am practicing, you see," Thomas said.

"Practicing?"

"To be a gentleman of leisure. Perhaps I should emulate your Mr. Audley."

"He is not my Mr. Audley," she immediately replied, even though she knew he had only said as much to provoke her.

"He shall not worry," Thomas continued, as if she'd not spoken. "I have left all of the affairs in perfect order. Every contract has been reviewed and every last number in every last column has been tallied. If he runs the estate into the ground, it shall be on his own head."

"Thomas, stop," she said, because she could not bear it. For either of them. "Don't talk this way. We don't know that he is the duke."

"Don't we?" His lip curled as he looked down at her. "Come now, Grace, we both know what we will find in Ireland."

"We don't," she insisted, and her voice sounded hollow. She *felt* hollow, as if she had to hold herself perfectly still just to keep from cracking.

He stared at her. For far longer than was comfortable. And then: "Do you love him?"

Grace felt the blood drain from her face.

"Do you love him?" he repeated, stridently this time. "Audley."

"I *know* who you're talking about," she said before she could think the better of it.

"I imagine you do."

She stood still, forcing herself to unclench her fists. She'd probably ruined the writing paper; she'd heard it crumple in her hand. He'd gone from apologetic to hateful in the space of a second, and she *knew* he was hurting inside, but so was she, damn it.

"How long have you been here?" he asked.

She drew back, her head turning slightly to the side. He was looking at her so strangely. "At Belgrave?" she said hesitantly. "Five years."

"And in all that time I haven't . . ." He shook his head. "I wonder why."

Without even thinking, she tried to step back, but the desk blocked her way. What was wrong with him? "Thomas," she said, wary now, "what are you talking about?"

He seemed to find that funny. "Damned if I know."

And then, while she was trying to think of a suitable reply, he let out a bitter laugh and said, "What's to become of us, Grace? We're doomed, you know. Both of us."

She knew it was true, but it was terrible to hear it confirmed.

"I don't know what you're talking about," she said.

"Oh, come now, Grace, you're far too intelligent for that."

"I should go."

But he was blocking her way.

"Thomas, I—"

And then—dear heavens—he was kissing her. His mouth was on hers, and her stomach flipped in horror, not because his kiss was repulsive, because it wasn't. It was the shock of it. Five years she'd been here, and he'd never even hinted at—

"Stop!" She wrenched herself away. "Why are you doing this?"

"I don't know," he said with a helpless shrug. "I'm here, you're here . . ."

"I'm leaving." But one of his hands was still on her arm. She needed him to release her. She could have pulled away; he was not holding her tightly. But she needed it to be his decision.

He needed it to be his decision.

"Ah, Grace," he said, looking almost defeated. "I am not Wyndham any longer. We both know it." He paused, shrugged, held out his hand in surrender.

"Thomas?" she whispered.

And then he said, "Why don't you marry me when this is all over?"

"What?" Something akin to horror washed over

her. "Oh, Thomas, you're mad." But she knew what he really meant. A duke could not marry Grace Eversleigh. But if he wasn't . . . If he was just plain Mr. Cavendish . . . Why not?

Acid rose in her throat. He didn't mean to insult. She didn't even feel insulted. She knew the world she inhabited. She knew the rules, and she knew her place.

Jack could never be hers. Not if he was the duke.

"What do you say, Gracie?" Thomas touched her chin, tipped her face up to look at him.

And she thought—*maybe*.

Would it be so very bad? She could not stay at Belgrave, that was for certain. And maybe she would learn to love him. She already did, really, as a friend.

He leaned down to kiss her again, and this time she let him, praying that her heart would pound and her pulse would race and that spot between her legs . . . Oh, please let it feel as it did when Jack touched her.

But there was nothing. Just a rather warm sense of friendship. Which she supposed wasn't the worst thing in the world.

"I can't," she whispered, turning her face to the side. She wanted to cry.

And then she did cry, because Thomas rested his chin on her head, comforting her like a brother.

Her heart twisted, and she heard him whisper, "I know."

Chapter Sixteen

Jack did not sleep well that night, which left him irritable and out of sorts, so he dispensed with breakfast, where he was sure to run into persons with whom he might be expected to converse, and instead went directly outside for his now customary morning ride.

It was one of the finest things about horses—they never expected conversation.

He had no idea what he was meant to say to Grace once he saw her again. *Lovely kissing you. Wish we'd done more.*

It was the truth, even if he'd been the one to cut them off. He'd been aching for her all night.

He might have to marry this one.

Jack stopped cold. Where had *that* come from?

From your conscience, a niggling little voice—probably his conscience—told him.

Damn. He really needed to get a better night's sleep. His conscience was never this loud.

But could he? Marry her? It was certainly the only way he'd ever be able to bed her. Grace was not the sort of woman one dallied with. It wasn't a question of her birth, although that certainly was a factor. It was just . . . *her*. The way she was. Her uncommon dignity, her quiet and sly humor.

Marriage. What a curious notion.

It wasn't that he'd been avoiding it. It was just that he'd never considered it. He was rarely in one place for long enough to form a lasting attachment. And his income was, by nature of his profession, sporadic. He wouldn't have dreamed of asking a woman to make a life with a highwayman.

Except he wasn't a highwayman. Not any longer. The dowager had seen to that.

"Lovely Lucy," Jack murmured, patting his gelding on the neck before dismounting at the stables. He supposed he ought to give the poor thing a man's name. They'd been together for so long, though. It'd be hard to make the change.

"My longest lasting attachment," Jack murmured to himself as he walked back to the house. "Now that's pathetic." Lucy was a prince, as far as horses went, but still, he was a horse.

What did he have to offer Grace? He looked up at Belgrave, looming over him like a stone monster, and almost laughed. A dukedom, possibly. Good Lord, but he didn't want the thing. It was too much.

And what if he wasn't the duke? He knew that he

was, of course. His parents had been married; he was quite certain of that. But what if there was no proof? What if there had been a church fire? Or a flood? Or mice? Didn't mice nibble at paper? What if a mouse—no, what if an entire legion of mice had chewed through the vicarage register?

It could happen.

But what did he have to offer her if he was not the duke?

Nothing. Nothing at all. A horse named Lucy, and a grandmother who, he was growing increasingly convinced, was the spawn of Satan. He had no skills to speak of—it was difficult to imagine parlaying his talents at highway thievery into any sort of honest employment. And he would not go back into the army. Even if it was respectable, it would take him away from his wife, and wasn't that the entire point?

He supposed that Wyndham would pension him off with some cozy little rural property, as far away from Belgrave as possible. He would take it, of course; he'd never been one for misplaced pride. But what did he know about cozy little rural properties? He'd grown up in one but never bothered to pay attention to how it was run. He knew how to muck out a stall and flirt with the maids, but he was quite certain there was more to it than that, if one wanted to make a decent go of it.

And then there was Belgrave, still looming over him, still blotting out the sun. Good Lord, if he did not think he could properly manage a small rural property, what the devil would he do with *this*? Not to mention the dozen or so other holdings in the Wyndham portfolio. The dowager had listed them one night at supper. He couldn't begin to imagine the paperwork he'd be required to review. Mounds of contracts, and ledgers, and proposals, and letters—his brain hurt just thinking of it.

And yet, if he did not take the dukedom, if he somehow found a way to stop it all before it engulfed him—what would he have to offer Grace?

His stomach was protesting his skipped breakfast, so he made haste up the steps to the castle's entrance and went inside. The hall was quite busy, with servants moving through, carrying out their myriad tasks, and his entrance went mostly unnoticed, which he did not mind. He pulled off his gloves and was rubbing his hands together to warm them back up when he glimpsed Grace at the other end of the hall.

He did not think she'd seen him, and he started to go to her, but as he passed one of the drawing rooms, he heard an odd collection of voices and could not contain his curiosity. Pausing, he peeked in.

"Lady Amelia," he said with surprise. She was standing rather stiffly, her hands clasped tightly in front of her. He could not blame her. He was sure he'd feel tense and pinched if he were engaged to marry Wyndham.

He entered the room to greet her. "I did not realize you had graced us with your lovely presence."

It was then that he noticed Wyndham. He couldn't not, really. The duke was emitting a rather macabre sound. Almost like laughter.

Standing next to him was an older gentleman of middling height and paunch. He looked every inch the aristocrat, but his complexion was tanned and wind-worn, hinting at time spent out of doors.

Lady Amelia coughed and swallowed, looking rather queasy. "Er, Father," she said to the older man, "may I present Mr. Audley? He is a houseguest at Belgrave. I made his acquaintance the other day when I was here visiting Grace."

"Where *is* Grace?" Wyndham said.

Something about his tone struck Jack as off, but nonetheless he said, "Just down the hall, actually. I was walking—"

"I'm sure you were," Wyndham snapped, not even looking at him. Then, to Lord Crowland: "Right. You wished to know my intentions."

Intentions? Jack stepped farther into the room. This could be nothing but interesting.

"This might not be the best time," Lady Amelia said.

"No," said Wyndham, his manner uncharacteristically grand. "This might be our only time."

While Jack was deciding what to make of *that*, Grace arrived. "You wished to see me, your grace?"

For a moment Wyndham was nonplussed. "Was I *that* loud?"

Graced motioned back toward the hall. "The footman heard you . . ."

Ah yes, footmen abounded at Belgrave. It did make one wonder why the dowager thought she might actually be able to keep the journey to Ireland a secret.

But if Wyndham minded, he did not show it. "Do come in, Miss Eversleigh," he said, sweeping his arm in welcome. "You might as well have a seat at this farce."

Jack began to feel uneasy. He did not know his new-found cousin well, nor did he wish to, but this was not his customary behavior. Wyndham was too dramatic, too grand. He was a man pushed to the edge and tee-tering badly. Jack recognized the signs. He had been there himself.

Should he intercede? He could make some sort of inane comment to pierce the tension. It might help, and it would certainly affirm what Wyndham al-ready thought of him—rootless joker, not to be taken seriously.

Jack decided to hold his tongue.

He watched as Grace entered the room, taking a spot near the window. He was able to catch her eye, but only briefly. She looked just as puzzled as he, and a good deal more concerned.

"I demand to know what is going on," Lord Crow-land said.

"Of course," Wyndham said. "How rude of me. Where *are* my manners?"

Jack looked over at Grace. She had her hand over her mouth.

"We've had quite an exciting week at Belgrave," Wyndham continued. "Quite beyond my wildest imag-inings."

"Your meaning?" Lord Crowland said curtly.

"Ah, yes. You probably should know—this man, right here"—Thomas flicked a wrist toward Jack—"is my cousin. He might even be the duke." He looked at Lord Crowland and shrugged. "We're not sure."

Silence. And then:

"Oh dear God."

Jack looked sharply over to Lady Amelia. She'd gone white. He could not imagine what she must be thinking.

"The trip to Ireland . . ." her father was saying.

"Is to determine his legitimacy," Wyndham confirmed. And then, with a morbidly jolly expression, he continued, "It's going to be quite a party. Even my grandmother is going."

Jack fought to keep the shock off his face, then looked over at Grace. She, too, was staring at the duke in horror.

Lord Crowland's countenance, on the other hand, was nothing but grim. "We will join you," he said.

Lady Amelia lurched forward. "Father?"

Her father didn't even turn around. "Stay out of this, Amelia."

"But—"

"I assure you," Wyndham cut in, "we will make our determinations with all possible haste and report back to you immediately."

"My daughter's future hangs in the balance," Crowland returned hotly. "I will be there to examine the papers."

Wyndham's expression grew lethal, and his voice dangerously low. "Do you think we try to deceive you?"

"I only look out for my daughter's rights."

"Father, please." Amelia had come up to Crowland and placed her hand on his sleeve. "Please, just a moment."

"I said stay out of this!" her father yelled, and he

shook her from his arm with enough force to cause her to stumble.

Jack stepped forward to aid her, but Wyndham was there before he could blink. "Apologize to your daughter," Wyndham said.

Crowland sputtered in confusion. "What the devil are you talking about?"

"Apologize to her!" Wyndham roared.

"Your grace," Amelia said, trying to insinuate herself between the two men. "Please, do not judge my father too harshly. These are exceptional circumstances."

"No one knows that more clearly than I." But Wyndham wasn't looking at her as he said it, nor did he remove his eyes from her father's face when he added, "Apologize to Amelia or I will have you removed from the estate."

And for the first time, Jack admired him. He had already realized that he respected him, but that was not the same thing. Wyndham was a bore, in his humble opinion, but everything he did, every last decision and action—they were for others. It was all for Wyndham—the heritage, not the person. It was impossible not to respect such a man.

But this was different. The duke wasn't standing up for his people, he was standing up for one person. It was a far more difficult thing to do.

And yet, looking at Wyndham now, he would say that it had come as naturally as breathing.

"I'm sorry," Lord Crowland finally said, looking as if he was not quite certain what had just happened. "Amelia, you know I—"

"I know," she said, cutting him off.

And then finally Jack found himself at center stage.

"Who is this man?" Lord Crowland asked, thrusting an arm in his direction.

Jack turned to Wyndham and quirked a brow, allowing him to answer.

"He is the son of my father's elder brother," Wyndham told Lord Crowland.

"Charles?" Amelia asked.

"John."

Lord Crowland nodded, still directing his questions to Wyndham. "Are you certain of this?"

Thomas only shrugged. "You may look at the portrait yourself."

"But his name—"

"Was Cavendish at birth," Jack cut in. If he was going to be the subject of the discussion, he would bloody well be given a place in it. "I went by Cavendish-Audley at school. You may check the records, should you wish."

"Here?" Crowland asked.

"In Enniskillen. I only came to England after serving in the army."

"I am satisfied that he is a blood relation," Wyndham said quietly. "All that remains is to determine whether he is also one by law."

Jack looked to him in surprise. It was the first time he had publicly acknowledged him aloud as a relative.

The earl did not comment. Not directly, at least. He just muttered, "This is a disaster," and walked over to the window.

And said nothing.

Nor did anyone else.

And then, in a voice low and furious, came the earl's comment. "I signed the contract in good faith," he said, still staring out over the lawn. "Twenty years ago, I signed the contract."

Still no one spoke.

Abruptly, he turned around. "Do you understand?" he demanded, glaring at Wyndham. "Your father came to me with his plans, and I agreed to them, believing you to be the rightful heir to the dukedom. She was to be a duchess. A duchess! Do you think I would have signed away my daughter had I known you were nothing but . . . but . . ."

But one such as me, Jack wanted to say. But for once it did not seem the time or the place for a light, sly quip.

And then Wyndham—*Thomas,* Jack suddenly decided he wished to call him— stared the earl down and said, "You may call me Mr. Cavendish, if you so desire. If you think it might help you to accustom yourself to the idea."

It was exactly what Jack would have wanted to say. If he'd been in Thomas's shoes. If he'd thought of it.

But the earl was not cowed by the sarcastic rebuke. He glared at Thomas, practically shaking as he hissed, "I will not allow my daughter to be cheated. If you do not prove to be the right and lawful Duke of Wyndham, you may consider the betrothal null and void."

"As you wish," Thomas said curtly. He made no argument, no indication that he might wish to fight for his betrothed.

Jack looked over at Lady Amelia, then looked away.

There were some things, some emotions, a gentleman could not watch.

But when he turned back, he found himself face-to-face with the earl. Her father. And the man's finger was pointed at his chest.

"If that is the case," he said, "if you are the Duke of Wyndham, then *you* will marry her."

It took a great deal to render Jack Audley speechless. This, however, had done it.

When he regained his voice, after a rather unattractive choking sound he assumed had come from his throat, he managed the following:

"Oh. *No.*"

"Oh, you will," Crowland warned him. "You will marry her if I have to march you to the altar with my blunderbuss at your back."

"Father," Lady Amelia cried out, "you cannot do this."

Crowland ignored his daughter completely. "My daughter is betrothed to the Duke of Wyndham, and the Duke of Wyndham she *will* marry."

"I am not the Duke of Wyndham," Jack said, recovering some of his composure.

"Not yet. Perhaps not ever. But I will be present when the truth comes out. And I will make sure she marries the right man."

Jack took his measure. Lord Crowland was not a feeble man, and although he did not exude quite the same haughty power as Wyndham, he clearly knew his worth and his place in society. He would not allow his daughter to be wronged.

Jack respected that. If he had a daughter, he supposed he'd do the same. But not, he hoped, at the expense of an innocent man.

He looked at Grace. Just for a moment. Fleeting, but he caught the expression in her eyes, the subdued horror at the unfolding scene.

He would not give her up. Not for any bloody title, and certainly not to honor someone else's betrothal contract.

"This is madness," Jack said, looking around the room, unable to believe that he was the only one speaking in his defense. "I do not even know her."

"That is hardly a concern," Crowland said gruffly.

"You are *mad*," Jack exclaimed. "I am not going to marry her." He looked quickly at Amelia, then wished he hadn't. "My pardons, my lady," he practically mumbled. "It is not personal."

Her head jerked a bit, fast and pained. It wasn't a yes, or a no, but more of a stricken acknowledgment, the sort of motion one made when it was all one was capable of.

It ripped Jack straight through his gut.

No, he told himself. *This is not your responsibility. You do not have to make it right.*

And all around him, no one said a word in his defense. Grace, he understood, since it was not her position to do so, but by God, what about Wyndham? Didn't he *care* that Crowland was trying to give his fiancée away?

But the duke just stood there, still as a stone, his eyes burning with something Jack could not identify.

"I did not agree to this," Jack said. "I signed no contract." Surely that had to mean something.

"Neither did he," Crowland responded, with a shrug in Wyndham's direction. "His father did it."

"In his *name*," Jack fairly yelled.

"That is where you are wrong, Mr. Audley. It did not specify his name at all. My daughter, Amelia Honoria Rose, was to marry the seventh Duke of Wyndham."

"Really?" This, *finally*, from Thomas.

"Have you not looked at the papers?" Jack demanded.

"No," Thomas said simply. "I never saw the need."

"Good God," Jack swore, "I have fallen in with a band of bloody idiots."

No one contradicted him, he noticed. He looked desperately to Grace, who had to be the one sane member of humanity left in the building. But she would not meet his eyes.

That was enough. He had to put an end to this. He stood straight and looked hard into Lord Crowland's face. "Sir," he said, "I will not marry your daughter."

"Oh, you will."

But this was not said by Crowland. It was Thomas, stalking across the room, his eyes burning with barely contained rage. He did not stop until they were nearly nose-to-nose.

"What did you say?" Jack asked, certain he'd heard incorrectly. From all he had seen, which, admittedly, wasn't much, Thomas rather liked his little fiancée.

"This woman," Thomas said, motioning back to Amelia, "has spent her entire life preparing to be the

Duchess of Wyndham. I will not permit you to leave her life in shambles."

Around them the room went utterly still.

Except for Amelia, who looked ready to crumble.

"Do you understand me?"

And Jack . . . Well, he was Jack, and so he simply lifted his brows, and he didn't quite smirk, but he was quite certain that his smile clearly lacked sincerity. He looked Thomas in the eye.

"No."

Thomas said nothing.

"No, I don't understand." Jack shrugged. "Sorry."

Thomas looked at him. And then: "I believe I will kill you."

Lady Amelia let out a shriek and leapt forward, grabbing onto Thomas seconds before he could attack Jack.

"You may steal my life away," Thomas growled, just barely allowing her to subdue him. "You may steal my very name, but by God you will not steal hers."

"She *has* a name," Jack said. "It's Willoughby. And for the love of God, she's the daughter of an earl. She'll find someone else."

"If you are the Duke of Wyndham," Thomas said furiously, "you will honor your commitments."

"If I'm the Duke of Wyndham, then you can't tell me what to do."

"Amelia," Thomas said with deadly calm, "release my arm."

If anything, she pulled him back. "I don't think that's a good idea."

Lord Crowland chose that moment to step between them. "Er, gentlemen, this is all hypothetical at this point. Perhaps we should wait until—"

And then Jack saw his escape. "I wouldn't be the seventh duke, anyway," he said.

"I beg your pardon?" Crowland said, as if Jack were some irritant and not the man he was attempting to bludgeon into marrying his daughter.

"I wouldn't." Jack thought furiously, trying to put together all the details of the family history he'd learned in the past few days. He looked at Thomas. "Would I? Because your father was the sixth duke. Except he wasn't. Would he have been? If I was?"

"What the devil are you talking about?" Crowland demanded.

But Jack saw that Thomas understood his point precisely. And indeed, he said, "Your father died before his own father. If your parents were married, then *you* would have inherited upon the fifth duke's death, eliminating my father—and myself—from the succession entirely."

"Which makes me number six," Jack said quietly.

"Indeed."

"Then I am not bound to honor the contract," Jack declared. "No court in the land would hold me to it. I doubt they'd do so even if I were the seventh duke."

"It is not to a legal court you must appeal," Thomas said, "but to the court of your own moral responsibility."

"I did not ask for this," Jack said.

"Neither," Thomas said softly, "did I."

Jack said nothing. His voice felt like it was trapped

in his chest, pounding and rumbling and squeezing out the air. The room was growing hot, and his cravat felt tight, and in that moment, as his life was flipping and spiraling out of his control, he knew only one thing for certain.

He had to get out.

He looked over for Grace, but she'd moved. She was standing now by Amelia, holding her hand.

He would not give her up. He could not. For the first time in his life he'd found someone who filled all the empty spaces in his heart.

He did not know who he would be, once they went to Ireland and found whatever it was they all thought they were looking for. But whoever he was—duke, highwayman, soldier, rogue—he wanted her by his side.

He loved her.

He loved her.

There were a million reasons he did not deserve her, but he loved her. And he was a selfish bastard, but he was going to marry her. He'd find a way. No matter who he was or what he owned.

Maybe he was engaged to Amelia. He probably wasn't smart enough to understand the legalities of it all—certainly not without the contract in hand and someone to translate the legalspeak for him.

He would marry Grace. He would.

But first he had to go to Ireland.

He couldn't marry Grace until he knew what he was, but more than that—he could not marry her until he'd atoned for his sins.

And that could only be done in Ireland.

Chapter Seventeen

Five days later, at sea

This was not the first time Jack had crossed the Irish Sea. It was not even the second or the third. He wondered if the unease would ever leave him, if he would someday be able to look down at the dark, swirling waters below and not think of his father slipping beneath the surface, meeting his death.

Even before he had met the Cavendishes, when his father was just a wispy figment in his mind, he'd disliked this crossing.

And yet here he stood. At the railing. He could not seem to help himself. He could not be on the water and not look out. Out, and then down.

It was a gentle voyage this time, although that did little to comfort him. It was not that he feared for his own safety. It was just that it all felt so morbid, skimming atop his father's grave. He wanted it done. He wanted to be back on land. Even, he supposed, if that land was Ireland.

The last time he'd been home . . .

Jack pinched his lips together, and then he pinched his eyes shut. The last time he had been home was to bring back Arthur's body.

It was the hardest thing he'd ever done. Not just because his heart had broken anew with every mile, and not even because he'd dreaded his arrival at home. How could he face his aunt and uncle, delivering to them their dead son?

As if all that hadn't been enough, it was damned *hard* to move a body from France to England to Ireland. He'd had to find a coffin, which was surprisingly difficult in the middle of a war. "Supply and demand," one of his friends told him after their first unsuccessful attempt to obtain a coffin. There were a lot of dead bodies strewn about. Coffins were the ultimate luxury on a battlefield.

But he had persisted, and he'd followed to the letter the directions he'd been given by the undertaker, filling the wooden coffin with sawdust and sealing it with tar. Even then the smell eventually seeped through, and by the time he reached Ireland, no driver would take the cargo. He'd had to buy his own wagon to get his cousin home.

The journey had disrupted his own life, too. The army refused his request to be allowed to move the body, and he was forced to sell off his commission. It was a small price to pay, to be able to do this one last service for his family. But it had meant that he'd had to leave a position for which he was—finally—a perfect fit. School had been a misery, failure after failure. He'd muddled through, mostly with help from Arthur, who, seeing his struggles, had come quietly to his aid.

But university—good God, he still could not believe he'd been encouraged to go. He had known it would be a disaster, but Portora Royal boys went on to university. It was as simple as that. But Arthur was a year behind, and without him, Jack didn't have a prayer. Failure would have been too mortifying, so he got himself booted out. Not that it took much imagination to find ways to behave in a manner unbecoming of a Trinity College student.

He had returned home, supposedly in disgrace, and it was decided that he might do well in the army. So off he went. It had been a perfect fit. Finally, a place he could succeed and thrive without books and papers and quills. It wasn't that he was unintelligent. It was just that he hated books and papers and quills. They gave him a headache.

But that was all over, and now here he was, on his way back to Ireland for the first time since Arthur's funeral service, and he might be the Duke of Wyndham, which would ensure him a bloody lifetime of books and papers and quills.

And headaches.

He glanced off to his left and saw Thomas standing by the bow with Amelia. He was pointing toward something—probably a bird, since Jack could not see anything else of interest. Amelia was smiling, perhaps not broadly, but enough at least to ease some of the guilt Jack was feeling about the scene back at Belgrave when he had refused to marry her. It wasn't as if he could have done anything else. Did they really think he would roll over and say, *Oh, yes, give me anyone! I'll just show up at the church and be grateful.*

Not that there was anything wrong with Lady Amelia. In fact, one could (and probably would) do much worse, if one were to be forced into marriage. And if he hadn't met Grace . . .

He might have been willing to do it.

He heard someone approaching, and when he turned, there she was, as if summoned by his thoughts. She'd left off her bonnet, and her dark hair was ruffling in the breeze.

"It's very pleasant out here," she said, leaning against the railing next to him.

He nodded. He had not seen much of her on the voyage. The dowager had elected to remain in her cabin, and Grace was required to attend to her. She did not complain, of course. She never complained, and in truth, he supposed she did not have reason to do so. It was her job, after all, to remain by the dowager's side. Still, he could not imagine a less palatable position. And he *knew* he could never have lasted in the post.

Soon, he thought. Soon she would be free. They would be married, and Grace would never have to even *see* the dowager again if that was her desire. Jack did not care if the old bat was his grandmother. She was unkind, selfish, and he had no intention of exchanging another word with her once this was all through. If he turned out to be the duke, he would damn well buy that farm in the Outer Hebrides and send her packing. And if he wasn't, he planned to take Grace by the hand, lead her from Belgrave and never look back.

It was a rather happy dream, to tell the truth.

Grace looked down, watching the water. "Isn't it strange," she mused, "how quickly it seems to move by."

Jack glanced up at the sail. "It is a good wind."

"I know. It makes perfect sense, of course." She looked up and smiled. "It is just that I have never been on a boat before."

"Never?" It did seem difficult to imagine.

She shook her head. "Not like this. My parents took me out rowing on a lake once, but that was just for merry." She looked back down. "I have never seen water rushing by like this. It makes me wish I could lean down and dip my fingers in."

"It's cold," Jack said.

"Well, yes, of course." She leaned out, her throat arching as she seemed to catch the wind on her face. "But I'd still like to touch it."

He shrugged. He ought to be more voluble, especially with her, but he thought he could see the first hint of land on the horizon, and his belly was clenching and twisting.

"Are you all right?" Grace asked.

"I'm fine."

"You look a bit green. Are you seasick?"

He wished. He never got seasick. He was land-sick. He didn't want to go back. He'd woken up in the middle of the night, stuck down in his small berth, clammy with sweat.

He had to go back. He knew he did. But that didn't mean a very large part of him didn't want to turn coward and flee.

He heard Grace's breath catch, and when he looked at her, she was pointing out, her face alight with excitement.

It was quite possibly the most beautiful thing he'd ever seen.

"Is that Dublin?" she asked. "Over there?"

He nodded. "The port. The town proper is a bit farther in."

She craned her neck, which would have been amusing had he not been in such a wretched mood. There was no way she could have seen anything from this distance. "I've heard it is a charming city," she said.

"There is much to entertain."

"It's a pity. I don't expect we shall be spending much time there."

"No. The dowager is eager to be on her way."

"Aren't you?" she asked.

At that, he took a breath and rubbed his eyes. He was tired, and he was nervous, and it felt as if he was being delivered to his downfall. "No," he said. "To be honest, I'd be quite happy to stay right here, on this boat, at this railing, for the rest of my life."

Grace turned to him with somber eyes.

"With you," he said softly. "Here at this railing, with you."

He looked back out. The port of Dublin was more

than a speck on the horizon now. Soon he would be able
to make out buildings and ships. Off to his left he could
hear Thomas and Amelia chatting. They were pointing
out over the water, too, watching the port as it seemed
to grow before their eyes.

Jack swallowed. The knot in his stomach was growing as well. Good God, it was almost funny. Here he
was, back in Ireland, forced to face his family, whom
he'd failed so many years before. And if that weren't
bad enough, he could very well find himself named
the Duke of Wyndham, a position for which he was
uniquely unqualified.

And then, because no injury should ever be without insult, he had to do it all in the company of the
dowager.

He wanted to laugh. It was funny. It *had* to be
funny. If it wasn't funny, then he'd have to bloody
well go and cry.

But he couldn't seem to laugh. He looked out at
Dublin, looming larger in the distance.

It was too late for laughter.

Several hours later, at the Queen's Arms, Dublin

"It is *not* too late!"

"Ma'am," Grace said, trying to be as calm and soothing as she could, "it is past seven. We are all tired and
hungry, and the roads are dark and unknown to us."

"Not to him," the dowager snapped, jerking her
head toward Jack.

"I am tired and hungry," Jack snapped right back,

"and thanks to you, I no longer travel the roads by moonlight."

Grace bit her lip. They had been traveling over three days now, and one could almost chart the progress of their journey by the shortness of his temper. Every mile that brought them closer to Ireland had taken a notch out of his patience. He'd grown silent and withdrawn, so wholly unlike the man she knew.

The man she'd fallen in love with.

They had reached the port of Dublin in the late afternoon, but by the time they collected their belongings and made their way into town, it was nearly time for supper. Grace had not eaten much on the sea journey, and now that she was back to standing on surfaces that did not pitch and roll beneath her, she was famished. The last thing she wanted was to press on toward Butlersbridge, the small village in County Cavan where Jack had grown up.

But the dowager was being her argumentative self, so they were standing in the front room of the inn, all six of them, while she attempted to dictate the speed and direction of their journey.

"Don't you wish to have this matter settled, once and for all?" the dowager demanded of Jack.

"Not really," was his insolent response. "Certainly not as much as I want a slice of shepherd's pie and a tankard of ale." Jack turned to the rest of them, and Grace ached at the expression in his eyes. He was haunted. But by what, she could not guess.

What demons awaited him here? Why had he gone so long between visits? He'd told her he had a lovely childhood, that he adored his adoptive family and would not have traded them for the world. Didn't everyone wish for that? Didn't he want to go home? Didn't he understand how lucky he was to have a home to return to?

Grace would have given anything for that.

"Miss Eversleigh," Jack said, with a courteous nod. "Lady Amelia."

The two ladies bobbed their curtsies as he departed.

"I do believe he has the right idea of it," Thomas murmured. "Supper sounds infinitely more appealing than a night on the roads."

The dowager whipped her head toward him and glared.

"Not," he said with an extremely dry look, "that I am attempting to delay the inevitable. Even soon-to-be-dispossessed dukes get hungry."

Lord Crowland laughed aloud at that. "He has you there, Augusta," he said jovially, and wandered off to the taproom.

"I shall take my supper in my room," the dowager announced. Her tone was defiant, as if she expected someone to protest, but of course, no one did. "Miss Eversleigh," she barked, "you may attend to me."

Grace sighed wearily and started to follow.

"No," Thomas said.

The dowager froze. "No?" she echoed, all ice.

Grace turned and looked at Thomas. What could he mean? There had been nothing unusual about the dowager's order. Grace was her companion. This was exactly the sort of thing she had been hired to do.

But Thomas stared down his grandmother, a tiny,

subversive smile tugging at the corners of his mouth. "Grace will dine with us. In the dining room."

"She is my companion," the dowager hissed.

"Not anymore."

Grace held her breath as she watched the exchange. Matters between Thomas and his grandmother were never cordial, but this seemed to go quite beyond the usual. Thomas almost appeared to be enjoying himself.

"As I have not yet been removed from my position," he said, speaking slowly, clearly savoring each word, "I took the liberty of making a few last minute provisions."

"What the devil are you talking about?" the dowager demanded.

"Grace," Thomas said, turning to her with friendship and memories in his eyes, "you are officially relieved of your duties to my grandmother. When you return home, you will find a cottage deeded in your name, along with funds enough to provide an income for the rest of your life."

"Are you mad?" the dowager sputtered.

Grace just stared at him in shock.

"I should have done it long ago," he said. "I was too selfish. I couldn't bear the thought of living with her"—he jerked his head toward his grandmother—"without you there to act as a buffer."

"I don't know what to say," she whispered.

"Normally, I'd advise 'thank you,' but as I am the one thanking *you*, a mere 'You are a prince among men' would suffice."

Grace managed a wobbly smile and whispered, "You are a prince among men."

"It is always lovely to hear it," Thomas said. "Now, would you care to join the rest of us for supper?"

Grace turned toward the dowager, who was red-faced with rage.

"You grasping little whore," she spat. "Do you think I don't know what you are? Do you think I would allow you in my home again?"

Grace stared at her in calm shock, then said, "I was about to say that I would offer you my assistance for the rest of the journey, since I would never dream of leaving a post without giving proper and courteous notice, but I believe I have reconsidered." She turned to Amelia, holding her hands carefully at her sides. She was shaking. She was not sure if it was from shock or delight, but she was shaking. "May I share your room this evening?" she asked Amelia. Because certainly she was not going to remain with the dowager.

"Of course," Amelia replied promptly. She linked her arm through Grace's. "Let us have some supper."

It was, Grace later decided, the finest shepherd's pie she'd ever tasted.

Several hours later, Grace was up in her room staring out the window while Amelia slept.

Grace had tried to go to sleep, but her mind was still all abuzz over Thomas's astounding act of generosity. Plus, she wondered where Jack had gone off to—he'd not been in the dining room when she and Thomas and Amelia arrived, and no one seemed to know what had happened to him.

Plus *plus*, Amelia snored.

Grace rather enjoyed the view of Dublin below. They were not in the city center, but the street was busy enough, with local folk going about their business, and plenty of travelers on their way into or out of the port.

It was strange, this newfound sense of freedom. She still could not believe that she was here, sharing a bed with Amelia and not curled up on an uncomfortable chair at the dowager's bedside.

Supper had been a merry affair. Thomas was in remarkably good spirits, all things considered. He had not said anything more of his generous gift, but Grace knew why he'd done it. If Jack was found to be the true duke—and Thomas was convinced this would be the case—then she could not remain at Belgrave.

To have her heart broken anew, every day for the rest of her life—that, she could not bear.

Thomas knew that she'd fallen in love with Jack. She had not said so, not expressly, but he knew her well. He had to know. For him to act with such generosity, when she'd gone and fallen in love with the man who might very well be the cause of his downfall—

It brought tears to her eyes every time she thought of it.

And so now she was independent. An independent woman! She liked the sound of that. She would sleep until noon every day. She would read books. She would wallow in the sheer laziness of it all, at least for a few months, and then find something constructive to do with her time. A charity, perhaps. Or maybe she would learn to paint watercolors.

It sounded decadent. It sounded perfect.

And lonely.

No, she decided firmly, she would find friends. She had many friends in the district. She was glad she would not be leaving Lincolnshire, even if it did mean that she might occasionally cross paths with Jack. Lincolnshire was home. She knew everyone, and they knew her, and her reputation would not be questioned, even if she did set up her own home. She would be able to live in peace and respectability.

It would be a good thing.

But lonely.

No. *Not* lonely. She would have funds. She could go visit Elizabeth, who would be married to her earl in the South. She could join one of those women's clubs her mother had so adored. They'd met every Tuesday afternoon, claiming they were there to discuss art and literature and the news of the day, but when the meetings were held at Sillsby, Grace had heard far too much laughter for those topics.

She would not be lonely.

She refused to be lonely.

She looked back at Amelia, snoring away on the bed. Poor thing. Grace had often envied the Willoughby girls their secure places in society. They were daughters of an earl, with impeccable bloodlines and generous dowries. It was odd, really, that her future should now be so well-defined while Amelia's was so murky.

But she had come to realize that Amelia was no more in control of her own fate than she herself had been. Her father had chosen her husband before she could even speak, before he knew who she was, what she was like. How could he know, looking upon an infant of less than one year, whether she would be suited for life as a duchess?

All of her life, Amelia had been stuck, waiting for Thomas to get around to marrying her. And even if she did not end up marrying either of the two Dukes of Wyndham, she'd still find herself obliged to follow her father's dictates.

Grace was turning back toward the window when she heard a noise in the hall. Footsteps, she decided. Male. And because she could not help herself, she hurried to her door, opened it a crack, and peered out.

Jack.

He looked rumpled and tired and achingly heartsick. He was squinting in the dark, trying to figure out which room was his.

Grace-the-companion might have retreated back into her room, but Grace-the-woman-of-independent-means was somewhat more daring, and she stepped out, whispering his name.

He looked up. His eyes flared, and Grace belatedly remembered that she was still in her nightgown. It was nothing remotely risqué; in fact, she was far more covered than she would have been in an evening dress. Still, she hugged her arms to her body as she moved forward.

"Where have you been?" she whispered.

He shrugged. "Out and about. Visiting old haunts."

Something about his voice was unsettling. "Really?" she asked.

"No." He looked at her, then rubbed his eyes. "I was across the street. Having my shepherd's pie."

She smiled. "And your pint of ale?"

"Two, actually." He smiled then, a sheepish, boyish thing that tried to banish the exhaustion from his face. "I missed it."

"Irish ale?"

"The English stuff is pig swill by comparison."

Grace felt herself warming inside. There was humor in his eyes, the first she'd seen in days. And it was strange—she'd thought it would be torture to be near him, to be with him and hear his voice and see his smile. But all she felt now was happiness. And relief.

She could not bear it when he was so unhappy. She needed for him to be *him*. Even if he could not be hers.

"You should not be out here like this," he said.

"No." She shook her head but did not move.

He grimaced and looked down at his key. "I cannot find my room."

Grace took the key from him and peered at it. "Fourteen," she said. She looked up. "The light is dim."

He nodded.

"It is that way," she told him, pointing down the hall. "I passed it on the way in."

"Is your room acceptable?" he asked. "Large enough for both you and the dowager?"

Grace gasped. He did not know. She'd completely forgotten. He had already left when Thomas gave her the cottage. "I'm not with the dowager," she said, unable to conceal all of her excitement. "I—"

"Someone's coming," he whispered harshly, and indeed, she heard voices and footsteps on the stairs. He started to steer her back to her room.

"No, I can't." She dug in her heels. "Amelia is there."

"Amelia? Why would she—" He muttered something under his breath and then yanked her along with him down the hall. Into Room 14.

Chapter Eighteen

hree minutes," Jack said, the moment he pulled the door shut. Because truly, he did not think he could last any longer than that. Not when she was dressed in her nightgown. It was an ugly thing, really, all rough and buttoned from chin to toe, but still, it was a *nightgown*.

And she was Grace.

"You will never believe what has happened," she said.

"Normally an excellent opening," he acknowledged, "but after everything that *has* happened in the last two weeks, I find myself willing to believe almost anything." He smiled and shrugged. Two pints of fine Irish ale had made him mellow.

But then she told him the most amazing story. Thomas had given her a cottage and an income. Grace was now an independent woman. She was free of the dowager.

Jack lit the lamp in his room, listening to her excitement. He felt a prickle of jealousy, though not because he did not think she should be receiving gifts from another man—the truth was, she'd more than earned anything the duke chose to portion off to her. Five years with the dowager—Good God, she ought to be given a title in her own right as penance for such as that. No one had done more for England.

No, his jealousy was a far more basic stripe. He heard the joy in her voice, and once he'd banished the dark of the room, he saw the joy in her eyes. And quite simply, it just felt wrong that someone else had given her that.

He wanted to do it. *He* wanted to light her eyes with exhilaration. *He* wanted to be the origin of her smile.

"I will still have to go with you to County Cavan," Grace was saying. "I can't stay here by myself, and I wouldn't want Amelia to be alone. This is all terribly difficult for her, you know."

She looked up at him, so he nodded in response. Truthfully, he hadn't been thinking very much of Amelia, selfish as that was.

"I'm sure it will be awkward with the dowager," Grace continued. "She was furious."

"I can imagine," Jack murmured.

"Oh, no." Her eyes grew very wide. "This was extraordinary, even for her."

He pondered that. "I am not certain if I am sorry or relieved that I missed it."

"It was probably for the best that you were not present," Grace replied, grimacing. "She was rather unkind."

He was about to say that it was difficult to imagine her any other way, but Grace suddenly brightened and said, "But do you know, I don't care!" She giggled then, the heady sound of someone who can't quite believe her good fortune.

He smiled for her. It was infectious, her happiness. He did not intend that she should ever live apart from him, and he rather suspected that Thomas had not given her the cottage with the intention that she live there as Mrs. Jack Audley, but he understood her delight. For the first time in years, Grace had something of her own.

"I'm sorry," she said, but she could not quite hide her smile. "I should not be here. I didn't mean to wait up for you, but I was just so excited, and I wanted to tell you, because I knew you'd understand."

And as she stood there, her eyes shining up at him, his demons slipped away, one by one, until he was just a man, standing before the woman he loved. In this room, in this minute, it didn't matter that he was back in Ireland, that there were so many bloody reasons he should be running for the door and finding passage on the next ship to anywhere.

In this room, in this minute, she was his everything.

"Grace," he said, and his hand rose to touch her cheek. She curled into it, and in that moment he knew he was lost. Whatever strength he'd thought he possessed, whatever will to do the right thing—

It was gone.

"Kiss me," he whispered.

Her eyes widened.

"Kiss me."

She wanted to. He could see it in her eyes, feel it in the air around them.

He leaned down, closer . . . but not enough so their lips touched. "Kiss me," he said, one last time.

She rose on her toes. She moved nothing else—her hands did not come up to caress him, she did not lean in, allowing her body to rest against his. She just rose on her toes until her lips brushed his.

And then she backed away.

"Jack?" she whispered.

"I—" He almost said it. The words were right there, on his lips. *I love you.*

But somehow he knew—he had no idea how, just that he did—if he said it then, if he gave voice to what he was certain she knew in her heart, it would scare her away.

"Stay with me," he whispered. He was through being noble. The current Duke of Wyndham could spend his life doing nothing but the right thing, but he could not be so unselfish.

He kissed her hand.

"I shouldn't," she whispered.

He kissed her other hand.

"Oh, Jack."

He raised them both to his lips, holding them to his face, inhaling her scent.

She looked at the door.

"Stay with me," he said again. And then he touched

her chin, tipped her face gently up, and laid one soft kiss on her lips. "Stay."

He watched her face, saw the conflicted shadows in her eyes. Her lips trembled, and she turned away from him before she spoke.

"If I—" Her voice was a whisper, shaky and unsure. "If I stay . . ."

He touched her chin but did not guide her back to face him. He waited until she was ready, until she turned on her own.

"If I stay . . ." She swallowed, and shut her eyes for a moment, as if summoning courage. "Can you . . . Is there a way you can make sure there is no baby?"

For a moment he could not speak. Then he nodded, because yes, he could make sure there was no baby. He had spent his adult life making sure there would be no babies.

But that had been with women he did not love, women he did not intend to adore and worship for the rest of their lives. This was Grace, and the idea of making a baby with her suddenly burned within him like a shining, magical dream. He could see them as a family, laughing, teasing. His own childhood had been like that—loud and boisterous, racing across fields with his cousins, fishing in streams and never catching a thing. Meals were never formal affairs; the icy gatherings at Belgrave had been as foreign to him as a Chinese banquet.

He wanted all of that, and he wanted it with Grace. Only he hadn't realized just how much until this very moment.

"Grace," he said, holding her hands tightly. "It does

not matter. I will marry you. I *want* to marry you."

She shook her head, the motion fast and jerky, almost frenzied. "No," she said. "You can't. Not if you are the duke."

"I will." And then, damn it all, he said it anyway. Some things were too big, too true, to keep inside. "I love you. I love you. I have never said that to another woman, and I never will. I love *you*, Grace Eversleigh, and I want to marry you."

She shut her eyes, looking almost pained. "Jack, you can't—"

"I *can*. I do. I will."

"Jack—"

"I am so tired of everyone telling me what I cannot do," he burst out, letting go of her hands to stalk across the room. "Do you understand that I don't care? I don't care about the bloody dukedom and I certainly don't care about the dowager. I care about you, Grace. You."

"Jack," she said again, "if you are the duke, you will be expected to marry a woman of high birth."

He swore under his breath. "You speak of yourself as if you were some dockside whore."

"No," she said, trying to be patient, "I do not. I know exactly what I am. I am an impoverished young lady of impeccable but undistinguished birth. My father was a country gentleman, my mother the daughter of a country gentleman. We have no connections to the aristocracy. My mother was the second cousin to a baronet, but that is all."

He stared at her as if he hadn't heard a word she'd said. Or as if he'd heard but hadn't listened.

No, Grace thought miserably. He'd listened but he hadn't heard. And sure enough, the first words from his mouth were: "I don't care."

"But everyone else does," she persisted. "And if you are the duke, there will be enough of an uproar as it is. The scandal will be amazing."

"I don't care."

"But you *should*." She stopped, forcing herself to take a breath before she continued. She wanted to grab her head and press her fingers into her scalp. She wanted to make fists until her fingernails bit into her skin. Anything—anything that would eat away at this awful frustration that was pulling her inside out. Why wasn't he listening? Why couldn't he hear that—

"Grace—" he began.

"No!" She cut him off, perhaps more loudly than she ought, but it had to be said: "You will need to tread carefully if you wish to be accepted into society. Your wife does not have to be Amelia, but it must be someone like her. With a similar background. Otherwise—"

"Are you listening to me?" he cut in. He grasped her shoulders, holding her in place until she looked up at him, directly into his eyes. "I don't care about 'otherwise.' I don't need for society to accept me. All I need is you, whether I live in a castle, a hovel, or anything in between."

"Jack . . ." she began. He was being naive. She loved him for it, nearly wept with joy that he adored her enough to think he could so thoroughly flout convention. But he didn't know. He had not lived at Belgrave for five years. He had not traveled to London with the dowager and seen firsthand what it meant to be a member of such a family. She had. She had watched, and she had observed, and she knew exactly what was expected of the Duke of Wyndham. His duchess could not be a nobody from the neighborhood. Not if he expected anyone to take him seriously.

"Jack," she said again, trying to find the right words. "I wish—"

"Do you love me?" he cut in.

She froze. He was staring at her with an intensity that left her breathless, immobile.

"Do you love me?"

"It doesn't—"

"Do . . . you . . . love me?"

She closed her eyes. She didn't want to say it. If she did, she would be lost. She would never be able to resist him—his words, his lips. If she gave him this, she would lose her last defense.

"Grace," he said, cradling her face in his hands. He leaned down and kissed her—once, with aching tenderness. "Do you love me?"

"Yes," she whispered. "Yes."

"Then that is all that matters."

She opened her lips to try one last time to talk sense into him, but he was already kissing her, his mouth hot and passionate on her own.

"I love you," he said, kissing her cheeks, her brows, her ears. "I love you."

"Jack," she whispered, but her body had already begun to hum with desire. She wanted him. She wanted this. She did not know what tomorrow would bring, but at this moment she was willing to pretend that she did not care. As long as—

"Promise me," she said urgently, grasping his face firmly in her hands. "Please. Promise me that there will be no baby."

His eyes shuttered and flared, but finally he said, "I promise you I will try."

"You will try?" she echoed. Surely he would not lie about this. He would not ignore her plea and later pretend that he'd "tried."

"I will do what I know how to do. It is not completely foolproof."

She loosened her grip and showed her acquiescence by allowing her fingers to trail along his cheeks. "Thank you," she whispered, leaning up for a kiss.

"But I promise you this," he said, sweeping her into his arms, "you *will* have our baby. I *will* marry you. No matter who I am, or what my name is, I will marry you."

But she no longer had the will to argue with him. Not now, not when he was carrying her to his bed. He laid her down atop the covers and stepped back, quickly undoing the top buttons of his shirt so he could pull it over his head.

And then he was back, half beside her, half atop her, kissing her as if his life depended upon it. "My God," he almost grunted, "this thing is ugly," and Grace could not help but giggle as his fingers attempted to do their magic on her buttons. He let out a frustrated growl when they did not comply, and he actually grasped the two sides of her nightgown, clearly intending to wrench it apart and let the buttons fly where they might.

"No, Jack, you can't!" She was laughing as she said

it; she didn't know why it was so funny—surely deflowerings were meant to be serious, life-altering affairs. But there was so much joy bubbling within her. It was difficult to keep it contained. Especially when he was trying so hard to complete such a simple task and failing so miserably.

"Are you sure?" His face was almost comical in its frustration. "Because I am fairly certain that I do a service to all mankind by destroying this."

She tried not to laugh. "It's my only nightgown."

This, he appeared to find interesting. "Are you saying that if I tear it off, you will have to sleep naked for the duration of our journey?"

She quickly moved his hand from her bodice. "Don't," she warned him.

"But it's so tempting."

"Jack . . ."

He sat back on his heels, gazing down at her with a mixture of hunger and amusement that made her shiver. "Very well," he said, "you do it."

She had been intending to do just that, but now, with him watching her so intently, his eyes heavy-lidded with desire, she felt almost frozen in place. How could she be so brazen as to strip before him? To peel her clothing from her body—to do it *herself.* There was a difference, she realized, in taking off her own clothing and allowing herself to be seduced.

Slowly, fingers trembling, she reached for the top button of her nightgown. She couldn't see it; it was far too high, almost to her chin. But her fingers knew the motions, knew the buttons, and almost without thinking, she slipped one free.

Jack sucked in his breath. "Another."

She obeyed.

"Another."

And again. And again, until she reached the one that lay between her breasts. He reached down then, his large hands slowly spreading the two sides of her gown open. It did not reveal her to him; she'd not un-buttoned enough for that. But she felt the cool air on her skin, felt the soft tickle of his breath as he leaned down to place one kiss on the flat plane of her chest.

"You are beautiful," he whispered. And when his fingers moved this time to the buttons on her night-gown, he mastered them with no difficulty at all. He took her hand and gave it a gentle tug, indicating for her to sit up. She did, closing her eyes as the night-gown fell away.

With her vision dark, she *felt* more keenly, and the fabric—nothing but a plain, serviceable cotton—raised shivers of sensation as it slid along her skin.

Or maybe it was just that she knew he was looking at her.

Was this what it had felt like for that woman? The one in the painting? She must have been a woman of some experience by the time she'd posed for Monsieur Boucher, but surely there had to be a first time for her, as well. Had she, too, closed her eyes so she could *feel* a man's gaze upon her body?

She felt Jack's hand touching her face, the tips of his fingers softly trailing along the line of her neck to the hollow of her shoulder. He paused there, but only for a moment, and Grace sucked in her breath, waiting for the intimacy that awaited her.

"Why are your eyes closed?" he murmured.

"I don't know."

"Are you afraid?"

"No."

She waited. She gasped. She even jumped, just a little, when his fingers slid along the outer curve of her breast.

She felt herself arching. It was strange. She'd never thought about this, never even wondered what it might be like to have a man's hands stroking her in this way, but now that the moment was upon her, she knew exactly what she wanted him to do.

She wanted to feel him cupping her, holding her entirely in his palm.

She wanted to feel his hand brushing against her nipples.

She wanted him to touch her . . . dear God, she wanted him to touch her so badly, and it was spreading. It had moved from her breasts to her belly, to the hidden spot between her legs. She felt hot, and tingly, and searingly hungry.

Hungry . . . *there.*

It was without a doubt the strangest and most compelling sensation. She could not ignore it. She didn't *want* to ignore it. She wanted to feed it, indulge it, let him teach her how to quench it.

"Jack," she moaned, and his hands moved until he was cradling both of her breasts. And then he kissed her.

Her eyes flew open.

His mouth was on her now, on the very tip, and she actually clasped one of her hands to her mouth, lest she scream with the pleasure of it. She hadn't imagined . . . She'd thought she'd known what she wanted, but this . . .

She hadn't known.

She clutched at his head, using him for support. It was torture, and it was bliss, and she was barely able to breathe by the time he dragged his mouth back up to hers.

"Grace . . . Grace . . ." he murmured, over and over, his voice sliding into her skin. It felt as if he was kissing her everywhere, and maybe he was—one moment it was her mouth, and next her ear, and then her neck. And his hands—they were wicked. And relentless.

He never stopped moving, never stopped touching her. His hands were on her shoulders, and then her hips, and then one of them started sliding down her leg, tugging at her nightgown until it slipped off her entirely.

She should have been embarrassed. She should have felt awkward. But she didn't. Not with him. Not when he was gazing down at her with such love and devotion.

He loved her. He'd said he did, and she believed him, but now she felt it. The heat, the warmth. It shone from his eyes. And she understood now how a woman might find herself ruined. How could anyone resist this? How could she resist him?

He stood then, breathing hard, working at the fastenings of his breeches with frantic fingers. His chest was already bare, and all she could think was—*He's beautiful. How could a man be so beautiful?* He'd not led a life of leisure; this, she could see. His body was lean and firm, his skin marred here and there with scars and calluses.

"Were you shot?" she asked, her eyes falling on a puckered scar on his upper arm.

He looked down, even as he pushed off his breeches. "A French sniper," he confirmed. He smiled, rather lopsidedly. "I am fortunate he was not better at his craft."

It should not have been so amusing. But the statement was so . . . *him*. So matter of fact, so understated and dry. She smiled in return. "I almost died, too."

"Really?"

"Fever."

He winced. "I hate fevers."

She nodded, pinching the corners of her lips to keep from smiling. "I should hate to be shot."

He looked back at her, his eyes alight with humor. "I don't recommend it."

And then she did laugh, because it was all so ludicrous. He was standing there naked, for heaven's sake, clearly aroused, and they were discussing the relative unpleasantness of gunshot wounds and fevers.

He crawled onto the bed, looming over her with a predatory expression. "Grace?" he murmured.

She looked up at him and nearly melted. "Yes?"

He smiled wolfishly. "I'm all better now."

And with that, there were no more words. When he kissed her this time, it was with an intensity and fervor that she knew would carry them through to completion. She felt it, too—this desire, this relentless need— and when he nudged his leg between hers, she opened to him immediately, without reservation, without fear.

How long he kissed her, she couldn't possibly have known. It seemed like nothing. It seemed like forever. It felt like she had been born for this moment, with this man. As if somehow, on the day of her birth, this had all been preordained—on October the twenty-eighth, the year of our Lord 1819, she would be in Room 14 of the Queen's Arms Inn, and she would give herself to this man, John Augustus Cavendish-Audley.

Nothing else could possibly have happened. This was how it was meant to be.

She kissed him back with equal abandon, clutching at his shoulders, his arms, anywhere she could gain purchase. And then, just when she thought she could handle no more, his hand slipped between her legs. His touch was gentle, but still, she thought she might scream from the shock and wonder of it.

"Jack," she gasped, not because she wanted him to stop, but because there was no way she could remain silent amidst the onslaught of sensation brought forth by that simple touch. He tickled and teased, and she panted and writhed. And then she realized that he was no longer just touching her, he was inside of her, his fingers exploring her in a manner so intimate it left her breathless.

She could feel herself clench around him, her muscles begging for more. She didn't know what to do, didn't know anything except that she wanted him. She wanted *him*, and something only he could give her.

He shifted position, and his fingers moved away.

His body lifted off hers, and when Grace looked up at him, he seemed to be straining against some irresistible force. He was holding himself above her, supporting himself on his forearms. Her tongue moved, preparing to say his name, but just then she felt him at her entrance, pressing gently forward.

Their eyes met.

"Shhh," he murmured. "Just wait . . . I promise . . ."

"I'm not scared," she whispered.

His mouth moved into a lopsided smile. "I am."

She wanted to ask what he meant and why he was smiling, but he began to move forward, opening her, stretching her, and it was the strangest, most amazing thing, but he was *inside* of her. That one person could enter another seemed the most spectacular thing. They were joined. She could not think of any other way to describe it.

"Am I hurting you?" he whispered.

She shook her head. "I like it," she whispered back.

He groaned at that, and thrust forward, the sudden motion sending a wave of sensation and pressure through her. She gasped his name and grabbed his shoulders, and then she found herself in an ancient rhythm, moving with him, as one. Moving, and pulsing, and straining, and then—

She shattered. She arched, she moaned, she nearly screamed. And when she finally came down and found the strength to breathe, she could not imagine how she could possibly still be alive. Surely a body could not feel that way and live to repeat it.

Then, abruptly, he pulled out of her and turned

away, grunting and groaning his own satisfaction. She touched his shoulder, feeling the spasms of his body. And when he cried out, she did not just hear it. She *felt* it, through his skin, through her body.

To her heart.

For a few moments he did not move, just lay there, his breathing slowly returning to normal. But then he rolled back over and gathered her into his arms. He whispered her name and kissed the top of her head.

And then he did it again.

And again.

And when she finally fell asleep, that was what she heard in her dreams. Jack's voice. Soft, whispering her name.

Jack knew the exact moment she fell asleep. He was not sure what it was—her breathing had already softened to a slow, even sigh, and her body had long since stilled.

But when she fell asleep, he knew.

He kissed her one last time, on her temple. And as he looked down at her peaceful face, he whispered, "I *will* marry you, Grace Eversleigh."

It did not matter who he was. He would not let her go.

Chapter Nineteen

The drive to Butlersbridge was everything Jack remembered. The trees, the birds, the precise shade of green as the wind ruffled the grass . . . These were the sights and sounds of his childhood. Nothing had changed. It ought to have been comforting.

It wasn't.

When he opened his eyes that morning, Grace had already slipped from the bed and made her way back to her own room. He was disappointed, of course; he'd been awakened by his own love and desire for her, and wanted nothing more than to gather her back into his arms.

But he had understood. Life was not as free for a woman as for a man, even a woman of independent means. Grace had her reputation to consider. Thomas and Amelia would never say a word against her, but Jack did not know Lord Crowland well enough to guess what he might do if Grace were caught in his bed. And as for the dowager. . .

Well, it went without saying that she'd happily destroy Grace now, if given the chance.

The traveling party—minus the dowager, to everyone's relief—met up in the inn's dining room for breakfast. Jack knew he'd been unable to keep his heart from his eyes when he saw Grace enter the room. Would it always be this way, he wondered. Would he see her and feel this indescribable, overwhelming rush of feeling?

It wasn't even desire. It was far more than that.

It was love.

Love. With a capital L and swirly script and hearts and flowers and whatever else the angels—and yes, all those annoying little cupids—wished to use for embellishment.

Love. It could be nothing else. He saw Grace and he felt joy. Not just his joy, but everyone's. The stranger seated behind him. The acquaintance across the room. He saw it all. He felt it all.

It was amazing. Humbling. Grace looked at him, and he was a better man.

And she thought he would allow anyone to keep them apart.

It would not happen. He would not let it happen.

Throughout breakfast she did not precisely avoid him—there were far too many shared glances and secret smiles for that. But she had been careful not to seek him out, and indeed, he'd not had an opportunity to speak with her even once. He probably wouldn't have been able to do so even if Grace was not so inclined to be circumspect; Amelia slipped her hand in Grace's right after breakfast and did not let go.

Safety in numbers, Jack decided. The two ladies were stuck in the coach all day with the dowager. He would have been blindly reaching for a hand if forced to endure the same.

The three gentlemen rode on horseback, taking advantage of the fine weather. Lord Crowland decided to take a seat in the carriage after their first stop to water the horses, but thirty minutes later he was staggering back out, declaring the ride far less exhausting than the dowager.

"You would abandon your daughter to the dowager's venom?" Jack asked mildly.

Crowland did not even try to make excuses. "I did not say I was proud of myself."

"The Outer Hebrides," Thomas said, trotting by. "I'm telling you, Audley, it's the key to your happiness. The Outer Hebrides."

"The Outer Hebrides?" Crowland echoed, looking from man to man for explanation.

"Almost as far as the Orkneys," Thomas said cheerfully. "And much more fun to say."

"Have you holdings there?" Crowland asked.

"Not yet," Thomas replied. He looked over at Jack. "Perhaps you can restore a nunnery. Something with insurmountable walls."

Jack found himself enjoying the mental picture. "How have you lived with her for so long?" he asked.

Thomas shook his head. "I have no idea."

They were talking as if it were already decided, Jack realized. They were talking as if he had already been named the duke. And Thomas did not seem to mind. If anything, he appeared to be looking forward to his imminent dispossession.

Jack looked back at the carriage. Grace had insisted that she could not marry him if he was the duke. And yet, he could not imagine doing it without her. He was unprepared for the duties that came with the title. Astoundingly so. But she knew what to do, didn't she? She'd lived at Belgrave for five years. She had to know how the place was run. She knew the name of every last servant, and as far as he could tell, their birthdays, too.

She was kind. She was gracious. She was innately fair, of impeccable judgment, and far more intelligent than he.

He could not imagine a more perfect duchess.

But he did not want to be the duke.

He truly didn't.

He'd gone over it in his mind countless times, reminding himself of all of the reasons why he'd make a very bad Duke of Wyndham, but had he ever actually come out and said it plainly?

He did not want to be the duke.

He looked over at Thomas, who was looking up at the sun, shading his eyes with his hand.

"It must be past noon," Lord Crowland said. "Shall we stop for lunch?"

Jack shrugged. It did not matter to him.

"For the sake of the ladies," Crowland said.

As one, they turned and looked over their shoulders toward the carriage.

Jack thought he saw Crowland cringe. "It's not pretty in there," he said in a low voice.

Jack quirked a brow.

"The dowager," Crowland said, shuddering. "Amelia begged me to let her ride after we watered the horses."

"That would be too cruel to Grace," Jack said.

"That's what I told Amelia."

"As you were fleeing the carriage," Thomas murmured, smiling just a little.

Crowland cocked his head. "I would never claim otherwise."

"And I would never chastise you for it."

Jack listened to the exchange with little interest. By his estimation, they were about halfway to Butlersbridge, and it was growing increasingly difficult to find humor in the inane. "There is a clearing a mile or so ahead," he said. "I've stopped there before. It's suitable for a picnic."

The two other men nodded their agreement, and about five minutes later they'd found the spot. Jack dismounted and went immediately to the carriage. A groom was helping the ladies down, but as Grace would be the last to alight, it was easy enough for him to position himself so he might take her hand when she emerged.

"Mr. Audley," Grace said. She was nothing but polite, but her eyes shone with a secret warmth.

"Miss Eversleigh." He looked down at her mouth. The corners were moving slightly . . . very slightly. She wanted to smile. He could see it.

He could feel it.

"I will eat in the carriage," the dowager announced sharply. "Only heathens eat on the ground."

Jack tapped his chest and grinned. "Proud to be a heathen." He quirked his head toward Grace. "And you?"

"Very proud."

The dowager marched once around the perimeter of the field—to stretch her legs, she said—and then disappeared back inside the carriage.

"That must have been very difficult for her," Jack commented, watching her go.

Grace had been examining the contents of a picnic basket, but at that she looked up. "Difficult?"

"There is no one to harass in the carriage," he explained.

"I think she feels that we have all ganged up upon her."

"We have."

Grace looked conflicted. "Yes, but—"

Oh . . . *no*. He was not going to listen to her make excuses for the dowager. "Don't tell me that you harbor any sympathy toward her."

"No." Grace shook her head. "I wouldn't say that, but—"

"You are far too softhearted."

At that she smiled. Sheepishly. "Perhaps."

Once the blankets were laid out, Jack maneuvered them so they were seated a bit apart from the others. It was not very difficult—or very obvious—to do so; Amelia had sat down next to her father, who appeared to be delivering some sort of lecture, and Thomas had wandered off, probably in search of a tree that needed watering.

"Is this the road you traveled when you went to school in Dublin?" Grace asked, reaching for a slice of bread and cheese.

"Yes."

He'd tried to keep the tightness out of his voice, but he must not have succeeded, because when he looked at her, she was regarding him in that unsettling way of hers. "Why don't you want to go home?" she asked.

It was on the tip of his tongue to say that her imagination was too active, or, since he really ought to be reverting to form, something clever and grandiose, involving sunshine, twittering birds, and milk of human kindness.

Statements like that had got him out of far more delicate situations than this.

But he hadn't the energy just now, nor the will.

And, anyway, Grace knew better. She knew *him* better. He could be his usual flip and funny self, and most of the time— he hoped—she would love him for it. But not when he was trying to hide the truth.

Or hide *from* the truth.

"It's complicated," he said, because at least that wasn't a lie.

She nodded and turned to her lunch. He waited for another question, but none were forthcoming. So he picked up an apple.

He looked over. She was cutting into a slice of roast chicken, her eyes on her utensils. He opened his mouth to speak, then decided not to, then brought the apple to his mouth.

Then didn't bite into it.

"It's been over five years," he blurted out.

She looked up. "Since you've been home?"

He nodded.

"That's a long time."

"Very long."

"Too long?"

His fingers tightened around the apple. "No."

She took a few bites of her meal, then looked up. "Would you like me to slice that apple for you?"

He handed it over, mostly because he'd forgotten he was holding it. "I had a cousin, you know." Bloody hell, where had that come from? He hadn't meant to say anything about Arthur. He'd spent the last five years trying not to think about him, trying to make sure that Arthur's was not the last face he saw before he fell asleep at night.

"I thought you'd said you had three cousins," Grace said. She wasn't looking at him; she gave every sign of giving her complete focus to the apple and knife in her hands.

"Only two now."

She looked up, her eyes large with sympathy. "I am sorry."

"Arthur died in France." The words sounded rusty. He realized it had been a long time since he'd said Arthur's name aloud. Five years, probably.

"With you?" Grace asked softly.

He nodded.

She looked down at the apple slices, now neatly arranged on a plate. She didn't seem to know what to do with them.

"You're not going to say that it wasn't my fault?" he said, and he *hated* the sound of his voice. It was hollow, and pained, and sarcastic, and desperate, and he couldn't believe what he'd just said.

"I wasn't there," she said.

His eyes flew to her face.

"I can't imagine how it would have been your fault, but I wasn't there." She reached across the food and laid her hand briefly atop his. "I'm sorry. Were you close?"

He nodded, turning away and pretending to look at the trees. "Not so much when we were young. But after we left for school . . ." He pinched the bridge of his nose, wondering how to explain just what Arthur had done for him. " . . . we found much more in common."

Her fingers tightened around his, and then she let go. "It is difficult to lose someone you love."

He looked back at her once he was satisfied that his eyes would remain dry. "When you lost your parents . . ."

"It was horrible," she answered. Her lips moved at the corners, but not into a smile. It was one of those flashes of movement—a tiny, little rush of emotion, escaping almost without notice. "I didn't think I should die," Grace said softly, "but I did not know how I would live."

"I wish . . ." But he didn't know what he wished. That he could have been there for her? What good would he have been? Five years ago he'd been broken, too.

"The dowager saved me," she said. She smiled wryly. "Isn't that funny?"

His brows rose. "Oh, come now. The dowager does nothing out of the goodness of her heart."

"I did not say why she did it, just that she did. I should have been forced to marry my cousin if she had not taken me in."

He took her hand and brought it to his lips. "I am glad you did not."

"So am I," she said, without any trace of tenderness. "He is awful."

Jack chuckled. "And here I'd hoped you were relieved to have waited for me."

She gave him an arch look and withdrew her hand. "You have not met my cousin."

He finally took one of the apple pieces and bit into it. "We have an overabundance of odious relations, you and I."

Her lips twisted in thought, and then her body twisted so that she could look back toward the carriage. "I should go to her," she said.

"No, you shouldn't," Jack said firmly.

Grace sighed. She did not want to feel sorry for the dowager, not after what the dowager had said to her the night before. But her conversation with Jack had brought back memories . . . and reminded her just how very much she was indebted to her.

She turned back to Jack. "She is all alone."

"She deserves to be alone." He said this with great conviction, and more than a touch of surprise, as if he could not believe the matter might be under discussion.

"No one deserves to be alone."

"Do you really believe that?"

She didn't, but . . . "I want to believe it."

He looked at her dubiously.

Grace started to rise. She looked this way and that, making sure no one could hear, and said, "You should not have been kissing my hand where people can see, anyway."

She stood then, stepping quickly away, before he had a chance to make a reply.

"Have you finished your lunch?" Amelia called out as she passed.

Grace nodded. "Yes. I am going to the carriage to see if the dowager needs anything."

Amelia looked at her as if she'd gone mad.

Grace gave a little shrug. "Everybody deserves a second chance." She thought about that, then added, mostly to herself, "*That,* I really do believe." She marched over to the carriage. It was too high for her to climb up herself, and the grooms were nowhere in sight, so she called out, "Your grace! Your grace!"

There was no reply, so she said, a little louder, "Ma'am!"

The dowager's irate visage appeared in the open doorway. "What do *you* want?"

Grace reminded herself that she had not spent a lifetime of Sunday mornings in church for nothing. "I wished to inquire if you needed anything, your grace."

"Why?"

Good heavens, she was suspicious. "Because I am a nice person," Grace said, somewhat impatiently. And then she crossed her arms, waiting to see what the dowager said to that.

The dowager stared down at her for several moments, then said, "It is my experience that nice people don't need to advertise themselves as such."

Grace wanted to inquire what sort of experience the dowager *had* with nice people, since it was her own experience that most nice people fled the dowager's presence.

But that seemed catty.

She took a breath. She did not have to do this. She did not have to help the dowager in any way. She was her own woman now, and she did not need to worry over her security.

But she was, as she had noted, a nice person. And she was determined to remain a nice person, regardless of her improved circumstances. She had waited upon the dowager for the last five years because she'd had to, not because she wanted to. And now . . .

Well, she still didn't want to. But she'd do it. Whatever the dowager's motives five years ago, she had saved Grace from a lifetime of unhappiness. And for that, she could spend an hour attending to the dowager. But more than that, she could *choose* to spend an hour attending to her.

It was amazing what a difference that made.

"Ma'am?" Grace said. That was all. Just *ma'am*. She'd said enough. It was up to the dowager now.

"Oh, very well," she said irritably. "If you feel you must."

Grace kept her face utterly serene as she allowed Lord Crowland (who had caught the latter half of the conversation and told Grace she was mad) to help her up. She took her prescribed seat—facing backward, as far from the dowager as possible—and folded her hands neatly in her lap. She did not know how long they would be sitting here; the others had not seemed quite ready to quit their lunch.

The dowager was looking out the window; Grace kept her eyes on her hands. Every now and then she'd steal a glance up, and every time, the dowager was still turned away, her posture hard and stiff, her lips pinched tight.

And then— perhaps the fifth time Grace looked up—the dowager was staring straight at her.

"You disappoint me," she said, her voice low—not quite hiss, but something close to it.

Grace held her silence. She held everything, it seemed—her posture, her breath. She did not know what to say, except that she would not apologize. Not for having the audacity to reach out for happiness.

"You were not supposed to leave."

"I was but a servant, ma'am."

"You were not supposed to leave," the dowager said again, but this time something within her seemed to shake. Not quite her body, and not quite her voice.

Her heart, Grace realized with a shock. Her heart was shaking.

"He is not what I expected," the dowager said.

Grace blinked, trying to follow. "Mr. Audley?"

"Cavendish," the dowager said sharply.

"You did not know that he existed," Grace said, as gently as she was able. "How could you have expected anything?"

The dowager did not answer. Not that question, anyway. "Do you know why I took you into my home?" she asked instead.

"No," Grace said softly.

The dowager's lips pressed together for a moment before she said, "It was not right. A person should not be alone in this world."

"No," Grace said again. And she believed it, with her whole heart.

"It was for the both of us. I took a terrible thing and turned it into good. For both of us." Her eyes narrowed, boring into Grace's. "*You were not supposed to leave.*"

And then—good heavens, Grace could not believe she was saying it, but: "I will come visit you, should you wish."

The dowager swallowed, and she looked straight ahead when she said, "That would be acceptable."

Grace was saved from further reply by the arrival of Amelia, who informed them that they would depart momentarily. And indeed, she'd had barely enough time to settle into her seat when the carriage wheels creaked into motion, and they began to roll forward.

No one spoke.

It was better that way.

Several hours later, Grace opened her eyes.

Amelia was staring at her. "You fell asleep," she said quietly, then put her finger to her lips as she motioned to the dowager, who had also dozed off.

Grace covered a yawn, then asked, "How much longer do you think we have until we get there?"

"I don't know." Amelia gave a little shrug. "Perhaps an hour? Two?" She sighed then, and leaned back. She looked tired, Grace thought. They were all tired.

And scared.

"What will you do?" Grace asked, before she had the chance to think better of it.

Amelia did not open her eyes. "I don't know."

It was not much of an answer, but then again, it hadn't been a fair question.

"Do you know what the funniest part of it is?" Amelia asked quite suddenly.

Grace shook her head, then remembered that Amelia's eyes were still closed and said, "No."

"I keep thinking to myself, 'This isn't fair. I should have a choice. I should not have to be traded and bartered like some sort of commodity.' But then I think, 'How is this any different? I was given to Wyndham years ago. I never made a complaint.'"

"You were just a baby," Grace said.

Still, Amelia did not open her eyes, and when she spoke, her voice was quiet and full of recrimination. "I have had many years to lodge a complaint."

"Amelia—"

"I have no one to blame but myself."

"That's not true."

Amelia finally opened her eyes. One of them, at least. "You're just saying that."

"No, I'm not. I would," Grace admitted, because it was true. "But as it happens, I am telling the truth. It isn't your fault. It's not anyone's fault, really." She took a breath. Let it out. "I wish it were. It would be so much easier that way."

"To have someone to blame?"

"Yes."

And then Amelia whispered, "I don't want to marry him."

"Thomas?" Grace asked. Amelia had spent so long as his fiancée, and they did not seem to have any great affection for one another.

Amelia looked at her curiously. "No. Mr. Audley."

"Really?"

"You sound so shocked."

"No, of course not," Grace said hurriedly. What was she to say to Amelia—that she was so desperately in love with him herself that she could not imagine anyone not wanting him? "It's just that he's so handsome," she improvised.

Amelia gave a little shrug. "I suppose."

She *supposed*? Hadn't she ever seen him *smile*?

But then Amelia said, "Don't you find him a little *too* charming?"

"No." Grace immediately looked down at her hands, because her *no* had come out in not at all the tone of voice she'd intended. And indeed, Amelia must have heard it, too, because her next words were—

"Grace Eversleigh, do you fancy Mr. Audley?"

Grace stammered and stumbled, and managed a rather croaky, "I—" before Amelia cut in with—

"You *do*."

"It does not signify," Grace said, because what was she supposed to say? To *Amelia*, who might or might not be engaged to marry him.

"Of course it signifies. Does he fancy you?"

Grace wanted to melt into the seat.

"No," Amelia said, sounding highly amused. "Don't answer. I can see from your face that he does. Well. I certainly shall not marry him now."

Grace swallowed. Her throat tasted bitter. "You should not refuse him on my account."

"*What* did you just say?"

"I can't marry him if he's the duke."

"Why not?"

Grace tried to smile, because really, it was sweet of Amelia to ignore the difference in their positions. But she could not quite manage it. "If he is the duke, he will need to marry someone suitable. Of *your* rank."

"Oh, don't be silly," Amelia scoffed. "It's not as if you grew up in an orphanage."

"There will be scandal enough. He must not add to it with a sensational marriage."

"An actress would be sensational. You will merely be a week's worth of gossip."

It would be more than that, but Grace saw no point in arguing further. But then Amelia said—

"I do not know Mr. Audley's mind, or his intentions, but if he is prepared to dare everything for love, then you should be, too."

Grace looked at her. How was it that Amelia suddenly looked so very wise? When had that happened? When had she stopped being Elizabeth's little sister and become . . . herself?

Amelia reached out and squeezed her hand. "Be a woman of courage, Grace." She smiled then, murmuring something to herself as she turned and looked out the window.

Grace stared straight ahead, thinking . . . wondering . . . was Amelia right? Or was it just that she had never faced hardship? It was easy to talk about being courageous when one had never come face-to-face with desperation.

What *would* happen if a woman of her background married a duke? Thomas's mother had not been an aristocrat, but when she married his father, he was only third in line to inherit, and no one had expected her to become a duchess. By all accounts, she had been dreadfully unhappy. Miserable, even.

But Thomas's parents had not loved each other. They had not even liked each other, from what Grace had heard.

But she loved Jack.

And he loved her.

Still, it would all be so much simpler if he turned out not to be the legitimate son of John Cavendish.

And then, out of nowhere, Amelia whispered, "We could blame the dowager." As Grace turned to her in confusion, Amelia clarified, "For this. You said it would be easier if we had someone to blame."

Grace looked over at the dowager, who was seated across from Amelia. She was snoring softly, and her head was perched at what had to be an uncomfortable angle. It was remarkable, but even in repose her mouth was pinched and unpleasant.

"It's certainly more her fault than anyone else's," Amelia added, but Grace noted that she tossed a nervous glance at the dowager as she spoke.

Grace nodded, murmuring, "I cannot disagree with that."

Amelia stared off into space for several seconds, and then, just when Grace was convinced that she did not plan to respond, she said, "It didn't make me feel any better."

"Blaming the dowager?"

"Yes." Amelia's shoulders slumped a bit. "It's still horrible. The whole thing."

"Dreadful," Grace agreed.

Amelia turned and looked at her directly. "Sodding bad."

Grace gasped. "Amelia!"

Amelia's face wrinkled in thought. "Did I use that correctly?"

"I wouldn't know."

"Oh, come now, don't tell me you haven't thought something just as unladylike."

"I wouldn't *say* it."

The look Amelia gave her was as clear as a dare. "But you thought it."

Grace felt her lips twitch. "It's a damned shame."

"A bloody inconvenience, if you ask me," Amelia responded, fast enough so Grace knew she'd been saving that one.

"I have an advantage, you know," Grace said archly.

"Oh, really?"

"Indeed. *I* am privy to the servants' talk."

"Oh, come now, you won't be convincing me that the housemaids at Belgrave talk like the fishmonger."

"No, but sometimes the footmen do."

"In front of you?"

"Not on purpose," Grace admitted, "but it happens."

"Very well." Amelia turned to her with quirked lips and humor in her eyes. "Do your worst."

Grace thought for a moment and then, after darting a quick glance across the carriage to make sure that the dowager was still asleep, she leaned forward and whispered in Amelia's ear.

When she was through, Amelia drew back and stared at her, blinking three times before saying, "I'm not sure I know what that means."

Grace frowned. "I don't think I do, either."

"It sounds bad, though."

"Sodding bad," Grace said with a smile, and she patted Amelia's hand.

Amelia sighed. "A damned shame."

"We're repeating ourselves," Grace pointed out.

"I *know*," Amelia said, with a fair bit of feeling. "But whose fault is it? Not ours. We've been far too sheltered."

"Now that," Grace announced with flair, "really *is* a damned shame."

"A bloody inconvenience, if you ask me."

"What the *devil* are the two of you talking about?"

Grace gulped, and she stole a glance at Amelia, who was staring at the now quite awake dowager with a similar look of horror.

"Well?" the dowager demanded.

"Nothing," Grace chirped.

The dowager regarded her with a most unpleasant expression, then turned her icy attentions to Amelia. "And *you*, Lady Amelia. Where is your breeding?"

And then Amelia—oh, dear heavens—she shrugged her shoulders and said, "Damned if I know."

Grace tried to hold still, but her shock positively burst out of her, and she rather feared she spat upon the dowager. Which did seem ironic, that the first time she did such a thing, it should be accidental.

"You are disgusting," the dowager hissed. "I cannot believe I considered forgiving you."

"Stop picking on Grace," Amelia said. With surprising force.

Grace turned to Amelia in surprise.

The dowager, however, was furious. "I *beg* your pardon."

"I said, stop picking on Grace."

"And who do you think you are, to order me about?"

As Grace watched Amelia, she would have sworn she changed right before her very eyes. Gone was the unsure girl, in her place was: "The future Duchess of Wyndham, or so I'm told."

Grace's lips parted in shock. And admiration.

"Because really," Amelia added disdainfully, "if I'm not, what the devil am I doing here, halfway across Ireland?"

Grace's eyes darted from Amelia to the dowager and back. And then back again. And then—

Well, suffice it to say, it was a monstrously long moment of silence.

"Do not speak again," the dowager finally said. "I cannot tolerate the sound of your voices."

And indeed, they all remained silent for the rest of the journey. Even the dowager.

Chapter Twenty

$\mathcal{O}$utside the carriage, the atmosphere was considerably less tense. The three men remained on horseback, never quite in a line. Every now and then one of them would increase his pace or fall behind, and one horse would pass another. Perfunctory greetings would be exchanged.

Occasionally someone would comment on the weather.

Lord Crowland seemed rather interested in the native birds.

Thomas didn't say much, but—Jack glanced over at him—good Lord, was he whistling?

"Are you *happy*?" Jack asked, his voice a bit short.

Thomas looked back in surprise. "Me?" He frowned, thinking about it. "I suppose I am. It's a rather fine day, don't you think?"

"A fine day," Jack echoed.

"None of us is trapped in the carriage with that evil old hag," Crowland announced. "We should all be happy." Then he added, "Pardon," since the evil old hag was, after all, grandmother to both of his companions.

"Pardons unnecessary on my account," Thomas said. "I agree with your assessment completely."

There had to be something significant in this, Jack thought—that their conversation kept returning to how relieved they all were not to be in the dowager's presence. It was damned strange, to tell the truth, and yet, it did make one think . . .

"Will I have to live with her?" he blurted out.

Thomas looked over and grinned. "The Outer Hebrides, my man, the Outer Hebrides."

"Why didn't you do it?" Jack demanded.

"Oh, believe me, I will, on the off chance I still possess any power over her tomorrow. And if I don't . . ." Thomas shrugged. "I'll need some sort of employment, won't I? I always wished to travel. Perhaps I shall be your scout. I'll find the oldest, coldest place on the island. I shall have a rollicking good time."

"For God's sake," Jack swore. "Stop talking like that." He did not want this to be preordained. He did not want it to be understood. Thomas ought to be fighting for his place in the world, not blithely handing it over.

Because he himself did not want it. He wanted Grace, and he wanted his freedom, and more than anything, right at that very moment, he wanted to be somewhere else. Anywhere else.

Thomas gave him a curious look but said nothing

more. And neither did Jack. Not when they reached Pollamore, or Cavan town, or even as they rode into Butlersbridge.

Night had long since fallen, but Jack knew every storefront, every last signpost and tree. There was the Derragarra Inn, where he'd got himself drunk on his seventeenth birthday. There was the butcher, and the blacksmith, and ah, yes, there was the oatmeal mill, behind which he'd stolen his first kiss.

Which meant that in five—no, make that four—more minutes, he would be home.

Home.

It was a word he had not uttered in years. It had had no meaning. He'd lived in inns and public houses and sometimes under the stars. He'd had his ragtag group of friends, but they drifted in and out of togetherness. They thieved together more by convenience than anything else. All they'd had in common was a shared past in the military, and a willingness to give a portion of their bounty to those who had returned from the war less fortunate than they.

Over the years, Jack had given money to men without legs, women without husbands, children without parents. No one ever questioned where he'd got the money. He supposed his bearing and accent were those of a gentleman, and that was enough. People saw what they wanted to see, and when a former officer (who never quite got around to sharing his name) came bearing gifts. . .

No one ever *wanted* to question it.

And through all this, he'd told no one. Who had there been to tell?

Grace.

Now there was Grace.

He smiled. She would approve. Perhaps not of the means, but certainly of the end. The truth was, he'd never taken anything from anyone who hadn't looked as if they could afford it. And he'd always been careful to more thoroughly rob the most annoying of his victims.

Such scruples would not have kept him from the gallows, but it had always made him feel a bit better about his chosen profession.

He heard a horse draw up next to his, and when he turned, there was Thomas, now keeping pace beside him. "Is this the road?" he asked quietly.

Jack nodded. "Just around the bend."

"They are not expecting you, are they?"

"No."

Thomas had far too much tact to question him further, and indeed, he allowed his mount to fall back by half a length, granting Jack his privacy.

And then there it was. Cloverhill. Just as he'd remembered it, except maybe the vines had taken over a bit more of the brick facade. The rooms were lit, and the windows shone with warmth. And even though the only sounds were those made by the traveling party, Jack could swear he could hear laughter and merriment seeping out through the walls.

Dear God, he'd thought he'd missed it, but this . . .

This was something more. This was an ache, a true, pounding pain in his chest; an empty hole; a sob, forever caught in his throat.

This was home.

Jack wanted to stop, to take a moment to gaze at the graceful old house, but he heard the carriage drawing closer and knew that he could not keep everyone at bay while he indulged his own nostalgia.

The last thing he wanted was for the dowager to barge in ahead of him (which he was quite certain she would do), so he rode up to the entrance, dismounted, and walked up the steps on his own. He closed his eyes and drew a long breath, and then, since he wasn't likely to amass any more courage in the next few minutes, he lifted the brass knocker and brought it down.

There was no immediate reply. This was not a surprise. It was late. They were unexpected. The butler might have retired for the night. There were so many reasons they should have got rooms in the village and made their way to Cloverhill in the morning. He didn't want—

The door opened. Jack held his hands tightly behind his back. He'd tried leaving them at his sides, but they started to shake.

He saw the light of the candle first, and then the man behind it, wrinkled and stooped.

"Master Jack?"

Jack swallowed. "Wimpole," he said. Good heavens, the old butler must be nearing eighty, but of course his aunt would have kept him on, for as long as he wished to work, which, knowing Wimpole, would be until the day he died.

"We were not expecting you," Wimpole said.

Jack tried for a smile. "Well, you know how I like a surprise."

"Come in! Come in! Oh, Master Jack, Mrs. Audley

will be so *pleased* to see you. As will—" Wimpole stopped, peering out the door, his wizened old eyes creasing into a squint.

"I am afraid that I brought a few guests," Jack explained. The dowager had already been helped down from the carriage, and Grace and Amelia were right behind her. Thomas had grabbed onto his grand-mother's arm—hard, from the looks of it—to give Jack a few moments alone, but the dowager was already showing signs of impending outrage.

"Wimpole?" came a feminine voice. "Who is here at this hour?"

Jack stood stiffly, hardly able to breathe. It was his aunt Mary. She sounded exactly the same. It was as if he'd never left. . .

Except it wasn't. If he'd never left, his heart wouldn't be pounding, his mouth wouldn't be dry. And most of all, he wouldn't feel so bloody terrified. Scared spitless at seeing the one person who had loved him his entire life, with her whole heart and without condition.

"Wimpole? I—" She'd rounded the corner and was staring at him like a ghost. "Jack?"

"In the flesh." He tried for a jovial tone but couldn't quite manage it, and deep inside, down where he kept his blackest moments, he wanted to cry. Right there, in front of everyone, it was twisting and writhing inside of him, bursting to get out.

"Jack!" she cried out, and she hurled herself forward, throwing her arms around him. "Oh, Jack. Jack, my dear sweet boy. We've missed you so." She was covering his face with kisses, like a mother would her son.

Like she should have been able to do for Arthur.

"It is good to see you, Aunt Mary," he said. He pulled her tight then and buried his face in the crook of her neck, because she *was* his mother, in every way that mattered. And he'd missed her. By God, he'd missed her, and in that moment it did not matter that he'd hurt her in the worst way imaginable. He just wanted to be held.

"Oh, Jack," she said, smiling through her tears, "I ought to horsewhip you for staying away so long. Why would you do such a thing? Don't you know how worried we were? How—"

"Ahem."

Mary stopped and turned, still holding Jack's face in her hands. The dowager had made her way to the front entrance and was standing behind him on the stone steps.

"You must be the aunt," she said.

Mary just stared at her. "Yes," she finally replied. "And you are . . . ?"

"Aunt Mary," Jack said hastily, before the dowager could speak again, "I am afraid I must introduce you to the dowager Duchess of Wyndham."

Mary let go of him and curtsied, stepping aside as the dowager swept past her. "The *Duchess* of Wyndham?" she echoed, looking at Jack with palpable shock. "Good heavens, Jack, couldn't you have sent notice?"

Jack smiled tightly. "It is better this way, I assure you."

The rest of the traveling party came forward at that moment, and Jack completed the introductions, trying not to notice his aunt going from paler to palest after he identified the Duke of Wyndham and the Earl of Crowland.

"Jack," she whispered frantically, "I haven't the rooms. We have nothing grand enough—"

"Please, Mrs. Audley," Thomas said with a deferential bow, "do not put yourself out on my accord. It was unforgivable for us to arrive without notice. I would not expect you to go to any great lengths. Although"—he glanced over at the dowager, who was standing in the hall with a sour look on her face—"perhaps your finest room for my grandmother. It will be easier for everyone."

"Of course," Mary said quickly. "Please, please, it's chilly. You must all come inside. Jack, I do need to tell you—"

"Where is your church?" the dowager demanded.

"Our church?" Mary asked, looking to Jack in confusion. "At this hour?"

"I do not intend to worship," the dowager snapped. "I wish to inspect the records."

"Does Vicar Beveridge still preside?" Jack asked, trying to cut the dowager off.

"Yes, but he will surely be abed. It's half nine, I should think, and he is an early riser. Perhaps in the morning. I—"

"This is a matter of dynastic importance," the dowager cut in. "I don't care if it's after midnight. We—"

"I care," Jack cut in, silencing her with an icy expression. "You are not going to pull the vicar out of bed. You have waited this long. You can bloody well wait until morning."

"Jack!" Mary gasped. She turned to the dowager. "I did not raise him to speak this way."

"No, you didn't," Jack said, which was the closest he was going to come to an apology while the dowager was staring him down.

"You were his mother's sister, weren't you?" the dowager said.

Mary looked a bit baffled at the sudden change of topic. "I am."

"Were you present at her wedding?"

"I was not."

Jack turned to her in surprise. "You weren't?"

"No. I could not attend. I was in confinement." She gave Jack a rueful look. "I never told you. It was a stillbirth." Her face softened. "Just one of the reasons I was so happy to have *you*."

"We shall make for the church in the morning," the dowager announced, uninterested in Mary's obstetrical history. "First thing. We shall find the papers and be done with it."

"The papers?" Mary echoed.

"Proof of the marriage," the dowager bit off. She looked upon Mary with icy condescension, then dismissed her with a flick of her head, adding, "Are you daft?"

It was a good thing Thomas pulled her back, because Jack would have gone for her throat.

"Louise was not married in the Butlersbridge church," Mary said. "She was married at Maguiresbridge. In County Fermanagh, where we grew up."

"How far is that?" the dowager demanded, trying to yank her arm free of Thomas's grasp.

"Twenty miles, your grace."

The dowager muttered something quite unpleasant. Jack could not make out the exact words, but Mary blanched. She turned to him with an expression nearing alarm. "Jack? What is this all about? Why do you need proof of your mother's marriage?"

He looked at Grace, who was standing a bit behind his aunt. She offered him a tiny nod of encouragement, and he cleared his throat and said, "My father was her son."

Mary looked over at the dowager in shock. "Your father . . . John Cavendish, you mean . . ."

Thomas stepped forward. "May I intercede?"

Jack felt exhausted. "Please do."

"Mrs. Audley," Thomas said, with more dignity and collection than Jack could ever have imagined, "if there is proof of your sister's marriage, then your nephew is the true Duke of Wyndham."

"The true Duke of—" Mary covered her mouth in shock. "No. It's not possible. I remember him. Mr. Cavendish. He was—" She waved her arms in the air as if trying to describe him with gestures. Finally, after several attempts at a more verbal explanation, she said, "He would not have kept such a thing from us."

"He was not the heir at the time," Thomas told her, "and had no reason to believe he would become so."

"Oh, my heavens. But if Jack is the duke, then you—"

"Are not," he finished wryly. "I am sure you can imagine our eagerness to have this settled."

Mary stared at him in shock. And then at Jack. And then looked as if she very much wanted to sit down.

"I am standing in the hall," the dowager announced haughtily.

"Don't be rude," Thomas chided.

"She should have seen to—"

Thomas shifted his grip on her arm and yanked her forward, brushing right past Jack and his aunt. "Mrs. Audley," he said, "we are most grateful for your hospitality. *All* of us."

Mary nodded gratefully and turned to the butler. "Wimpole, would you—"

"Of course, ma'am," he said, and Jack had to smile as he moved away. No doubt he was rousing the housekeeper to have her prepare the necessary bedrooms. Wimpole had always known what Aunt Mary needed before she'd had to utter the words.

"We shall have rooms readied in no time," Mary said, turning to Grace and Amelia, who were standing off to the side. "Would the two of you mind sharing? I don't have—"

"It is no trouble at all," Grace said warmly. "We enjoy each other's company."

"Oh, thank you," Mary said, sounding relieved. "Jack, you shall have to take your old bed in the nursery, and—oh, this is silly, I should not be wasting your time here in the hall. Let us retire to the drawing room, where you may warm yourselves by the fire until your rooms are ready."

She ushered everyone in, but when Jack made to go, she placed her hand on his arm, gently holding him back.

"We missed you," she said.

He swallowed, but the lump in his throat would

not dislodge. "I missed you, too," he said. He tried to smile. "Who is home? Edward must have—"

"Married," she finished for him. "Yes. As soon as we were out of mourning for Arthur. And Margaret soon after. They both live close by, Edward just down the lane, Margaret in Belturbet."

"And Uncle William?" Jack had last seen him at Arthur's funeral. He'd looked older. Older, and tired. And stiff with grief. "He is well?"

Mary was silent, and then an unbearable sorrow filled her eyes. Her lips parted but she did not speak. She did not need to.

Jack stared at her in shock. "No," he whispered, because it could not be true. He was supposed to have had a chance to say he was sorry. He'd come all the way to Ireland. He wanted to say he was sorry.

"He died, Jack." Mary blinked several times, her eyes glistening. "It was two years ago. I didn't know how to find you. You never gave us an address."

Jack turned, taking a few steps toward the rear of the house. If he stayed where he was, someone could see him. Everyone was in the drawing room. If they looked through the doorway, they would see him, struck, ready to cry, maybe ready to scream.

"Jack?" It was Mary, and he could hear her steps moving cautiously toward him. He looked up at the ceiling, taking a shaky, open-mouthed breath. It didn't help, but it was all he could manage.

Mary laid her hand on his arm. "He told me to tell you he loved you."

"Don't say that." It was the one thing he couldn't hear. Not just now.

"He did. He told me he knew you would come home. And that he loved you, and you were his son. In his heart, you were his son."

He covered his face with his hands and found himself pressing tight, tighter, as if he could squeeze this all away. Why was he surprised? There was no reason he should be. William was not a young man; he'd been nearly forty when he married Mary. Did he think that life would have stood still in his absence? That no one would have changed, or grown . . . or died?

"I should have come back," he said. "I should have— Oh, God, I'm such an idiot."

Mary touched his hand, pulled it gently down and held it. And then she pulled him out of the hall, into the nearest room. His uncle's study.

Jack walked over to the desk. It was a hulking, behemoth of a thing, the wood dark and scuffed and smelling like the paper and ink that always lain atop it.

But it had never been imposing. Funny, he'd always liked coming in here. It seemed odd, really. He'd been an out of doors sort of boy, always running and racing, and covered in mud. Even now, he hated a room with fewer than two windows.

But he had always liked it here.

He turned to look at his aunt. She was standing in the middle of the room. She'd closed the door most of the way and set her candle down on a shelf. She turned and looked back at him and said, very softly, "He knew you loved him."

He shook his head. "I did not deserve him. Or you."

"Stop this talk. I won't hear it."

"Aunt Mary, you know . . ." He put his fisted hand to his mouth, biting down on his knuckle. The words were there, but they burned in his chest, and it was so damned hard to speak them. "You know that Arthur would not have gone to France if not for me."

She stared at him in bewilderment, then gasped and said, "Good heavens, Jack, you do not blame yourself for his death?"

"Of course I do. He went for me. He would never have—"

"He wanted to join the army. He knew it was that or the clergy, and heaven knows he did not want that. He'd always planned—"

"*No,*" Jack cut in, with all the force and anger in his heart. "He hadn't. Maybe he told you he had, but—"

"You cannot take responsibility for his death. I will not let you."

"Aunt Mary—"

"Stop! Stop it!"

The heels of her hands were pressed against her temples, her fingers wrapping up and over her skull. More than anything, she looked as if she were trying to shut him out, to put a stop to whatever it was he was trying to tell her.

But it had to be said. It was the only way she would understand.

And it would be the first time he'd uttered the words aloud.

"I cannot read."

Three words. That's all it was. Three words. And a lifetime of secrets.

Her brow wrinkled, and Jack could not tell—did she not believe him? Or was it simply that she thought she'd misheard?

People saw what they expected to see. He'd acted like an educated man, and so that was how she'd seen him.

"I can't read, Aunt Mary. I've never been able to. Arthur was the only one who ever realized."

She shook her head. "I don't understand. You were in school. You were graduated—"

"By the skin of my teeth," Jack cut in, "and only then, with Arthur's help. Why do you think I had to leave university?"

"Jack . . ." She looked almost embarrassed. "We were told you misbehaved. You drank too much, and there was that woman, and— and— that awful prank with the pig, and— Why are you shaking your head?"

"I didn't want to embarrass you."

"You think that wasn't embarrassing?"

"I could not do the work without Arthur's help," he explained. "And he was two years behind me."

"But we were told—"

"I'd rather have been dismissed for bad behavior than stupidity," he said softly.

"You did it all on purpose?"

He dipped his chin.

"Oh, my God." She sank into a chair. "Why didn't you say something? We could have hired a tutor."

"It wouldn't have helped." And then, when she looked up at him in confusion he said, almost helplessly, "The letters dance. They flip about. I can never tell the difference between a d and a b, unless they are uppercase, and even then I—"

"You're not stupid," she cut in, and her voice was sharp.

He stared at her.

"You are *not* stupid. If there is a problem it is with your eyes, not your mind. I know you." She stood, her movements shaky but determined, and then she touched his cheek with her hand. "I was there the moment you were born. I was the first to hold you. I have been with you for every scrape, every tumble. I have watched your eyes light, Jack. I have watched you *think*.

"How clever you must have been," she said softly, "to have fooled us all."

"Arthur helped me all through school," he said as evenly as he was able. "I never asked him to. He said he liked—" He swallowed then, because the memory was rising in his throat like a cannonball. "He said he liked to read aloud."

"I think he did like that." A tear began to roll down her cheek. "He idolized you, Jack."

Jack fought the sobs that were choking his throat. "I was supposed to protect him."

"Soldiers die, Jack. Arthur was not the only one. He was merely . . ." She closed her eyes and turned away, but not so fast that Jack didn't see the flash of pain on her face.

"He was merely the only one who mattered to me," she whispered. She looked up, straight into his eyes. "Please, Jack, I don't want to lose two sons."

She held out her arms, and before Jack knew it, he was there, in her embrace. Sobbing.

He had not cried for Arthur. Not once. He'd been so

full of anger—at the French, at himself—that he had not left room for grief.

But now here it was, rushing in. All the sadness, all the times he'd witnessed something amusing and Arthur had not been there to share it with. All the milestones he had celebrated alone. All the milestones Arthur would never celebrate.

He cried for all of that. And he cried for himself, for his lost years. He'd been running. Running from himself. And he was tired of it. He wanted to stop. To stay in one place.

With Grace.

He would not lose her. He did not care what he had to do to ensure their future, but ensure it he would. If Grace said that she could not marry the Duke of Wyndham, then he would not *be* the Duke of Wyndham. Surely there was some measure of his destiny that was still under his control.

"I need to see to the guests," Mary whispered, pulling gently away.

Jack nodded, wiping the last of his tears from his eyes. "The dowager . . ." Good lord, what was there to say about the dowager, except: "I'm so sorry."

"She shall have my bedchamber," Mary said.

Normally Jack would have forbidden her to give up her room, but he was tired, and he suspected she was tired, and tonight seemed like the perfect time to put ease before pride. And so he nodded. "That is very kind of you."

"I suspect it's something closer to self-preservation."

He smiled at that. "Aunt Mary?"

She'd reached the door, but she stopped with her hand

on the knob, turning back around to face him. "Yes?"

"Miss Eversleigh," he said.

Something lit in his aunt's eyes. Something romantic. "Yes?"

"I love her."

Mary's entire being seemed to warm and glow. "I am so happy to hear it."

"She loves me, too."

"Even better."

"Yes," he murmured, "it is."

She motioned toward the hall. "Will you return with me?"

Jack knew he should, but the evening's revelations had left him exhausted. And he did not want anyone to see him thus, his eyes still red and raw. "Would you mind if I remained here?" he asked.

"Of course not." She smiled wistfully and left the room.

Jack turned back toward his uncle's desk, running his fingers slowly along the smooth surface. It was peaceful here, and the Lord knew, he needed a spot of peace.

It was going to be a long night. He would not sleep. There was no sense in trying. But he did not want to *do* anything. He did not want to go anywhere, and most of all, he did not want to think.

For this moment . . . for this night . . . he just wanted to *be*.

Grace liked the Audleys' drawing room, she decided. It was quite elegant, decorated in soft tones of burgundy and cream, with two seating areas, a writing desk, and several cozy reading chairs in the corners. Signs of family life were everywhere—from the stack of letters on the desk to the embroidery Mrs. Audley must have abandoned on the sofa when she'd heard Jack at the door. On the mantel sat six miniatures in a row. Grace walked over, pretending to warm her hands by the fire.

It was their family, she instantly realized, probably painted fifteen years ago. The first was surely Jack's uncle, and the next Grace recognized as Mrs. Audley. After that was . . . Good heavens, was that Jack? It had to be. How could someone change so little? He looked younger, yes, but everything else was the same—the expression, the sly smile.

It nearly took her breath away.

The other three miniatures were the Audley children, or so Grace assumed. Two boys and one girl. She dipped her head and said a little prayer when she reached the younger of the boys. Arthur. Jack had loved him.

Was that what he was talking about with his aunt? Grace had been the last to enter the drawing room; she'd seen Mrs. Audley pull him gently through another doorway.

After a few minutes the butler arrived, announcing that their rooms had been prepared, but Grace loitered near the fireplace. She was not ready to leave this room.

She was not sure why.

"Miss Eversleigh."

She looked up. It was Jack's aunt.

"You walk softly, Mrs. Audley," she said. "I did not hear you approach."

"That one is Jack," Mrs. Audley said, reaching out and removing his miniature from the mantel.

"I recognized him," Grace murmured.

"Yes, he is much the same. This one is my son Edward. He lives just down the lane. And this is Margaret. She has two daughters of her own now."

Grace looked at Arthur. They both did.

"I am sorry for your loss," Grace finally said.

Mrs. Audley swallowed, but she did not seem to be near tears. "Thank you." She turned then, and took Grace's hand in hers. "Jack is in his uncle's study. At the far end of the hall, on the right. Go to him."

Grace's lips parted.

"Go," Mrs. Audley said, even more softly than before.

Grace felt herself nod, and before she'd had time to consider her actions, she was already in the hall, hurrying down toward the end.

To the door on the right.

"Jack?" she said softly, pushing the door open a few inches.

He was sitting in a chair, facing the window, but he turned quickly and stood at the sound of her voice.

She let herself in and closed the door gently behind her. "Your aunt said—"

He was right there. Right there in front of her. And then her back was against the door, and he was kissing her, hard, fast, and—*dear God*—thoroughly.

And then he stepped away. She couldn't breathe, she

could barely stand, and she knew she could not have put together a sentence if her life had depended on it.

Never in her life had she wanted anything as much as she wanted this man.

"Go to bed, Grace."

"What?"

"I cannot resist you," he said, his voice soft, haggard, and everything in between.

She reached toward him. She could not help it.

"Not in this house," he whispered.

But his eyes burned for her.

"Go," he said hoarsely. "Please."

She did. She ran up the stairs, found her room, and crawled between her sheets.

But she shivered all night.

She shivered and she burned.

Chapter Twenty-one

"Can't sleep?"

Jack looked up from where he was still sitting in his uncle's study. Thomas was standing in the doorway. "No," he said.

Thomas walked in. "Nor I."

Jack held out the bottle of brandy he'd taken from the shelf. There had not been a speck of dust on it, even though he was quite certain it had gone untouched since his uncle's death. Aunt Mary had always run a pristine household.

"It's good," Jack said. "I think my uncle was saving it." He blinked, looking down at the label, then murmured, "Not for this, I imagine."

He motioned to a set of crystal snifters near the window, waiting with the bottle in hand as Thomas walked across the room and took one. When Thomas returned, he sat in the study's other wingback chair, setting his snifter down on the small, low table between them. Jack reached out and poured. Generously.

Thomas took the brandy and drank, his eyes narrowing as he stared out the window. "It will be dawn soon."

Jack nodded. There were no hints of pink in the sky, but the pale silvery glow of morning had begun to permeate the air. "Has anyone awakened?" he asked.

"Not that I've heard."

They sat in silence for several moments. Jack finished his drink and considered another. He picked up the bottle to pour, but as the first drops splashed down, he realized he didn't really want it. He looked up. "Do you ever feel as if you are on display?"

Thomas's face remained impassive. "All the time."

"How do you bear it?"

"I don't know anything else."

Jack placed his fingers to his forehead and rubbed. He had a blistering headache and no reason to suppose it might improve. "It's going to be hideous today."

Thomas nodded.

Jack closed his eyes. It was easy to picture the scene. The dowager would insist upon reading the register first, and Crowland would be right over his shoulder, cackling away, ready to sell his daughter off to the highest bidder. His aunt would probably want to come, and Amelia, too—and who could blame her? She had as much at stake as anyone.

The only person who would not be there was Grace.

The only person he needed by his side.

"It's going to be a bloody circus," Jack muttered.

"Indeed."

They sat there, doing nothing, and then they both looked up at precisely the same moment. Their eyes met, and Jack watched Thomas's face as his gaze slid over toward the window.

Outside.

"Shall we?" Jack asked, and he felt the first glimmerings of a smile.

"Before anyone—"

"Right now." Because really, no one else had a place at this table.

Thomas stood. "Lead the way."

Jack rose to his feet and headed out the door, Thomas right behind. And as they mounted their horses and took off, the air still heavy with night, it occurred to him—

They were cousins.

And for the first time, that felt like a good thing.

Morning was well under way when they reached the Maguiresbridge church. Jack had been there several times before, visiting his mother's family, and the old gray stone felt comfortable and familiar. The building was small, and humble, and in his opinion, everything a church ought to be.

"It does not look as if anyone is about," Thomas said. If he was unimpressed by the plainness of the architecture, he did not indicate as much.

"The register will likely be at the rectory," Jack said.

Thomas nodded, and they dismounted, tying their horses to a hitching post before making their way to the front of the rectory. They knocked several times before they heard footsteps moving toward them from within.

The door opened, revealing a woman of middling years, clearly the housekeeper.

"Good day, ma'am," Jack said, offering her a polite bow. "I am Jack Audley, and this is—"

"Thomas Cavendish," Thomas cut in, nodding in greeting.

Jack gave him a bit of a dry look at that, which the housekeeper would surely have noticed if she hadn't been so obviously irritated by their arrival.

"We would like to see the parish register," Jack said.

She stared at them for a moment and a half and then jerked her head toward the rear. "It's in the back room," she said. "The vicar's office."

"Er, is the vicar present?" Jack asked, although the last bit of the last word was covered by a grunt, brought on by Thomas's elbow pressing into his side.

"No vicar just now," the housekeeper said. "The position is vacant." She walked over to a well-worn sofa in front of the fire and sat down. "We're supposed to get someone new soon. They send someone from Enniskillen every Sunday to deliver a sermon."

She then picked up a plate of toast and turned her back on them completely.

Jack looked over at Thomas. Who he found was looking over at him.

He supposed they were just meant to go in.

So they did.

The office was larger than Jack would have expected, given the tight quarters of the rest of the rectory. There were three windows, one on the north wall and then two on the west, flanking the fireplace. A small but tidy flame was burning; Jack walked over to warm his hands.

"Do you know what a parish register looks like?" Thomas asked.

Jack shrugged and shook his head. He stretched his fingers, then flexed his feet as best as he could within the confines of his boots. His muscles were growing tense and jumpy, and everytime he tried to hold still, he realized that his fingers were drumming a frantic tattoo on his leg.

He wanted to jump out of his skin. He wanted to jump right out of his—

"This may be it."

Jack turned. Thomas was holding a large book. It was bound in brown leather, and the cover showed signs of age.

"Shall we?" Thomas asked. His voice was even, but Jack saw him swallow spasmodically. And his hands were trembling.

"You can do it," Jack said. He could not fake it this time. He could not stand there and pretend to read. Some things were simply too much to bear.

Thomas stared at him in shock. "You don't want to look with me?"

"I trust you." It was true. Thomas could not think of a more inherently trustworthy person. Thomas would not lie. Not even about this.

"No," Thomas said, dismissing this entirely. "I won't do it without you."

For a moment Jack just stood there unmoving, and then, cursing under his breath, he went over to join Thomas at the desk.

"You're too bloody noble," Jack bit off.

Thomas muttered something Jack could not quite make out and set the book down, opening it to one of the first pages.

Jack looked down. It was a blur, all swirls and dips, dancing before his eyes. He swallowed, stealing a glance at Thomas to see if he'd seen anything. But Thomas was staring down at the register, his eyes moving quickly from left to right as he flipped through the pages.

And then he slowed down.

Jack clenched his teeth, trying to make it out. Sometimes he could tell the bigger letters, and frequently the numbers. It was just that they were so often not where he thought they should be, or not *what* he thought they should be.

Ah, idiocy. It ought to have been familiar by now. But it never was.

"Do you know what month your parents would have married in?" Thomas asked.

"No." But it was a small parish. How many weddings could there have been?

Jack watched Thomas's fingers. They moved along the edge of the page, then slid around the edge.

And flipped it. And stopped.

Jack looked at Thomas. He was still.

He'd closed his eyes. And it was clear. On his face. It was clear.

"Dear God." The words fell from Jack's lips like tears. It wasn't a surprise, and yet, he'd been hoping . . . praying . . .

That his parents hadn't married. Or the proof had been lost. That someone, anyone, had been wrong because *this* was wrong. It could not be happening. He could not do this.

Just look at him now. He was standing there bloody well *pretending* to read the register. How in God's name did anyone think he could be a duke?

Contracts?

Oh, that would be fun.

Rents?

He'd better get a trustworthy steward, since it wasn't as if *he* could check to see if he was being cheated.

And then—he choked back a horrified laugh—it was a damned good thing he could sign his documents with a seal. The Lord knew how long it would take to learn to sign his new name without looking as if he had to think about it.

John Cavendish-Audley had taken months. Was it any wonder he'd been so eager to drop the Cavendish?

Jack brought his face to his hands, closing his eyes tight. This could not be happening. He'd known it would happen, and yet, here he was, convinced it was an impossibility.

He was going mad.

He felt like he couldn't breathe.

"Who is Philip?" Thomas asked.

"What?" Jack practically snapped.

"Philip Galbraith. He was a witness."

Jack looked up. And then down at the register. At the swirls and dips that apparently spelled out his uncle's name. "My mother's brother."

"Does he still live?"

"I don't know. He did the last I knew. It has been five years." Jack thought furiously. Why was Thomas asking? Would it mean anything if Philip was dead? The proof was still right there in the register.

The register.

Jack stared at it, his lips parted and slack. It was the enemy. That one little book.

Grace had said she could not marry him if he was the Duke of Wyndham.

Thomas had made no secret of the mountains of paperwork that lay ahead.

If he was the Duke of Wyndham.

But there was only that book. There was only that page.

Just one page, and he could remain Jack Audley. All his problems would be solved.

"Tear it out," Jack whispered.

"What did you say?"

"Tear it out."

"Are you mad?"

Jack shook his head. "You are the duke."

Thomas looked down at the register. "No," he said softly, "I'm not."

"No." Jack's voice grew urgent, and he grabbed Thomas by the shoulders. "You are what Wyndham needs. What everyone needs."

"Stop, you—"

"Listen to me," Jack implored. "You are born and

bred to the job. I will ruin everything. Do you understand? I cannot do it. I *cannot* do it."

But Thomas just shook his head. "I may be bred to it, but you were born to it. And I cannot take what is yours."

"I don't want it!" Jack burst out.

"It is not yours to accept or deny," Thomas said, his voice numbingly calm. "Don't you understand? It is not a possession. It is who you are."

"Oh, for God's sake," Jack swore. He raked his hands through his hair. He grabbed at it, pulled entire fistfuls until his scalp felt as if it were stretching off the bone. "I am *giving* it to you. On a bloody silver platter. You stay the duke, and I shall leave you alone. I'll be *your* scout in the Outer Hebrides. Anything. Just tear the page out."

"If you didn't want the title, why didn't you just say that your parents hadn't been married at the outset?" Thomas shot back. "I asked you if your parents were married. You could have said no."

"I didn't *know* that I was in line to inherit when you questioned my legitimacy." Jack gulped. His throat tasted acrid and afraid. He stared at Thomas, trying to gauge his thoughts.

How could he be so bloody upright and noble? Anyone else would have ripped that page to shreds. But no, not Thomas Cavendish. He would do what was right. Not what was best, but what was right.

Bloody fool.

Thomas was just standing there, staring at the register. And he—he was ready to climb the walls. His entire body was shaking, his heart pounding, and he—

What was that noise?

"Do you hear that?" Jack whispered urgently.

Horses.

"They're here," Thomas said.

Jack stopped breathing. Through the window he could see a carriage approaching.

He was out of time.

He looked at Thomas.

Thomas was staring down at the register. "I can't do it," he whispered.

Jack didn't think. He just moved. He leapt past Thomas to the church register and tore.

Thomas tackled him, trying to grab the paper away, but Jack slid out from his grasp, launching himself toward the fire.

"Jack, no!" Thomas yelled, but Jack was too quick, and even as Thomas caught hold of his arm, Jack managed to hurl the paper into the fire.

The fight drained from both of them in an instant, and they both stood transfixed, watching the paper curl and blacken.

"God in heaven," Thomas whispered. "What have you done?"

Jack could not take his eyes off the fire. "I have saved us all."

Grace had not expected to be included in the journey to the Maguiresbridge church. No matter how closely involved she had become in the matter of the Wyndham inheritance, she was not a member of the family. She wasn't even a member of the household any longer.

But when the dowager discovered that Jack and Thomas went to the church without her, she had—and Grace did not believe this an exaggeration—gone mad. It required but a minute for her to recover, but for those first sixty seconds it was a terrifying sight. Even Grace had never witnessed the like.

And so when it was time to depart, Amelia had refused to leave without her. "Do not leave me alone with that woman," she hissed in Grace's ear.

"You won't be alone," Grace tried to explain. Her father would be going, of course, and Jack's aunt had claimed a spot in the carriage as well.

"Please, Grace," Amelia begged. She did not know Jack's aunt, and she could not bear to sit next to her father. Not this morning.

The dowager had pitched a fit, which was not unexpected, but her tantrum only made Amelia more firm. She grabbed hold of Grace's hand and nearly crushed her fingers.

"Oh, do what you wish," the dowager had snapped. "But if you are not in the carriage in three minutes, I shall leave without you."

Which was how it came to pass that Amelia, Grace, and Mary Audley were squeezed together on one side of the carriage, with the dowager and Lord Crowland on the other.

The ride to Maguiresbridge had seemed interminably long. Amelia looked out her window, the dowager out hers, and Lord Crowland and Mary Audley did the same. Grace, squeezed in the middle facing backwards, could do nothing but stare at the spot midway between the dowager's and Lord Crowland's heads.

Every ten minutes or so the dowager would turn to Mary and demand to know how much longer it would be until they reached their destination. Mary answered each query with admirable deference and patience, and then finally, to everyone's relief, she said, "We are here."

The dowager hopped down first, but Lord Crowland was close on her heels, practically dragging Amelia behind him. Mary Audley hurried out next, leaving Grace alone at the rear. She sighed. It seemed somehow fitting.

By the time Grace reached the front of the rectory, the rest of them were already inside, pushing through the door to another room, where, she presumed, Jack and Thomas were, along with the all-important church register.

An open-mouthed woman stood in the center of the front room, a cup of tea balanced precariously in her fingers.

"Good day," Grace said with a rushed smile, wondering if the others had even bothered to knock.

"Where is it?" she heard the dowager demand, followed by the crash of a door slamming against a wall. "How dare you leave without me! Where is it? I demand to see the register!"

Grace made it to the doorway, but it was still blocked by the others. She couldn't see in. And then she did the last thing she'd ever have expected of herself.

She shoved. Hard.

She loved him. She loved Jack. And whatever the day brought, she would be there. He would not be alone. She would not allow it.

She stumbled inside just as the dowager was screaming, "What did you find?"

Grace steadied herself and looked up. There he was. Jack. He looked awful.

Haunted.

Her lips formed his name, but she made no sound. She couldn't have. It was as if her voice had been yanked right out of her. She had never seen him thus. His color was wrong—too pale, or maybe too flushed—she couldn't quite tell. And his fingers were trembling. Couldn't anyone else see that?

Grace turned to Thomas, because surely he would do something. *Say* something.

But he was staring at Jack. Just like everyone else. No one was speaking. Why wasn't anyone speaking?

"He is Wyndham," Jack finally said. "As he should be."

Grace should have jumped for joy, but all she could think was—*I don't believe him.*

He didn't look right. He didn't sound right.

The dowager turned on Thomas. "Is this true?"

Thomas did not speak.

The dowager growled with frustration and grabbed his arm. "Is . . . it . . . true?" she demanded.

Still, Thomas did not speak.

"There is no record of a marriage," Jack insisted.

Grace wanted to cry. He was lying. It was so obvious . . . to her, to everyone. There was desperation in his voice, and fear, and— Dear God, was he doing this for her? Was he trying to forsake his birthright for *her*?

"Thomas is the duke," Jack said again, looking

frantically from person to person. "Why aren't you listening? Why isn't anyone listening to me?"

But there was only silence. And then:

"He lies."

It was Thomas, in a voice that was low and even, and absolutely true.

Grace let out a choked sob and turned away. She could not bear to watch.

"No," Jack said, "I'm telling you—"

"Oh, for God's sake," Thomas snapped. "Do you think no one will find you out? There will be witnesses. Do you really think there won't be any witnesses to the wedding? For God's sake, you can't rewrite the past."

Grace closed her eyes.

"Or burn it," Thomas said ominously. "As the case may be."

Oh, Jack, she thought. *What have you done?*

"He tore the page from the register," Thomas said. "He threw it into the fire."

Grace opened her eyes, unable to *not* look at the hearth. There was no sign of paper. Nothing but black soot and ash under the steady orange flame.

"It's yours," Thomas said, turning to Jack. He looked him in the eye and then bowed.

Jack looked sick.

Thomas turned, facing the rest of the room. "I am—" He cleared his throat, and when he continued, his voice was even and proud. "I am Mr. Cavendish," he said, "and I bid you all a good day."

And then he left. He brushed past them and walked right out the door.

At first no one could speak. And then, in a moment

that was almost grotesque, Lord Crowland turned to Jack and bowed. "Your grace," he said.

"No," Jack said, shaking his head. He turned to the dowager. "Do not allow this. He will make a better duke."

"True enough," Lord Crowland said, completely oblivious to Jack's distress. "But you'll learn."

And then—Jack couldn't help it—he started to laugh. From deep within him, his sense of the absurd rose to the fore, and he laughed. Because good God, if there was one thing he'd never be able to do, it was learn. Anything.

"Oh, you have no idea," he said. He looked at the dowager. His desperation was gone, replaced by something else—something bitter and fatalistic, something cynical and grim. "You have no idea what you've done," he told her. "No idea at all."

"I have restored you to your proper place," she said sharply. "As is my duty to my son."

Jack turned. He couldn't bring himself to look at her for one moment more. But there was Grace, standing near the doorway. She looked shocked, she looked scared. But when she looked at *him*, he saw his entire world, falling softly into place.

She loved him. He didn't know how or why, but he was not enough of a fool to question it. And when her eyes met his, he saw hope. He saw the future, and it was shining like the sunrise.

His entire life, he'd been running. From himself, from his faults. He'd been so desperate that no one should truly know him, that he'd denied himself the chance to find his place in the world.

He smiled. He finally knew where he belonged.

He had seen Grace when she entered the room, but she'd stood back, and he couldn't go to her, not when he'd been trying so hard to keep the dukedom in Thomas's hands, where it belonged.

But it seemed he'd failed in that measure.

He would not fail in *this*.

"Grace," he said, and went to her, taking both of her hands in his.

"What the devil are you doing?" the dowager demanded.

He dropped to one knee.

"Marry me," he said, squeezing her hands. "Be my bride, be my—" He laughed, a bubble of absurdity rising from within. "Be my duchess." He smiled up at her. "It's a lot to ask, I know."

"Stop that," the dowager hissed. "You can't marry her."

"Jack," Grace whispered. Her lips were trembling, and he knew she was thinking about it. She was teetering.

And he could bring her over the edge.

"For once in your life," he said fervently, "make *yourself* happy."

"Stop this!" Crowland blustered. He grabbed Jack under his arm and tried to haul him to his feet, but Jack would not budge. He would remain on one knee for eternity if that was what it took.

"Marry me, Grace," he whispered.

"You will marry Amelia!" Crowland cut in.

Jack did not take his eyes off Grace's face. "Marry me."

"Jack . . ." she said, and he could hear it in her voice that she thought she should make an excuse, should say something about his duty or her place.

"Marry me," he said again, before she could go on.

"She is not acceptable," the dowager said coldly.

He brought Grace's hands to his lips. "I will marry no one else."

"She is not of your rank!"

He turned and gave his grandmother an icy look. He felt rather ducal, actually. It was almost entertaining. "Do you wish for me to produce an heir? Ever?"

The dowager's face pinched up like a fish.

"I shall take that as a yes," he announced. "Which means that Grace shall have to marry me." He shrugged. "It's the only way, if I am to give Wyndham a legitimate heir."

Grace started to blink, and her mouth—the corners were moving. She was fighting herself, telling herself she should say no. But she loved him. He knew that she did, and he would not allow her to throw that away.

"Grace—" He scowled, then laughed. "What the devil is your middle name, anyway?"

"Catriona," she whispered.

"Grace Catriona Eversleigh," he said, loud and sure, "I love you. I love you with every inch of my heart, and I swear right now, before all who are assembled . . ." He looked around, catching sight of the rectory housekeeper, who was standing open-mouthed in the doorway. " . . . even—devil it," he muttered, "what is your name?"

"Mrs. Broadmouse," she said, eyes wide.

Jack cleared his throat. He was beginning to feel like himself. For the first time in days, he felt like himself. Maybe he was stuck with this bloody title, but with Grace at his side, he could find a way to do some good with it.

"I swear to you," he said, "before Mrs. Broad-mouse—"

"Stop this!" the dowager yelled, grabbing hold of his other arm. "Get on your feet!"

Jack gazed up at Grace and smiled. "Was there ever a proposal so beleaguered?"

She smiled back, even as tears threatened to spill from her eyes.

"You are supposed to marry Amelia!" Lord Crowland growled.

And then there was Amelia . . . poking her head around her father's shoulder. "I won't have him," she announced, rather matter-of-fact. She caught Jack's eye and smiled.

The dowager gasped. "You would refuse my grandson?"

"*This* grandson," Amelia clarified.

Jack tore his eyes off Grace for just long enough to grin approvingly at Amelia. She grinned back, motioning with her head toward Grace, telling him in no uncertain terms to get back to the matter at hand.

"Grace," Jack said, rubbing her hands softly with his. "My knee is beginning to hurt."

She started to laugh.

"Say yes, Grace," Amelia said.

"Listen to Amelia," Jack said.

"What the devil am I going to do with you?" Lord

Crowland said. To Amelia, that was, not that she seemed to care.

"I love you, Grace," Jack said.

She was grinning now. It seemed her whole body was grinning, as if she'd been enveloped in a happiness that would not let go. And then she said it. Right in front of everyone.

"I love you, too."

He felt all the happiness in the world swirling into him, straight to his heart. "Grace Catriona Eversleigh," he said again, "will you marry me?"

"Yes," she whispered. "Yes."

He stood. "I'm going to kiss her now," he called out.

And he did. Right in front of the dowager, in front of Amelia and her father, even in front of Mrs. Broadmouse.

He kissed her. And then he kissed her some more. He was kissing her when the dowager departed in an angry huff, and he was kissing her when Lord Crowland dragged Amelia away, muttering something about delicate sensibilities.

He kissed her, and he kissed her, and he would have kept kissing her except that he realized that Mrs. Broadmouse was still standing in the doorway, staring at them with a rather benign expression.

Jack grinned at her. "A spot of privacy, if you don't mind?"

She sighed and toddled away, but before she shut the door, they heard her say—

"I do like a good love story."

Epilogue

My dearest Amelia—

Can it only have been three weeks since I last
wrote? It feels as if I have gathered at least a
year of news. The children continue to thrive.
Arthur is so studious! Jack declares himself
boggled, but his delight is evident. We visited
the Happy Hare earlier this week to discuss
plans for the village fair with Harry Gladdish,
and Jack complained to no end about how difficult it has been to find a new tutor now that
Arthur has exhausted the last.

 Harry was not fooled. Jack was proud as puff.
 We were delighted to—

"Mama!"

Grace looked up from her correspondence. Her
third child (and only daughter) was standing in the
doorway, looking much aggrieved.

"What is it, Mary?" she asked.

"John was—"

"Just strolling by," John said, sliding along the polished floor until he came to a stop next to Mary.

"John!" Mary howled.

John looked at Grace with utter innocence. "I barely touched her."

Grace fought the urge to close her eyes and groan. John was only ten, but already he possessed his father's lethal charm.

"Mama," Mary said. "I was walking to the conservatory when—"

"What Mary *means* to say," John cut in, "is that *I* was walking to the *orangery* when she bumped into me and—"

"No!" Mary protested. "That is not what I meant to say." She turned to her mother in obvious distress. "Mama!"

"John, let your sister finish," Grace said, almost automatically. It was a sentence she uttered several times a day.

John smiled at her. Meltingly. Good gracious, Grace thought, it would not be long before she'd be beating the girls away with a stick.

"Mother," he said, in *exactly* the same tone Jack used when he was trying to charm his way out of a tight spot, "I would not dream of interrupting her."

"You just did!" Mary retorted.

John held up his hands, as if to say—*Poor dear*.

Grace turned to Mary with what she hoped was visible compassion. "You were saying, Mary?"

"He smashed an orange into my sheet music!"

Grace turned to her son. "John, is this—"

"No," he said quickly.

Grace gave him a dubious stare. It did not escape her that she had not finished her question before he answered. She supposed she ought not read too much into it. *John, is this true?* was another of the sentences she seemed to spend a great deal of time repeating.

"Mother," he said, his green eyes profoundly solemn, "upon my honor I swear to you that I did not smash an orange—"

"You lie," Mary seethed.

"*She* crushed the orange."

"After you put it under my foot!"

And then came a new voice: "Grace!"

Grace smiled with delight. Jack could now sort the children out.

"Grace," he said, turning sideways so that he might slip by them and into the room. "I need you to—"

"Jack!" she cut in.

He looked at her, and then behind him. "What did I do?"

She motioned to the children. "Did you not notice them?"

He quirked a smile—the very same one his son had tried to use on her a few moments earlier. "Of course I noticed them," he said. "Did you not notice me stepping around them?" He turned to the children. "Haven't we taught you that it is rude to block the doorway?"

It was a good thing she hadn't been to the orangery herself, Grace thought, because she would have peened him with one. As it was, she was beginning to think she ought to keep a store of small, round, easily throwable objects in her desk drawer.

"Jack," she said, with what she thought was amazing patience, "would you be so kind as to settle their dispute?"

He shrugged. "They'll work it out."

"Jack," she sighed.

"It's not your fault you had no siblings," he told her. "You have no experience in intrafamilial squabbles. Trust me, it all works out in the end. I predict we shall manage to get all four to adulthood with at least fifteen of their major limbs intact."

Grace leveled a stare. "You, on the other hand, are in supreme danger of—"

"Children!" Jack cut in. "Listen to your mother."

"She didn't say anything," John pointed out.

"Right," Jack said. He frowned for a moment. "John, leave your sister alone. Mary, next time don't step on the orange."

"But—"

"I'm done here," he announced.

And amazingly, they went on their way.

"That wasn't too difficult," he said. He stepped into the room. "I have some papers for you."

Grace immediately set aside her correspondence and took the documents he held forth.

"They arrived this afternoon from my solicitor," Jack explained.

She read the first paragraph. "About the Ennigsly building in Lincoln?"

"That's what I was expecting," he confirmed.

She nodded and then gave the document a thorough perusal. After a dozen years of marriage, they had fallen into an easy routine. Jack conducted all of his business affairs face-to-face, and when correspondence arrived, Grace was his reader.

It was almost amusing. It had taken Jack a year or so to find his footing, but he'd turned into a marvelous steward of the dukedom. His mind was razor sharp, and his judgment was such that Grace could not believe he'd not been trained in land management. The tenants adored him, the servants worshipped him (especially once the dowager was banished to the far side of the estate), and London society had positively fallen at his feet. It had helped, of course, that Thomas made it clear that he believed Jack was the rightful Duke of Wyndham, but still, Grace did not think herself biased to believe that Jack's charm and wit had something to do with it as well.

The only thing it seemed he could not do was read.

When he first told her, she had not believed him. Oh, she believed that *he* believed it. But surely he'd had poor teachers. Surely there had been some gross negligence on *someone's* part. A man of Jack's intelligence and education did not reach adulthood illiterate.

And so she'd sat with him. Tried her best. And he put up with it. In retrospect, she couldn't believe that he had not exploded with frustration. It was, perhaps, the oddest imaginable show of love—he'd let her try, again and again, to teach him to read. With a smile on his face, even.

But in the end she'd given up. She still did not understand what he meant when he told her the letters "danced," but she believed him when he insisted that all he ever got from a printed page was a headache.

"Everything is in order," she said now, handing the documents back to Jack. He had discussed the matter with her the week prior, after all of the decisions had been made. He always did that. So that she would know precisely what she was looking for.

"Are you writing to Amelia?" he asked.

She nodded. "I can't decide if I should tell her about John's escapade in the church belfry."

"Oh, do. They shall get a good laugh."

"But it makes him seem such a ruffian."

"He is a ruffian."

She felt herself deflate. "I know. But he's sweet."

Jack chuckled and kissed her, once, on the forehead. "He's just like me."

"I know."

"You needn't sound so despairing." He smiled then, that unbelievably devilish thing of his. It still got her, every time, just the way he wanted it to.

"Look how nicely I turned out," he added.

"Just so you understand," she told him, "if he takes to robbing coaches, I shall expire on the spot."

Jack laughed at that. "Give my regards to Amelia."

Grace was about to say *I shall*, but he was already gone. She picked up her pen and dipped it in ink, pausing briefly so she might recall what she'd been writing.

We were delighted to see Thomas on his visit. He made his annual pilgrimage to the dowager, who, I am sad to report, has not grown any less severe

in her old age. She is as healthy as can be—it is
my suspicion that she shall outlive us all.

Grace shook her head. She made the half-mile journey to the dower house but once a month. Jack had
said she needn't do even that, but she still felt an odd
loyalty toward the dowager. Not to mention a fierce
devotion and sympathy for the woman they'd hired to
replace her as the dowager's companion.

No servant had ever been so well-paid. Already the
woman earned (at Grace's insistence) double what she
herself had been paid. Plus, they promised her a cottage when the dowager finally expired. The very same
one Thomas had given to her so many years earlier.

Grace smiled to herself and continued writing, telling Amelia this and that—all those funny little an-
ecdotes mothers loved to share. Mary looked like a
squirrel with her front tooth missing. And little Oliver,
only eighteen months old, had skipped crawling entirely, going straight from the oddest belly-scoot to
full-fledged running. Already they'd lost him twice in
the hedgerow maze.

I do miss you, dear Amelia. You must promise
to visit this summer. You know how marvel-
ous Lincolnshire is when all the flowers are in
bloom. And of course—

"Grace?"
It was Jack, suddenly back in her doorway.
"I missed you," he explained.
"In the last five minutes?"

He stepped inside, closed the door. "It doesn't take long."

"You are incorrigible." But she set down her pen.

"It does seem to serve me well," he murmured, stepping around the desk. He took her hand and tugged her gently to her feet. "And you, too."

Grace fought the urge to groan. Only Jack would say such a thing. Only Jack would—

She let out a yelp as his lips—

Well, suffice to say, only Jack would do *that*.

Oh. And that.

She melted into him. And absolutely *that* . . .

Thomas Cavendish
&
Amelia Willoughby

Can this betrothal be saved?

Find out in
Julia Quinn's next bestseller

Mr. Cavendish,
I Presume

Coming from

Avon Books
October 2008

ENTER FOR A CHANCE TO WIN

A NOVEL BEACH ESCAPE FOR TWO AT SOUTH SEAS ISLAND RESORT

Seemingly adrift off of Florida's Gulf coast, **South Seas Island Resort** has redefined the luxury travel experience for guests following an extensive $140 million renovation. Tucked away at the northern end of Captiva Island, FL, **South Seas Island Resort** is situated on two-and-a-half miles of powder white beaches lapped by turquoise tides--and is the perfect place to get lost in time and explore the natural charm of "Olde Florida." Between 465 fully refurbished guest accommodations, a brand new pool and cabana oasis overlooking Pine Island Sound, and miles of private beach, **South Seas Island Resort** is the ideal spot to escape and relax with a great novel in hand.

Visit www.harpercollins.com/novelbeachescape, select one of our free newsletters, and you will be automatically entered into this random drawing. Official rules will be posted online on May 27, 2008.

SOUTH SEAS ISLAND RESORT

CAPTIVA ISLAND, FLORIDA

www.SouthSeas.com

 **AVON** *An Imprint of HarperCollinsPublishers* www.harpercollins.com   BEC0608

Want more Bridgertons?

YOU GOT IT!

Announcing the Bridgerton 2nd Epilogues...
where you get the story *after* the story.

Because when you're a *Bridgerton*,
happily ever after is a whole lot of fun.

Available online at **www.harpercollinsebooks.com**.

And visit **www.juliaquinn.com** to find Bridgerton
FAQs, the complete Bridgerton family tree,
and your e-book questions answered.

JULIA QUINN

juliaquinn.com

JQE 0207